# WALUK

## The Great Journey

## Ana Miralles · Emilio Ruiz

MAGNETIC™

WRITTEN BY

# EMILIO RUIZ

ILLUSTRATED BY

# ANA MIRALLES

Translation, Layout, and Editing by Mike Kennedy

**MAGNETIC™**

ISBN: 978-1-951719-05-0

Library of Congress Control Number: 2020919569

ABANDONED AS A CUB, YOUNG WALUK WANDERED THE TUNDRA IN SEARCH OF FOOD. THERE, HE MET ESKIMO, AN OLDER BEAR WITH A LOT OF KNOWLEDGE AND EXPERIENCE, BUT NOT AS MANY TEETH AS HE USED TO HAVE. TOGETHER, THE TWO NEW FRIENDS SET OUT ON VARIOUS ADVENTURES, HELPING EACH OTHER SURVIVE IN A LAND THAT SEEMED TO CHANGE EVERY DAY. WALUK WOULD HELP THE OLDER BEAR HUNT, AND ESKIMO WOULD TEACH THE YOUNGER BEAR HOW TO BE GREAT.

MAYBE, SOMEDAY, EVEN AS GREAT AS NANOOK, THE BIG BEAR IN THE SKY...

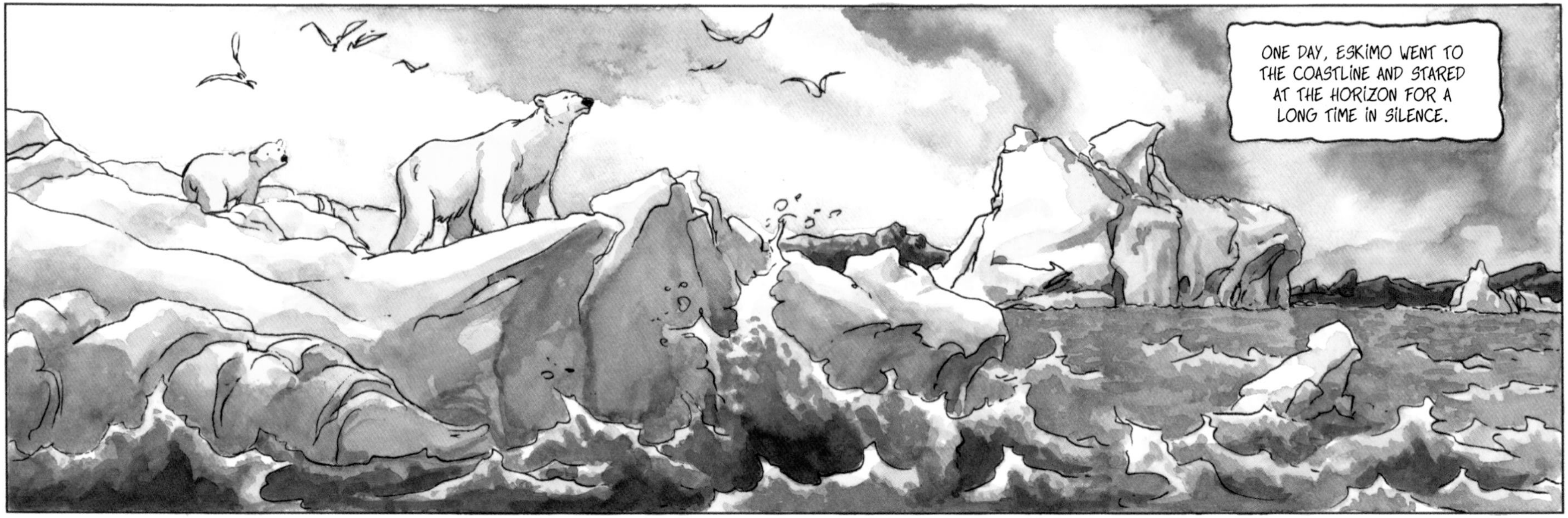
ONE DAY, ESKIMO WENT TO THE COASTLINE AND STARED AT THE HORIZON FOR A LONG TIME IN SILENCE.

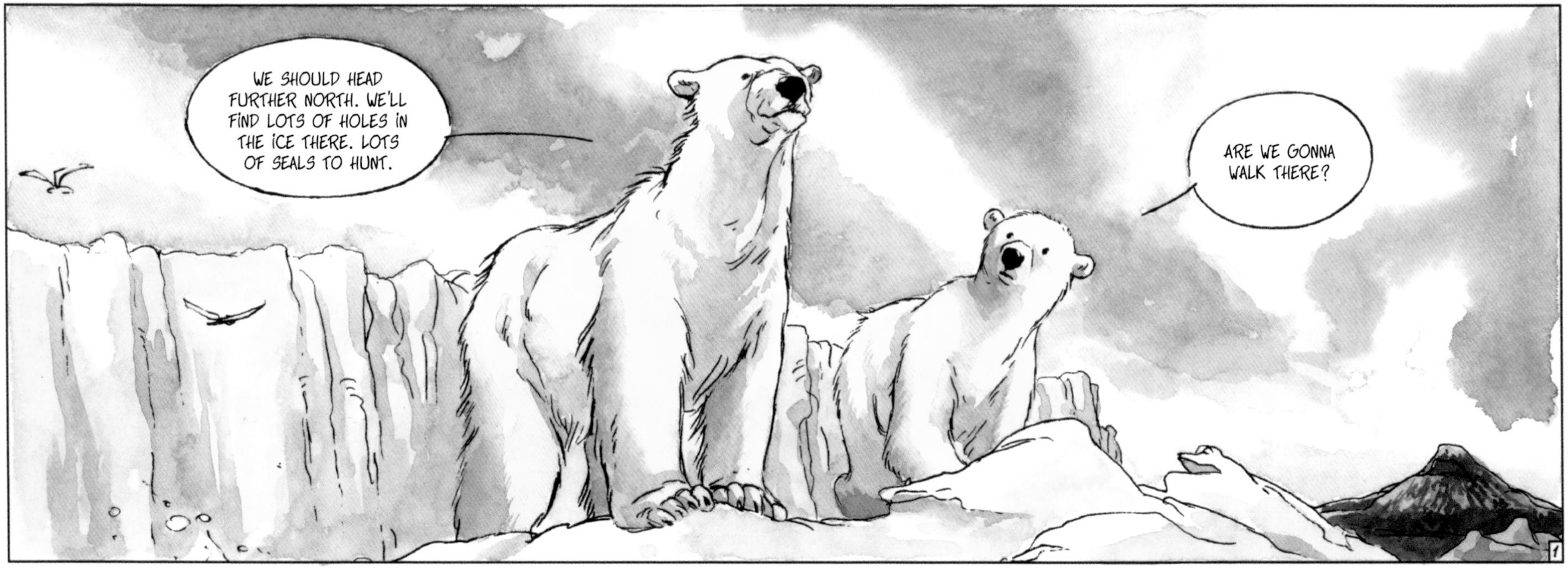
WE SHOULD HEAD FURTHER NORTH. WE'LL FIND LOTS OF HOLES IN THE ICE THERE. LOTS OF SEALS TO HUNT.
ARE WE GONNA WALK THERE?
1

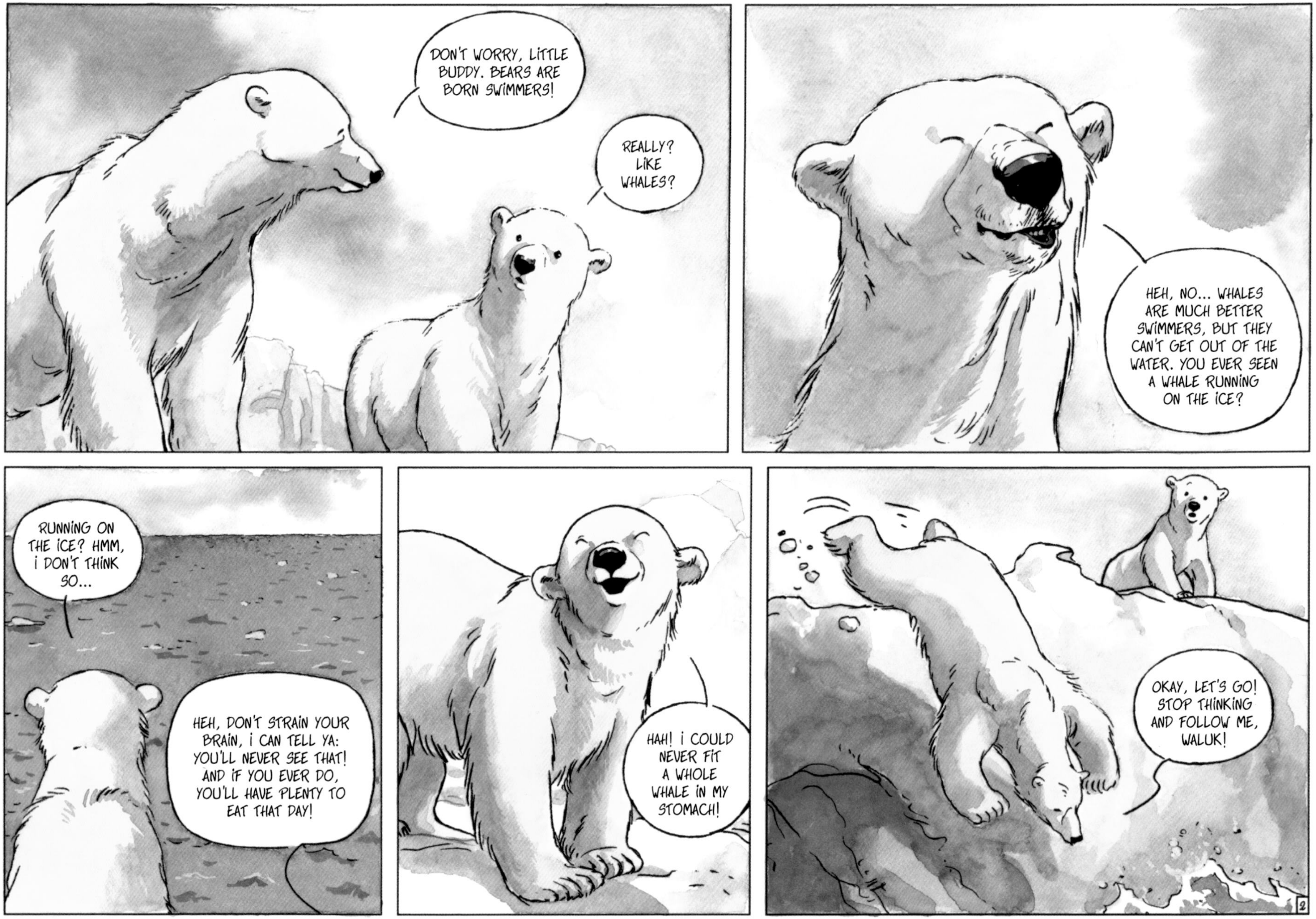
DON'T WORRY, LITTLE BUDDY. BEARS ARE BORN SWIMMERS!
REALLY? LIKE WHALES?
HEH, NO... WHALES ARE MUCH BETTER SWIMMERS, BUT THEY CAN'T GET OUT OF THE WATER. YOU EVER SEEN A WHALE RUNNING ON THE ICE?
RUNNING ON THE ICE? HMM, I DON'T THINK SO...
HEH, DON'T STRAIN YOUR BRAIN, I CAN TELL YA: YOU'LL NEVER SEE THAT! AND IF YOU EVER DO, YOU'LL HAVE PLENTY TO EAT THAT DAY!
HAH! I COULD NEVER FIT A WHOLE WHALE IN MY STOMACH!
OKAY, LET'S GO! STOP THINKING AND FOLLOW ME, WALUK!

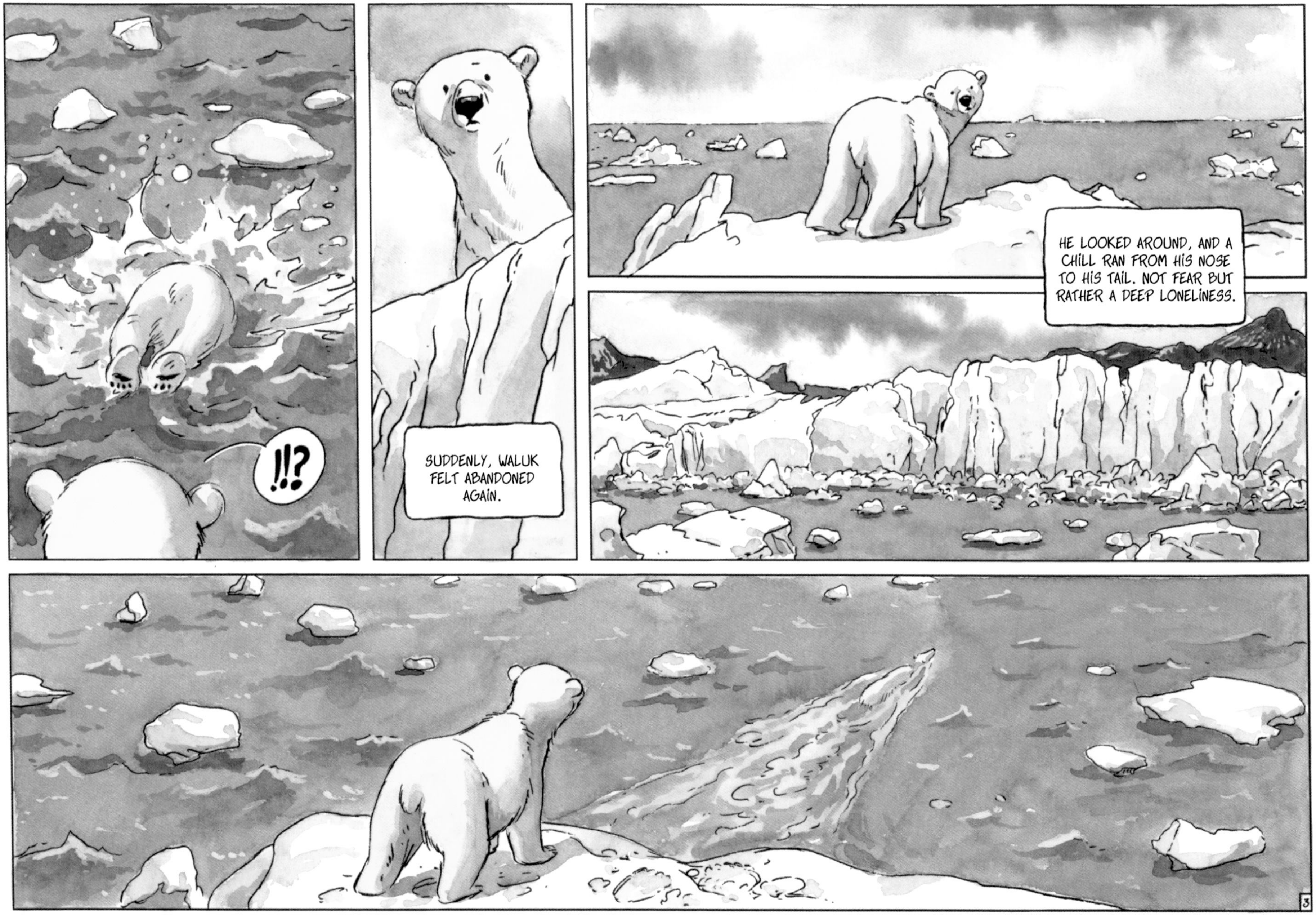
!!?
SUDDENLY, WALUK FELT ABANDONED AGAIN.
HE LOOKED AROUND, AND A CHILL RAN FROM HIS NOSE TO HIS TAIL. NOT FEAR BUT RATHER A DEEP LONELINESS.
3

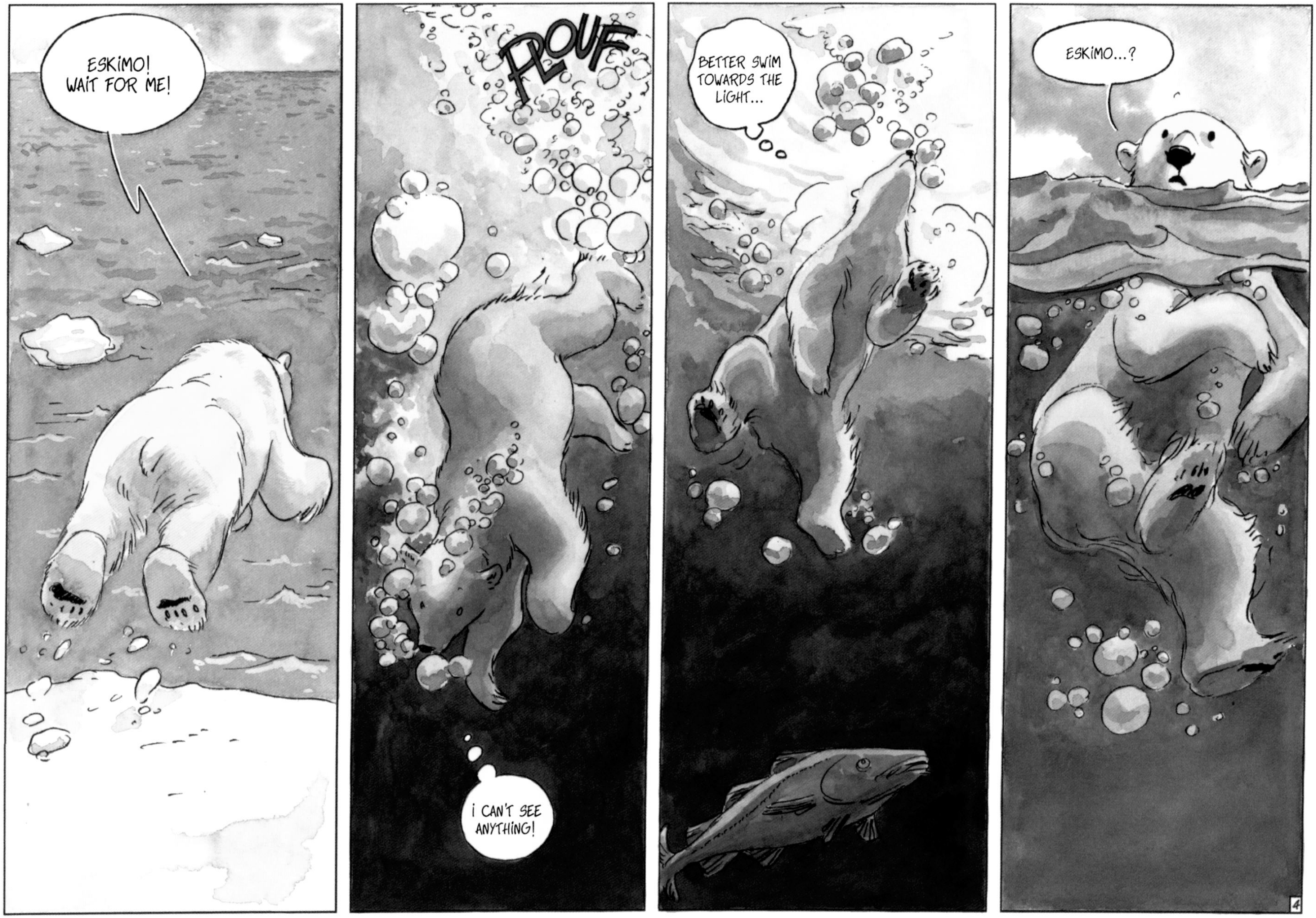
ESKiMO! WAiT FOR ME!
FLOUF
i CAN'T SEE ANYTHiNG!
BETTER SWiM TOWARDS THE LiGHT...
ESKiMO...?
4

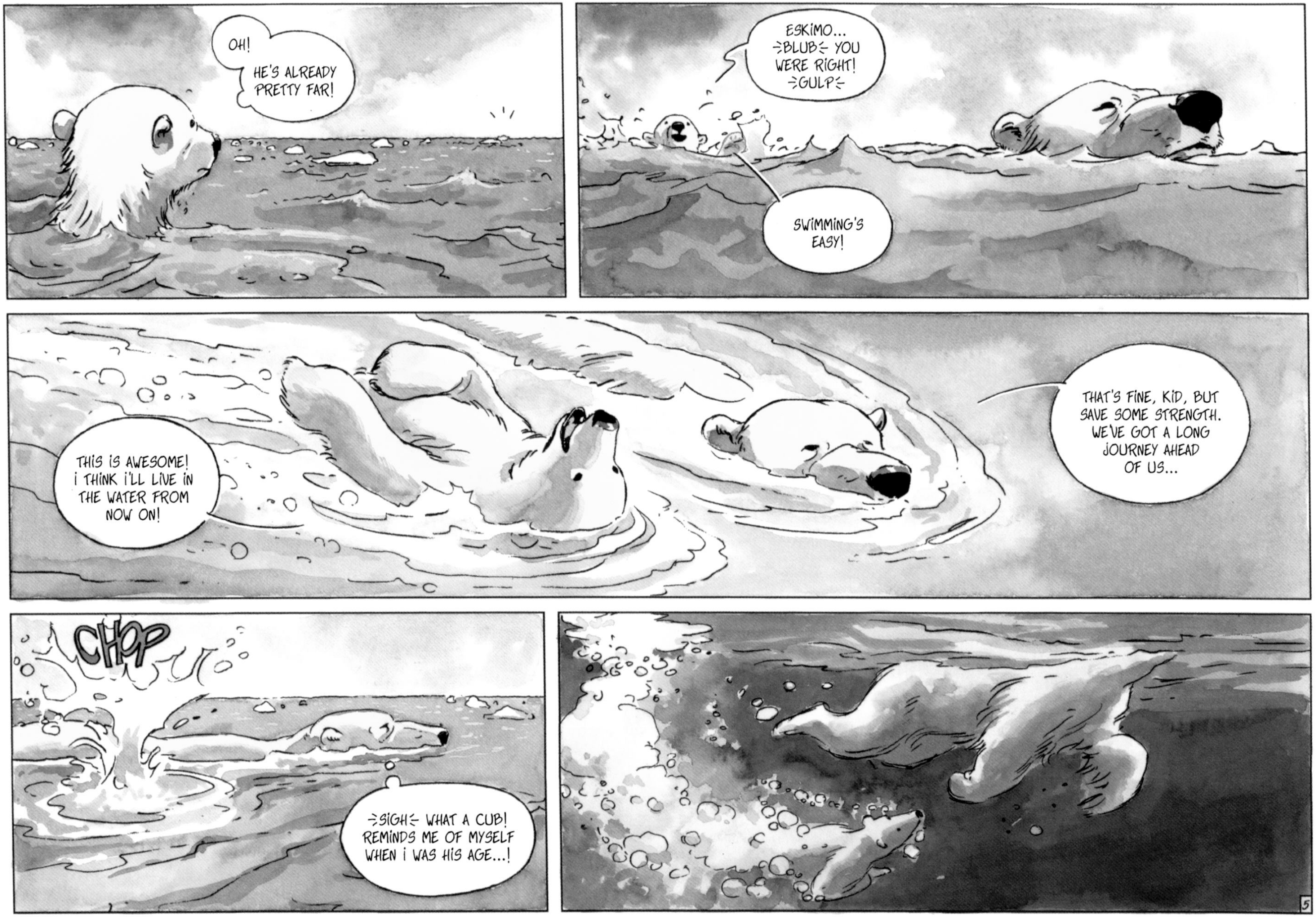
OH!
HE'S ALREADY PRETTY FAR!
ESKIMO... -BLUB- YOU WERE RIGHT! -GULP-
SWIMMING'S EASY!
THIS IS AWESOME! I THINK I'LL LIVE IN THE WATER FROM NOW ON!
THAT'S FINE, KID, BUT SAVE SOME STRENGTH. WE'VE GOT A LONG JOURNEY AHEAD OF US...
CHOP
-SIGH- WHAT A CUB! REMINDS ME OF MYSELF WHEN I WAS HIS AGE...!
5

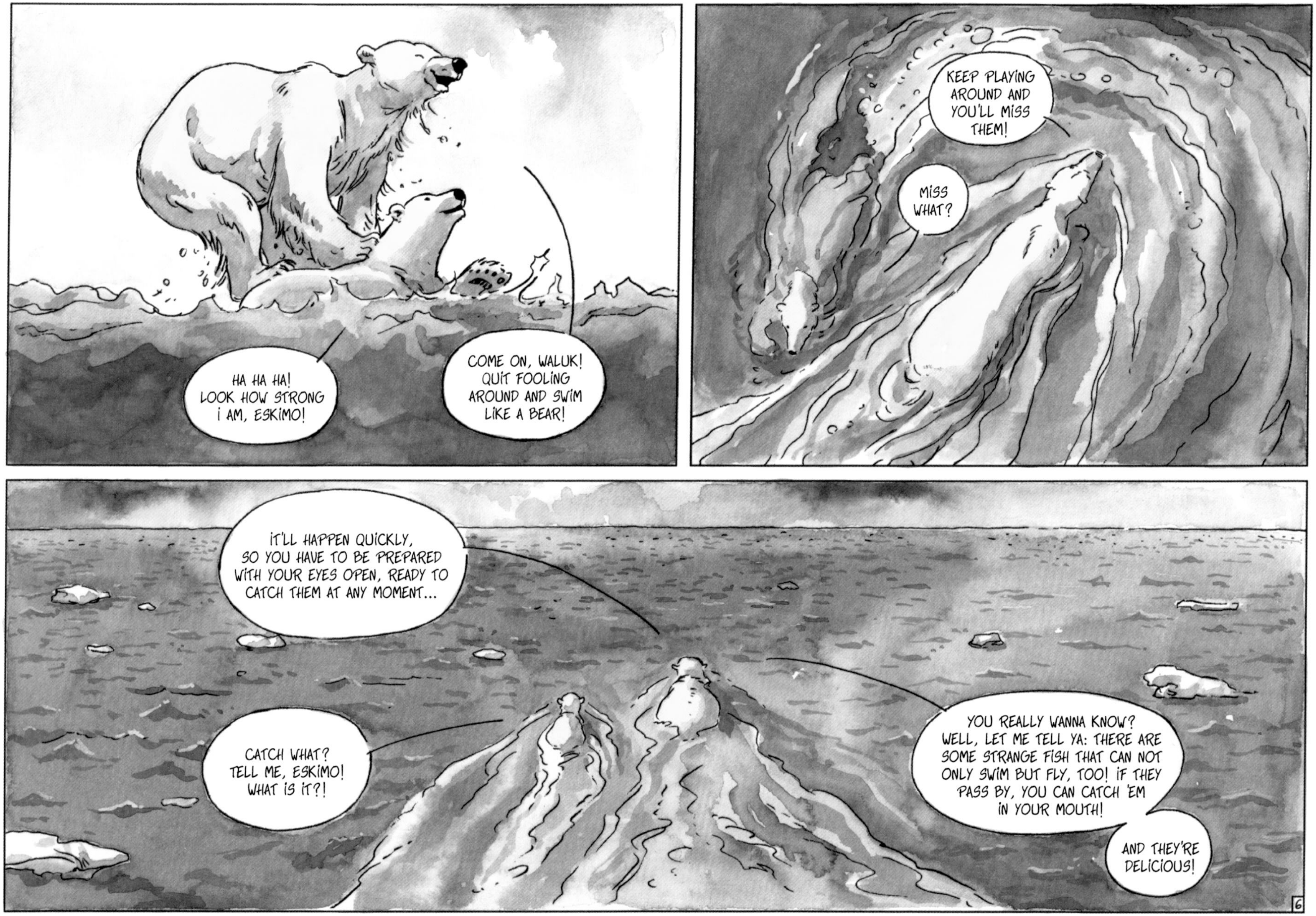
HA HA HA! LOOK HOW STRONG I AM, ESKIMO!
COME ON, WALUK! QUIT FOOLING AROUND AND SWIM LIKE A BEAR!
KEEP PLAYING AROUND AND YOU'LL MISS THEM!
MISS WHAT?
IT'LL HAPPEN QUICKLY, SO YOU HAVE TO BE PREPARED WITH YOUR EYES OPEN, READY TO CATCH THEM AT ANY MOMENT...
CATCH WHAT? TELL ME, ESKIMO! WHAT IS IT?!
YOU REALLY WANNA KNOW? WELL, LET ME TELL YA: THERE ARE SOME STRANGE FISH THAT CAN NOT ONLY SWIM BUT FLY, TOO! IF THEY PASS BY, YOU CAN CATCH 'EM IN YOUR MOUTH!
AND THEY'RE DELICIOUS!
6

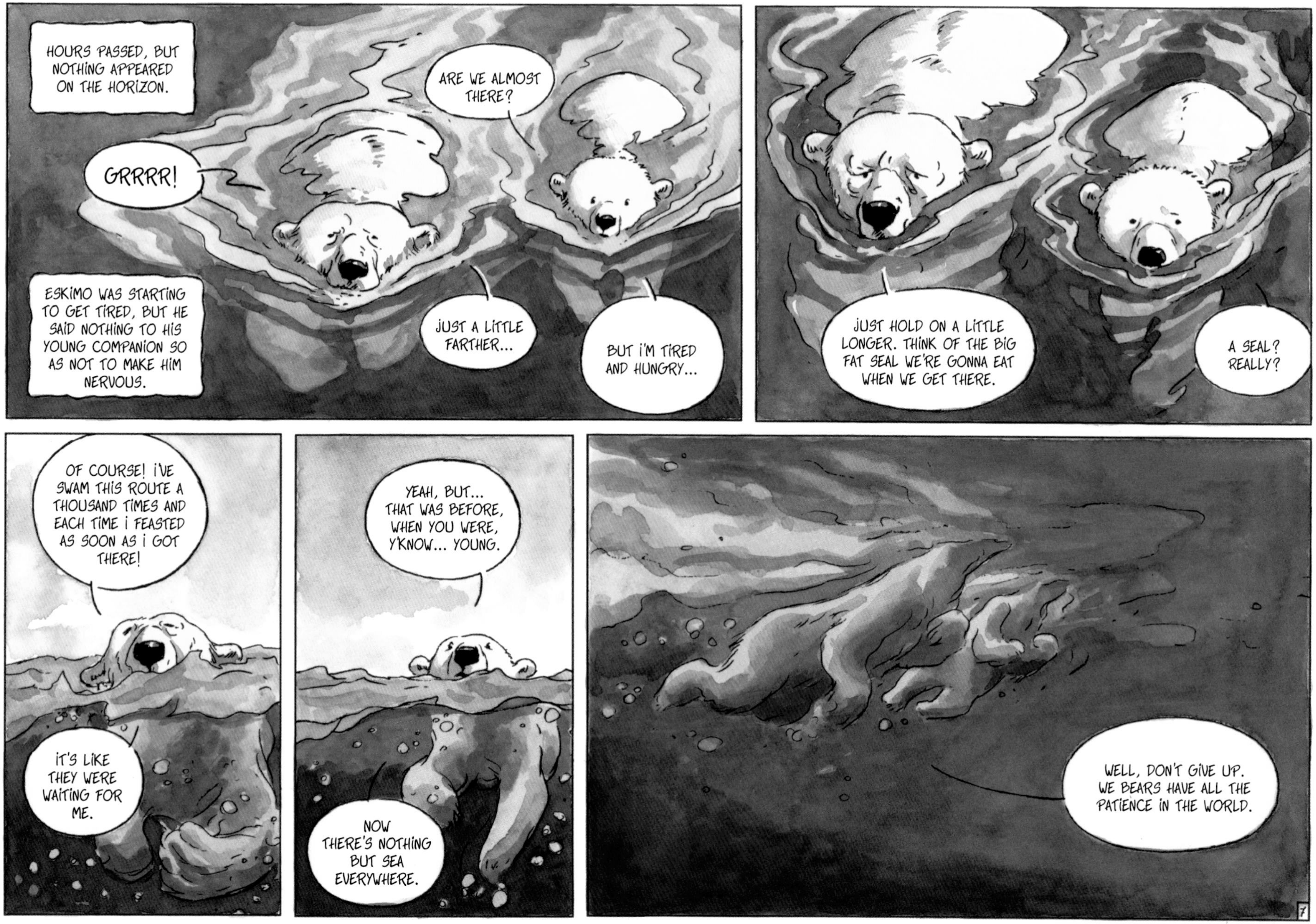
HOURS PASSED, BUT NOTHING APPEARED ON THE HORIZON.
ARE WE ALMOST THERE?
GRRRR!
ESKIMO WAS STARTING TO GET TIRED, BUT HE SAID NOTHING TO HIS YOUNG COMPANION SO AS NOT TO MAKE HIM NERVOUS.
JUST A LITTLE FARTHER...
BUT I'M TIRED AND HUNGRY...
JUST HOLD ON A LITTLE LONGER. THINK OF THE BIG FAT SEAL WE'RE GONNA EAT WHEN WE GET THERE.
A SEAL? REALLY?
OF COURSE! I'VE SWAM THIS ROUTE A THOUSAND TIMES AND EACH TIME I FEASTED AS SOON AS I GOT THERE!
IT'S LIKE THEY WERE WAITING FOR ME.
YEAH, BUT... THAT WAS BEFORE, WHEN YOU WERE, Y'KNOW... YOUNG.
NOW THERE'S NOTHING BUT SEA EVERYWHERE.
WELL, DON'T GIVE UP. WE BEARS HAVE ALL THE PATIENCE IN THE WORLD.
7

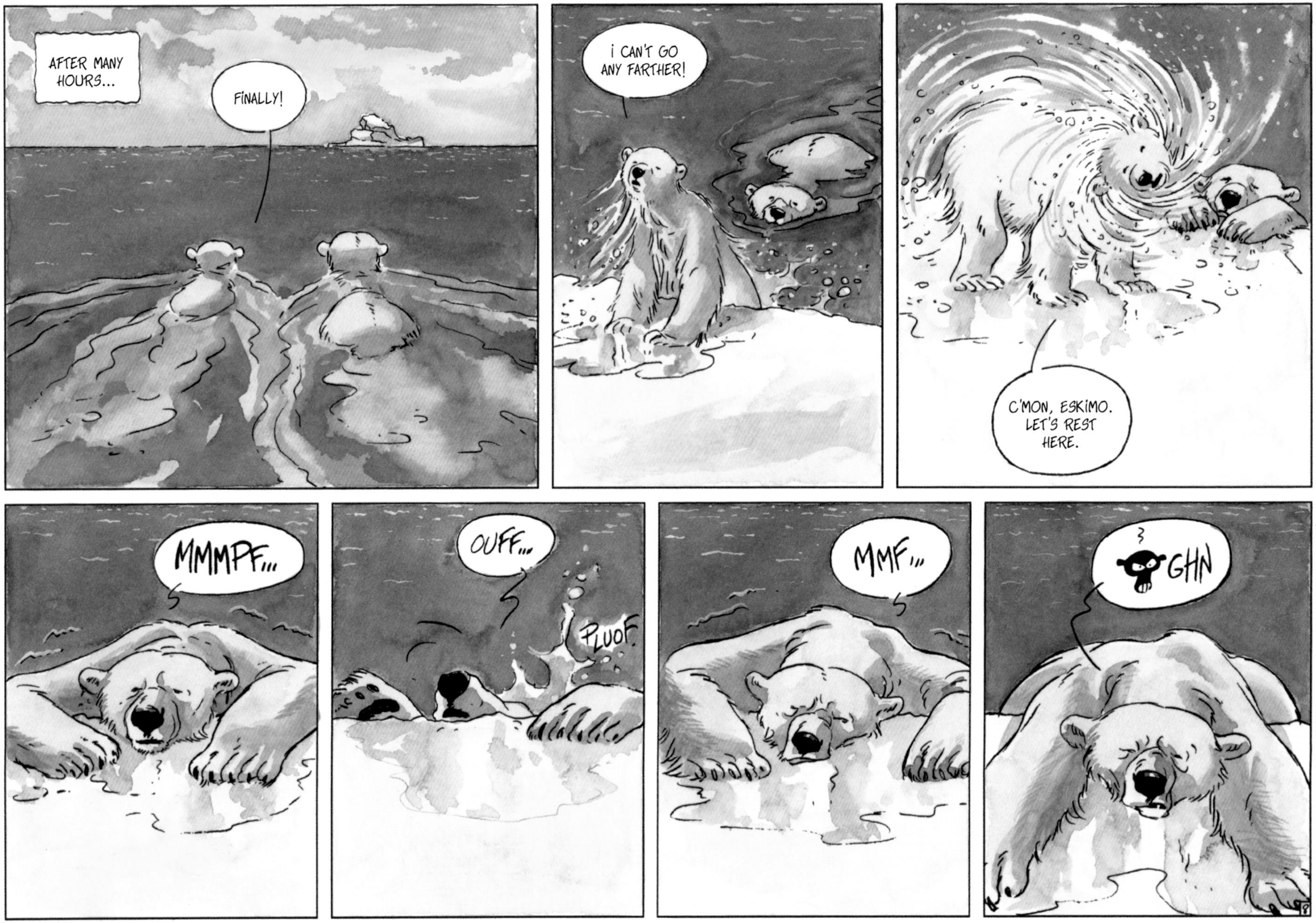
AFTER MANY HOURS...
FINALLY!
I CAN'T GO ANY FARTHER!
C'MON, ESKIMO. LET'S REST HERE.
MMMPF...
OUFF...
PLUOF
MMF...
GHN

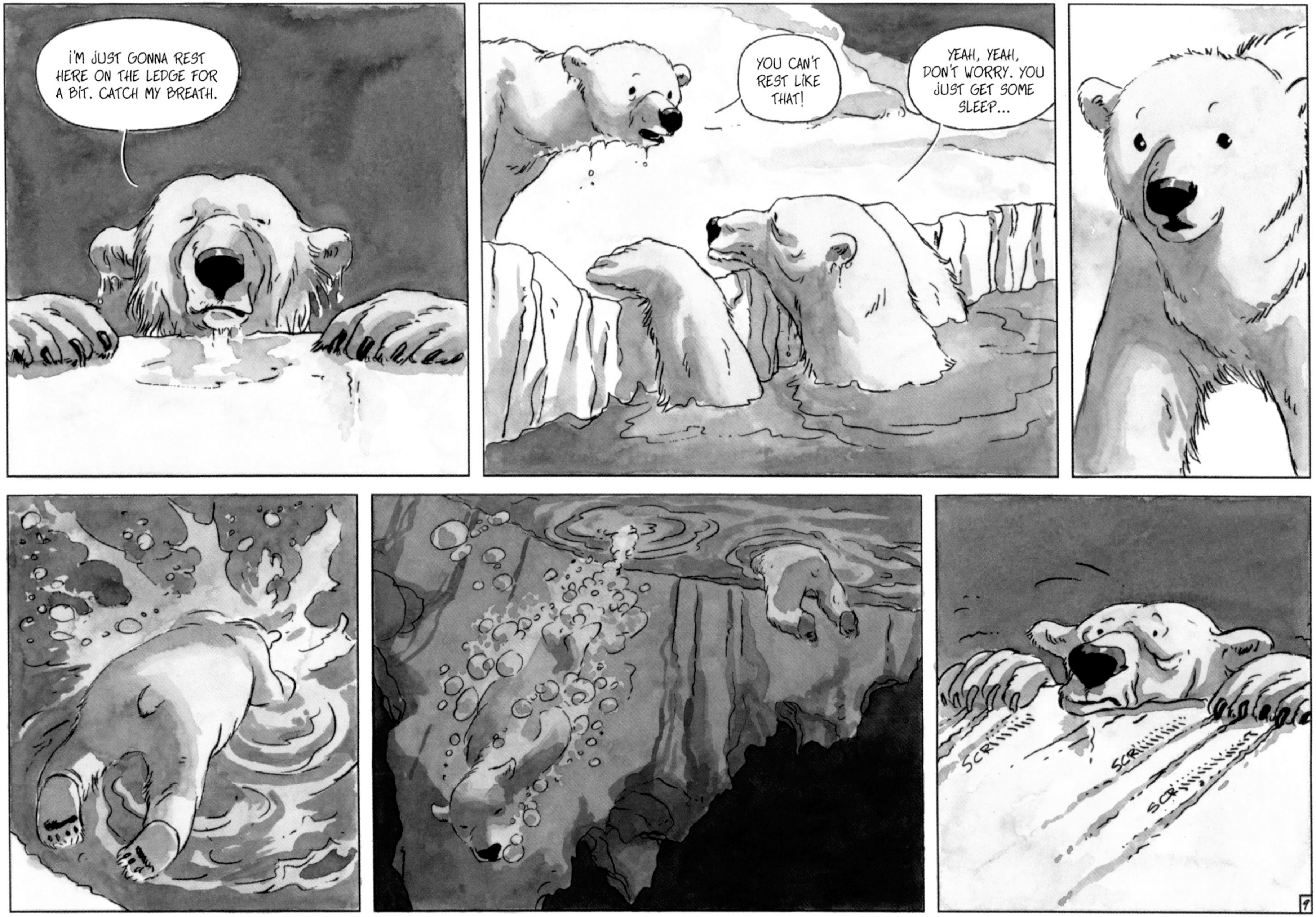
I'M JUST GONNA REST HERE ON THE LEDGE FOR A BIT. CATCH MY BREATH.
YOU CAN'T REST LIKE THAT!
YEAH, YEAH, DON'T WORRY. YOU JUST GET SOME SLEEP...
SCRiiiiiiii
SCRiiiiiiiiii
SCRiiiiiii
9

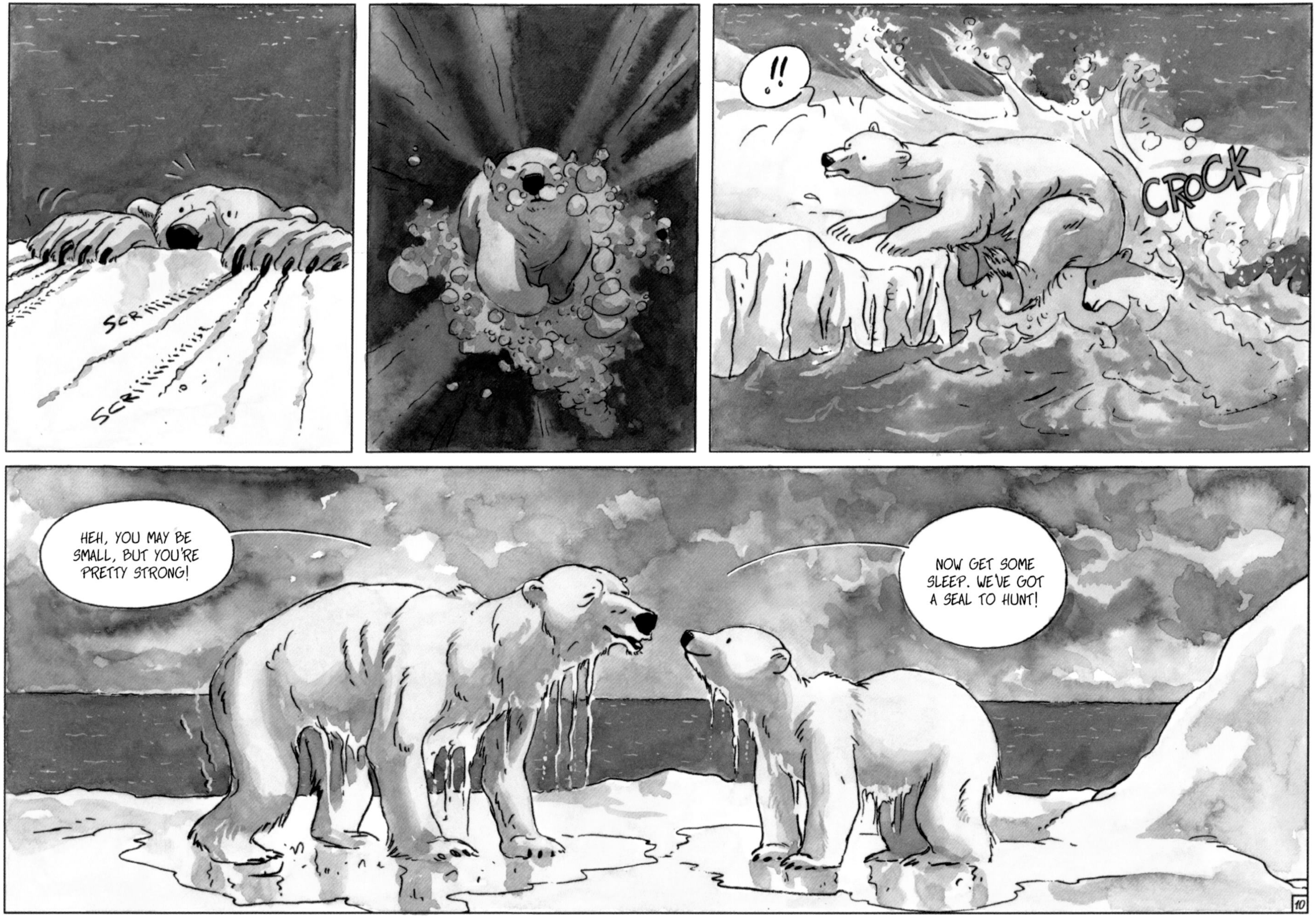
SCR
SCR
!!
CROCK
HEH, YOU MAY BE SMALL, BUT YOU'RE PRETTY STRONG!
NOW GET SOME SLEEP. WE'VE GOT A SEAL TO HUNT!
10

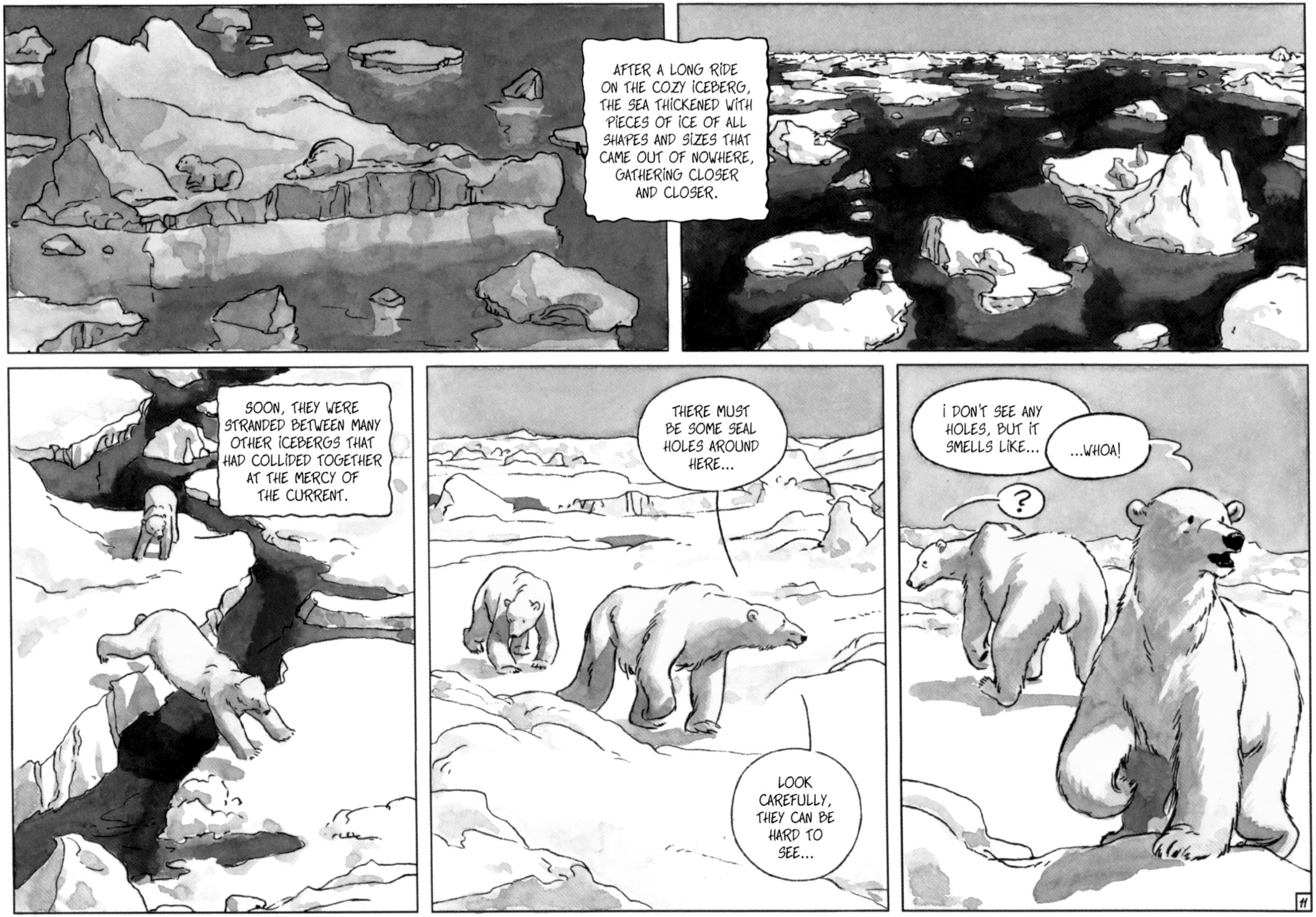
AFTER A LONG RIDE ON THE COZY ICEBERG, THE SEA THICKENED WITH PIECES OF ICE OF ALL SHAPES AND SIZES THAT CAME OUT OF NOWHERE, GATHERING CLOSER AND CLOSER.
SOON, THEY WERE STRANDED BETWEEN MANY OTHER ICEBERGS THAT HAD COLLIDED TOGETHER AT THE MERCY OF THE CURRENT.
THERE MUST BE SOME SEAL HOLES AROUND HERE...
LOOK CAREFULLY, THEY CAN BE HARD TO SEE...
I DON'T SEE ANY HOLES, BUT IT SMELLS LIKE...
...WHOA!
?
11

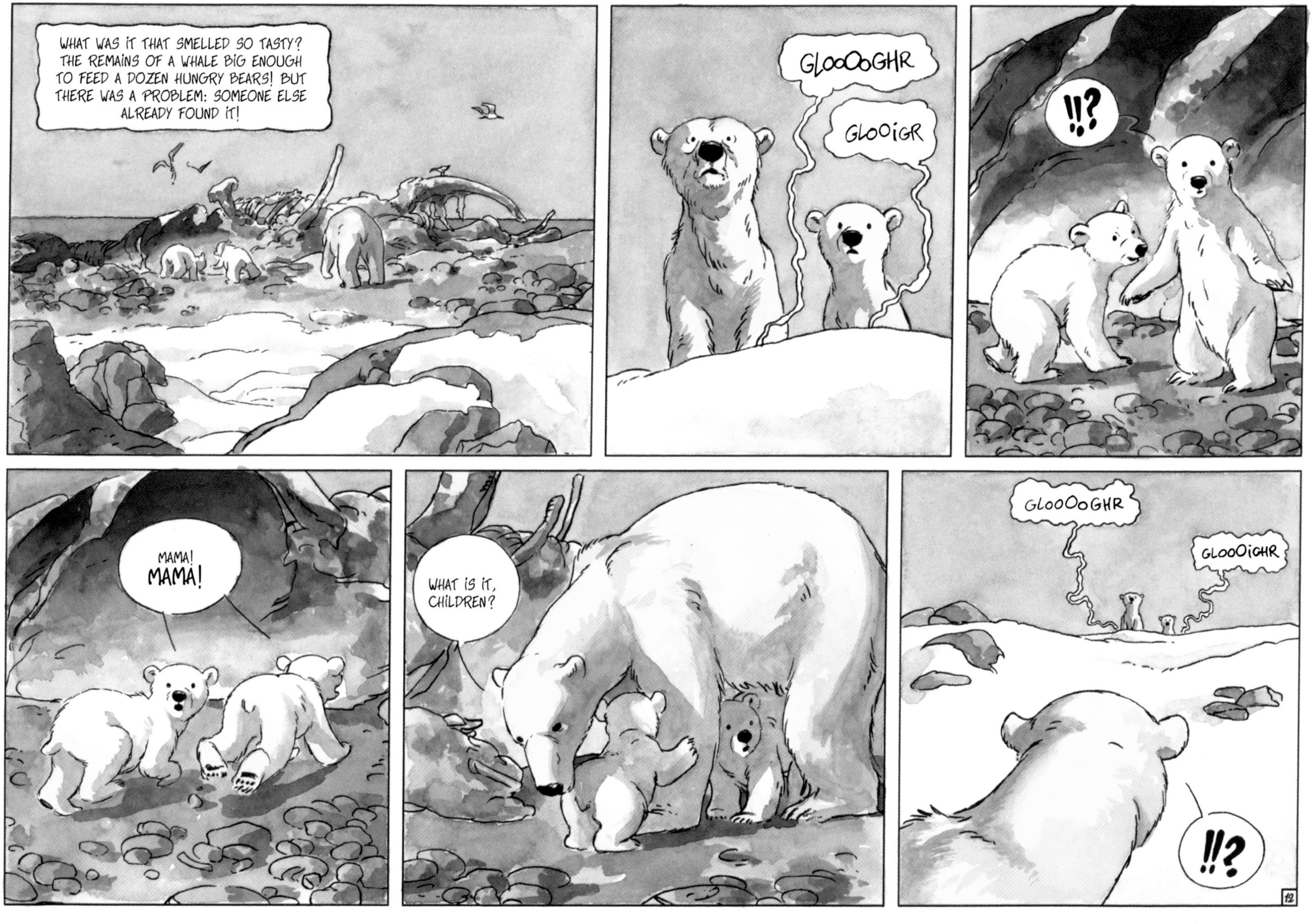
WHAT WAS IT THAT SMELLED SO TASTY? THE REMAINS OF A WHALE BIG ENOUGH TO FEED A DOZEN HUNGRY BEARS! BUT THERE WAS A PROBLEM: SOMEONE ELSE ALREADY FOUND IT!
GLOOOOGHR
GLOOIGR
!!?
MAMA! MAMA!
WHAT IS IT, CHILDREN?
GLOOOOGHR
GLOOOIGHR
!!?
12

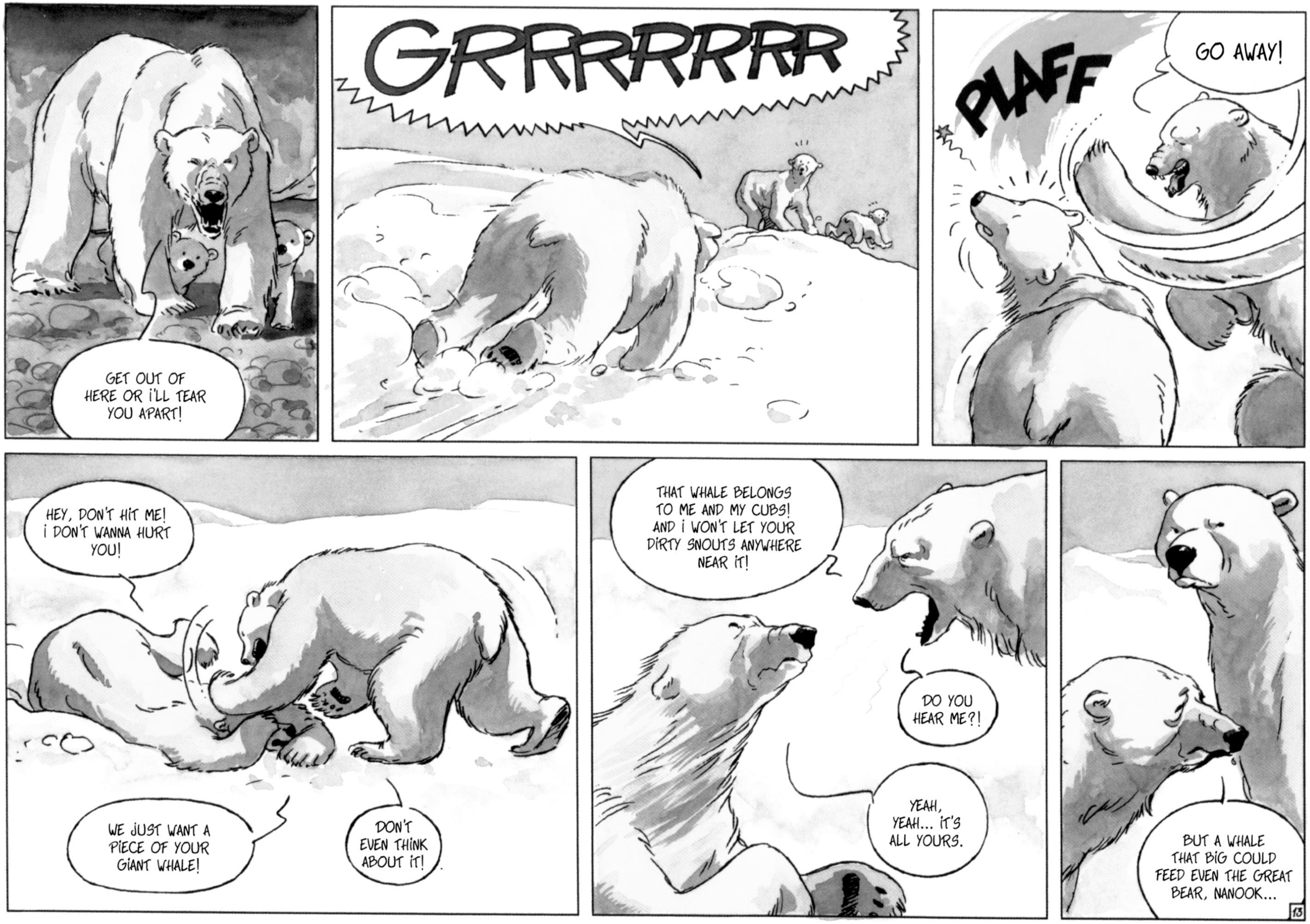
GET OUT OF HERE OR I'LL TEAR YOU APART!
GRRRRRRRR
PLAFF
GO AWAY!
HEY, DON'T HIT ME! I DON'T WANNA HURT YOU!
WE JUST WANT A PIECE OF YOUR GIANT WHALE!
DON'T EVEN THINK ABOUT IT!
THAT WHALE BELONGS TO ME AND MY CUBS! AND I WON'T LET YOUR DIRTY SNOUTS ANYWHERE NEAR IT!
DO YOU HEAR ME?!
YEAH, YEAH... IT'S ALL YOURS.
BUT A WHALE THAT BIG COULD FEED EVEN THE GREAT BEAR, NANOOK...
13

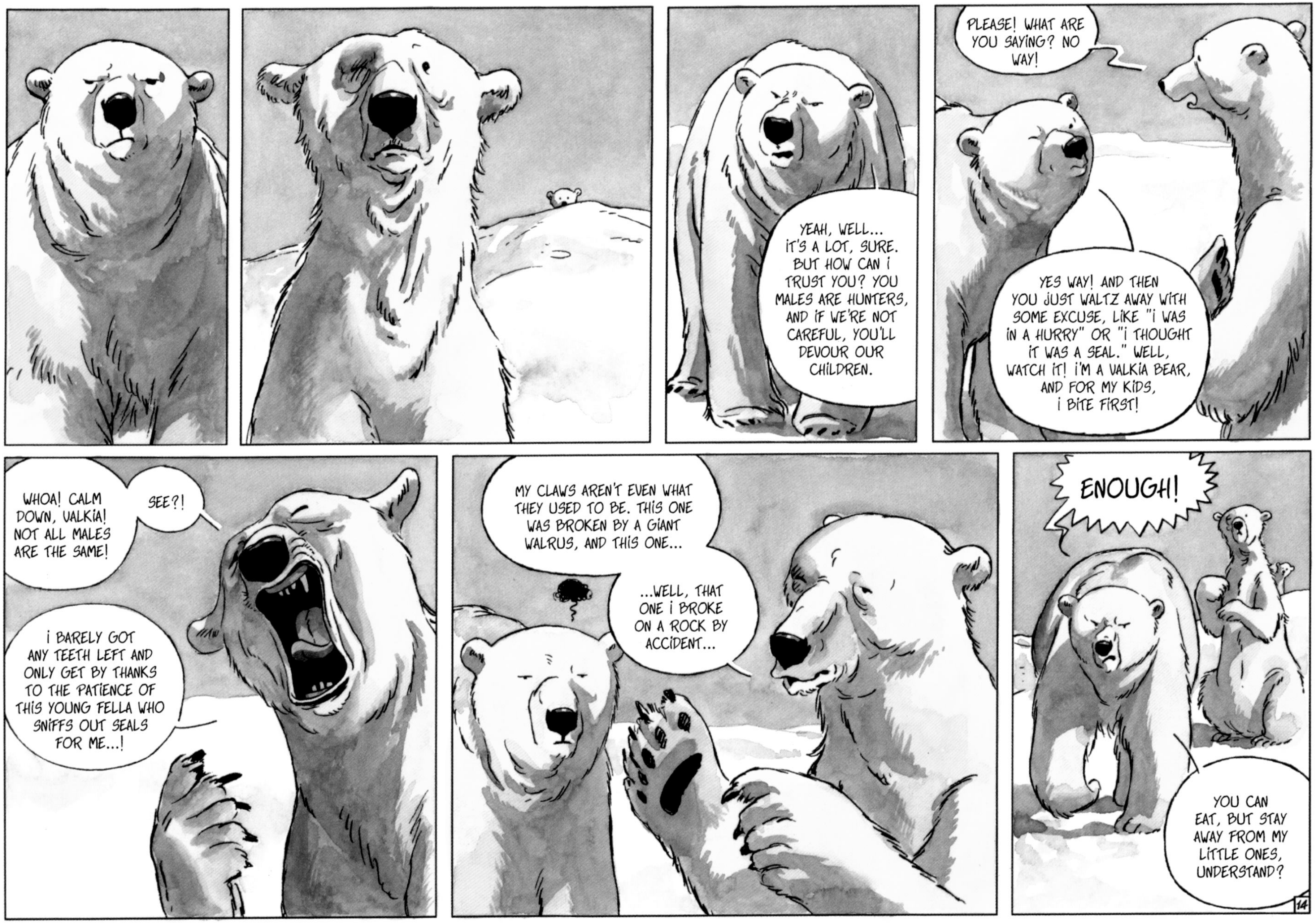

YEAH, WELL... IT'S A LOT, SURE. BUT HOW CAN I TRUST YOU? YOU MALES ARE HUNTERS, AND IF WE'RE NOT CAREFUL, YOU'LL DEVOUR OUR CHILDREN.
PLEASE! WHAT ARE YOU SAYING? NO WAY!
YES WAY! AND THEN YOU JUST WALTZ AWAY WITH SOME EXCUSE, LIKE "I WAS IN A HURRY" OR "I THOUGHT IT WAS A SEAL." WELL, WATCH IT! I'M A VALKIA BEAR, AND FOR MY KIDS, I BITE FIRST!
WHOA! CALM DOWN, VALKIA! NOT ALL MALES ARE THE SAME!
SEE?!
I BARELY GOT ANY TEETH LEFT AND ONLY GET BY THANKS TO THE PATIENCE OF THIS YOUNG FELLA WHO SNIFFS OUT SEALS FOR ME...!
MY CLAWS AREN'T EVEN WHAT THEY USED TO BE. THIS ONE WAS BROKEN BY A GIANT WALRUS, AND THIS ONE...
...WELL, THAT ONE I BROKE ON A ROCK BY ACCIDENT...
ENOUGH!
YOU CAN EAT, BUT STAY AWAY FROM MY LITTLE ONES, UNDERSTAND?
14

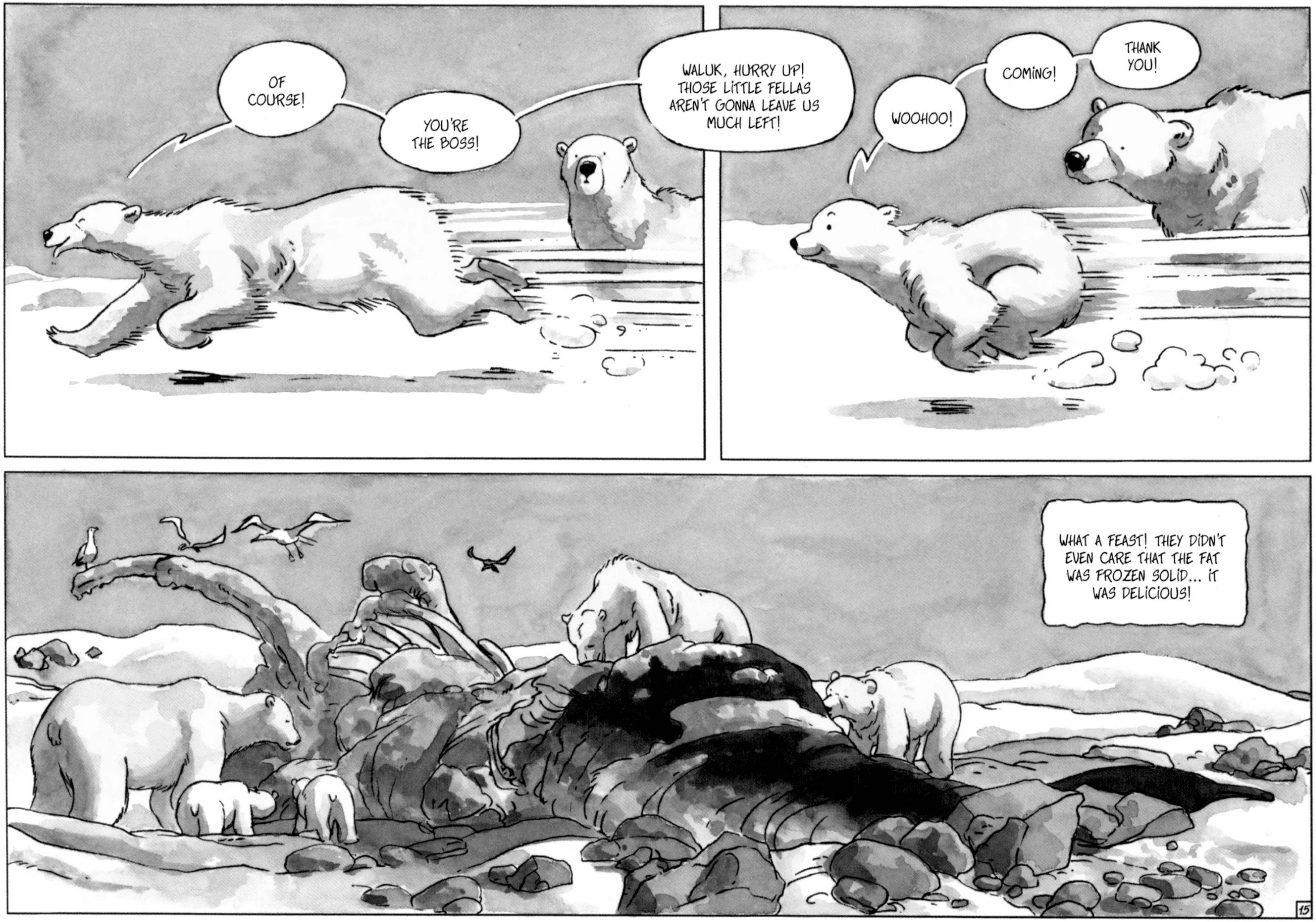
OF COURSE!
YOU'RE THE BOSS!
WALUK, HURRY UP! THOSE LITTLE FELLAS AREN'T GONNA LEAVE US MUCH LEFT!
WOOHOO!
COMING!
THANK YOU!
WHAT A FEAST! THEY DIDN'T EVEN CARE THAT THE FAT WAS FROZEN SOLID... IT WAS DELICIOUS!
15

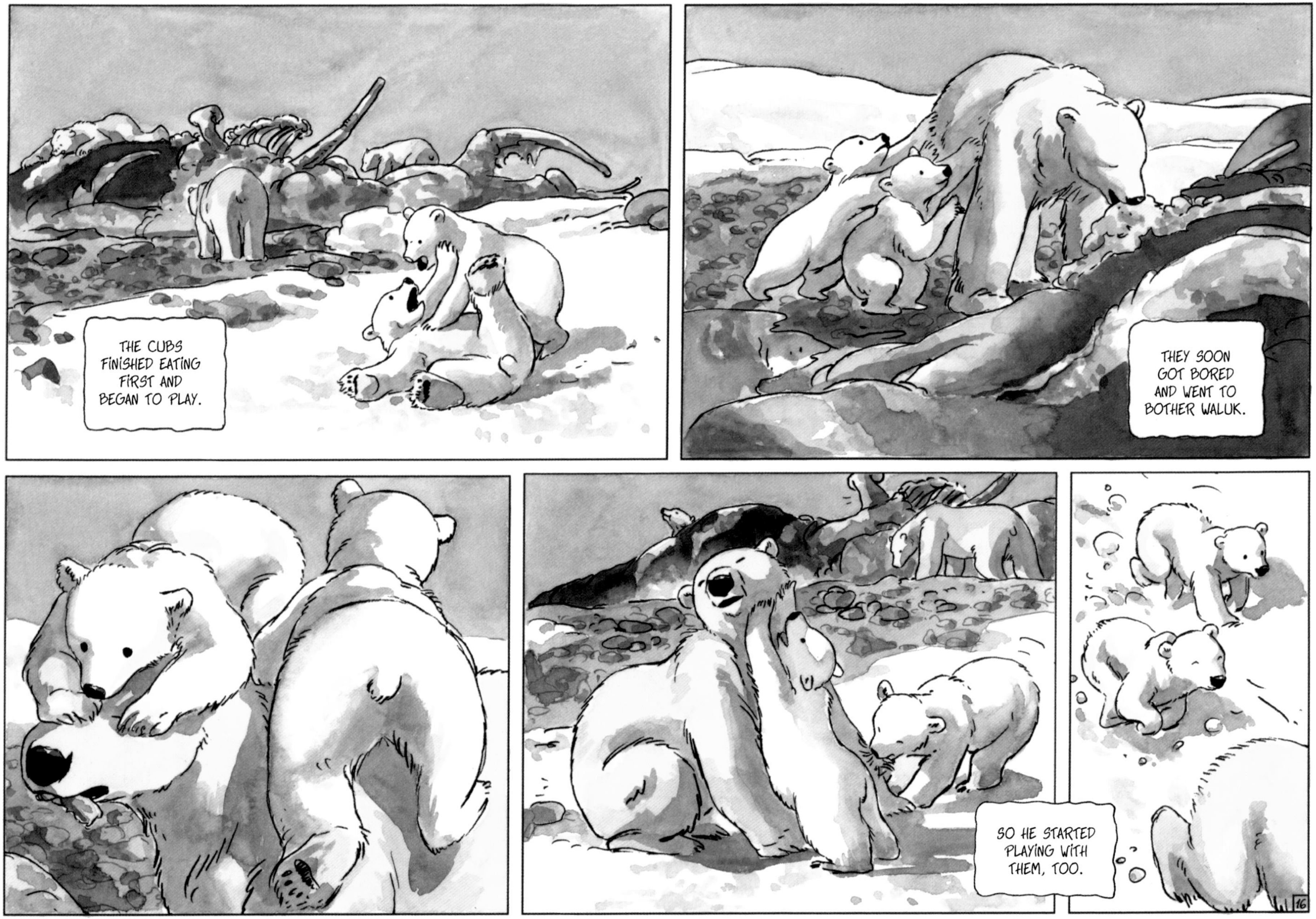
THE CUBS FINISHED EATING FIRST AND BEGAN TO PLAY.
THEY SOON GOT BORED AND WENT TO BOTHER WALUK.
SO HE STARTED PLAYING WITH THEM, TOO.
16

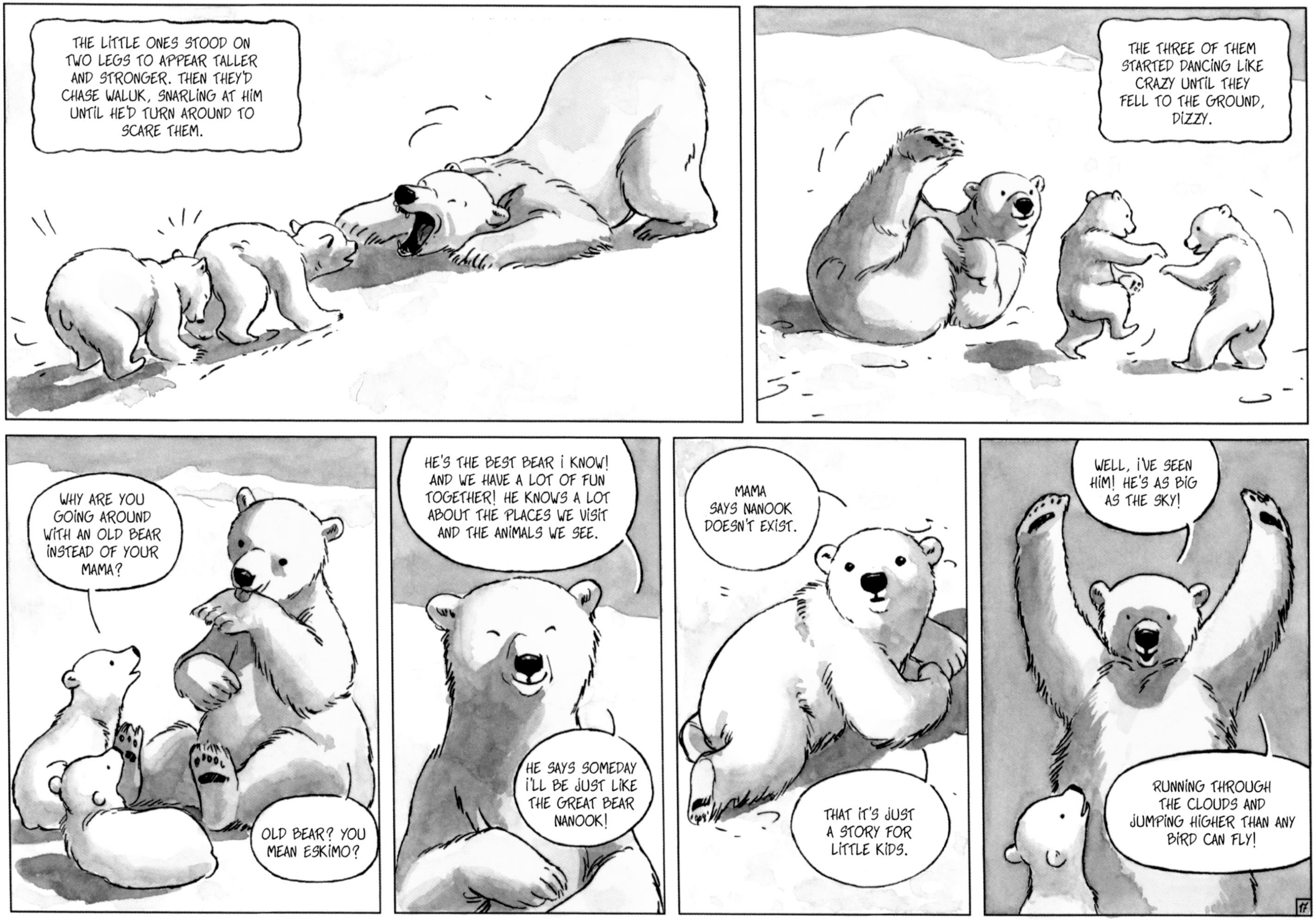

THE LITTLE ONES STOOD ON TWO LEGS TO APPEAR TALLER AND STRONGER. THEN THEY'D CHASE WALUK, SNARLING AT HIM UNTIL HE'D TURN AROUND TO SCARE THEM.
THE THREE OF THEM STARTED DANCING LIKE CRAZY UNTIL THEY FELL TO THE GROUND, DIZZY.
WHY ARE YOU GOING AROUND WITH AN OLD BEAR INSTEAD OF YOUR MAMA?
OLD BEAR? YOU MEAN ESKIMO?
HE'S THE BEST BEAR I KNOW! AND WE HAVE A LOT OF FUN TOGETHER! HE KNOWS A LOT ABOUT THE PLACES WE VISIT AND THE ANIMALS WE SEE.
HE SAYS SOMEDAY I'LL BE JUST LIKE THE GREAT BEAR NANOOK!
MAMA SAYS NANOOK DOESN'T EXIST.
THAT IT'S JUST A STORY FOR LITTLE KIDS.
WELL, I'VE SEEN HIM! HE'S AS BIG AS THE SKY!
RUNNING THROUGH THE CLOUDS AND JUMPING HIGHER THAN ANY BIRD CAN FLY!

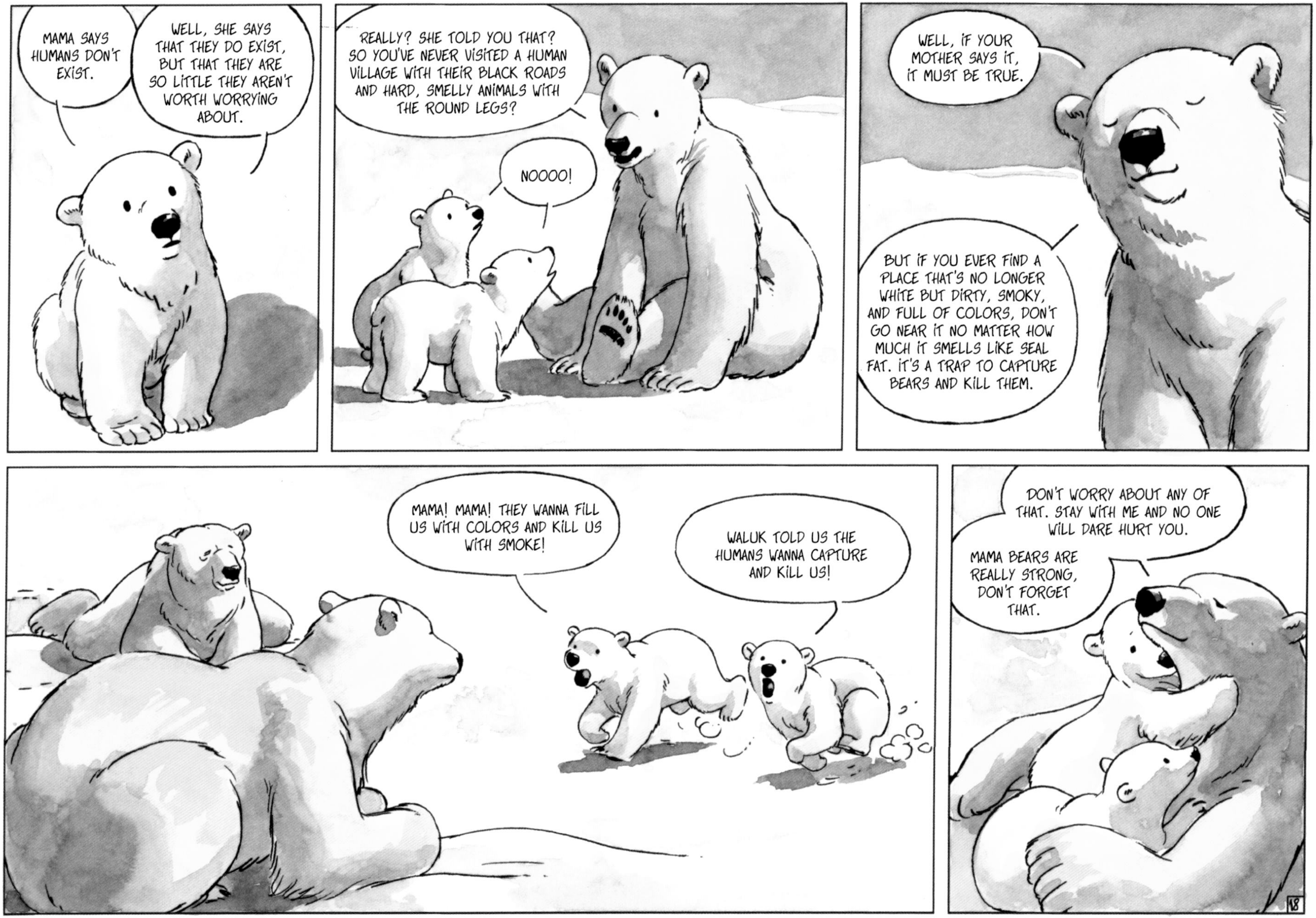
MAMA SAYS HUMANS DON'T EXIST.
WELL, SHE SAYS THAT THEY DO EXIST, BUT THAT THEY ARE SO LITTLE THEY AREN'T WORTH WORRYING ABOUT.
REALLY? SHE TOLD YOU THAT? SO YOU'VE NEVER VISITED A HUMAN VILLAGE WITH THEIR BLACK ROADS AND HARD, SMELLY ANIMALS WITH THE ROUND LEGS?
NOOOO!
WELL, IF YOUR MOTHER SAYS IT, IT MUST BE TRUE.
BUT IF YOU EVER FIND A PLACE THAT'S NO LONGER WHITE BUT DIRTY, SMOKY, AND FULL OF COLORS, DON'T GO NEAR IT NO MATTER HOW MUCH IT SMELLS LIKE SEAL FAT. IT'S A TRAP TO CAPTURE BEARS AND KILL THEM.
MAMA! MAMA! THEY WANNA FILL US WITH COLORS AND KILL US WITH SMOKE!
WALUK TOLD US THE HUMANS WANNA CAPTURE AND KILL US!
DON'T WORRY ABOUT ANY OF THAT. STAY WITH ME AND NO ONE WILL DARE HURT YOU.
MAMA BEARS ARE REALLY STRONG, DON'T FORGET THAT.
18

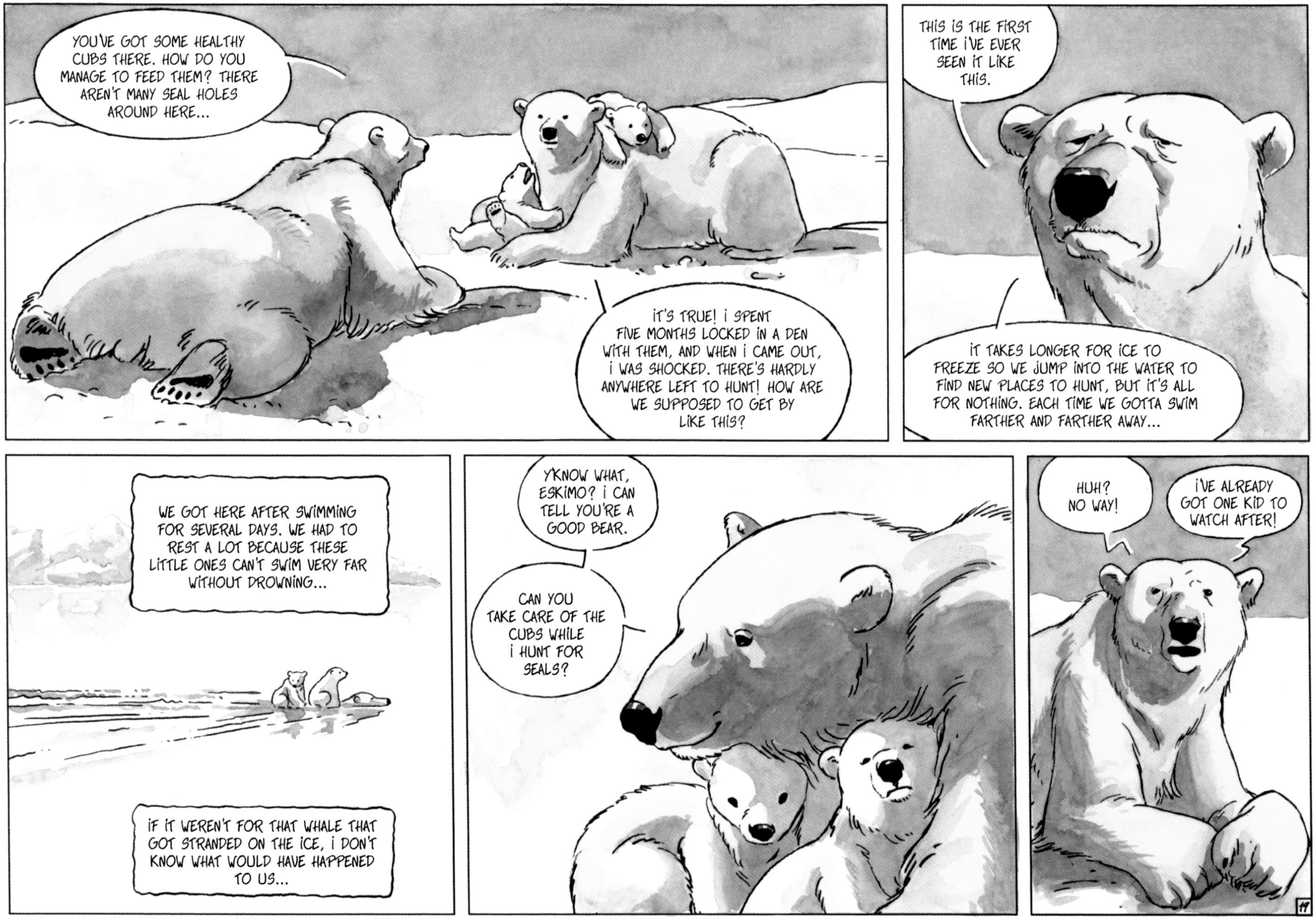

YOU'VE GOT SOME HEALTHY CUBS THERE. HOW DO YOU MANAGE TO FEED THEM? THERE AREN'T MANY SEAL HOLES AROUND HERE...
IT'S TRUE! I SPENT FIVE MONTHS LOCKED IN A DEN WITH THEM, AND WHEN I CAME OUT, I WAS SHOCKED. THERE'S HARDLY ANYWHERE LEFT TO HUNT! HOW ARE WE SUPPOSED TO GET BY LIKE THIS?
THIS IS THE FIRST TIME I'VE EVER SEEN IT LIKE THIS.
IT TAKES LONGER FOR ICE TO FREEZE SO WE JUMP INTO THE WATER TO FIND NEW PLACES TO HUNT, BUT IT'S ALL FOR NOTHING. EACH TIME WE GOTTA SWIM FARTHER AND FARTHER AWAY...
WE GOT HERE AFTER SWIMMING FOR SEVERAL DAYS. WE HAD TO REST A LOT BECAUSE THESE LITTLE ONES CAN'T SWIM VERY FAR WITHOUT DROWNING...
IF IT WEREN'T FOR THAT WHALE THAT GOT STRANDED ON THE ICE, I DON'T KNOW WHAT WOULD HAVE HAPPENED TO US...
Y'KNOW WHAT, ESKIMO? I CAN TELL YOU'RE A GOOD BEAR.
CAN YOU TAKE CARE OF THE CUBS WHILE I HUNT FOR SEALS?
HUH? NO WAY!
I'VE ALREADY GOT ONE KID TO WATCH AFTER!
19

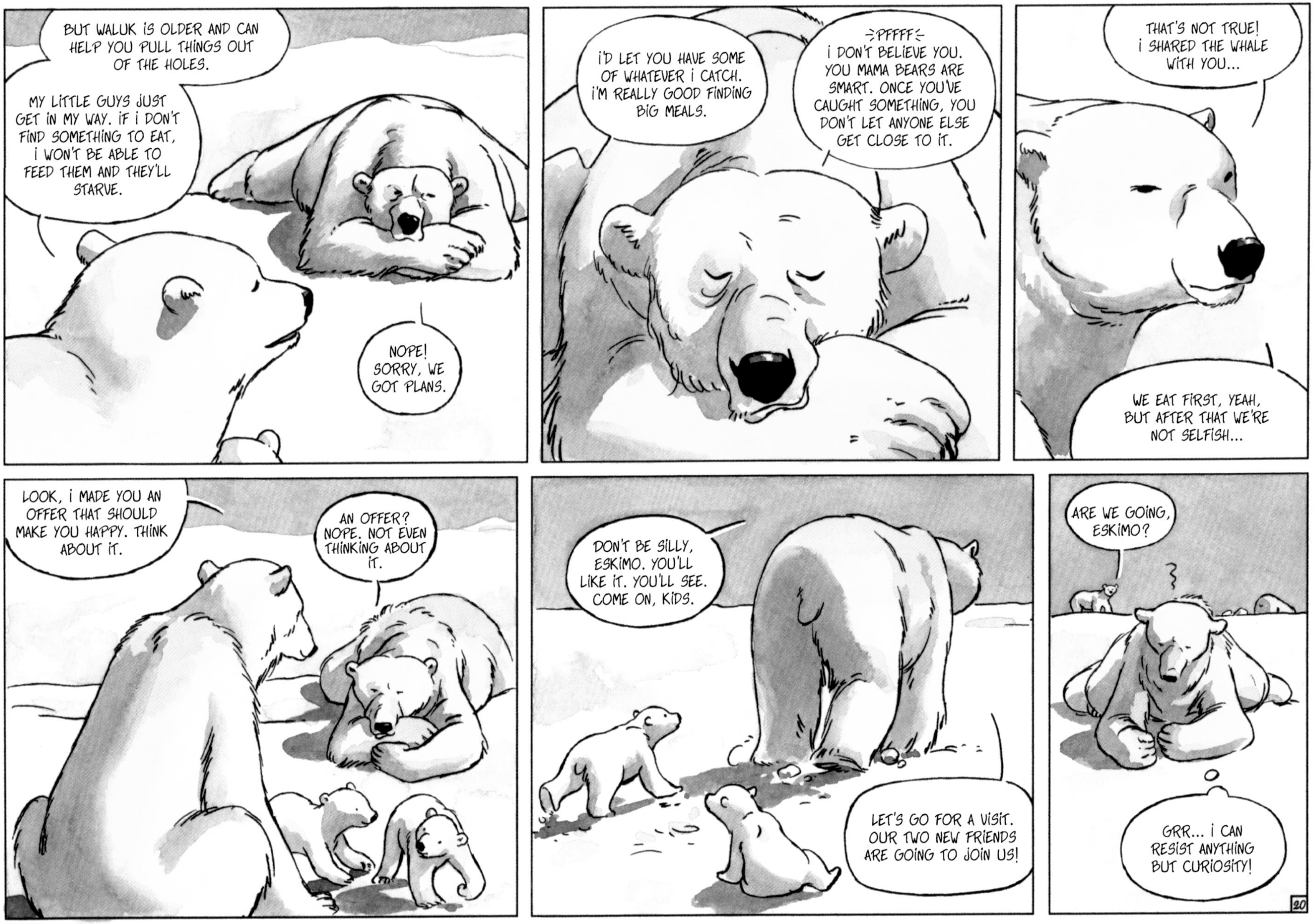

BUT WALUK IS OLDER AND CAN HELP YOU PULL THINGS OUT OF THE HOLES.
MY LITTLE GUYS JUST GET IN MY WAY. IF I DON'T FIND SOMETHING TO EAT, I WON'T BE ABLE TO FEED THEM AND THEY'LL STARVE.
NOPE! SORRY, WE GOT PLANS.
I'D LET YOU HAVE SOME OF WHATEVER I CATCH. I'M REALLY GOOD FINDING BIG MEALS.
PFFFF
I DON'T BELIEVE YOU. YOU MAMA BEARS ARE SMART. ONCE YOU'VE CAUGHT SOMETHING, YOU DON'T LET ANYONE ELSE GET CLOSE TO IT.
THAT'S NOT TRUE! I SHARED THE WHALE WITH YOU...
WE EAT FIRST, YEAH, BUT AFTER THAT WE'RE NOT SELFISH...
LOOK, I MADE YOU AN OFFER THAT SHOULD MAKE YOU HAPPY. THINK ABOUT IT.
AN OFFER? NOPE. NOT EVEN THINKING ABOUT IT.
DON'T BE SILLY, ESKIMO. YOU'LL LIKE IT. YOU'LL SEE. COME ON, KIDS.
LET'S GO FOR A VISIT. OUR TWO NEW FRIENDS ARE GOING TO JOIN US!
ARE WE GOING, ESKIMO?
GRR... I CAN RESIST ANYTHING BUT CURIOSITY!
20

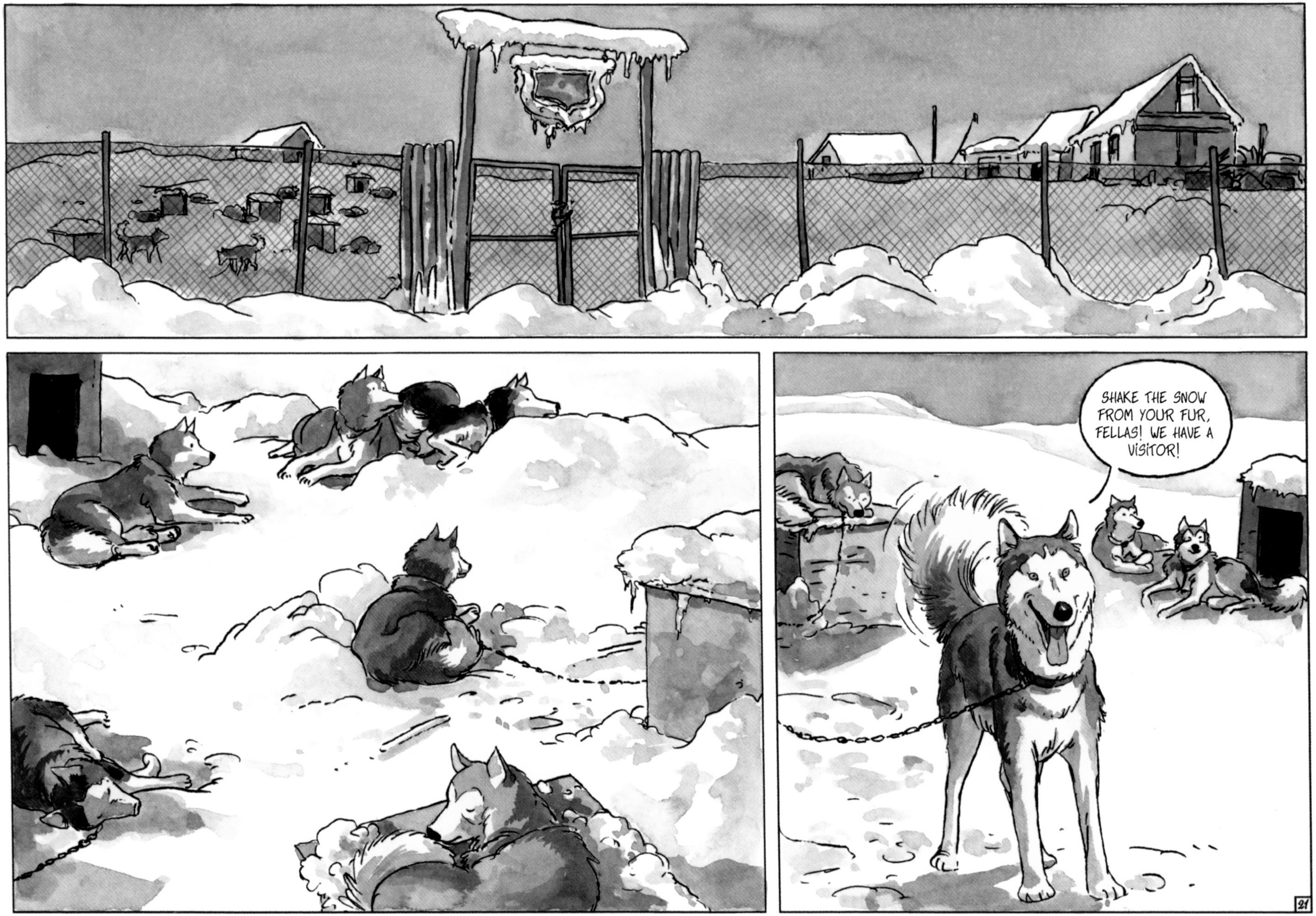
SHAKE THE SNOW FROM YOUR FUR, FELLAS! WE HAVE A VISITOR!
21

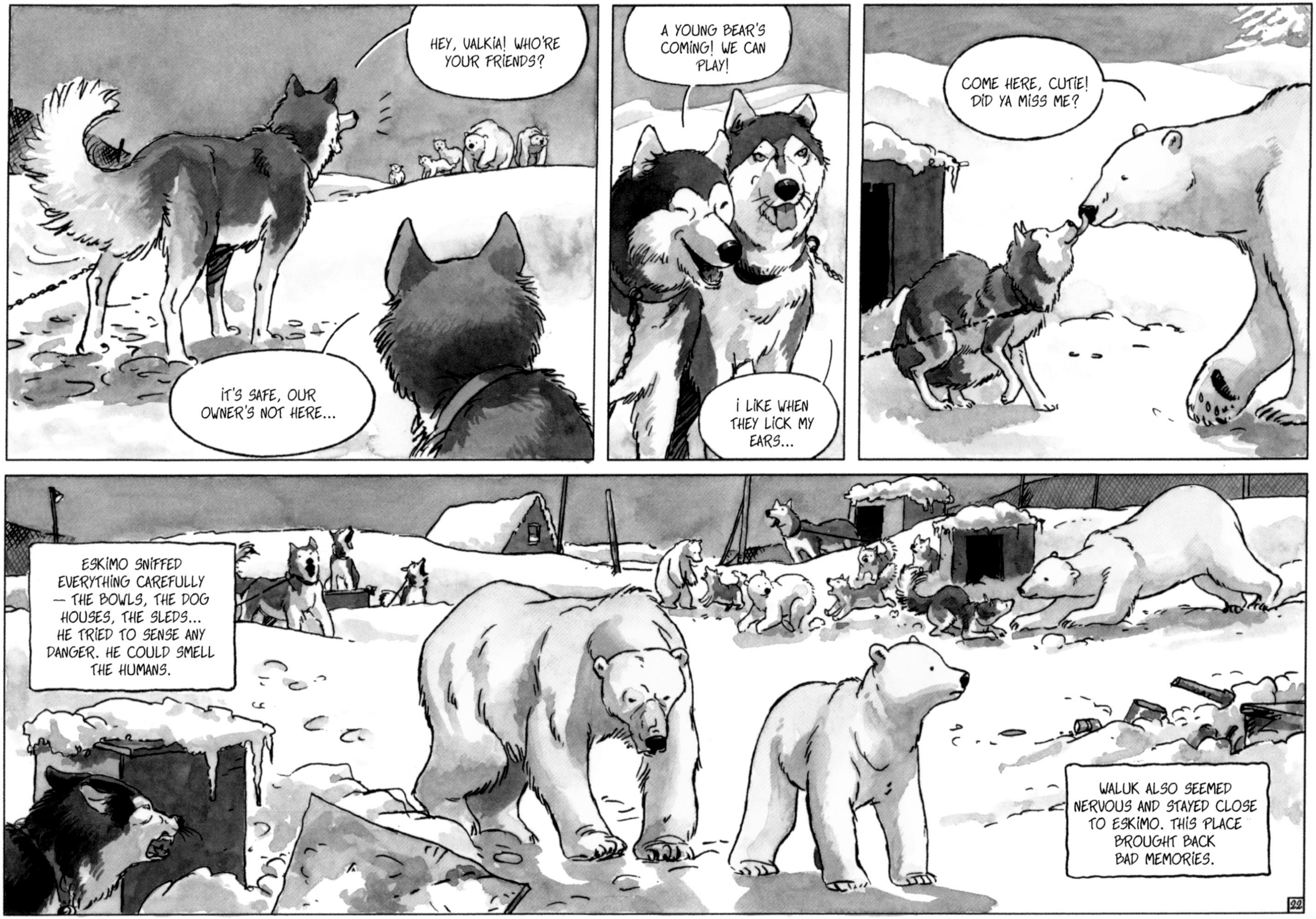
HEY, VALKIA! WHO'RE YOUR FRIENDS?
IT'S SAFE, OUR OWNER'S NOT HERE...
A YOUNG BEAR'S COMING! WE CAN PLAY!
I LIKE WHEN THEY LICK MY EARS...
COME HERE, CUTIE! DID YA MISS ME?
ESKIMO SNIFFED EVERYTHING CAREFULLY -- THE BOWLS, THE DOG HOUSES, THE SLEDS... HE TRIED TO SENSE ANY DANGER. HE COULD SMELL THE HUMANS.
WALUK ALSO SEEMED NERVOUS AND STAYED CLOSE TO ESKIMO. THIS PLACE BROUGHT BACK BAD MEMORIES.
22

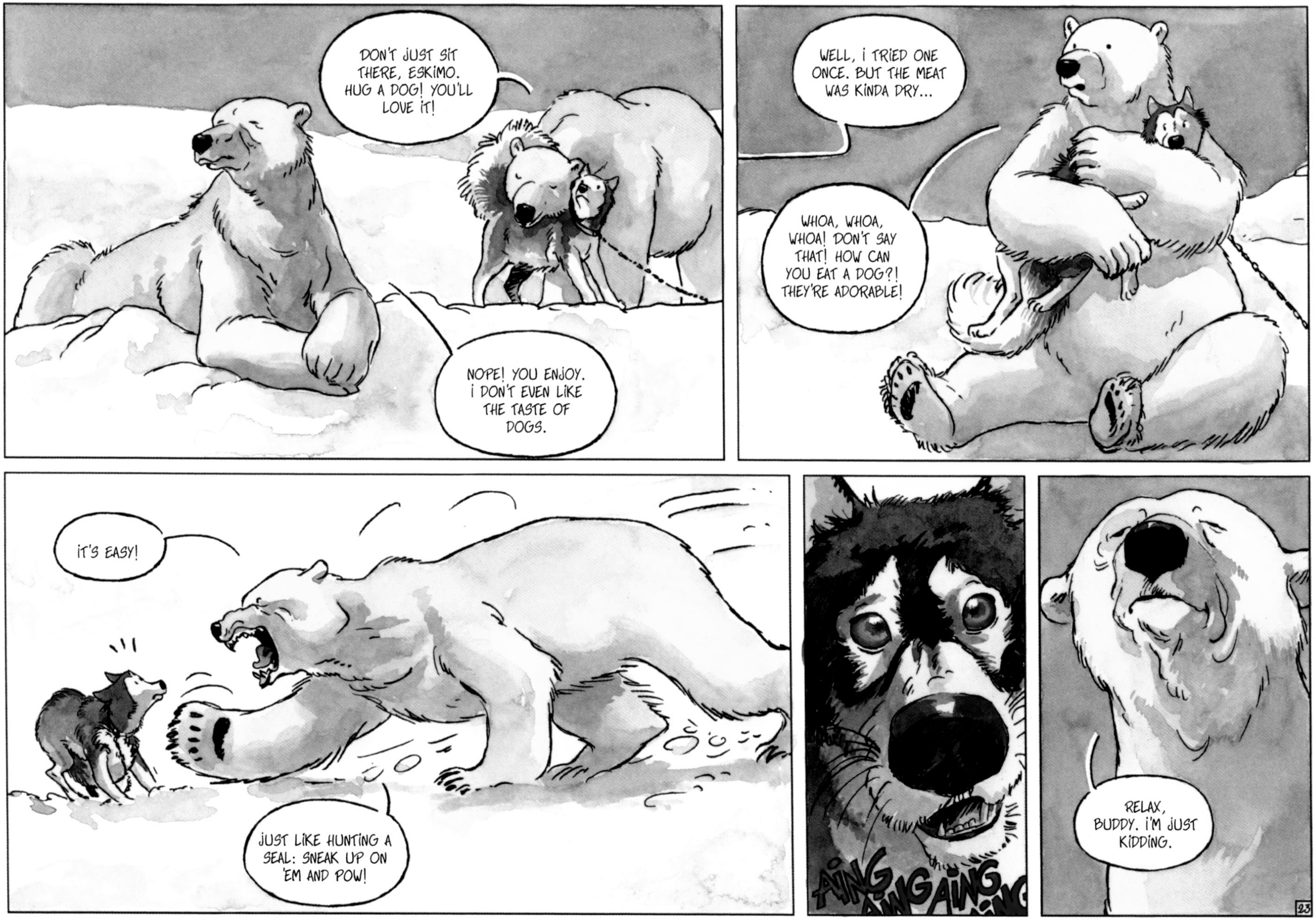
DON'T JUST SIT THERE, ESKIMO. HUG A DOG! YOU'LL LOVE IT!
NOPE! YOU ENJOY. I DON'T EVEN LIKE THE TASTE OF DOGS.
WELL, I TRIED ONE ONCE. BUT THE MEAT WAS KINDA DRY...
WHOA, WHOA, WHOA! DON'T SAY THAT! HOW CAN YOU EAT A DOG?! THEY'RE ADORABLE!
IT'S EASY!
JUST LIKE HUNTING A SEAL: SNEAK UP ON 'EM AND POW!
AING AINGAING
RELAX, BUDDY. I'M JUST KIDDING.
23

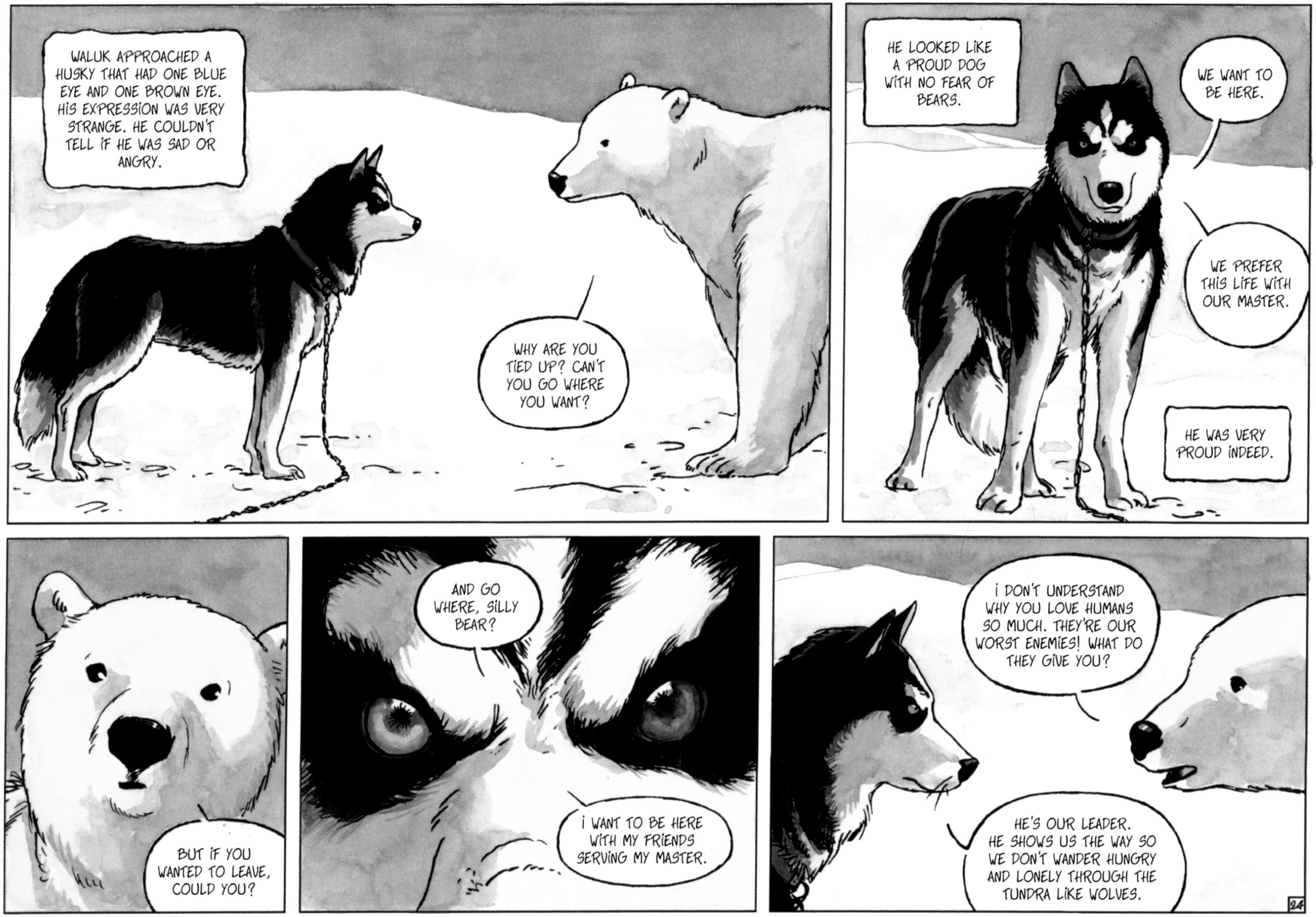
WALUK APPROACHED A HUSKY THAT HAD ONE BLUE EYE AND ONE BROWN EYE. HIS EXPRESSION WAS VERY STRANGE. HE COULDN'T TELL IF HE WAS SAD OR ANGRY.
WHY ARE YOU TIED UP? CAN'T YOU GO WHERE YOU WANT?
HE LOOKED LIKE A PROUD DOG WITH NO FEAR OF BEARS.
WE WANT TO BE HERE.
WE PREFER THIS LIFE WITH OUR MASTER.
HE WAS VERY PROUD INDEED.
BUT IF YOU WANTED TO LEAVE, COULD YOU?
AND GO WHERE, SILLY BEAR?
I WANT TO BE HERE WITH MY FRIENDS SERVING MY MASTER.
I DON'T UNDERSTAND WHY YOU LOVE HUMANS SO MUCH. THEY'RE OUR WORST ENEMIES! WHAT DO THEY GIVE YOU?
HE'S OUR LEADER. HE SHOWS US THE WAY SO WE DON'T WANDER HUNGRY AND LONELY THROUGH THE TUNDRA LIKE WOLVES.
24

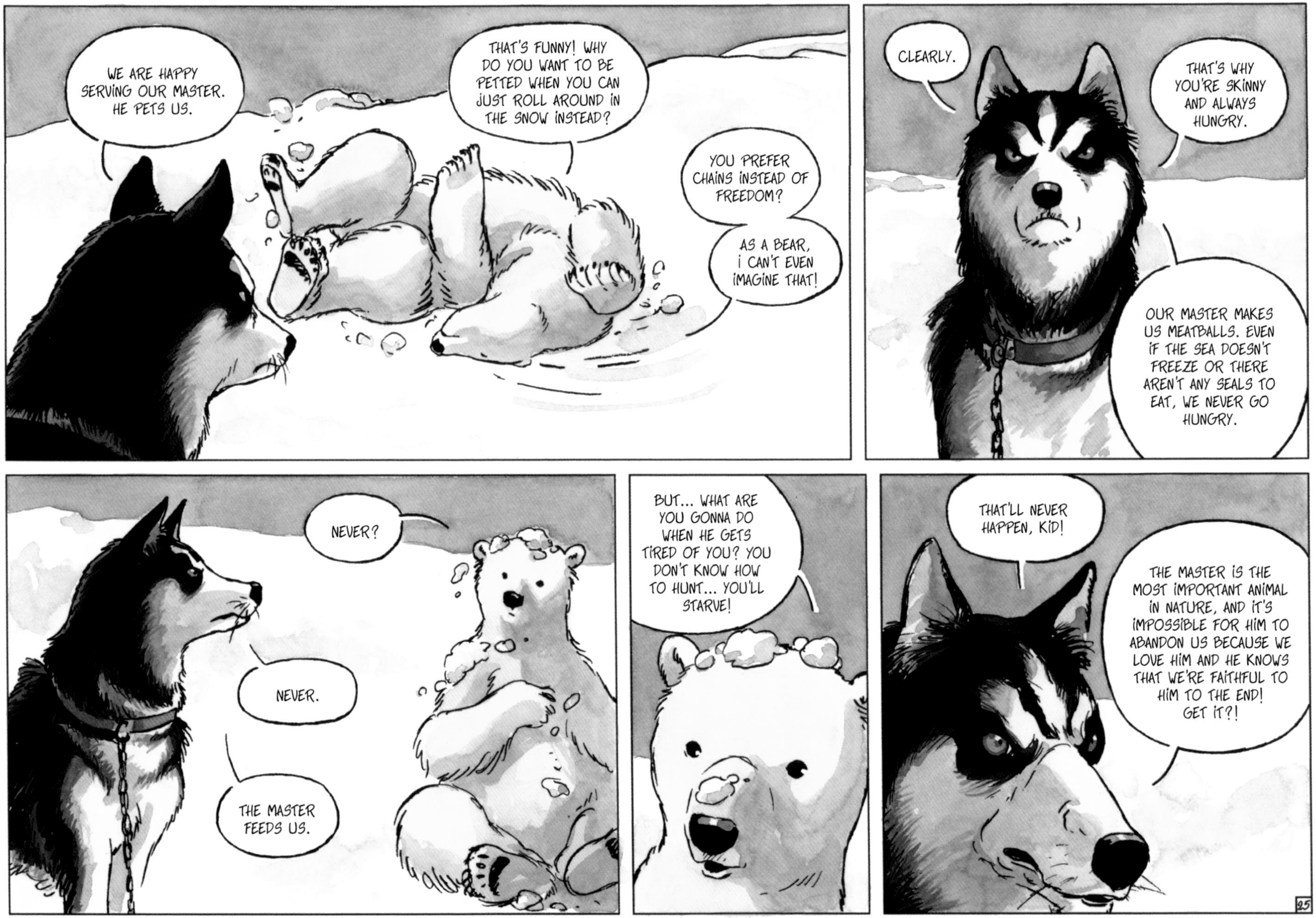
WE ARE HAPPY SERVING OUR MASTER. HE PETS US.
THAT'S FUNNY! WHY DO YOU WANT TO BE PETTED WHEN YOU CAN JUST ROLL AROUND IN THE SNOW INSTEAD?
YOU PREFER CHAINS INSTEAD OF FREEDOM?
AS A BEAR, I CAN'T EVEN IMAGINE THAT!
CLEARLY.
THAT'S WHY YOU'RE SKINNY AND ALWAYS HUNGRY.
OUR MASTER MAKES US MEATBALLS. EVEN IF THE SEA DOESN'T FREEZE OR THERE AREN'T ANY SEALS TO EAT, WE NEVER GO HUNGRY.
NEVER?
NEVER.
THE MASTER FEEDS US.
BUT... WHAT ARE YOU GONNA DO WHEN HE GETS TIRED OF YOU? YOU DON'T KNOW HOW TO HUNT... YOU'LL STARVE!
THAT'LL NEVER HAPPEN, KID!
THE MASTER IS THE MOST IMPORTANT ANIMAL IN NATURE, AND IT'S IMPOSSIBLE FOR HIM TO ABANDON US BECAUSE WE LOVE HIM AND HE KNOWS THAT WE'RE FAITHFUL TO HIM TO THE END! GET IT?!

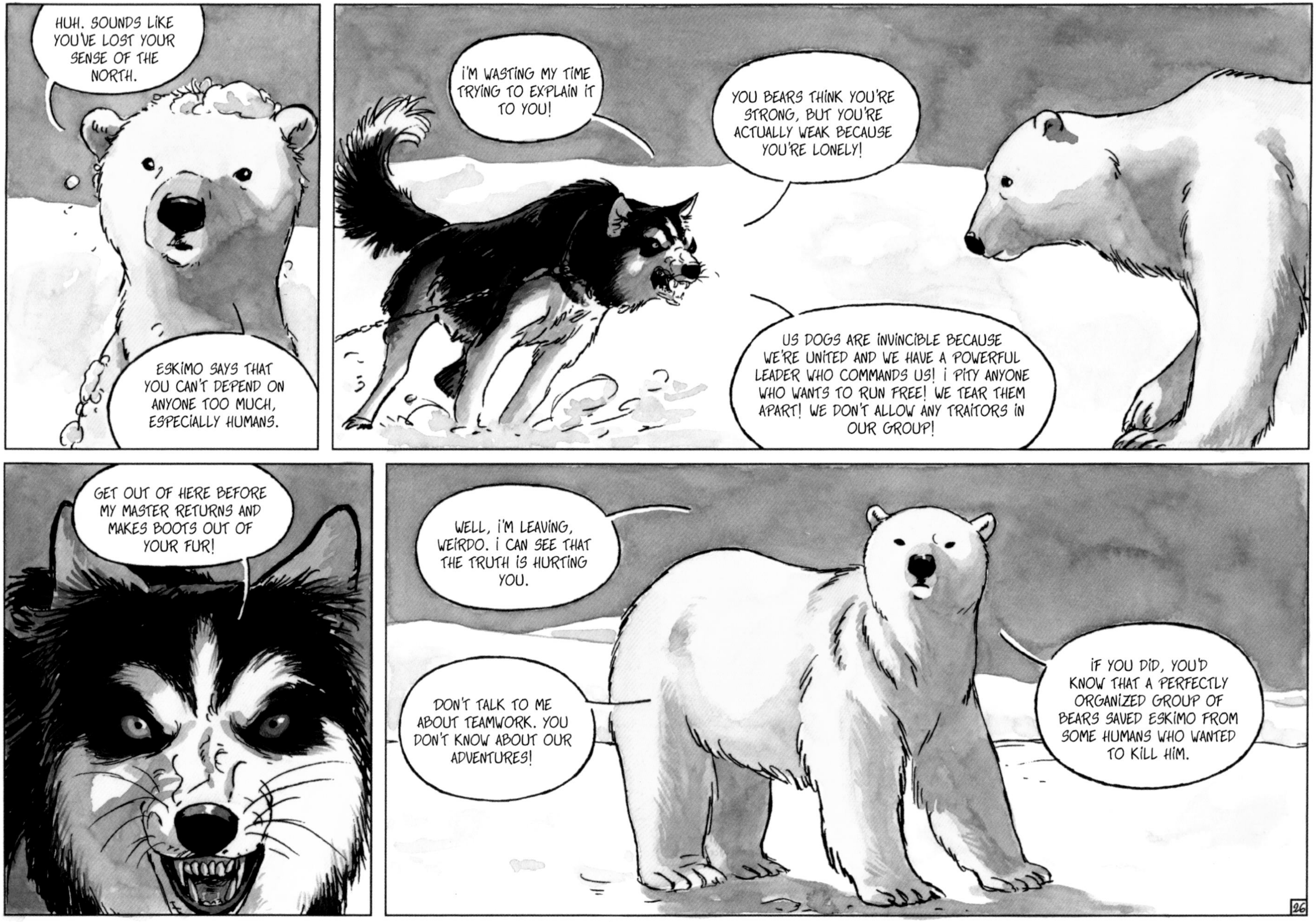
HUH. SOUNDS LIKE YOU'VE LOST YOUR SENSE OF THE NORTH.
ESKIMO SAYS THAT YOU CAN'T DEPEND ON ANYONE TOO MUCH, ESPECIALLY HUMANS.
I'M WASTING MY TIME TRYING TO EXPLAIN IT TO YOU!
YOU BEARS THINK YOU'RE STRONG, BUT YOU'RE ACTUALLY WEAK BECAUSE YOU'RE LONELY!
US DOGS ARE INVINCIBLE BECAUSE WE'RE UNITED AND WE HAVE A POWERFUL LEADER WHO COMMANDS US! I PITY ANYONE WHO WANTS TO RUN FREE! WE TEAR THEM APART! WE DON'T ALLOW ANY TRAITORS IN OUR GROUP!
GET OUT OF HERE BEFORE MY MASTER RETURNS AND MAKES BOOTS OUT OF YOUR FUR!
WELL, I'M LEAVING, WEIRDO. I CAN SEE THAT THE TRUTH IS HURTING YOU.
DON'T TALK TO ME ABOUT TEAMWORK. YOU DON'T KNOW ABOUT OUR ADVENTURES!
IF YOU DID, YOU'D KNOW THAT A PERFECTLY ORGANIZED GROUP OF BEARS SAVED ESKIMO FROM SOME HUMANS WHO WANTED TO KILL HIM.
26

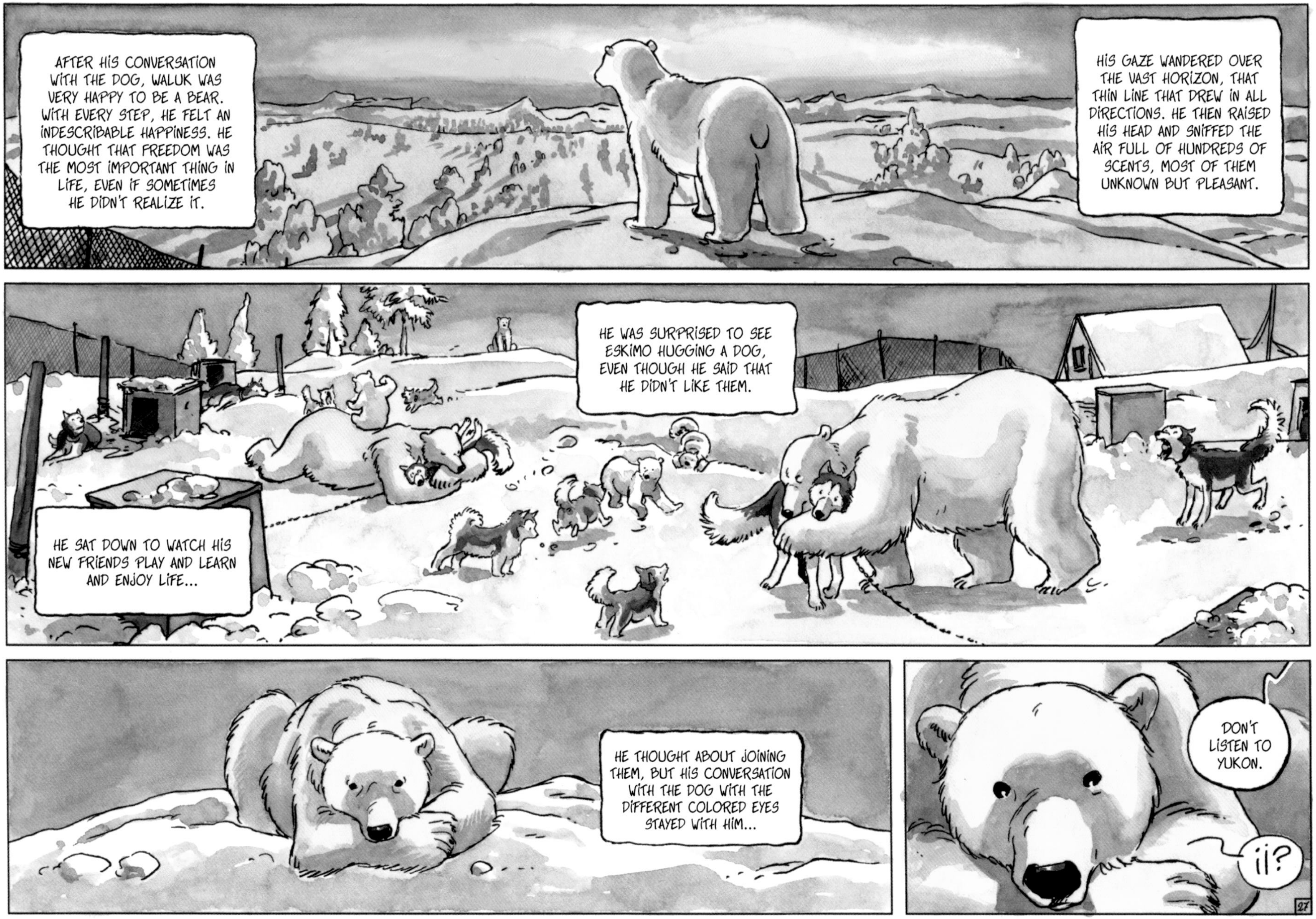
AFTER HIS CONVERSATION WITH THE DOG, WALUK WAS VERY HAPPY TO BE A BEAR. WITH EVERY STEP, HE FELT AN INDESCRIBABLE HAPPINESS. HE THOUGHT THAT FREEDOM WAS THE MOST IMPORTANT THING IN LIFE, EVEN IF SOMETIMES HE DIDN'T REALIZE IT.
HIS GAZE WANDERED OVER THE VAST HORIZON, THAT THIN LINE THAT DREW IN ALL DIRECTIONS. HE THEN RAISED HIS HEAD AND SNIFFED THE AIR FULL OF HUNDREDS OF SCENTS, MOST OF THEM UNKNOWN BUT PLEASANT.
HE WAS SURPRISED TO SEE ESKIMO HUGGING A DOG, EVEN THOUGH HE SAID THAT HE DIDN'T LIKE THEM.
HE SAT DOWN TO WATCH HIS NEW FRIENDS PLAY AND LEARN AND ENJOY LIFE...
HE THOUGHT ABOUT JOINING THEM, BUT HIS CONVERSATION WITH THE DOG WITH THE DIFFERENT COLORED EYES STAYED WITH HIM...
DON'T LISTEN TO YUKON.
i!?

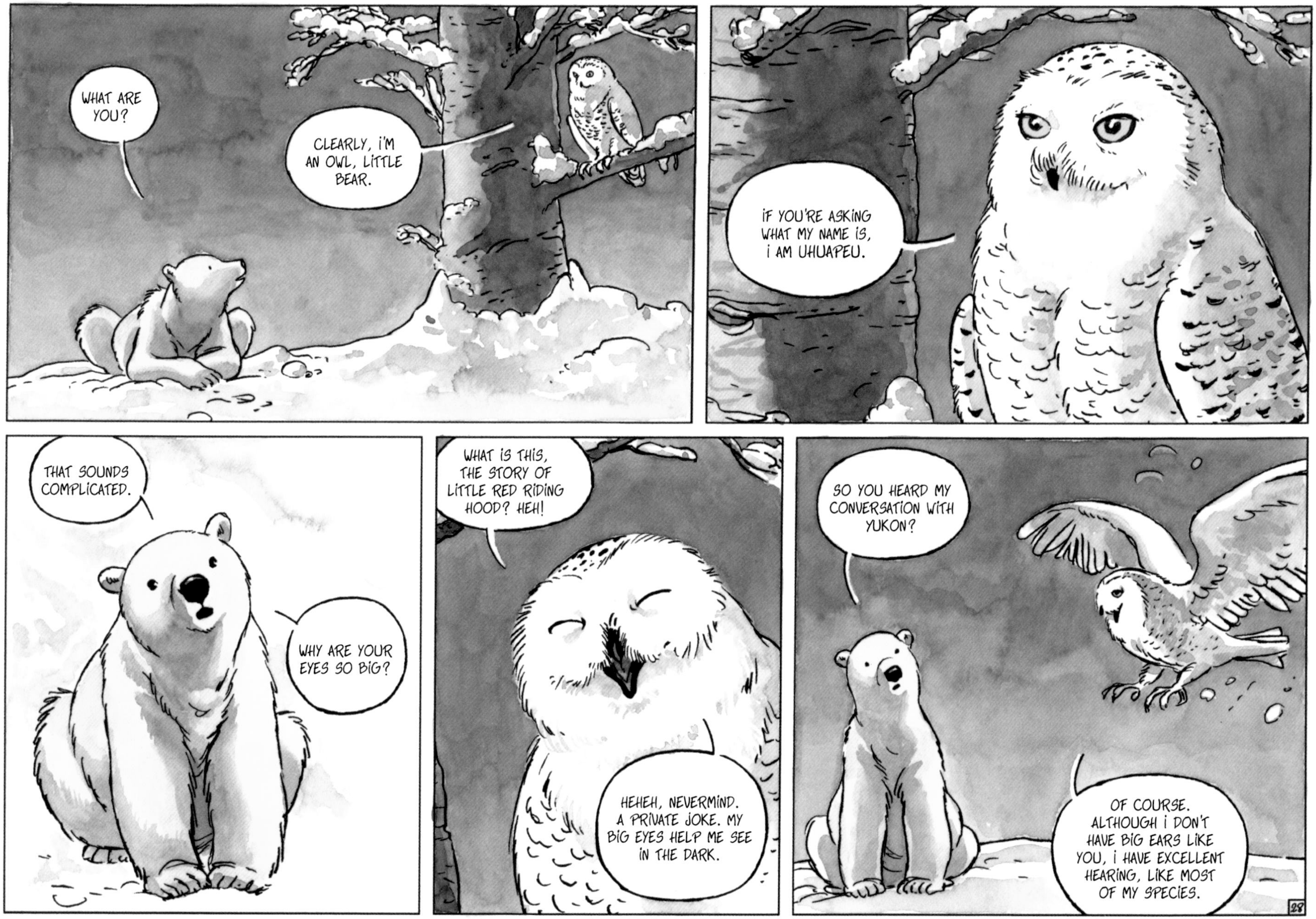
WHAT ARE YOU?
CLEARLY, I'M AN OWL, LITTLE BEAR.
IF YOU'RE ASKING WHAT MY NAME IS, I AM UHUAPEU.
THAT SOUNDS COMPLICATED.
WHY ARE YOUR EYES SO BIG?
WHAT IS THIS, THE STORY OF LITTLE RED RIDING HOOD? HEH!
HEHEH, NEVERMIND. A PRIVATE JOKE. MY BIG EYES HELP ME SEE IN THE DARK.
SO YOU HEARD MY CONVERSATION WITH YUKON?
OF COURSE. ALTHOUGH I DON'T HAVE BIG EARS LIKE YOU, I HAVE EXCELLENT HEARING, LIKE MOST OF MY SPECIES.
28

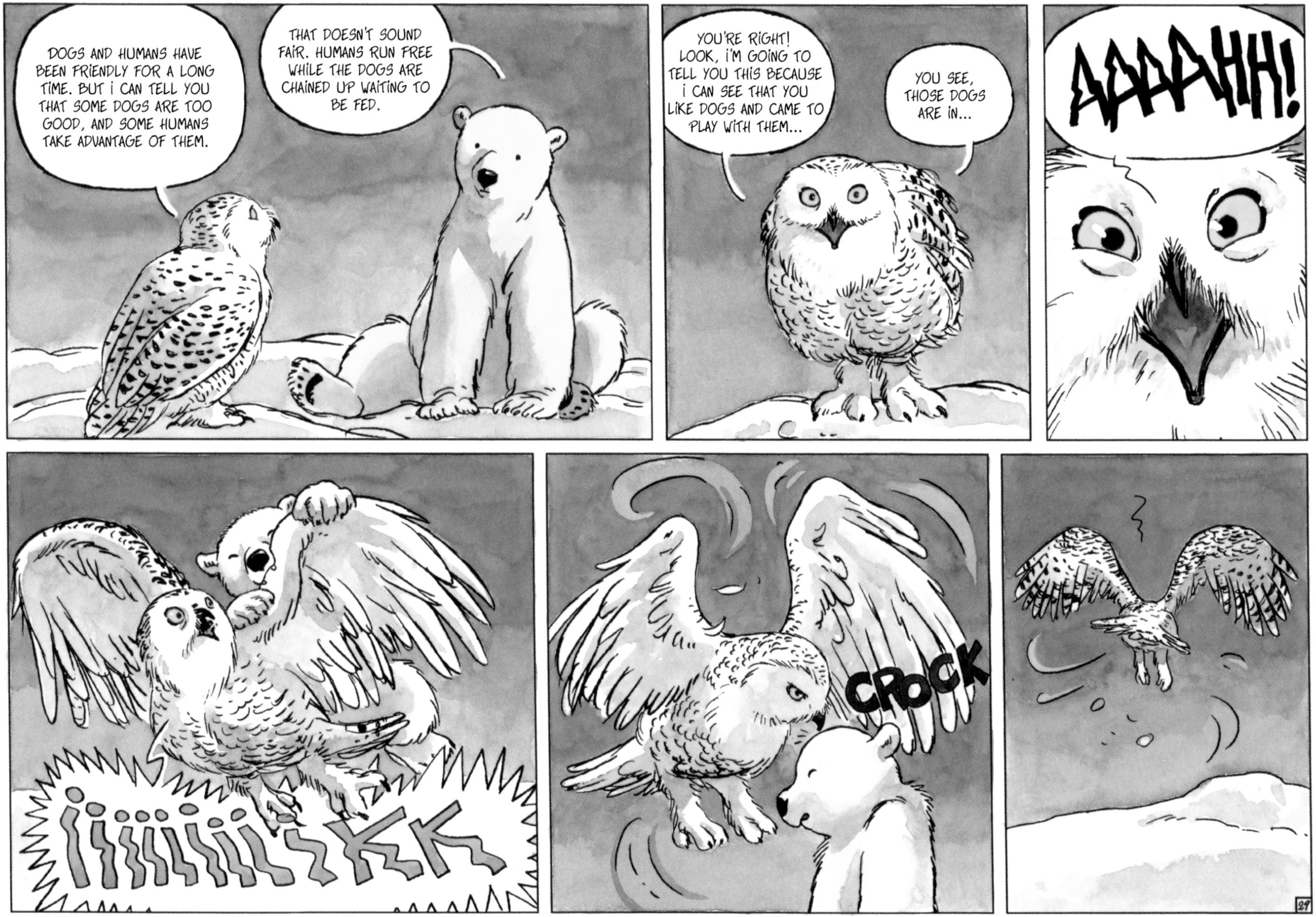
DOGS AND HUMANS HAVE BEEN FRIENDLY FOR A LONG TIME. BUT I CAN TELL YOU THAT SOME DOGS ARE TOO GOOD, AND SOME HUMANS TAKE ADVANTAGE OF THEM.
THAT DOESN'T SOUND FAIR. HUMANS RUN FREE WHILE THE DOGS ARE CHAINED UP WAITING TO BE FED.
YOU'RE RIGHT! LOOK, I'M GOING TO TELL YOU THIS BECAUSE I CAN SEE THAT YOU LIKE DOGS AND CAME TO PLAY WITH THEM...
YOU SEE, THOSE DOGS ARE IN...
AAAAHH!
IIIIIIIIZKZK
CROCK
29

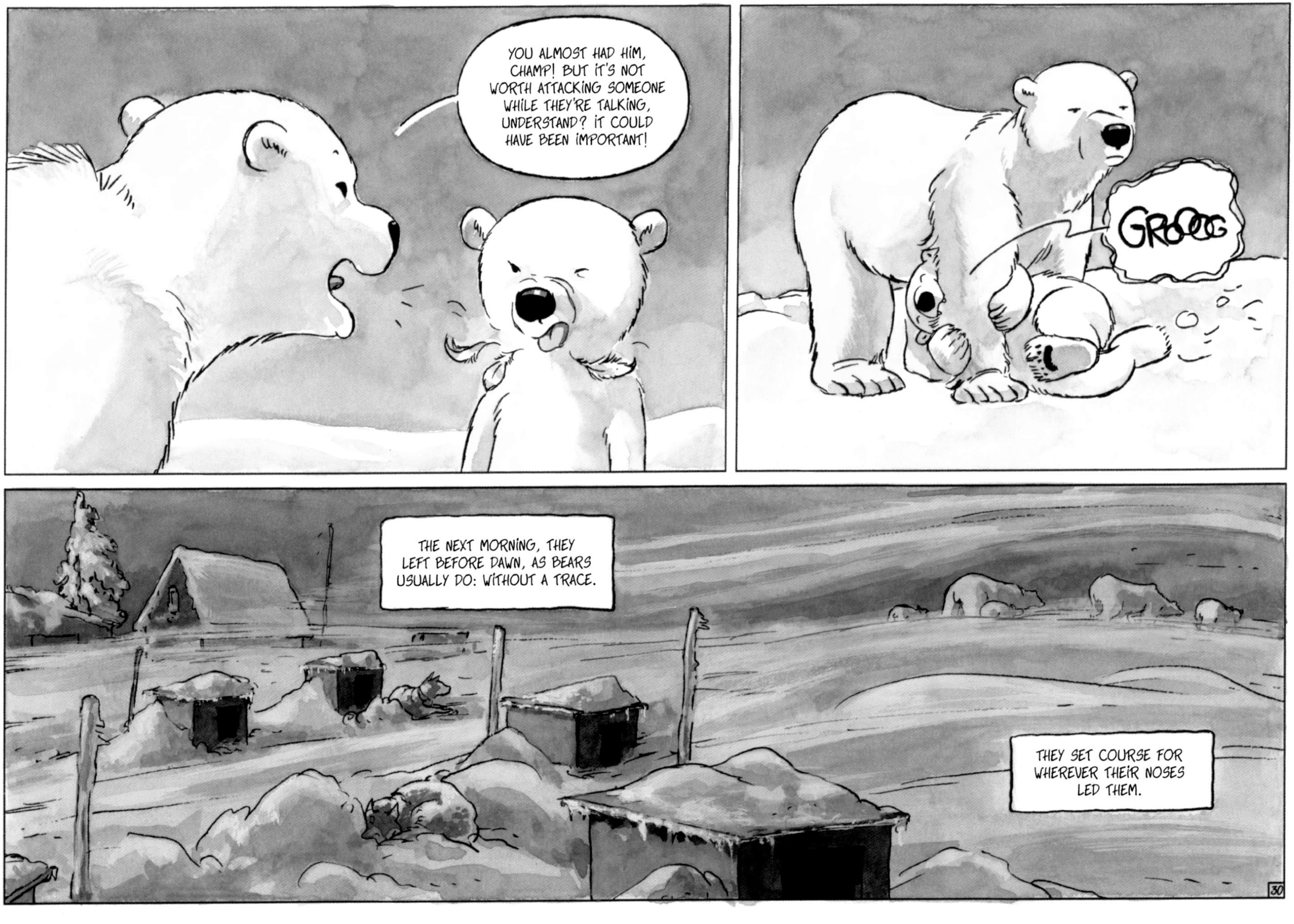
YOU ALMOST HAD HIM, CHAMP! BUT IT'S NOT WORTH ATTACKING SOMEONE WHILE THEY'RE TALKING, UNDERSTAND? IT COULD HAVE BEEN IMPORTANT!
GROOOG
THE NEXT MORNING, THEY LEFT BEFORE DAWN, AS BEARS USUALLY DO: WITHOUT A TRACE.
THEY SET COURSE FOR WHEREVER THEIR NOSES LED THEM.
30

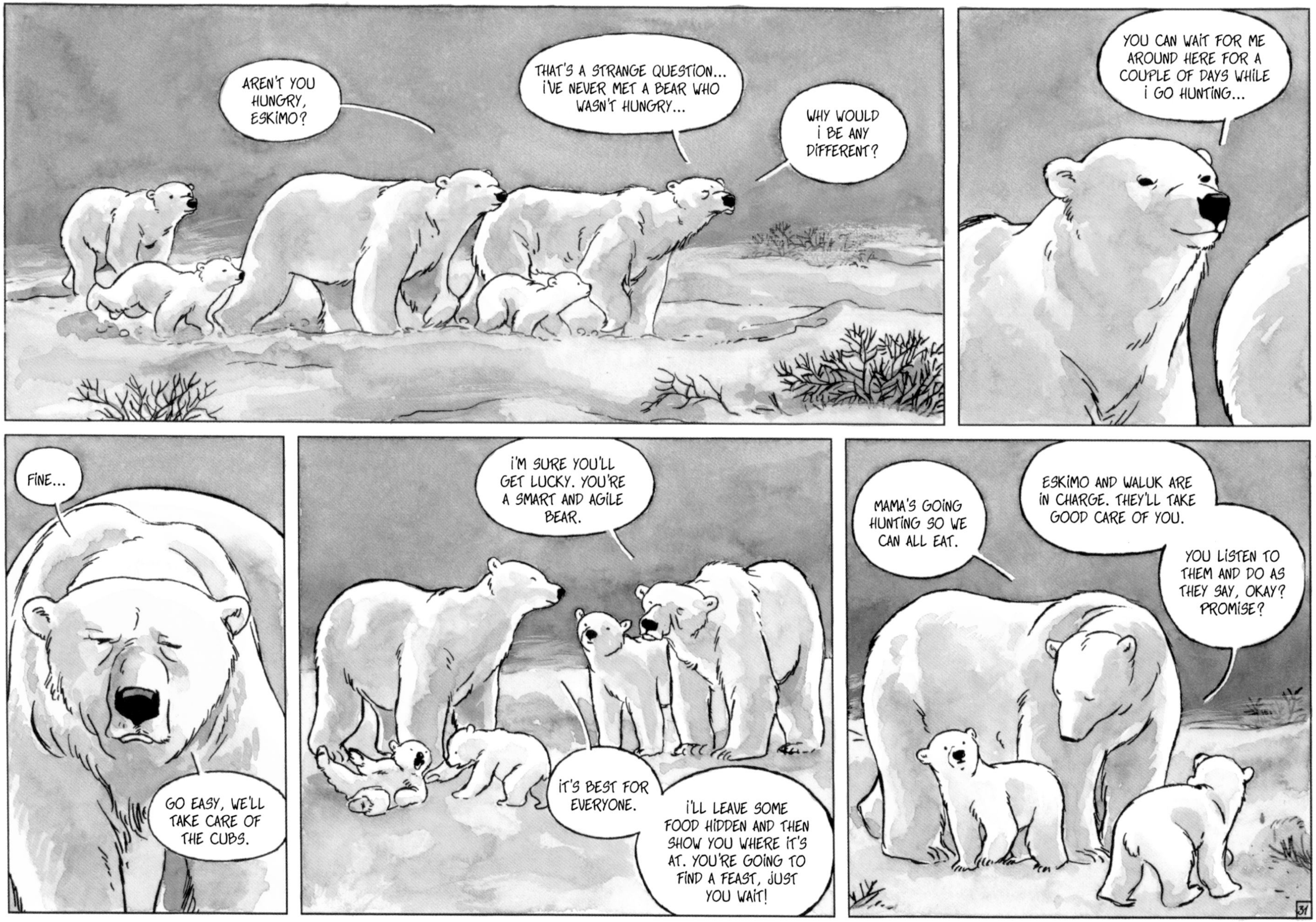
AREN'T YOU HUNGRY, ESKIMO?
THAT'S A STRANGE QUESTION... I'VE NEVER MET A BEAR WHO WASN'T HUNGRY...
WHY WOULD I BE ANY DIFFERENT?
YOU CAN WAIT FOR ME AROUND HERE FOR A COUPLE OF DAYS WHILE I GO HUNTING...
FINE...
GO EASY, WE'LL TAKE CARE OF THE CUBS.
I'M SURE YOU'LL GET LUCKY. YOU'RE A SMART AND AGILE BEAR.
IT'S BEST FOR EVERYONE.
I'LL LEAVE SOME FOOD HIDDEN AND THEN SHOW YOU WHERE IT'S AT. YOU'RE GOING TO FIND A FEAST, JUST YOU WAIT!
MAMA'S GOING HUNTING SO WE CAN ALL EAT.
ESKIMO AND WALUK ARE IN CHARGE. THEY'LL TAKE GOOD CARE OF YOU.
YOU LISTEN TO THEM AND DO AS THEY SAY, OKAY? PROMISE?
31

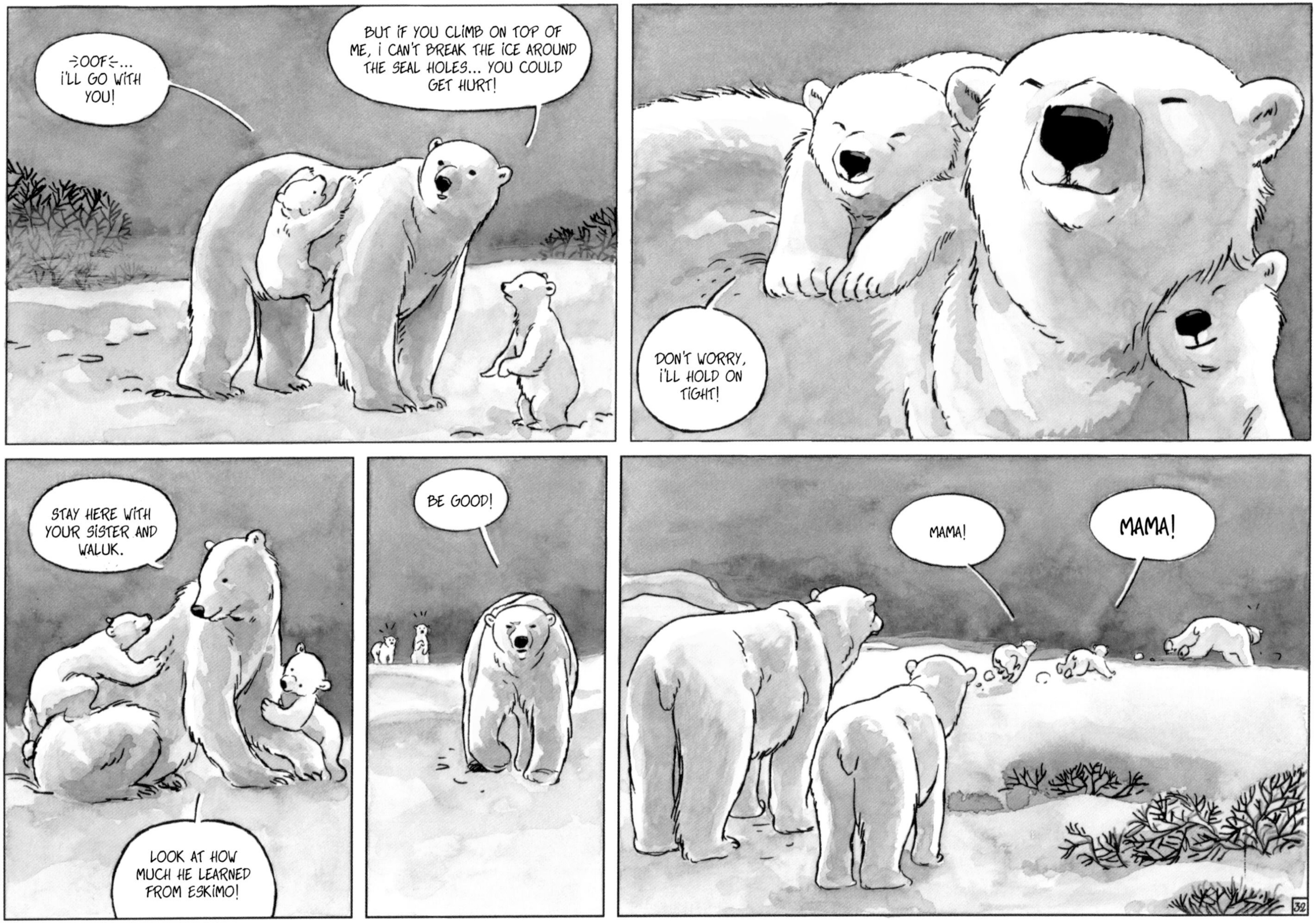

≡OOF≡... I'LL GO WITH YOU!
BUT IF YOU CLIMB ON TOP OF ME, I CAN'T BREAK THE ICE AROUND THE SEAL HOLES... YOU COULD GET HURT!
DON'T WORRY, I'LL HOLD ON TIGHT!
STAY HERE WITH YOUR SISTER AND WALUK.
LOOK AT HOW MUCH HE LEARNED FROM ESKIMO!
BE GOOD!
MAMA!
MAMA!
32

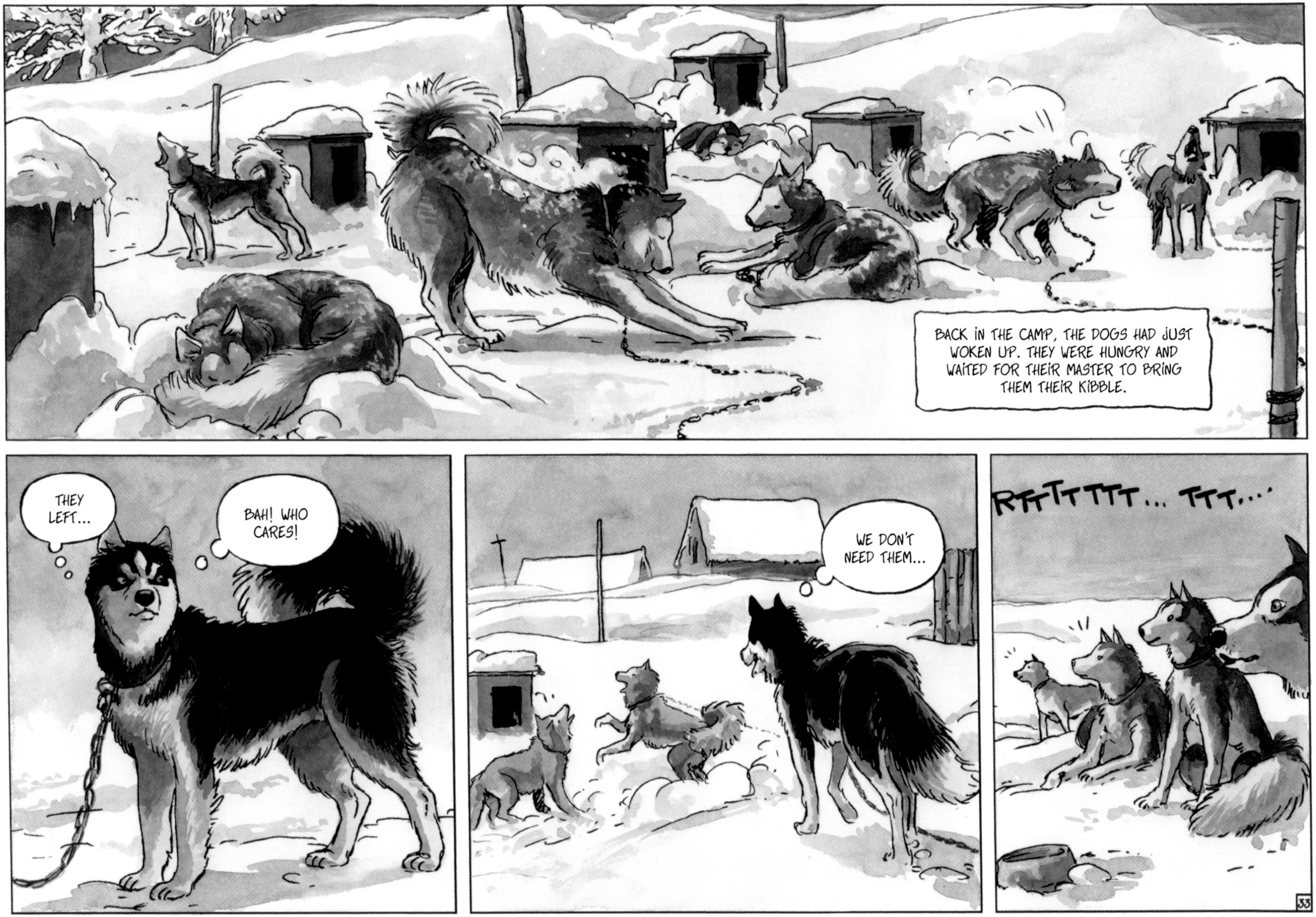
BACK IN THE CAMP, THE DOGS HAD JUST WOKEN UP. THEY WERE HUNGRY AND WAITED FOR THEIR MASTER TO BRING THEM THEIR KIBBLE.
THEY LEFT...
BAH! WHO CARES!
WE DON'T NEED THEM...
RTTTTTTT... TTT...
33

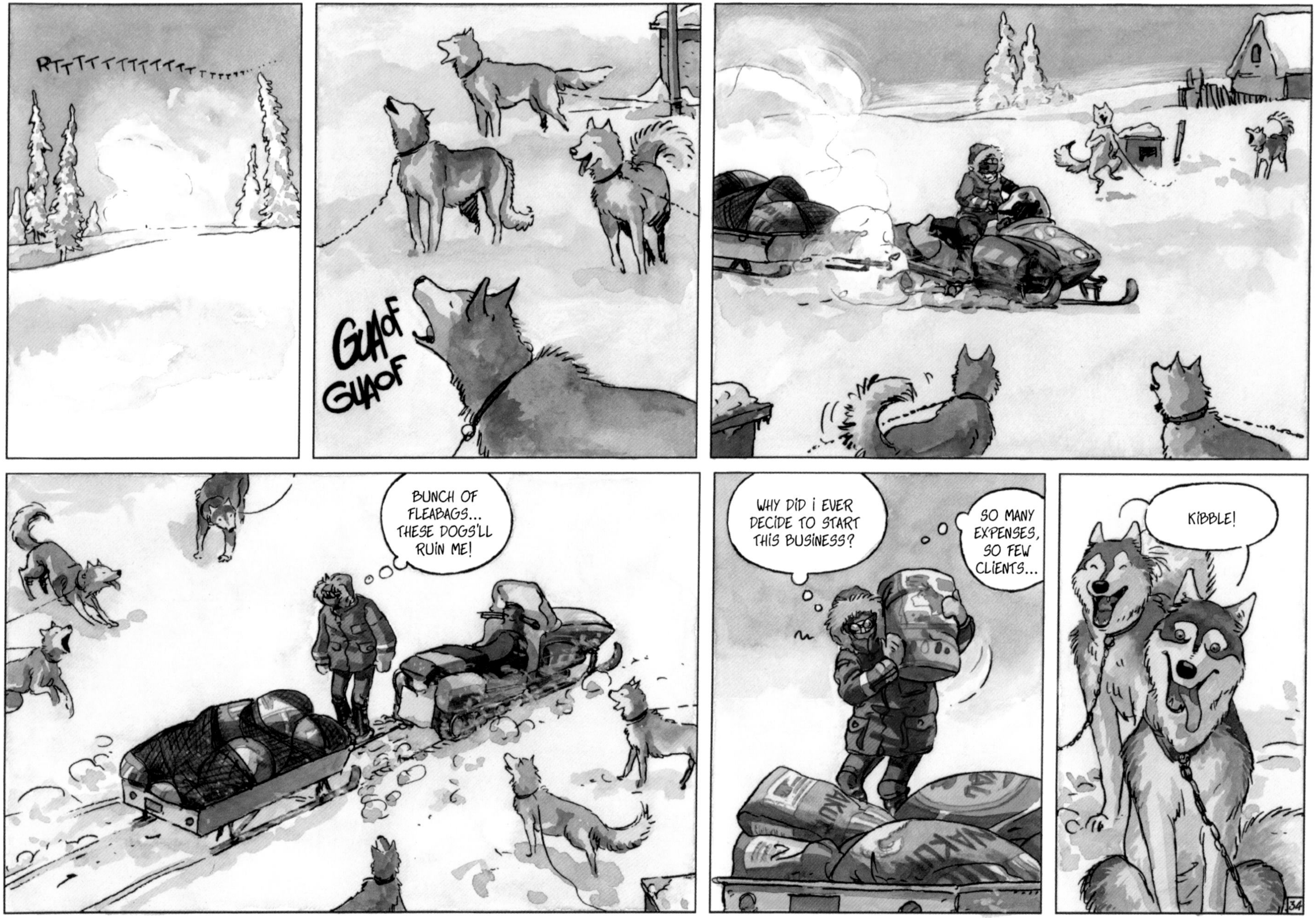
RTTTTTTTTTTTTTTTT
GUAOF
GUAOF
BUNCH OF FLEABAGS... THESE DOGS'LL RUIN ME!
WHY DID I EVER DECIDE TO START THIS BUSINESS?
SO MANY EXPENSES, SO FEW CLIENTS...
KIBBLE!
34

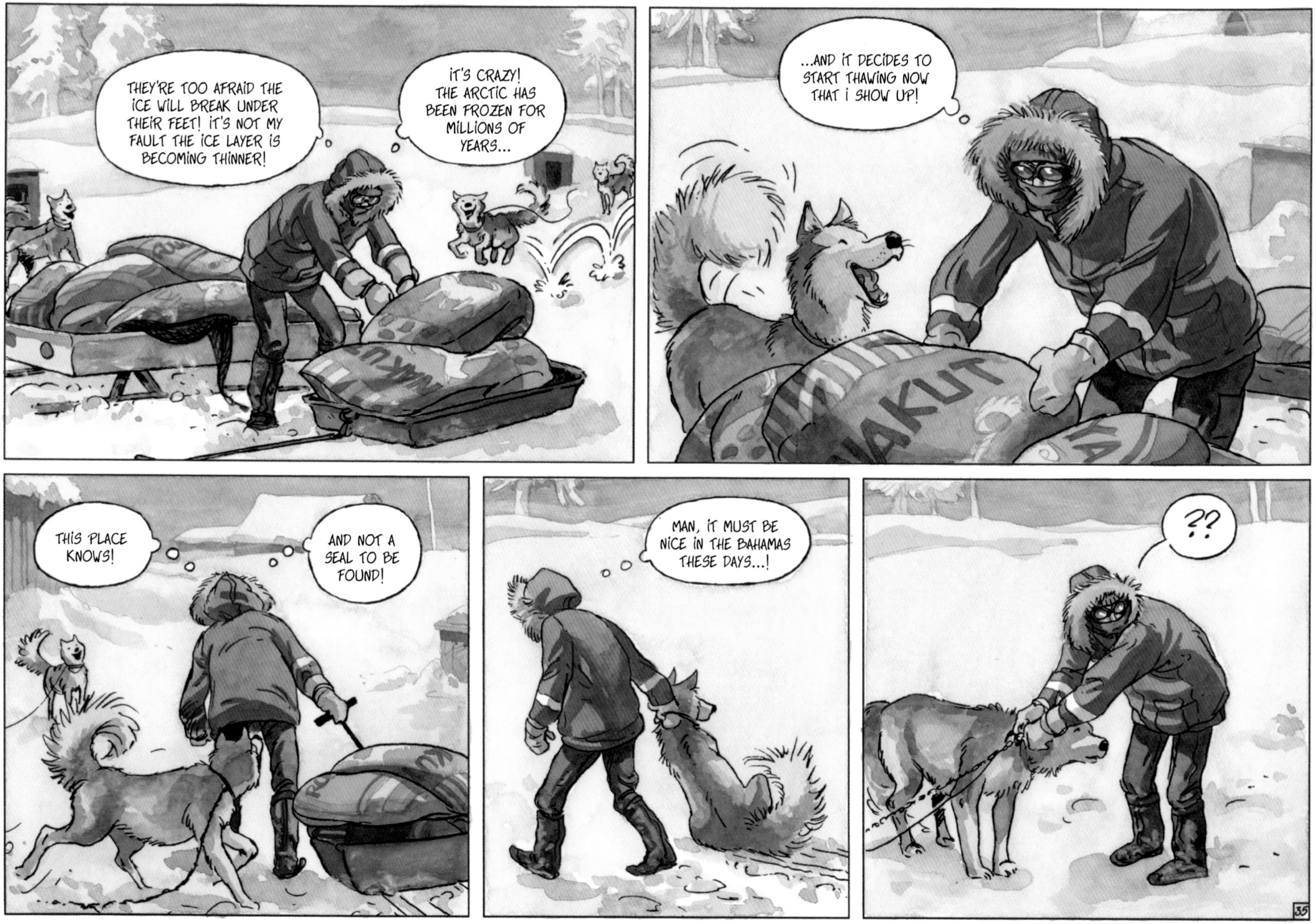
THEY'RE TOO AFRAID THE ICE WILL BREAK UNDER THEIR FEET! IT'S NOT MY FAULT THE ICE LAYER IS BECOMING THINNER!
IT'S CRAZY! THE ARCTIC HAS BEEN FROZEN FOR MILLIONS OF YEARS...
...AND IT DECIDES TO START THAWING NOW THAT I SHOW UP!
NAKUT
THIS PLACE KNOWS!
AND NOT A SEAL TO BE FOUND!
MAN, IT MUST BE NICE IN THE BAHAMAS THESE DAYS...!
??
35

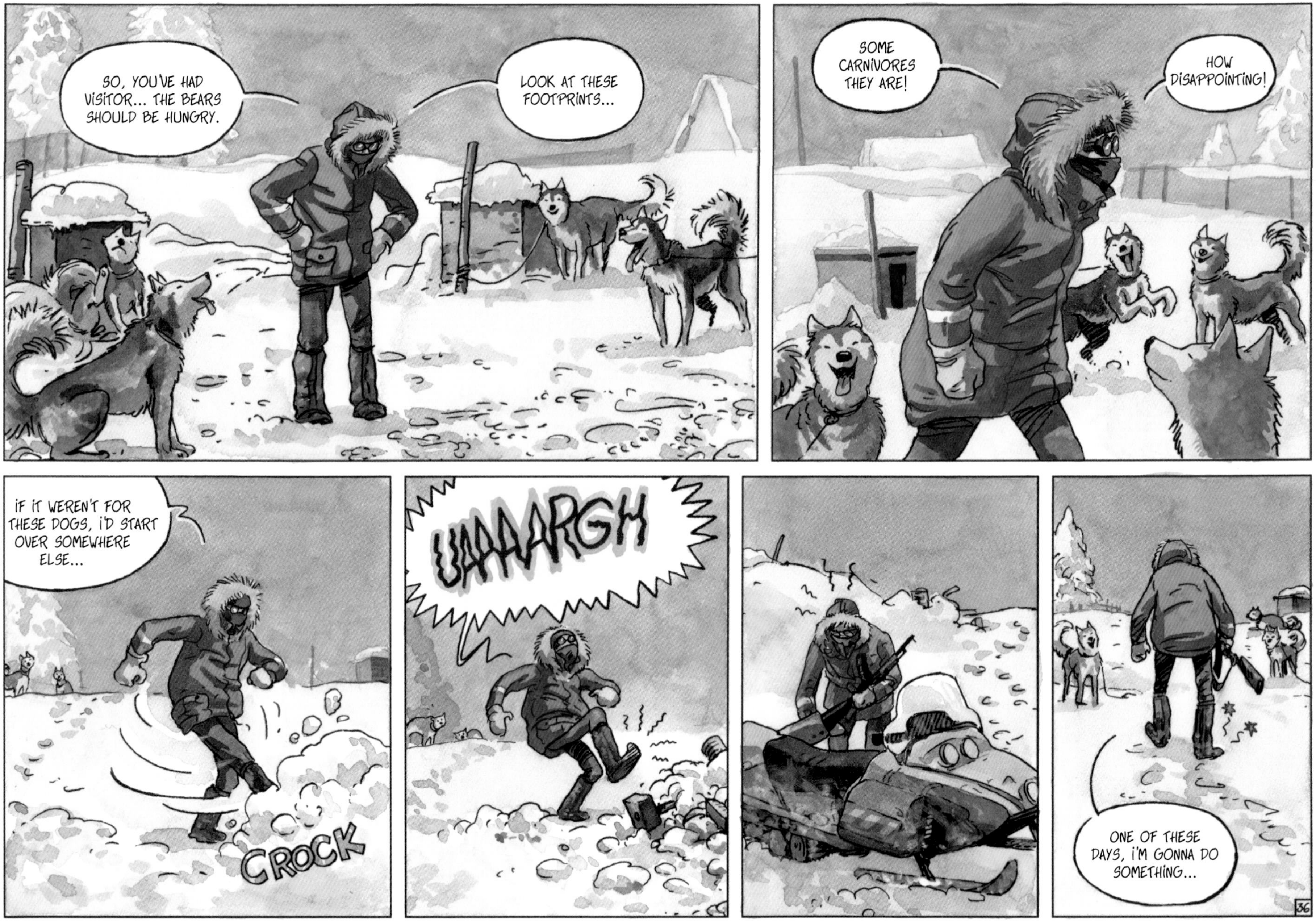
SO, YOU'VE HAD VISITOR... THE BEARS SHOULD BE HUNGRY.
LOOK AT THESE FOOTPRINTS...
SOME CARNIVORES THEY ARE!
HOW DISAPPOINTING!
IF IT WEREN'T FOR THESE DOGS, I'D START OVER SOMEWHERE ELSE...
CROCK
UAAARGH
ONE OF THESE DAYS, I'M GONNA DO SOMETHING...
36

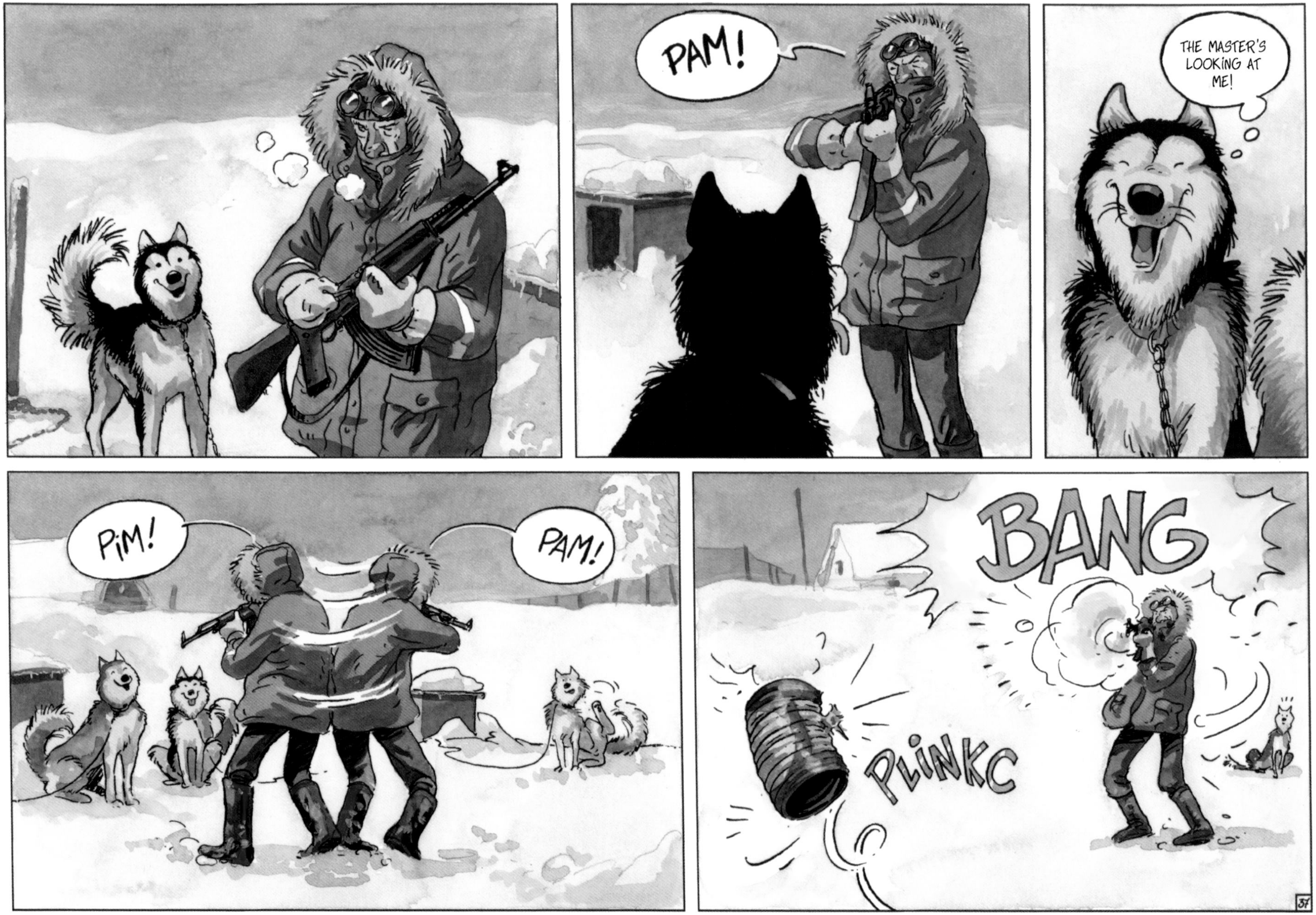
PAM!
THE MASTER'S LOOKING AT ME!
PIM!
PAM!
BANG
PLINKC
37

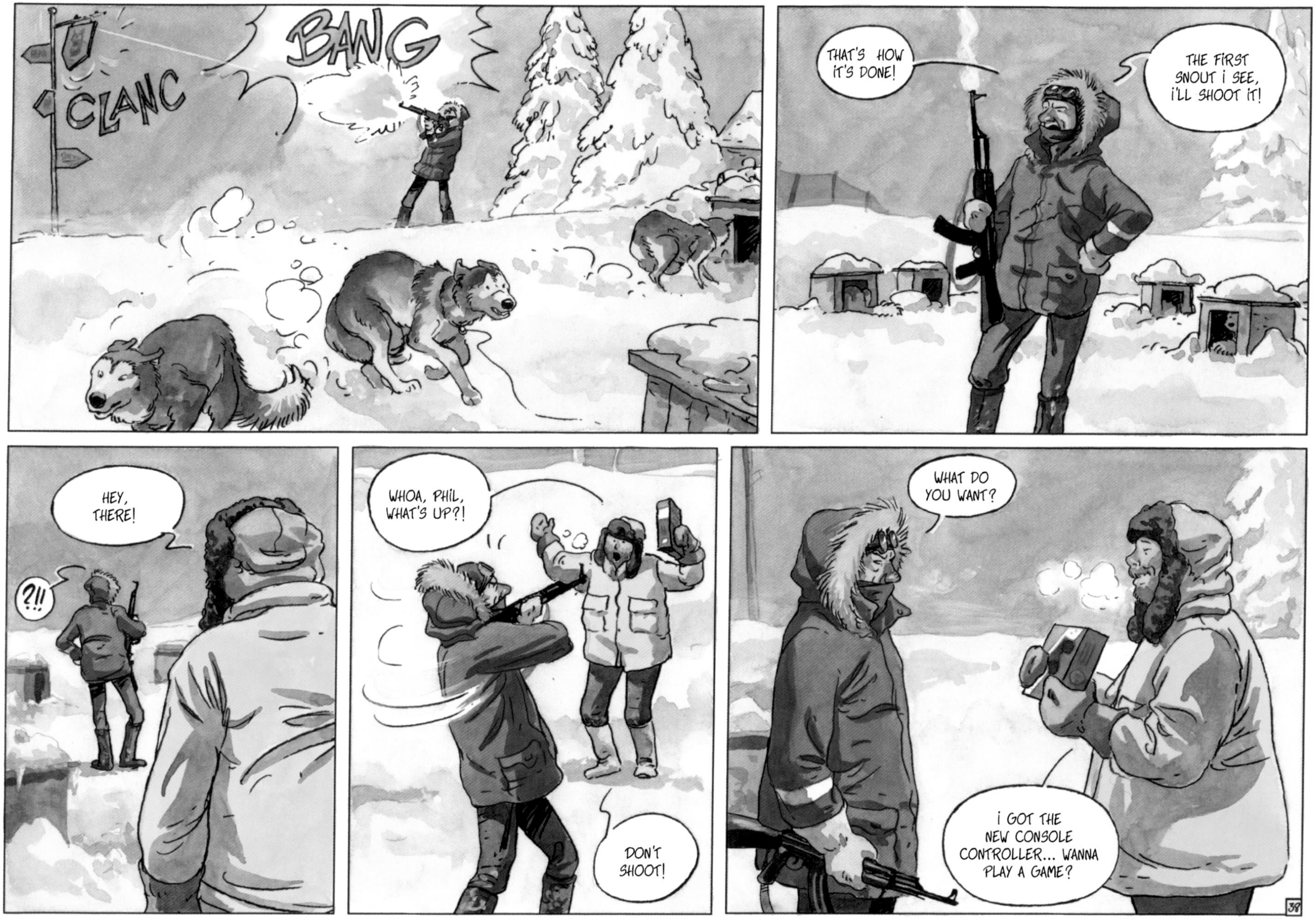
BANG
CLANC
THAT'S HOW IT'S DONE!
THE FIRST SNOUT I SEE, I'LL SHOOT IT!
HEY, THERE!
?!!
WHOA, PHIL, WHAT'S UP?!
DON'T SHOOT!
WHAT DO YOU WANT?
I GOT THE NEW CONSOLE CONTROLLER... WANNA PLAY A GAME?
38

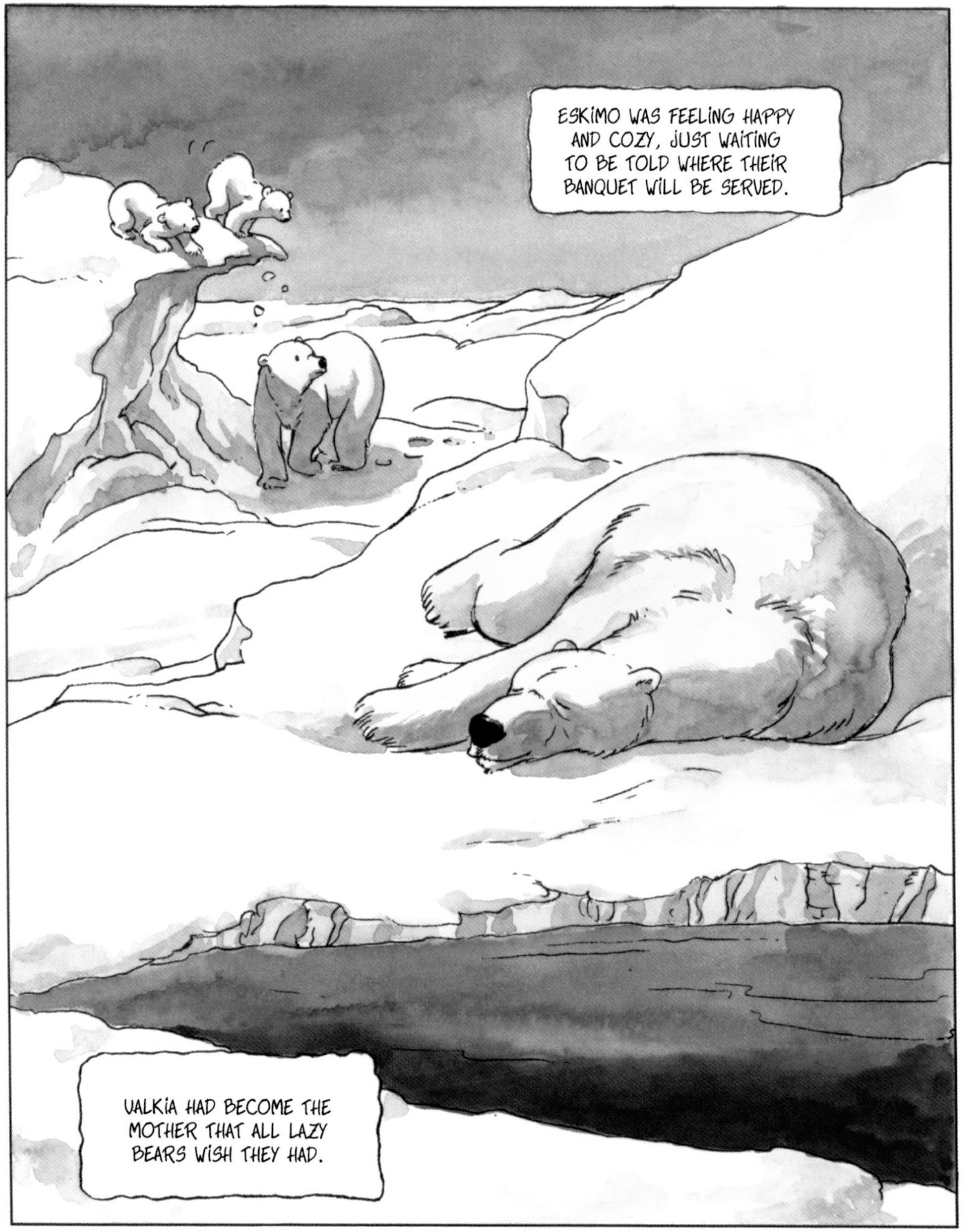
ESKiMO WAS FEELiNG HAPPY AND COZY, JUST WAiTiNG TO BE TOLD WHERE THEiR BANQUET WiLL BE SERVED.
VALKiA HAD BECOME THE MOTHER THAT ALL LAZY BEARS WiSH THEY HAD.

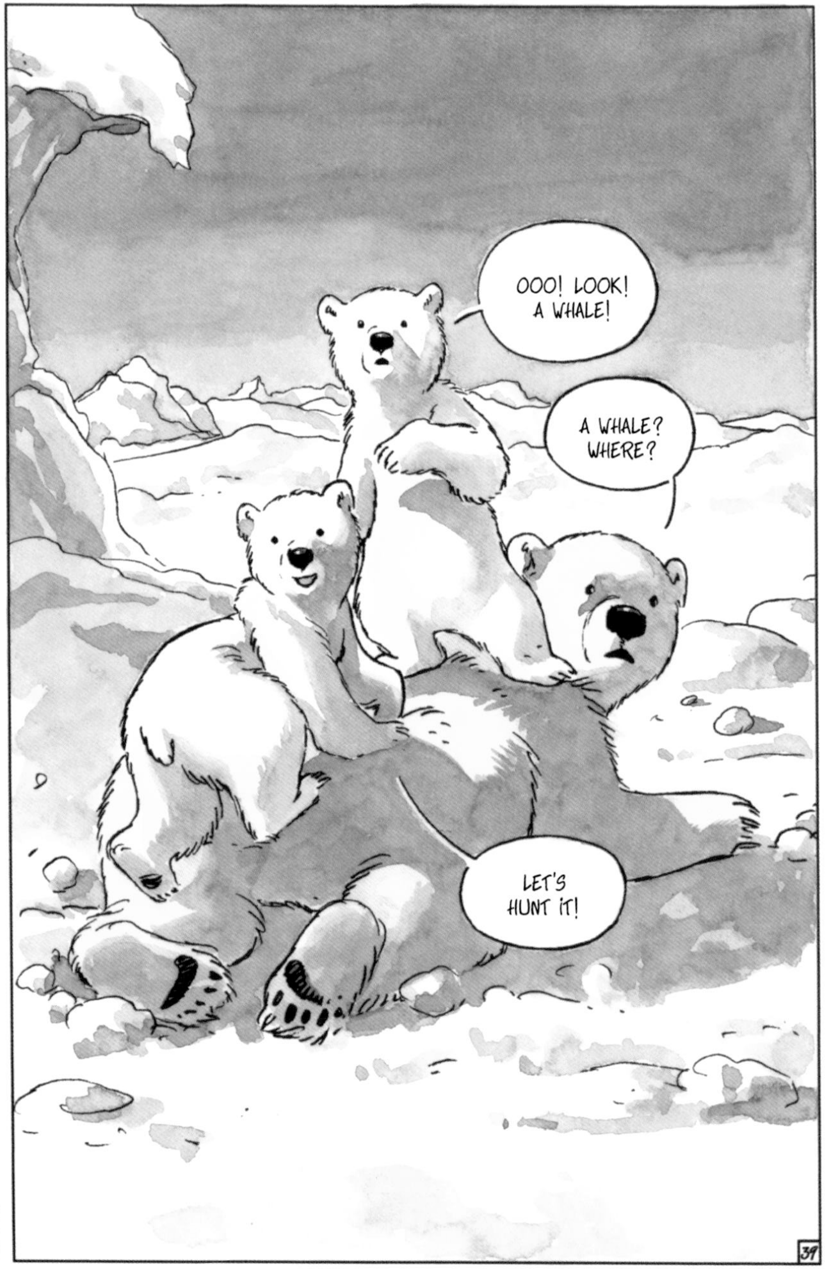
OOO! LOOK! A WHALE!
A WHALE? WHERE?
LET'S HUNT iT!
39

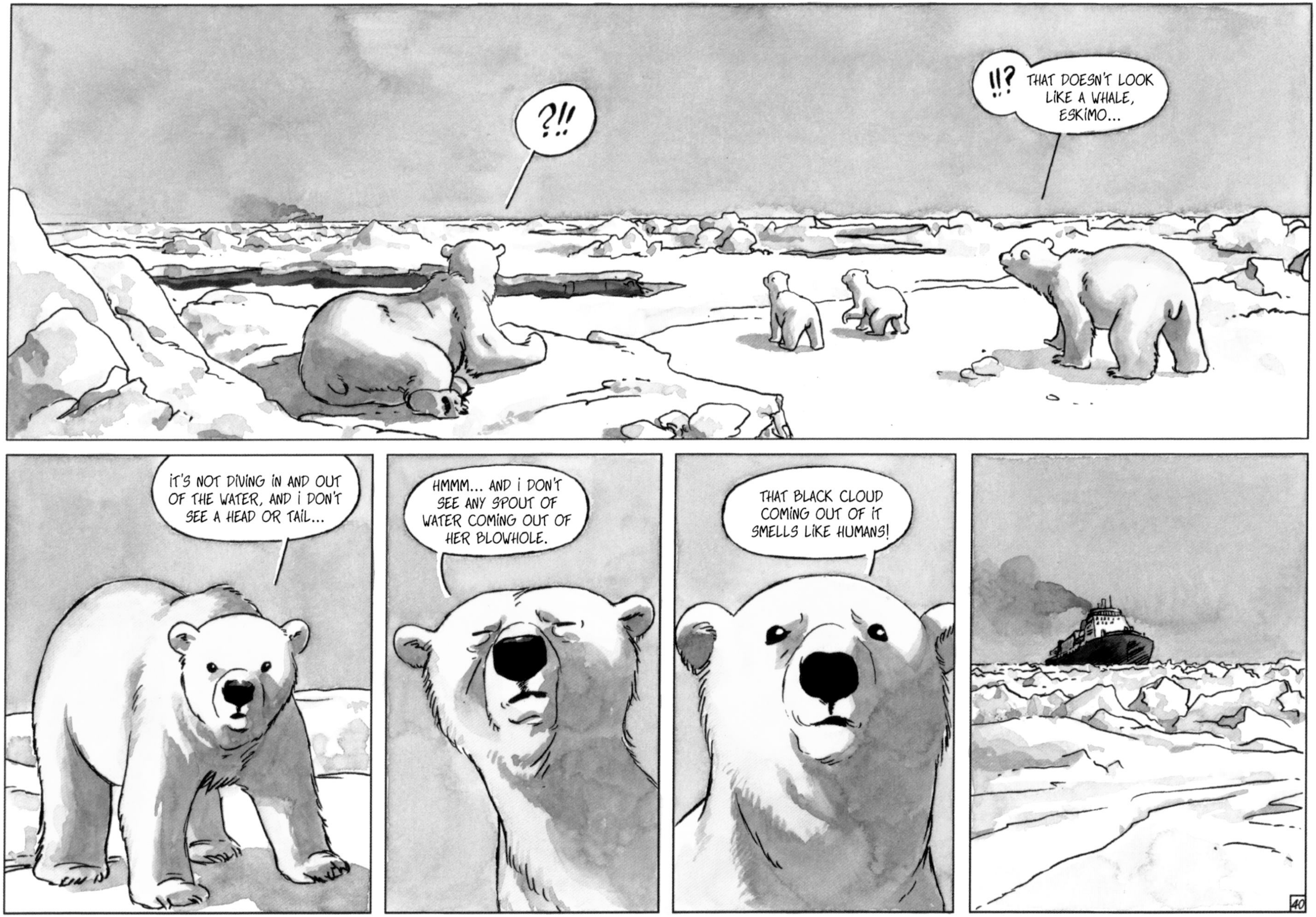
?!!
!!? THAT DOESN'T LOOK LIKE A WHALE, ESKIMO...
IT'S NOT DIVING IN AND OUT OF THE WATER, AND I DON'T SEE A HEAD OR TAIL...
HMMM... AND I DON'T SEE ANY SPOUT OF WATER COMING OUT OF HER BLOWHOLE.
THAT BLACK CLOUD COMING OUT OF IT SMELLS LIKE HUMANS!
40

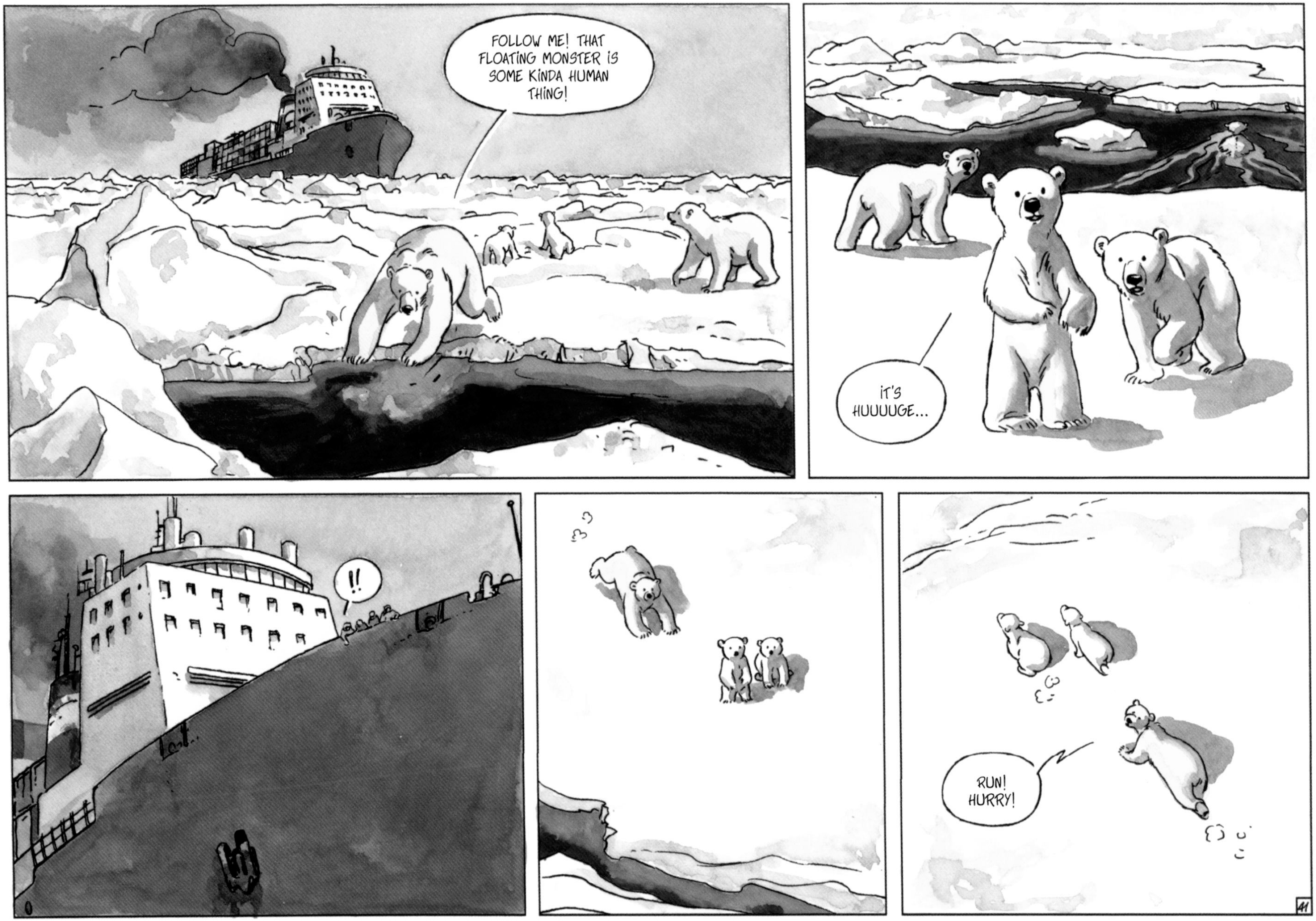
FOLLOW ME! THAT FLOATING MONSTER IS SOME KINDA HUMAN THING!
IT'S HUUUUGE...
!!
RUN! HURRY!
41

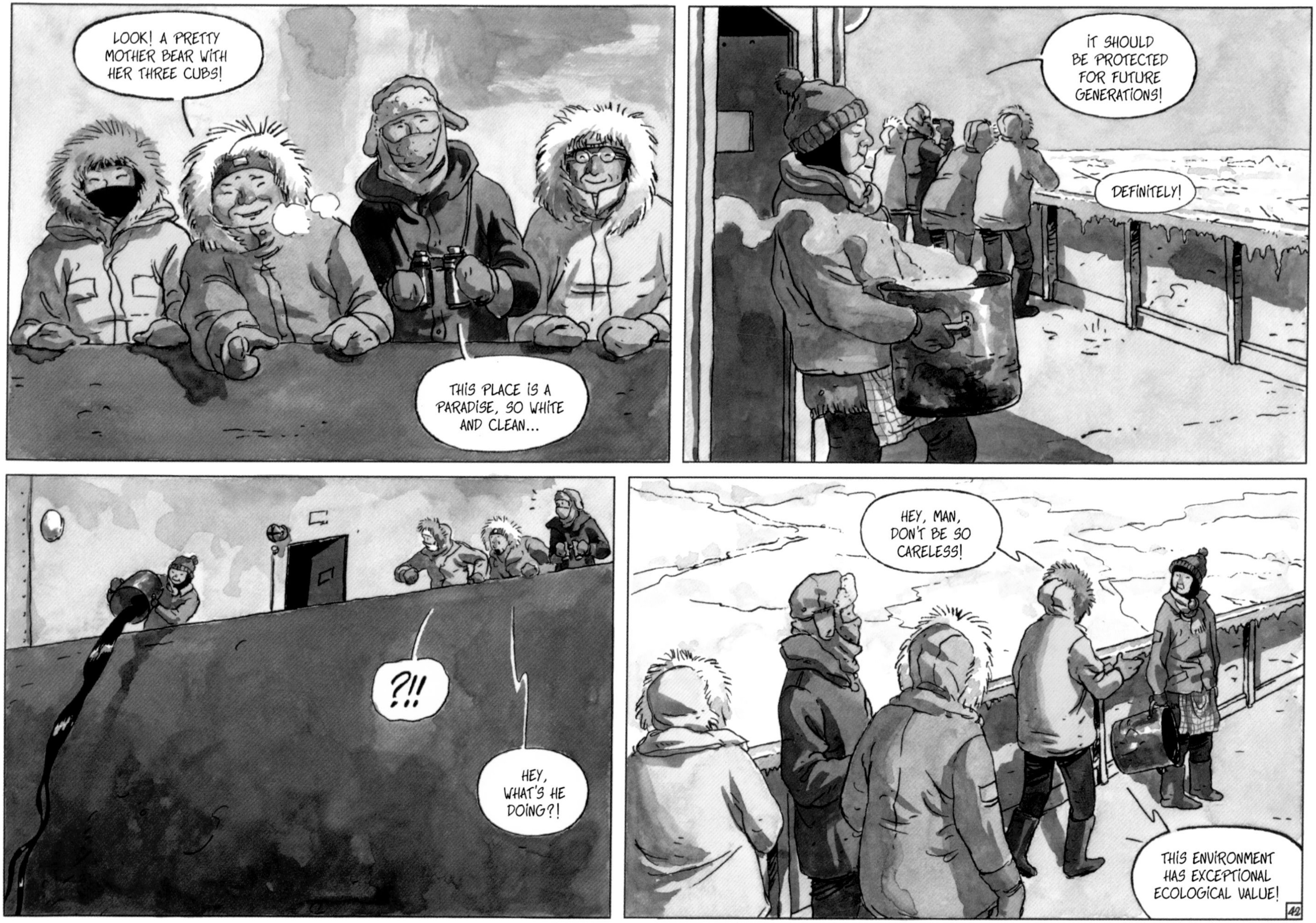
LOOK! A PRETTY MOTHER BEAR WITH HER THREE CUBS!
THIS PLACE IS A PARADISE, SO WHITE AND CLEAN...
IT SHOULD BE PROTECTED FOR FUTURE GENERATIONS!
DEFINITELY!
?!!
HEY, WHAT'S HE DOING?!
HEY, MAN, DON'T BE SO CARELESS!
THIS ENVIRONMENT HAS EXCEPTIONAL ECOLOGICAL VALUE!
42

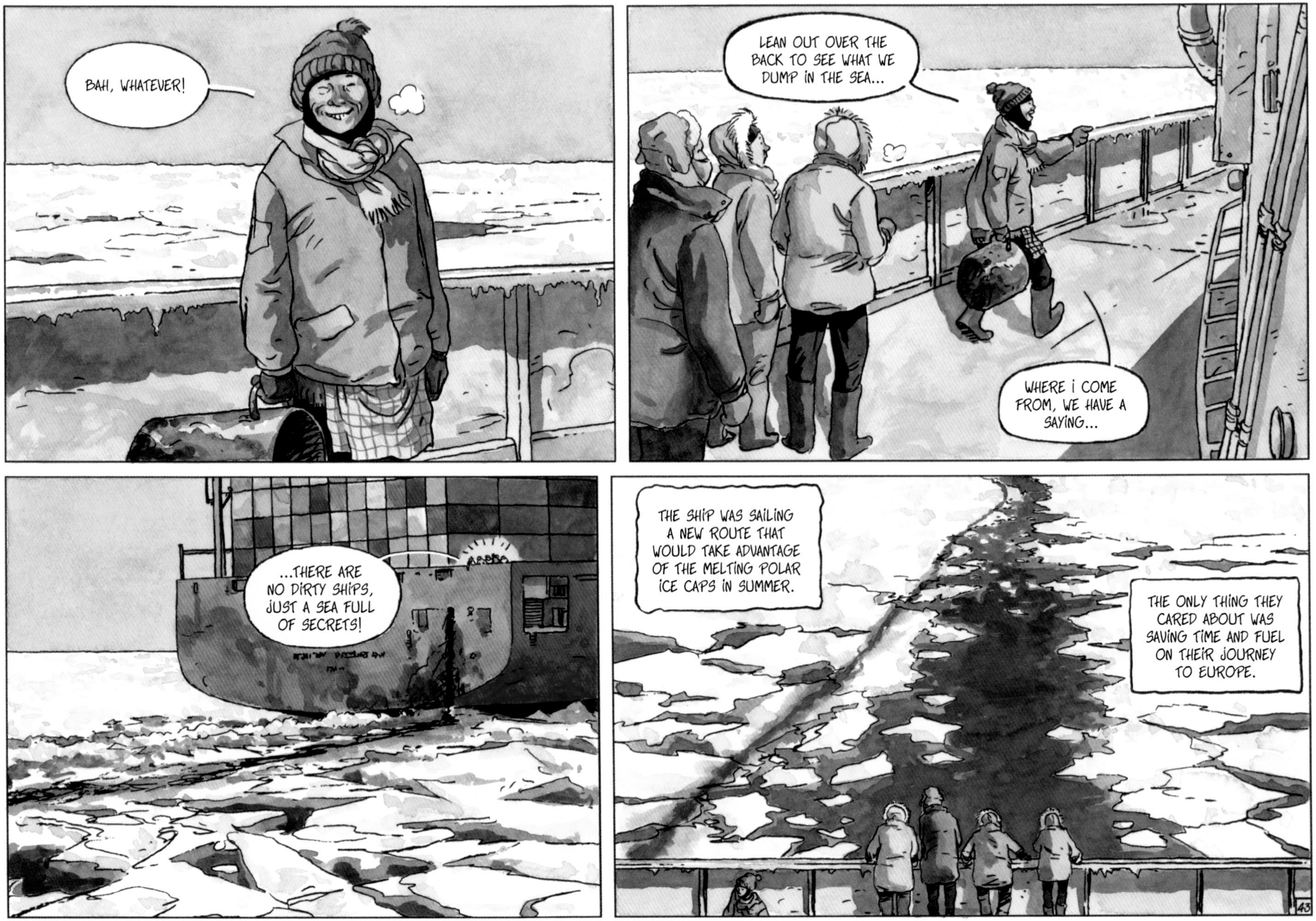
BAH, WHATEVER!
LEAN OUT OVER THE BACK TO SEE WHAT WE DUMP IN THE SEA...
WHERE I COME FROM, WE HAVE A SAYING...
...THERE ARE NO DIRTY SHIPS, JUST A SEA FULL OF SECRETS!
THE SHIP WAS SAILING A NEW ROUTE THAT WOULD TAKE ADVANTAGE OF THE MELTING POLAR ICE CAPS IN SUMMER.
THE ONLY THING THEY CARED ABOUT WAS SAVING TIME AND FUEL ON THEIR JOURNEY TO EUROPE.

THEY HADN'T EVEN LOOKED OUT FOR TEN SECONDS WHEN THE SHIP RAN AGROUND ON THE PACKED ICE.

THE IMPACT WAS INTENSE!

SHRIEKKKKK

THE HUNDREDS OF SHIPPING CONTAINERS ON BOARD, ALTHOUGH FIRMLY ATTACHED, SCREECHED LIKE THE TEETH OF AN ANGRY GIANT...

...AND THE SHIP'S ALARM BEGAN TO WAIL ACROSS THE DESOLATE LANDSCAPE.

UUUUUU UUUUUUU

UUUUUUUUUUUUUU UUUUUU

48

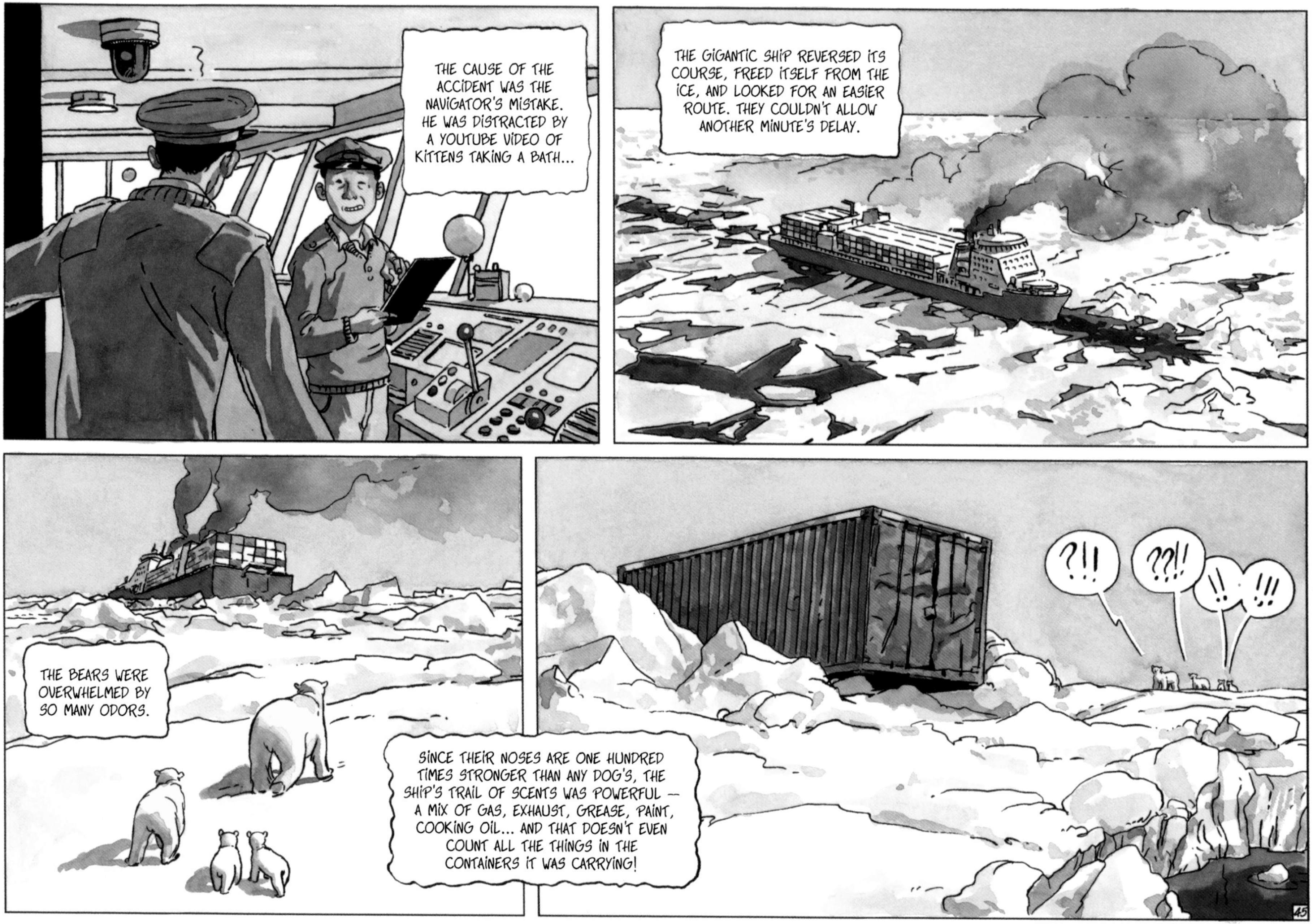
THE CAUSE OF THE ACCIDENT WAS THE NAVIGATOR'S MISTAKE. HE WAS DISTRACTED BY A YOUTUBE VIDEO OF KITTENS TAKING A BATH...
THE GIGANTIC SHIP REVERSED ITS COURSE, FREED ITSELF FROM THE ICE, AND LOOKED FOR AN EASIER ROUTE. THEY COULDN'T ALLOW ANOTHER MINUTE'S DELAY.
THE BEARS WERE OVERWHELMED BY SO MANY ODORS.
SINCE THEIR NOSES ARE ONE HUNDRED TIMES STRONGER THAN ANY DOG'S, THE SHIP'S TRAIL OF SCENTS WAS POWERFUL — A MIX OF GAS, EXHAUST, GREASE, PAINT, COOKING OIL... AND THAT DOESN'T EVEN COUNT ALL THE THINGS IN THE CONTAINERS IT WAS CARRYING!
?!!
??!!
!!
!!!

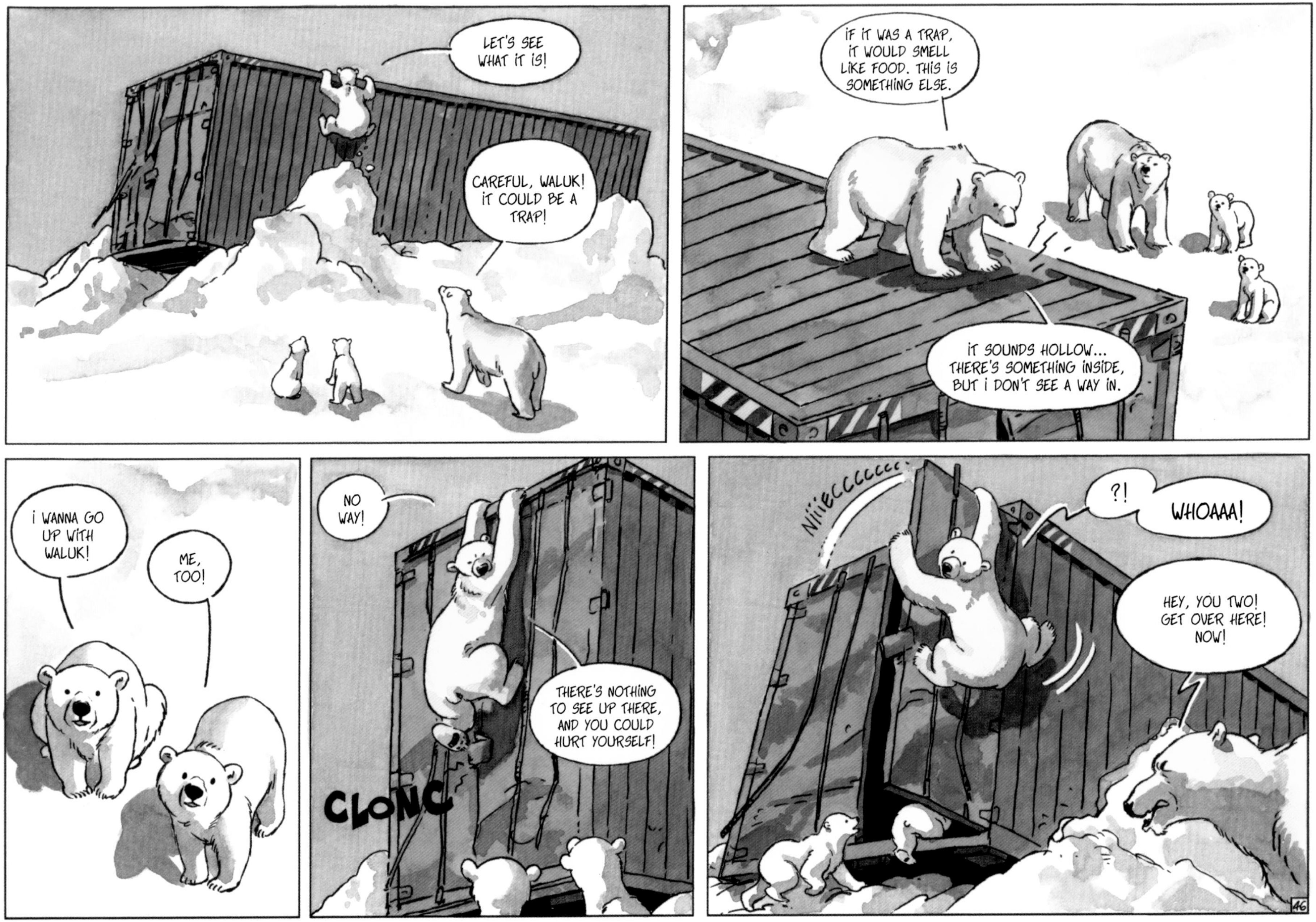
LET'S SEE WHAT IT IS!
CAREFUL, WALUK! IT COULD BE A TRAP!
IF IT WAS A TRAP, IT WOULD SMELL LIKE FOOD. THIS IS SOMETHING ELSE.
IT SOUNDS HOLLOW... THERE'S SOMETHING INSIDE, BUT I DON'T SEE A WAY IN.
I WANNA GO UP WITH WALUK!
ME, TOO!
NO WAY!
THERE'S NOTHING TO SEE UP THERE, AND YOU COULD HURT YOURSELF!
CLONC
NIIIECCCCCCC
?!
WHOAAA!
HEY, YOU TWO! GET OVER HERE! NOW!
46

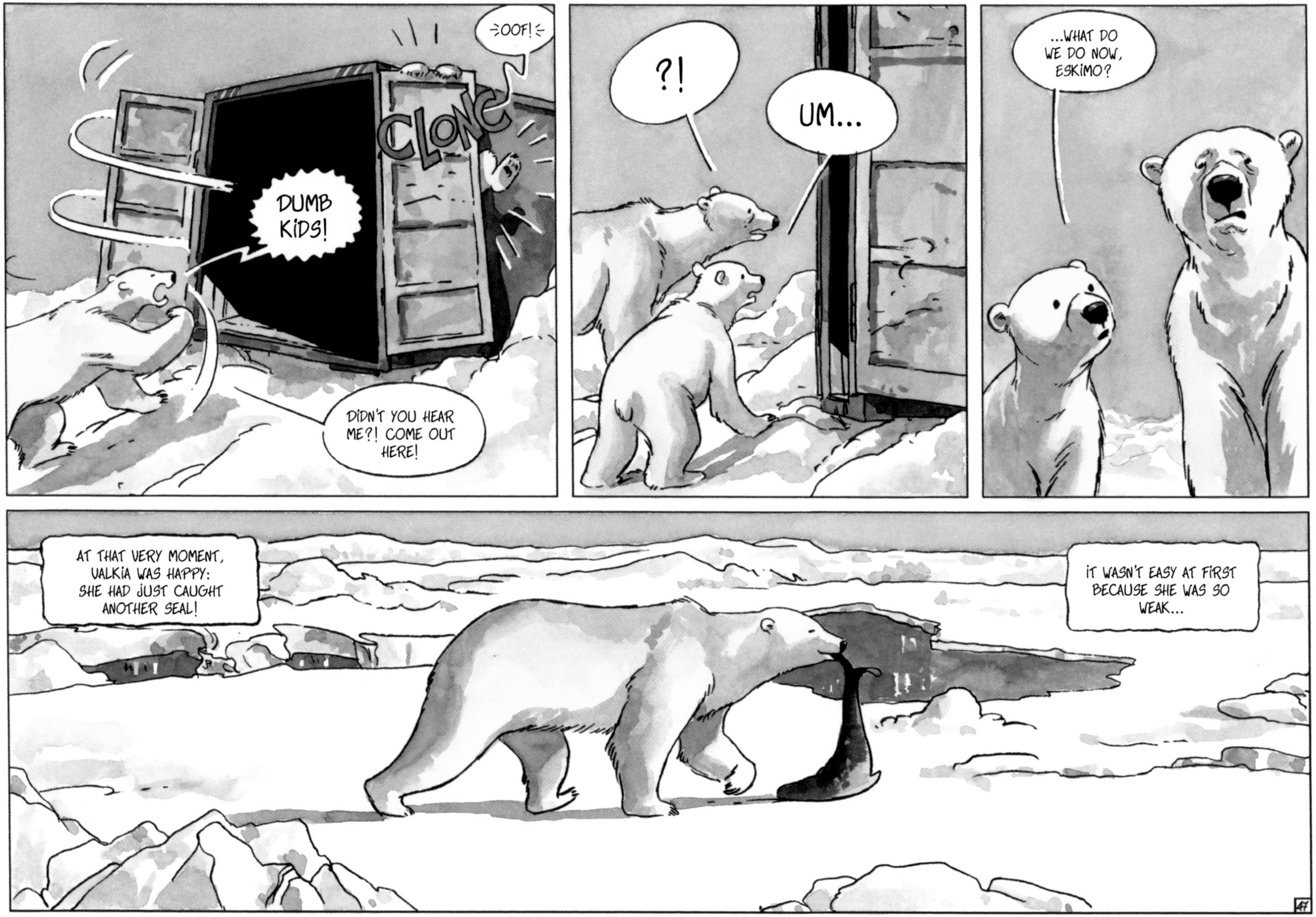
OOF!
CLONC
DUMB KIDS!
DIDN'T YOU HEAR ME?! COME OUT HERE!
?!
UM...
...WHAT DO WE DO NOW, ESKIMO?
AT THAT VERY MOMENT, VALKIA WAS HAPPY: SHE HAD JUST CAUGHT ANOTHER SEAL!
IT WASN'T EASY AT FIRST BECAUSE SHE WAS SO WEAK...

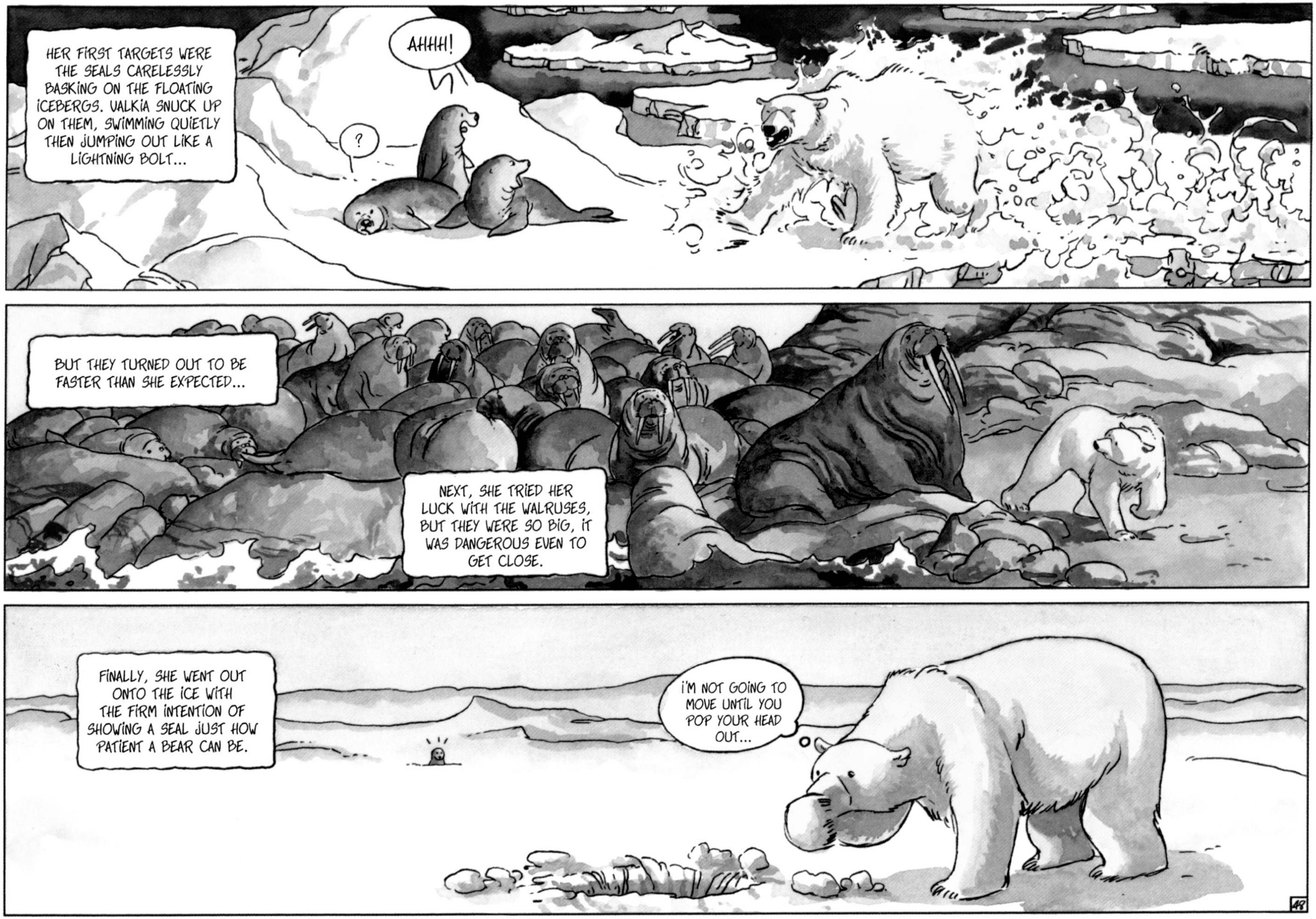
HER FIRST TARGETS WERE THE SEALS CARELESSLY BASKING ON THE FLOATING ICEBERGS. VALKIA SNUCK UP ON THEM, SWIMMING QUIETLY THEN JUMPING OUT LIKE A LIGHTNING BOLT...
?
AHHH!
BUT THEY TURNED OUT TO BE FASTER THAN SHE EXPECTED...
NEXT, SHE TRIED HER LUCK WITH THE WALRUSES, BUT THEY WERE SO BIG, IT WAS DANGEROUS EVEN TO GET CLOSE.
FINALLY, SHE WENT OUT ONTO THE ICE WITH THE FIRM INTENTION OF SHOWING A SEAL JUST HOW PATIENT A BEAR CAN BE.
I'M NOT GOING TO MOVE UNTIL YOU POP YOUR HEAD OUT...
48

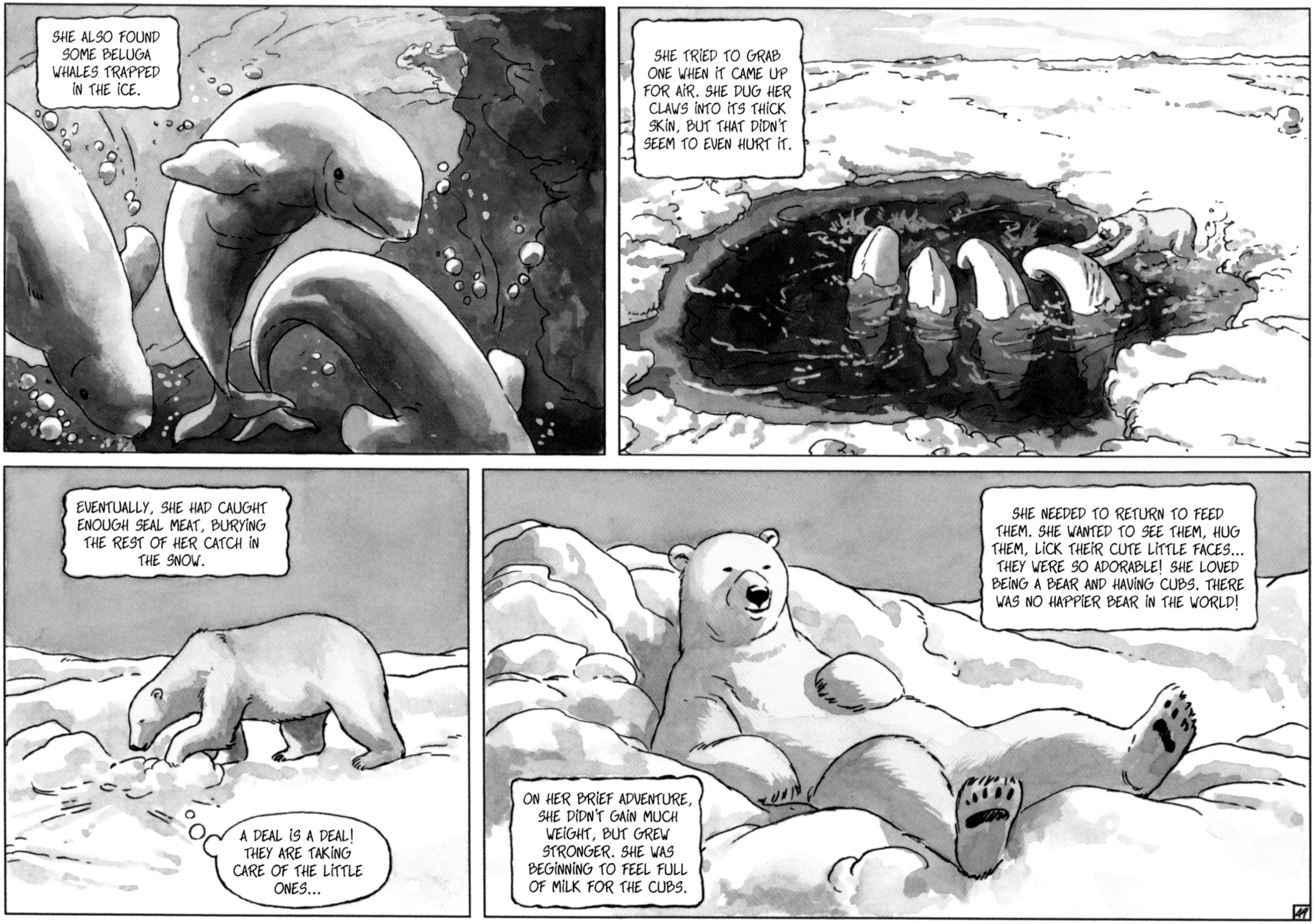
SHE ALSO FOUND SOME BELUGA WHALES TRAPPED IN THE ICE.
SHE TRIED TO GRAB ONE WHEN IT CAME UP FOR AIR. SHE DUG HER CLAWS INTO ITS THICK SKIN, BUT THAT DIDN'T SEEM TO EVEN HURT IT.
EVENTUALLY, SHE HAD CAUGHT ENOUGH SEAL MEAT, BURYING THE REST OF HER CATCH IN THE SNOW.
A DEAL IS A DEAL! THEY ARE TAKING CARE OF THE LITTLE ONES...
SHE NEEDED TO RETURN TO FEED THEM. SHE WANTED TO SEE THEM, HUG THEM, LICK THEIR CUTE LITTLE FACES... THEY WERE SO ADORABLE! SHE LOVED BEING A BEAR AND HAVING CUBS. THERE WAS NO HAPPIER BEAR IN THE WORLD!
ON HER BRIEF ADVENTURE, SHE DIDN'T GAIN MUCH WEIGHT, BUT GREW STRONGER. SHE WAS BEGINNING TO FEEL FULL OF MILK FOR THE CUBS.
49

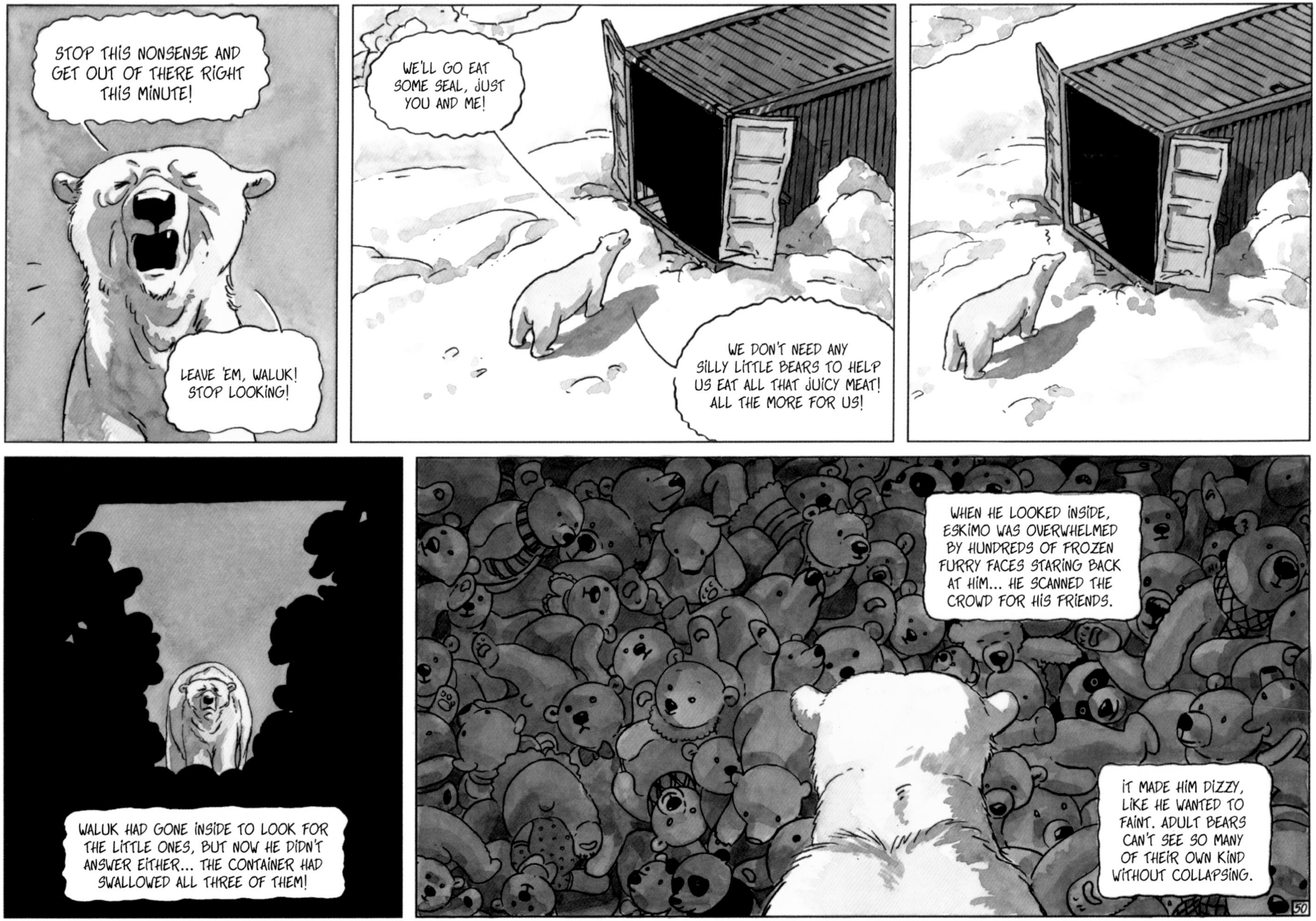
STOP THIS NONSENSE AND GET OUT OF THERE RIGHT THIS MINUTE!
LEAVE 'EM, WALUK! STOP LOOKING!
WE'LL GO EAT SOME SEAL, JUST YOU AND ME!
WE DON'T NEED ANY SILLY LITTLE BEARS TO HELP US EAT ALL THAT JUICY MEAT! ALL THE MORE FOR US!
WALUK HAD GONE INSIDE TO LOOK FOR THE LITTLE ONES, BUT NOW HE DIDN'T ANSWER EITHER... THE CONTAINER HAD SWALLOWED ALL THREE OF THEM!
WHEN HE LOOKED INSIDE, ESKIMO WAS OVERWHELMED BY HUNDREDS OF FROZEN FURRY FACES STARING BACK AT HIM... HE SCANNED THE CROWD FOR HIS FRIENDS.
IT MADE HIM DIZZY, LIKE HE WANTED TO FAINT. ADULT BEARS CAN'T SEE SO MANY OF THEIR OWN KIND WITHOUT COLLAPSING.
50

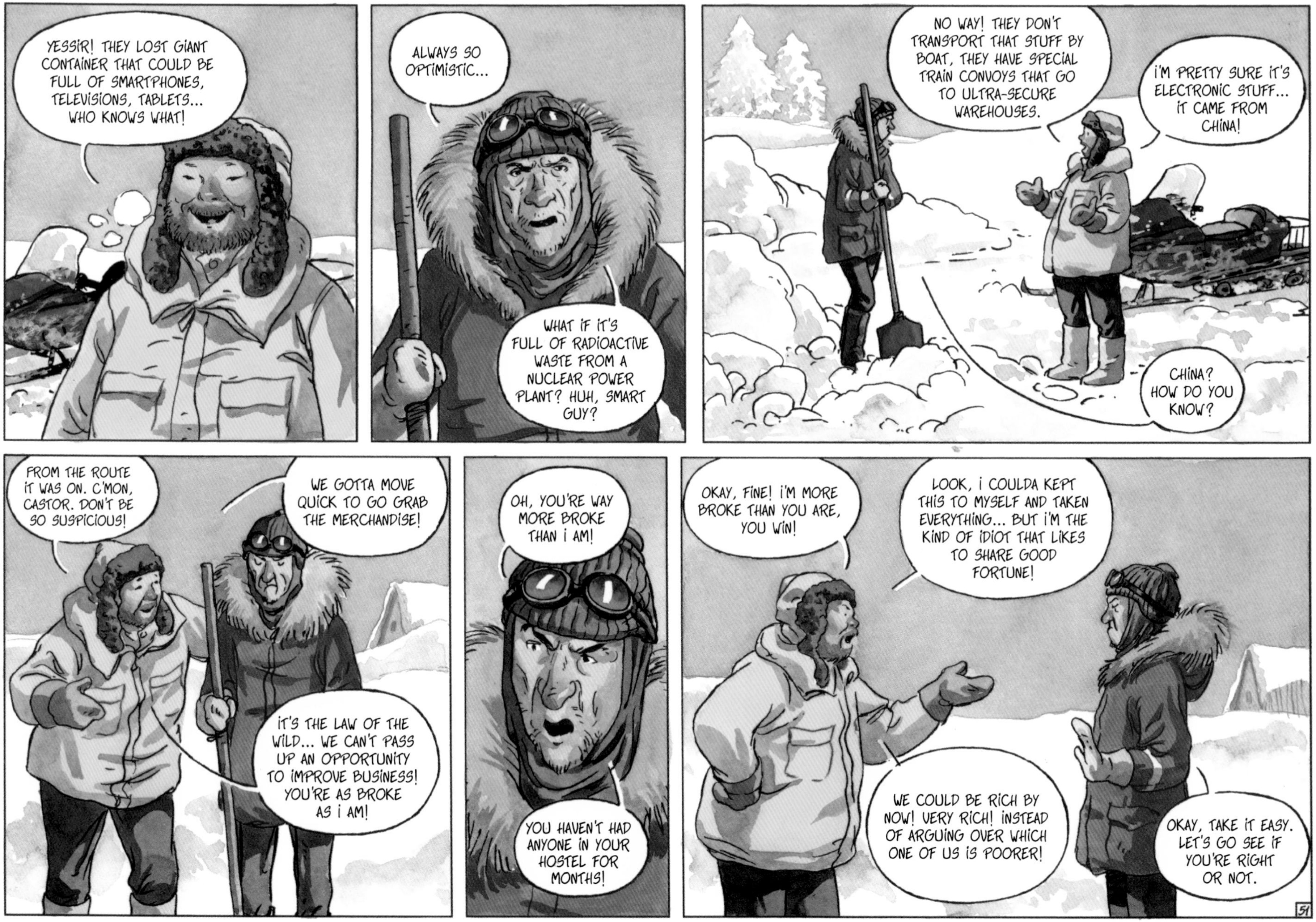
YESSIR! THEY LOST GIANT CONTAINER THAT COULD BE FULL OF SMARTPHONES, TELEVISIONS, TABLETS... WHO KNOWS WHAT!
ALWAYS SO OPTIMISTIC...
WHAT IF IT'S FULL OF RADIOACTIVE WASTE FROM A NUCLEAR POWER PLANT? HUH, SMART GUY?
I'M PRETTY SURE IT'S ELECTRONIC STUFF... IT CAME FROM CHINA!
NO WAY! THEY DON'T TRANSPORT THAT STUFF BY BOAT, THEY HAVE SPECIAL TRAIN CONVOYS THAT GO TO ULTRA-SECURE WAREHOUSES.
CHINA? HOW DO YOU KNOW?
FROM THE ROUTE IT WAS ON. C'MON, CASTOR. DON'T BE SO SUSPICIOUS!
WE GOTTA MOVE QUICK TO GO GRAB THE MERCHANDISE!
IT'S THE LAW OF THE WILD... WE CAN'T PASS UP AN OPPORTUNITY TO IMPROVE BUSINESS! YOU'RE AS BROKE AS I AM!
OH, YOU'RE WAY MORE BROKE THAN I AM!
YOU HAVEN'T HAD ANYONE IN YOUR HOSTEL FOR MONTHS!
OKAY, FINE! I'M MORE BROKE THAN YOU ARE, YOU WIN!
LOOK, I COULDA KEPT THIS TO MYSELF AND TAKEN EVERYTHING... BUT I'M THE KIND OF IDIOT THAT LIKES TO SHARE GOOD FORTUNE!
WE COULD BE RICH BY NOW! VERY RICH! INSTEAD OF ARGUING OVER WHICH ONE OF US IS POORER!
OKAY, TAKE IT EASY. LET'S GO SEE IF YOU'RE RIGHT OR NOT.
51

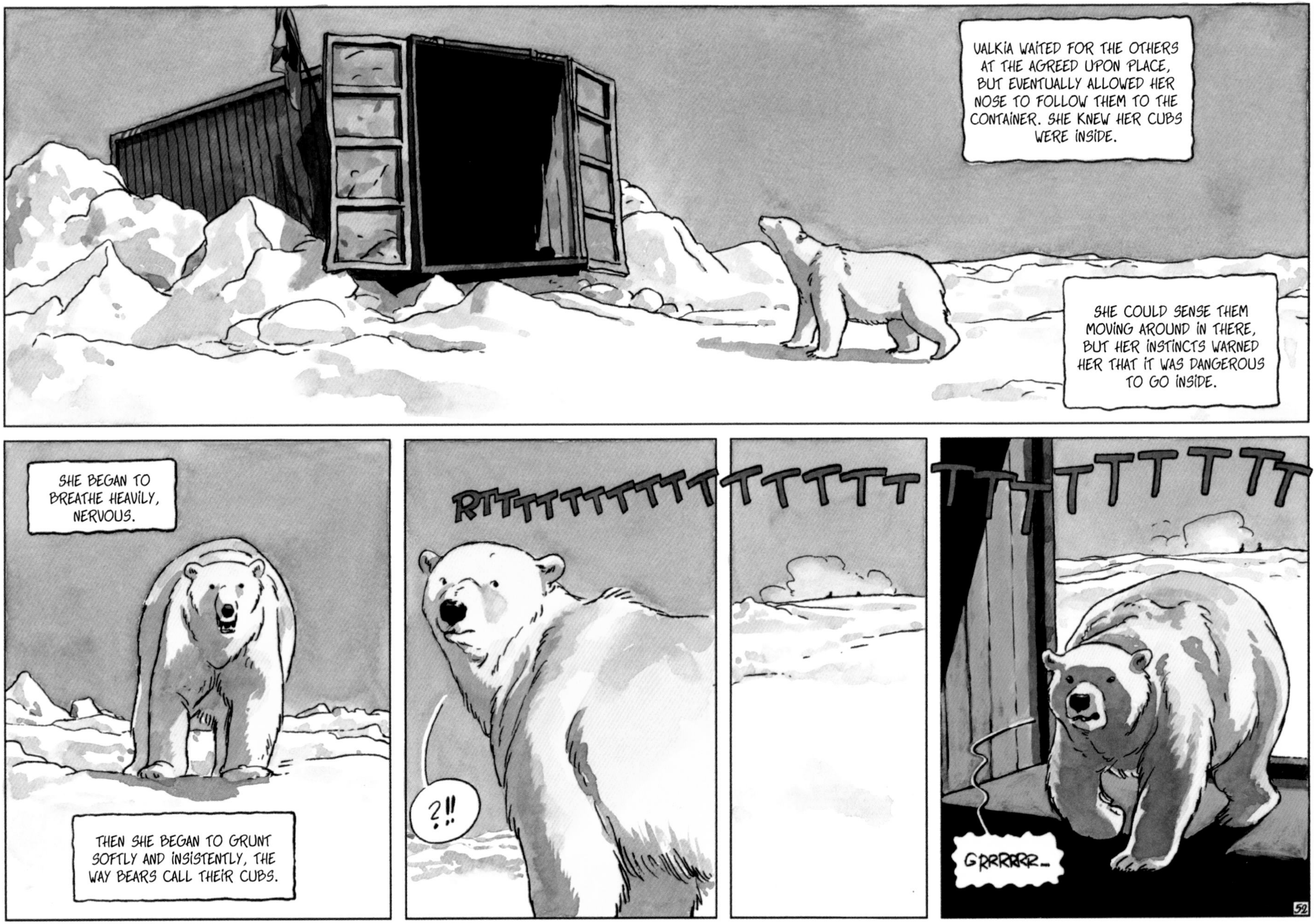
VALKIA WAITED FOR THE OTHERS AT THE AGREED UPON PLACE, BUT EVENTUALLY ALLOWED HER NOSE TO FOLLOW THEM TO THE CONTAINER. SHE KNEW HER CUBS WERE INSIDE.
SHE COULD SENSE THEM MOVING AROUND IN THERE, BUT HER INSTINCTS WARNED HER THAT IT WAS DANGEROUS TO GO INSIDE.
SHE BEGAN TO BREATHE HEAVILY, NERVOUS.
THEN SHE BEGAN TO GRUNT SOFTLY AND INSISTENTLY, THE WAY BEARS CALL THEIR CUBS.
RTTTTTTTTTTTTTTTTTTTTTTTTTT
?!!
GRRRRRR...
52

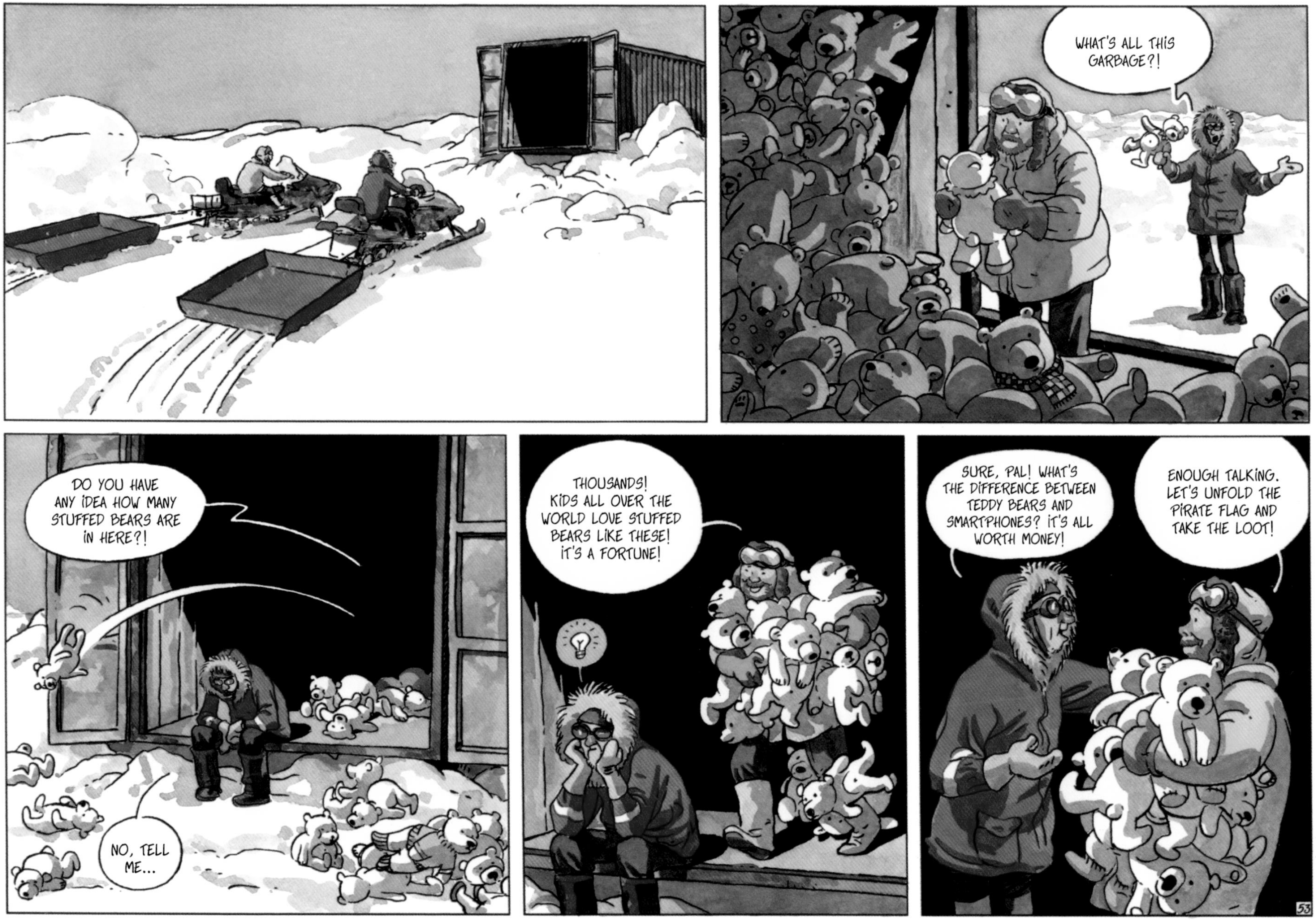
WHAT'S ALL THIS GARBAGE?!
DO YOU HAVE ANY IDEA HOW MANY STUFFED BEARS ARE IN HERE?!
NO, TELL ME...
THOUSANDS! KIDS ALL OVER THE WORLD LOVE STUFFED BEARS LIKE THESE! IT'S A FORTUNE!
SURE, PAL! WHAT'S THE DIFFERENCE BETWEEN TEDDY BEARS AND SMARTPHONES? IT'S ALL WORTH MONEY!
ENOUGH TALKING. LET'S UNFOLD THE PIRATE FLAG AND TAKE THE LOOT!
53

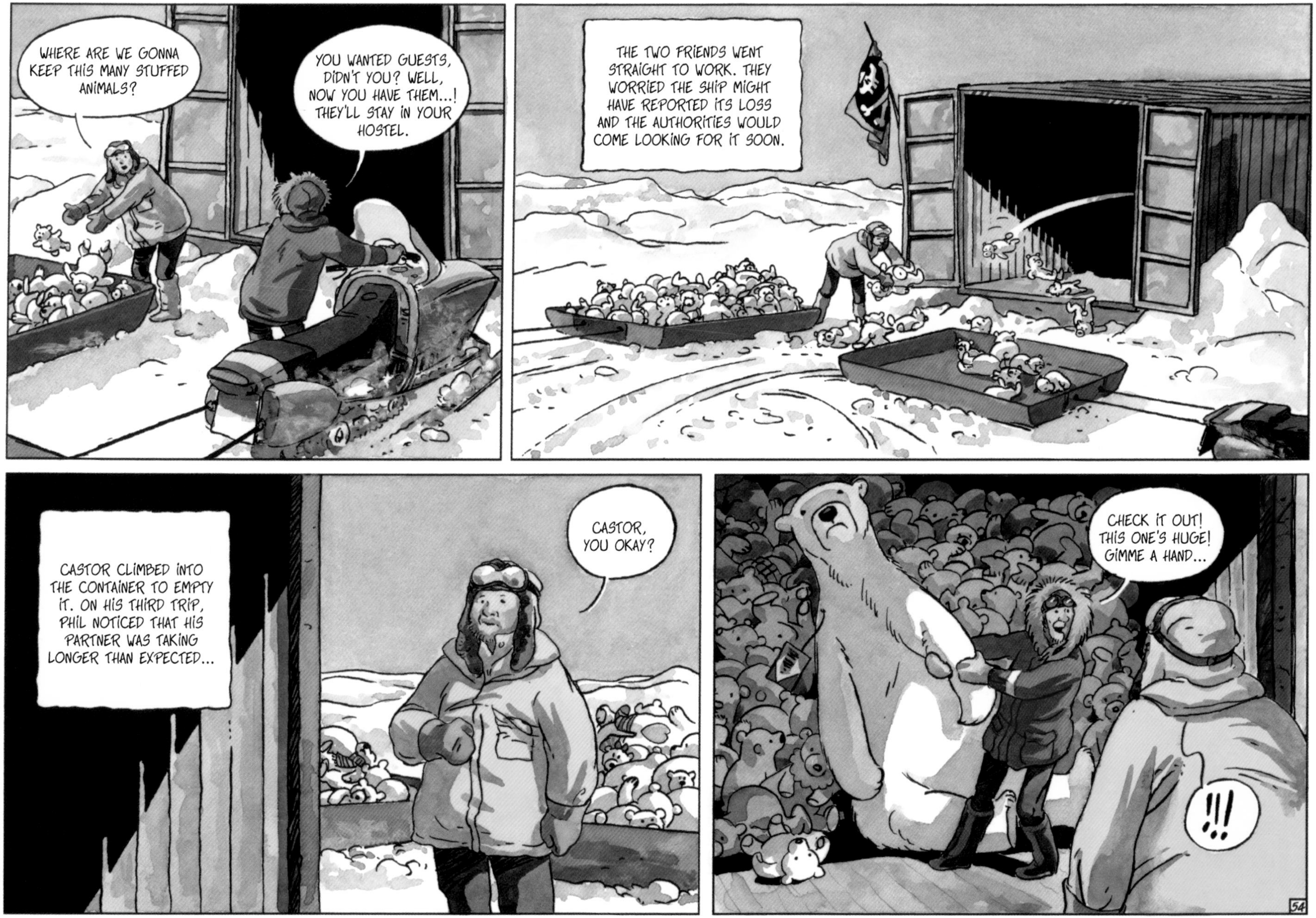
WHERE ARE WE GONNA KEEP THIS MANY STUFFED ANIMALS?
YOU WANTED GUESTS, DIDN'T YOU? WELL, NOW YOU HAVE THEM...! THEY'LL STAY IN YOUR HOSTEL.
THE TWO FRIENDS WENT STRAIGHT TO WORK. THEY WORRIED THE SHIP MIGHT HAVE REPORTED ITS LOSS AND THE AUTHORITIES WOULD COME LOOKING FOR IT SOON.
CASTOR CLIMBED INTO THE CONTAINER TO EMPTY IT. ON HIS THIRD TRIP, PHIL NOTICED THAT HIS PARTNER WAS TAKING LONGER THAN EXPECTED...
CASTOR, YOU OKAY?
CHECK IT OUT! THIS ONE'S HUGE! GIMME A HAND...
!!!
54

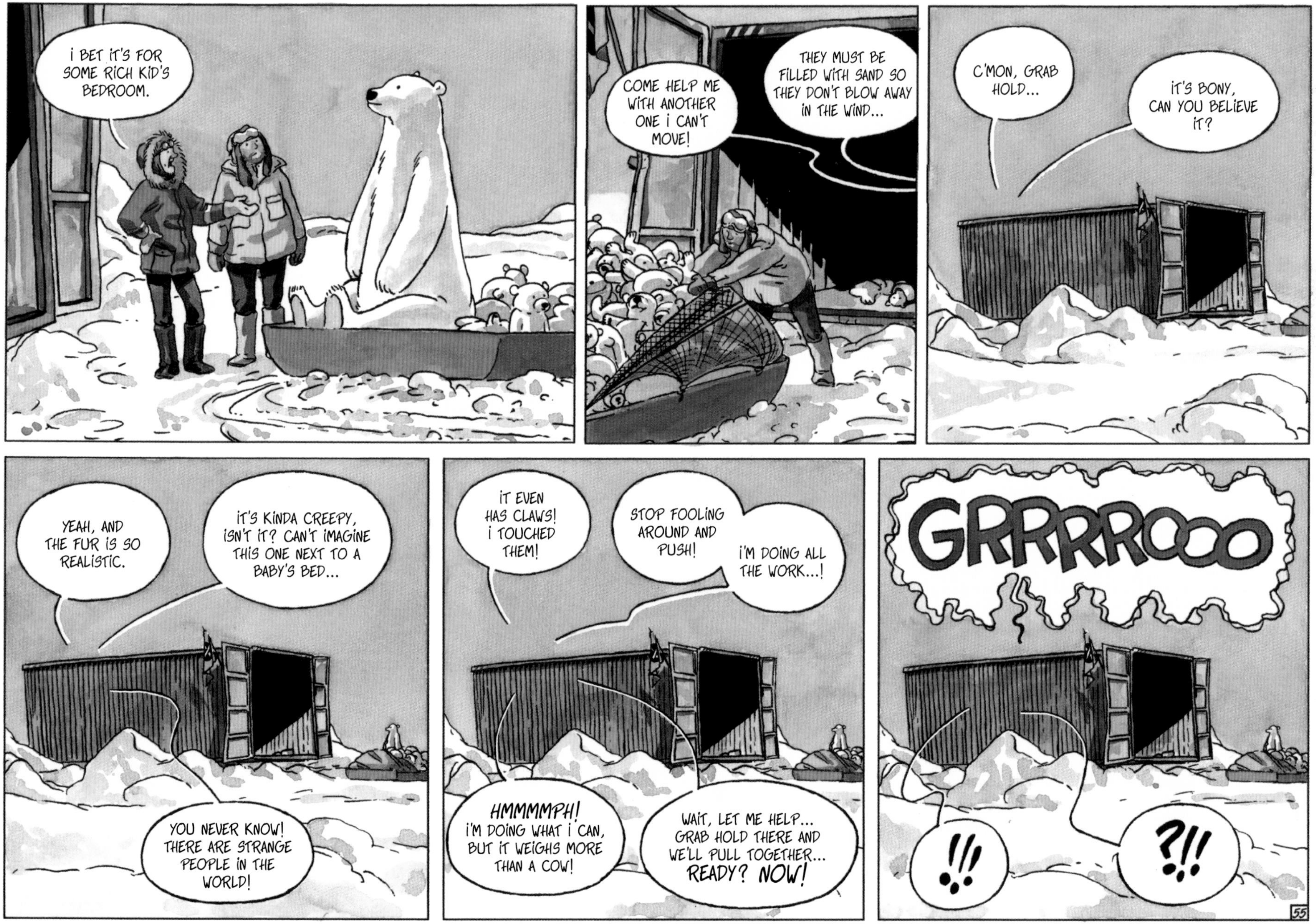
I BET IT'S FOR SOME RICH KID'S BEDROOM.
COME HELP ME WITH ANOTHER ONE I CAN'T MOVE!
THEY MUST BE FILLED WITH SAND SO THEY DON'T BLOW AWAY IN THE WIND...
C'MON, GRAB HOLD...
IT'S BONY, CAN YOU BELIEVE IT?
YEAH, AND THE FUR IS SO REALISTIC.
IT'S KINDA CREEPY, ISN'T IT? CAN'T IMAGINE THIS ONE NEXT TO A BABY'S BED...
YOU NEVER KNOW! THERE ARE STRANGE PEOPLE IN THE WORLD!
IT EVEN HAS CLAWS! I TOUCHED THEM!
STOP FOOLING AROUND AND PUSH!
I'M DOING ALL THE WORK...!
HMMMMPH! I'M DOING WHAT I CAN, BUT IT WEIGHS MORE THAN A COW!
WAIT, LET ME HELP... GRAB HOLD THERE AND WE'LL PULL TOGETHER... READY? NOW!
GRRRROOO
!!!
?!!
55

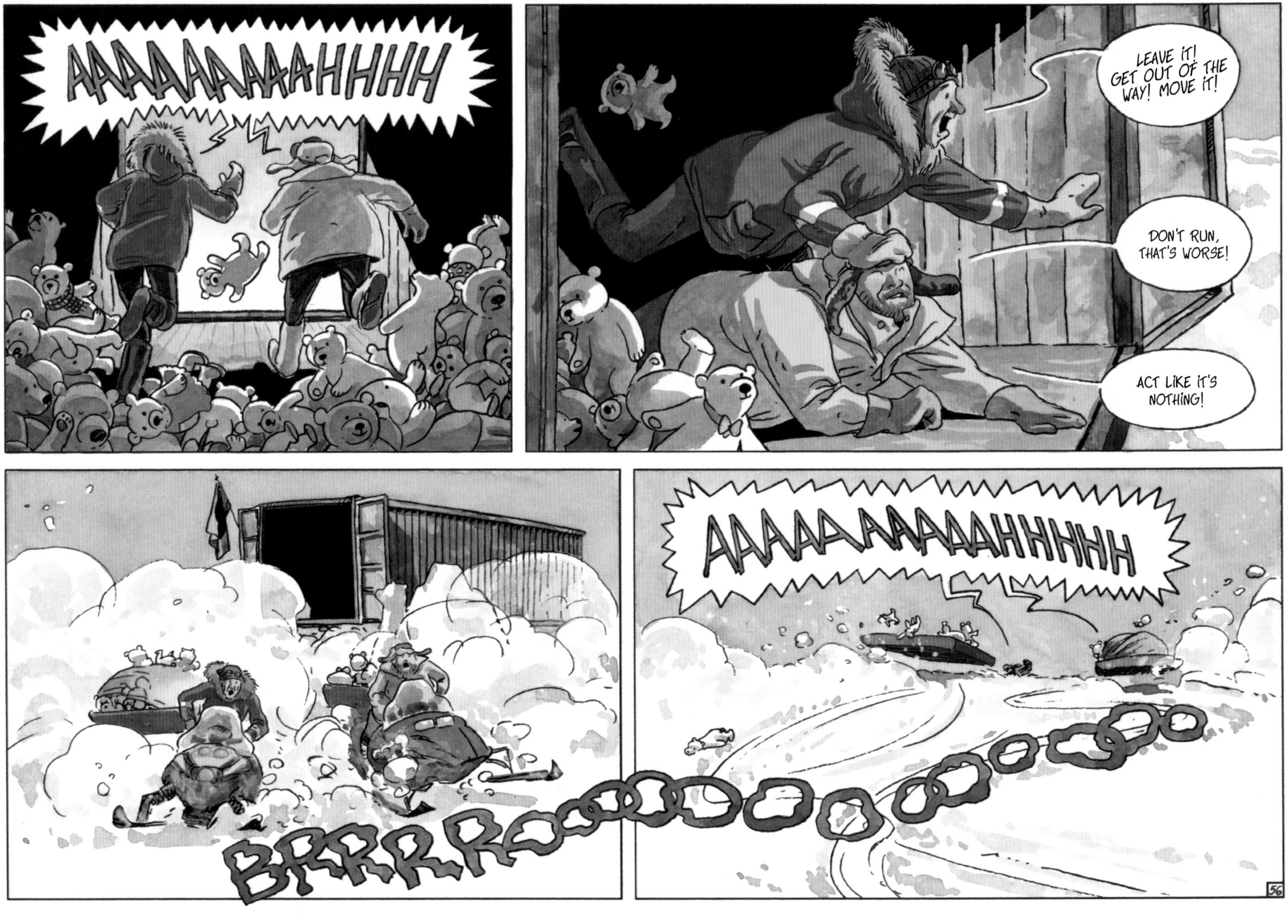
AAAAAAAAAHHHH
LEAVE IT! GET OUT OF THE WAY! MOVE IT!
DON'T RUN, THAT'S WORSE!
ACT LIKE IT'S NOTHING!
BRRRROOOOOOOOOOOOOOO
AAAAAAAAAAHHHHH
56

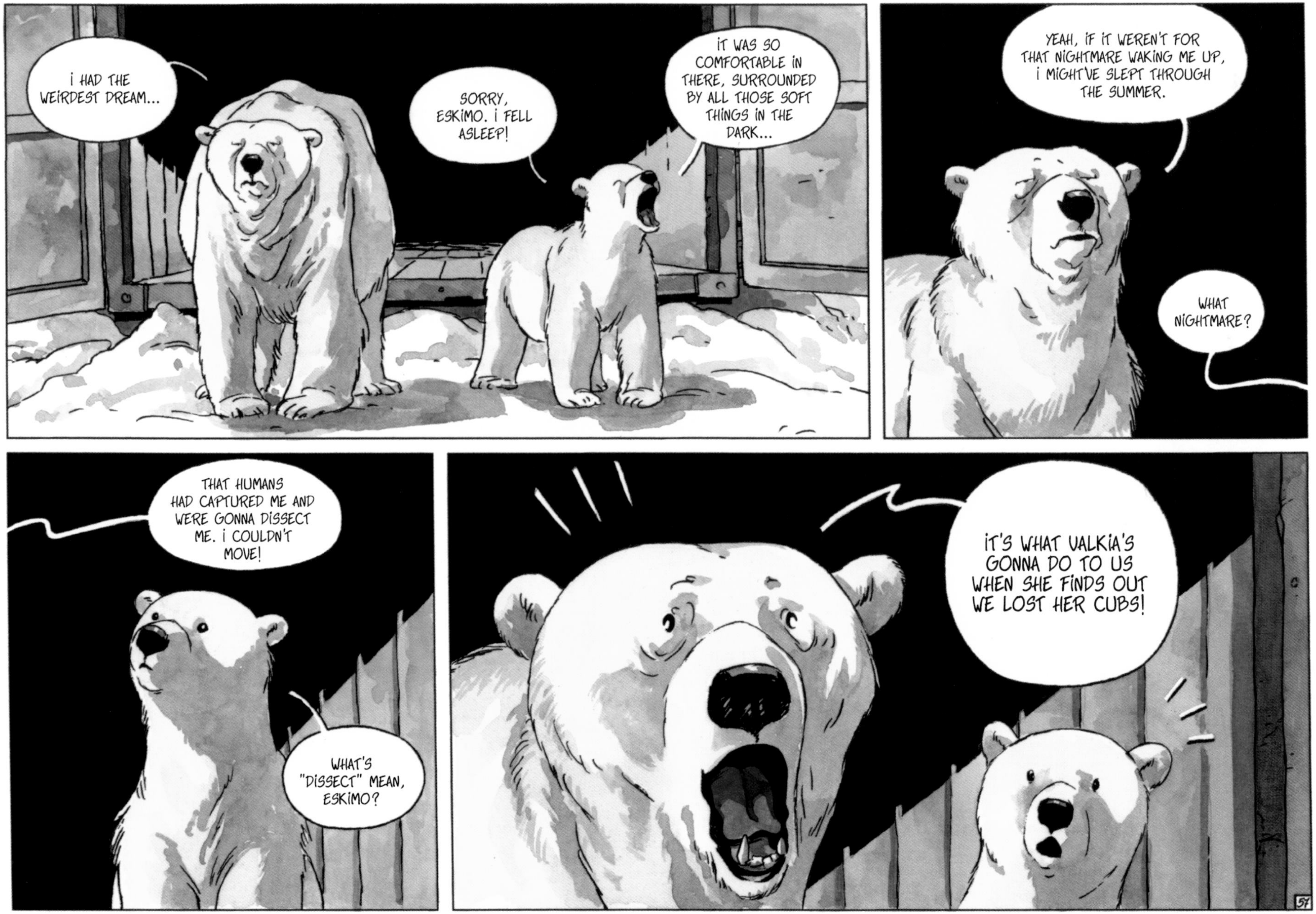
I HAD THE WEIRDEST DREAM...
SORRY, ESKIMO. I FELL ASLEEP!
IT WAS SO COMFORTABLE IN THERE, SURROUNDED BY ALL THOSE SOFT THINGS IN THE DARK...
YEAH, IF IT WEREN'T FOR THAT NIGHTMARE WAKING ME UP, I MIGHT'VE SLEPT THROUGH THE SUMMER.
WHAT NIGHTMARE?
THAT HUMANS HAD CAPTURED ME AND WERE GONNA DISSECT ME. I COULDN'T MOVE!
WHAT'S "DISSECT" MEAN, ESKIMO?
IT'S WHAT VALKIA'S GONNA DO TO US WHEN SHE FINDS OUT WE LOST HER CUBS!
57

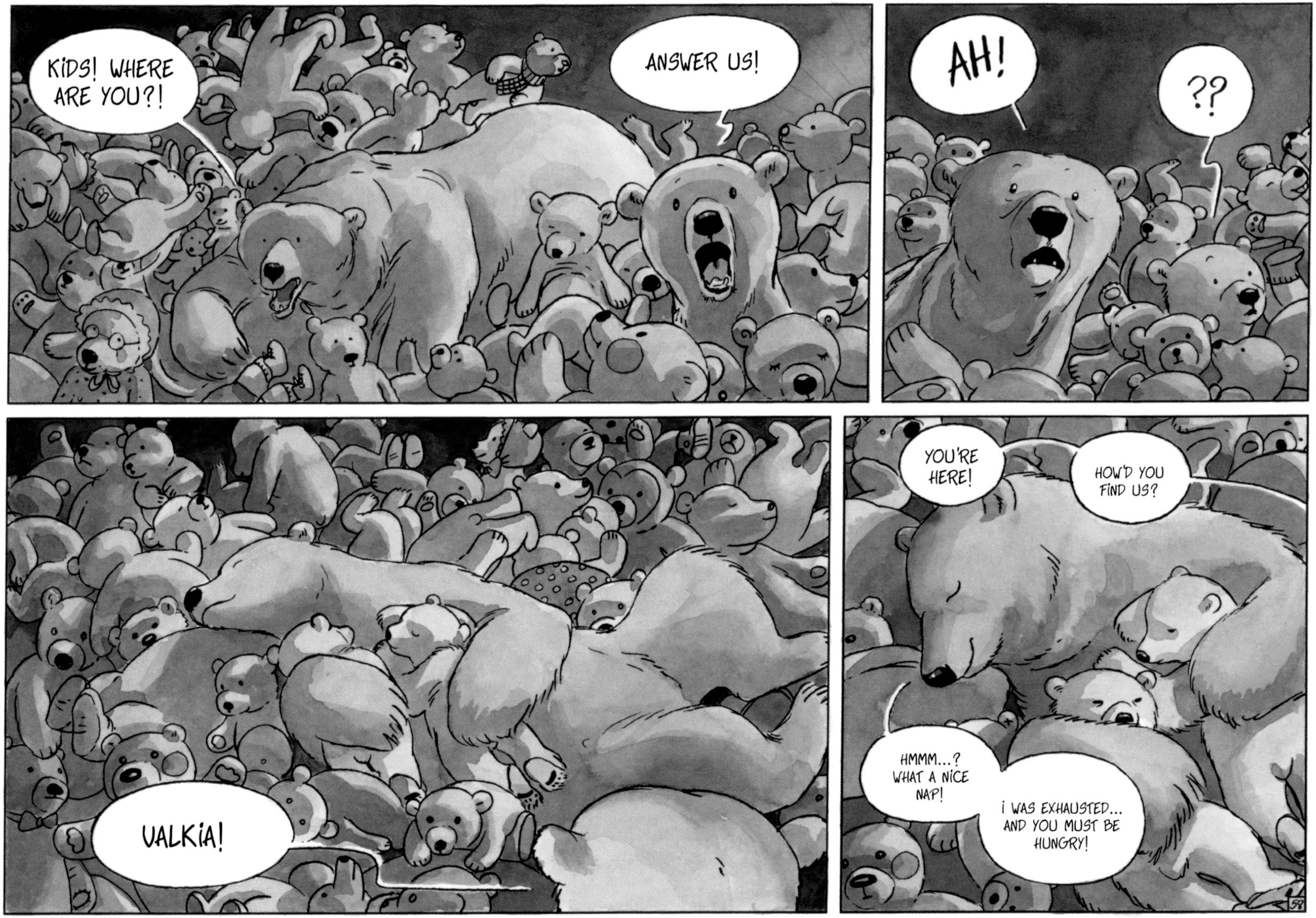

KiDS! WHERE ARE YOU?!
ANSWER US!
AH!
??
VALKiA!
YOU'RE HERE!
HOW'D YOU FiND US?
HMMM...? WHAT A NiCE NAP!
i WAS EXHAUSTED... AND YOU MUST BE HUNGRY!
58

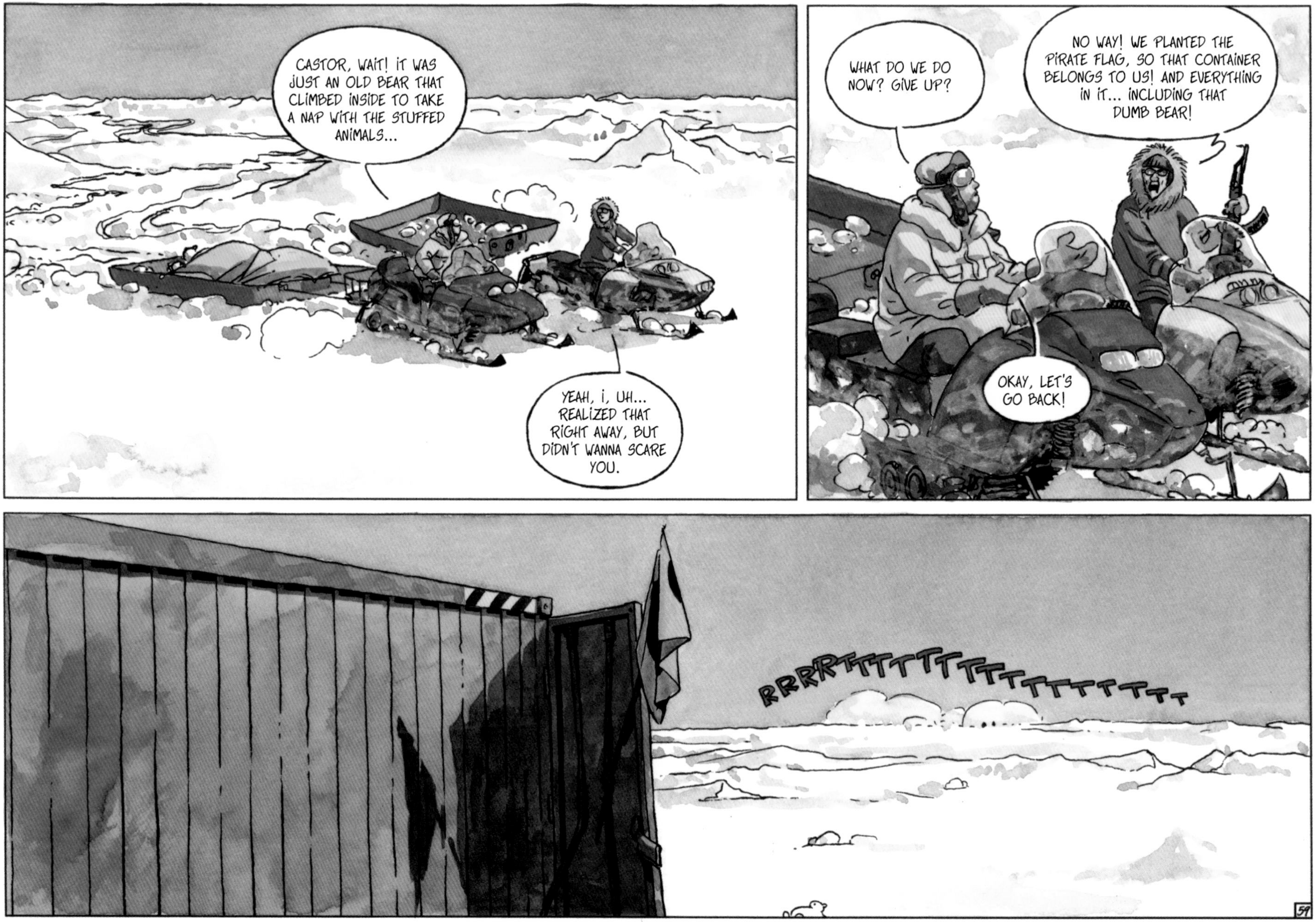
CASTOR, WAIT! IT WAS JUST AN OLD BEAR THAT CLIMBED INSIDE TO TAKE A NAP WITH THE STUFFED ANIMALS...
YEAH, I, UH... REALIZED THAT RIGHT AWAY, BUT DIDN'T WANNA SCARE YOU.
WHAT DO WE DO NOW? GIVE UP?
NO WAY! WE PLANTED THE PIRATE FLAG, SO THAT CONTAINER BELONGS TO US! AND EVERYTHING IN IT... INCLUDING THAT DUMB BEAR!
OKAY, LET'S GO BACK!
RRRRTTTTTTTTTTTTTTTTTT
59

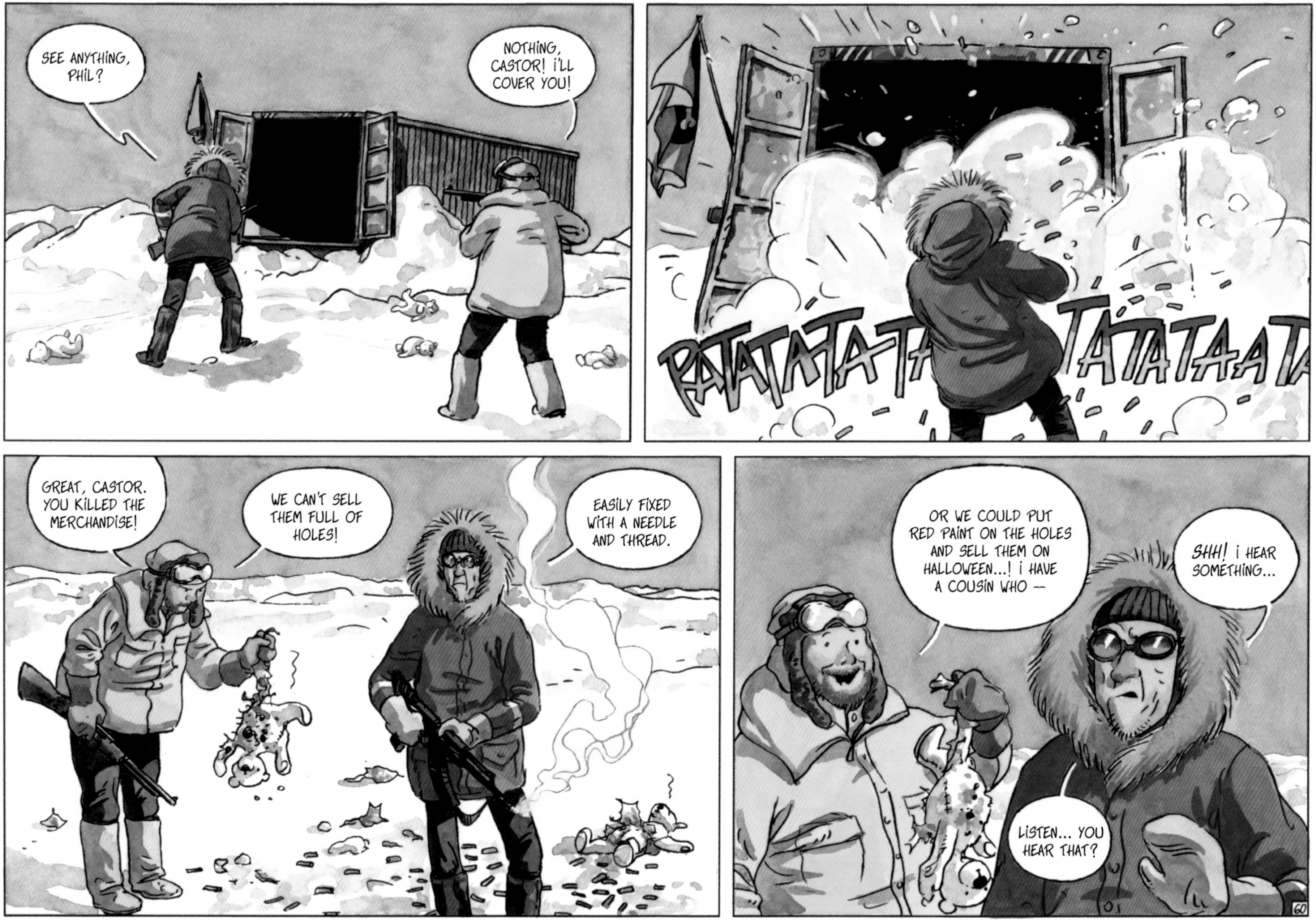
SEE ANYTHING, PHIL?
NOTHING, CASTOR! I'LL COVER YOU!
PATATATATA TATATAATA
GREAT, CASTOR. YOU KILLED THE MERCHANDISE!
WE CAN'T SELL THEM FULL OF HOLES!
EASILY FIXED WITH A NEEDLE AND THREAD.
OR WE COULD PUT RED PAINT ON THE HOLES AND SELL THEM ON HALLOWEEN...! I HAVE A COUSIN WHO —
SHH! I HEAR SOMETHING...
LISTEN... YOU HEAR THAT?
60

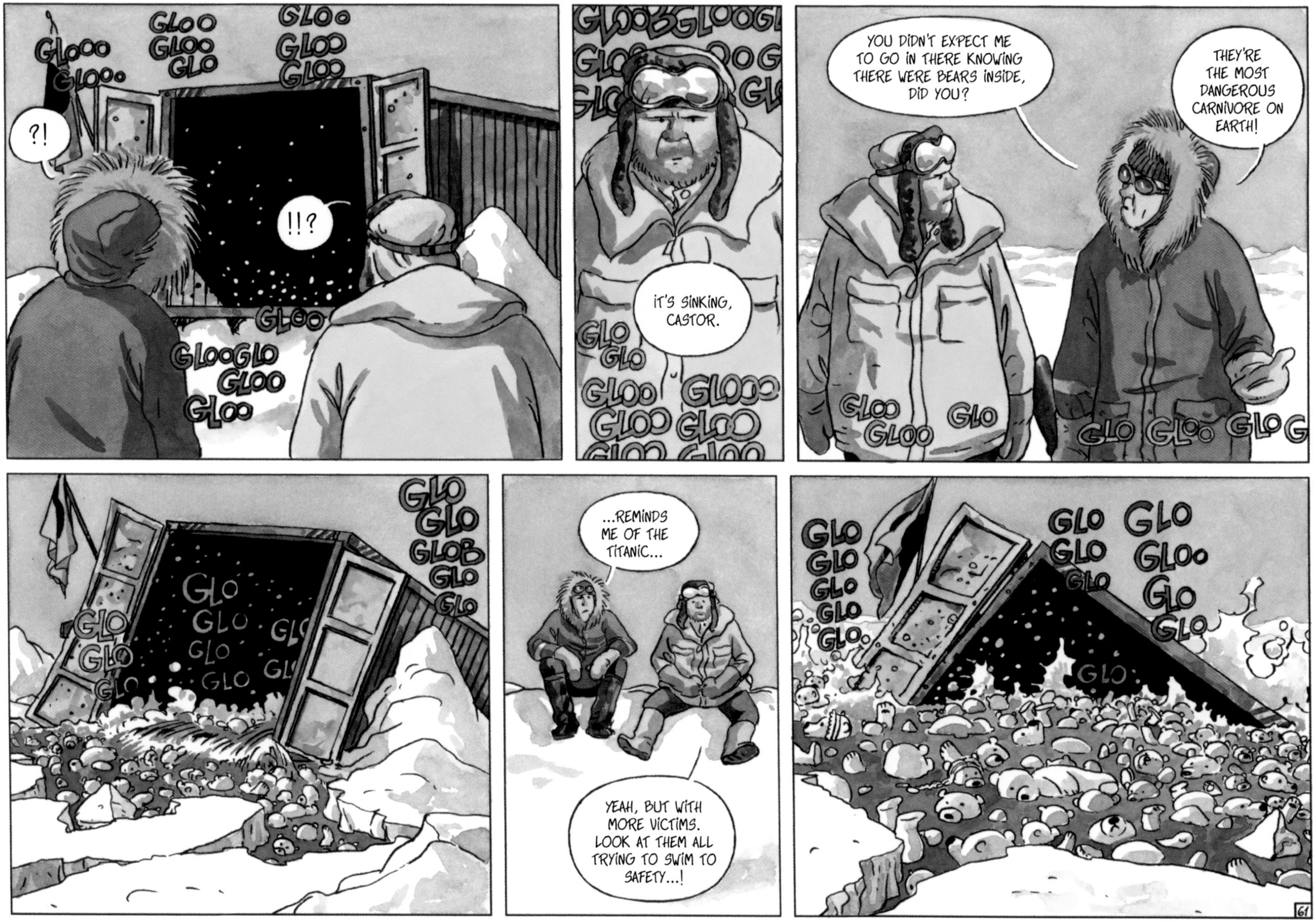
GLOOO GLOOO
GLOO GLOO GLO
GLOO GLOO GLOO
?!
!!?
GLOO
GLOOGLO GLOO GLOO
GLOOBGLOOGL
IT'S SINKING, CASTOR.
GLO GLO
GLOO GLOOO GLOO GLOO
YOU DIDN'T EXPECT ME TO GO IN THERE KNOWING THERE WERE BEARS INSIDE, DID YOU?
THEY'RE THE MOST DANGEROUS CARNIVORE ON EARTH!
GLOO GLOO GLO
GLO GLOO GLOG
GLO GLO GLOB GLO GLO
GLO GLO GLO GLO
GLO GLO GLO
...REMINDS ME OF THE TITANIC...
YEAH, BUT WITH MORE VICTIMS. LOOK AT THEM ALL TRYING TO SWIM TO SAFETY...!
GLO GLO GLO GLO GLO
GLO GLO GLO
GLO GLOO GLO GLO
GLO
61

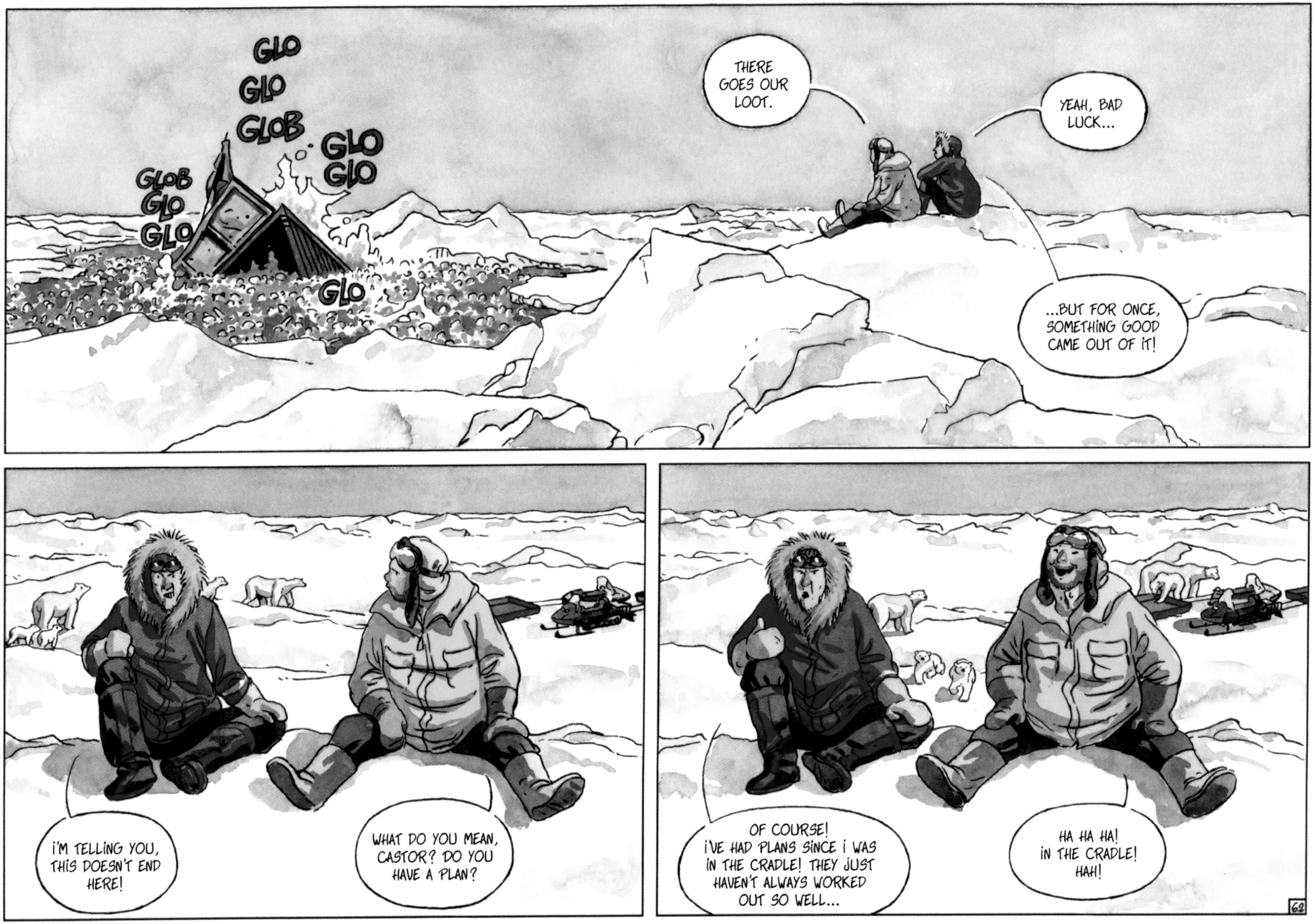
GLO
GLO
GLOB
GLO GLO
GLOB GLO GLO
GLO
THERE GOES OUR LOOT.
YEAH, BAD LUCK...
...BUT FOR ONCE, SOMETHING GOOD CAME OUT OF IT!
I'M TELLING YOU, THIS DOESN'T END HERE!
WHAT DO YOU MEAN, CASTOR? DO YOU HAVE A PLAN?
OF COURSE! I'VE HAD PLANS SINCE I WAS IN THE CRADLE! THEY JUST HAVEN'T ALWAYS WORKED OUT SO WELL...
HA HA HA! IN THE CRADLE! HAH!
62

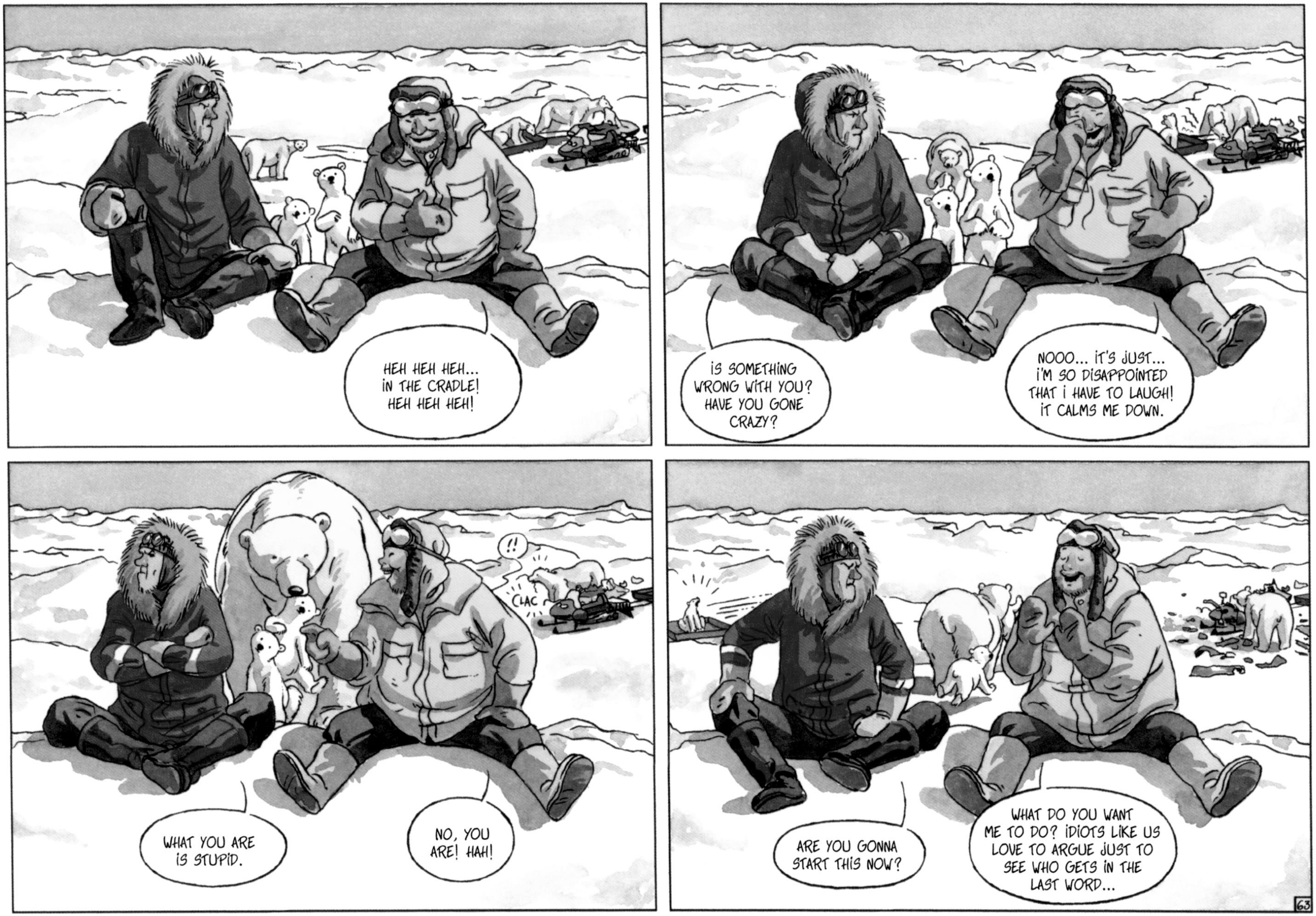
HEH HEH HEH...
IN THE CRADLE!
HEH HEH HEH!
IS SOMETHING WRONG WITH YOU? HAVE YOU GONE CRAZY?
NOOO... IT'S JUST... I'M SO DISAPPOINTED THAT I HAVE TO LAUGH! IT CALMS ME DOWN.
!!
CLAC
WHAT YOU ARE IS STUPID.
NO, YOU ARE! HAH!
ARE YOU GONNA START THIS NOW?
WHAT DO YOU WANT ME TO DO? IDIOTS LIKE US LOVE TO ARGUE JUST TO SEE WHO GETS IN THE LAST WORD...
63

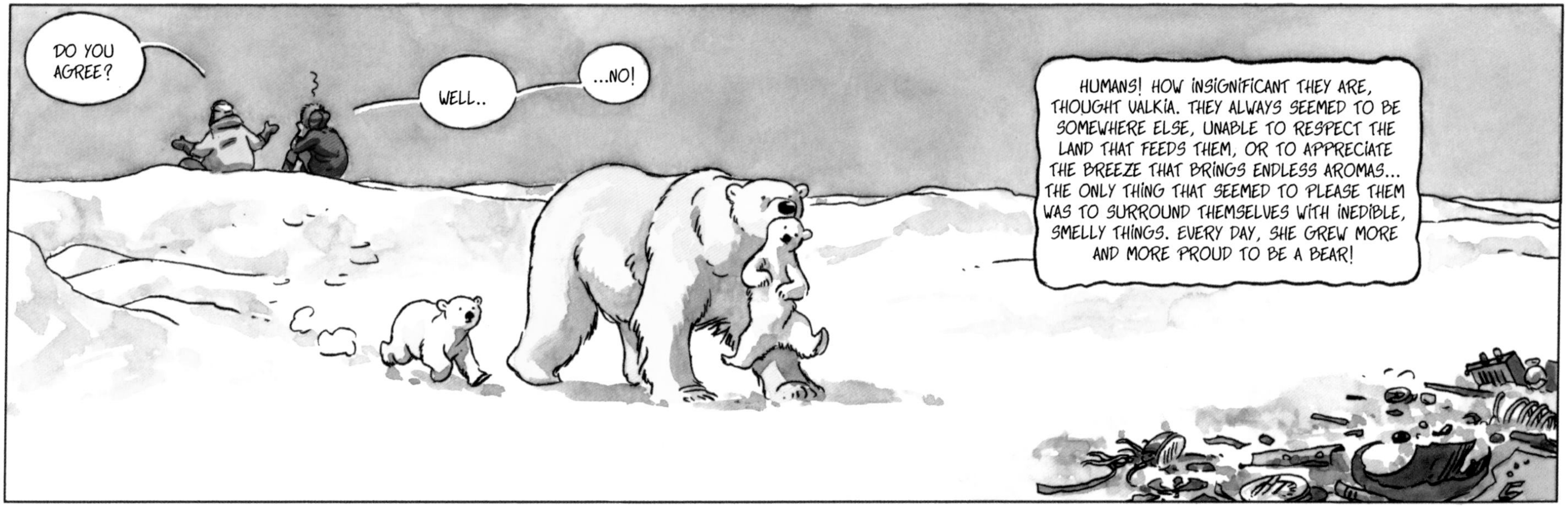
DO YOU AGREE?
WELL..
...NO!
HUMANS! HOW INSIGNIFICANT THEY ARE, THOUGHT VALKIA. THEY ALWAYS SEEMED TO BE SOMEWHERE ELSE, UNABLE TO RESPECT THE LAND THAT FEEDS THEM, OR TO APPRECIATE THE BREEZE THAT BRINGS ENDLESS AROMAS... THE ONLY THING THAT SEEMED TO PLEASE THEM WAS TO SURROUND THEMSELVES WITH INEDIBLE, SMELLY THINGS. EVERY DAY, SHE GREW MORE AND MORE PROUD TO BE A BEAR!

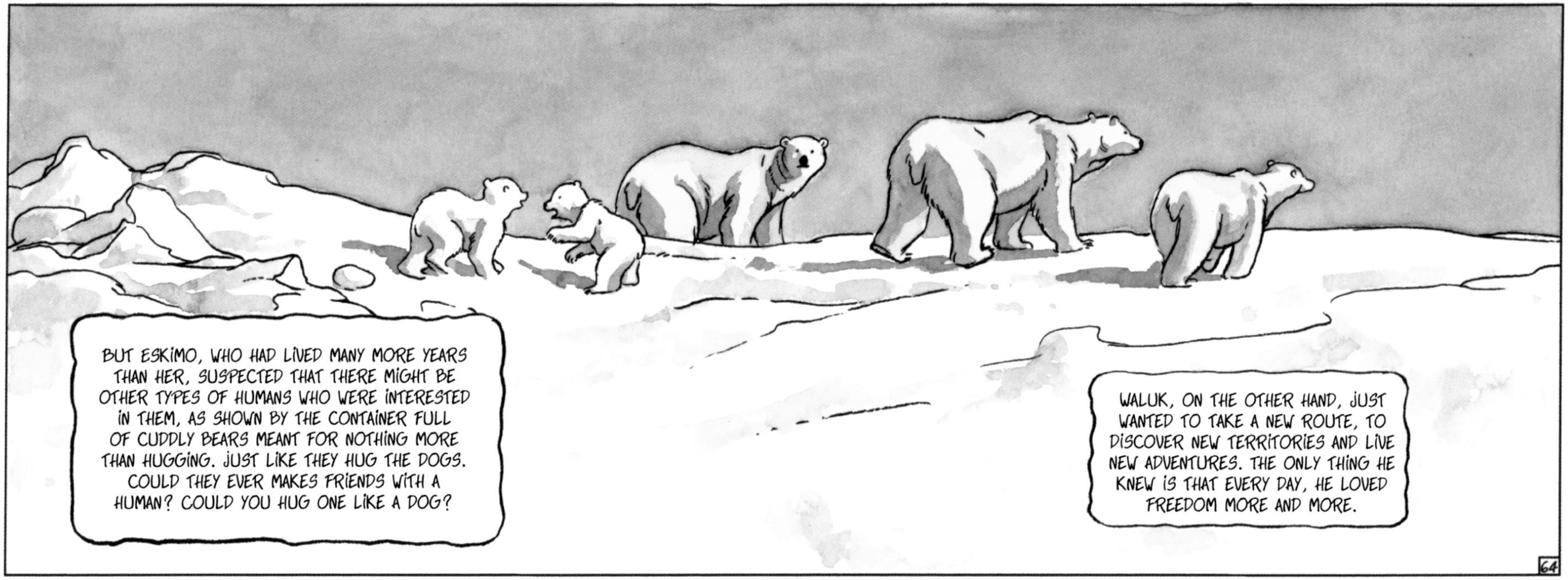
BUT ESKIMO, WHO HAD LIVED MANY MORE YEARS THAN HER, SUSPECTED THAT THERE MIGHT BE OTHER TYPES OF HUMANS WHO WERE INTERESTED IN THEM, AS SHOWN BY THE CONTAINER FULL OF CUDDLY BEARS MEANT FOR NOTHING MORE THAN HUGGING. JUST LIKE THEY HUG THE DOGS. COULD THEY EVER MAKES FRIENDS WITH A HUMAN? COULD YOU HUG ONE LIKE A DOG?
WALUK, ON THE OTHER HAND, JUST WANTED TO TAKE A NEW ROUTE, TO DISCOVER NEW TERRITORIES AND LIVE NEW ADVENTURES. THE ONLY THING HE KNEW IS THAT EVERY DAY, HE LOVED FREEDOM MORE AND MORE.
64

# THE PATH OF THE GREAT DOG

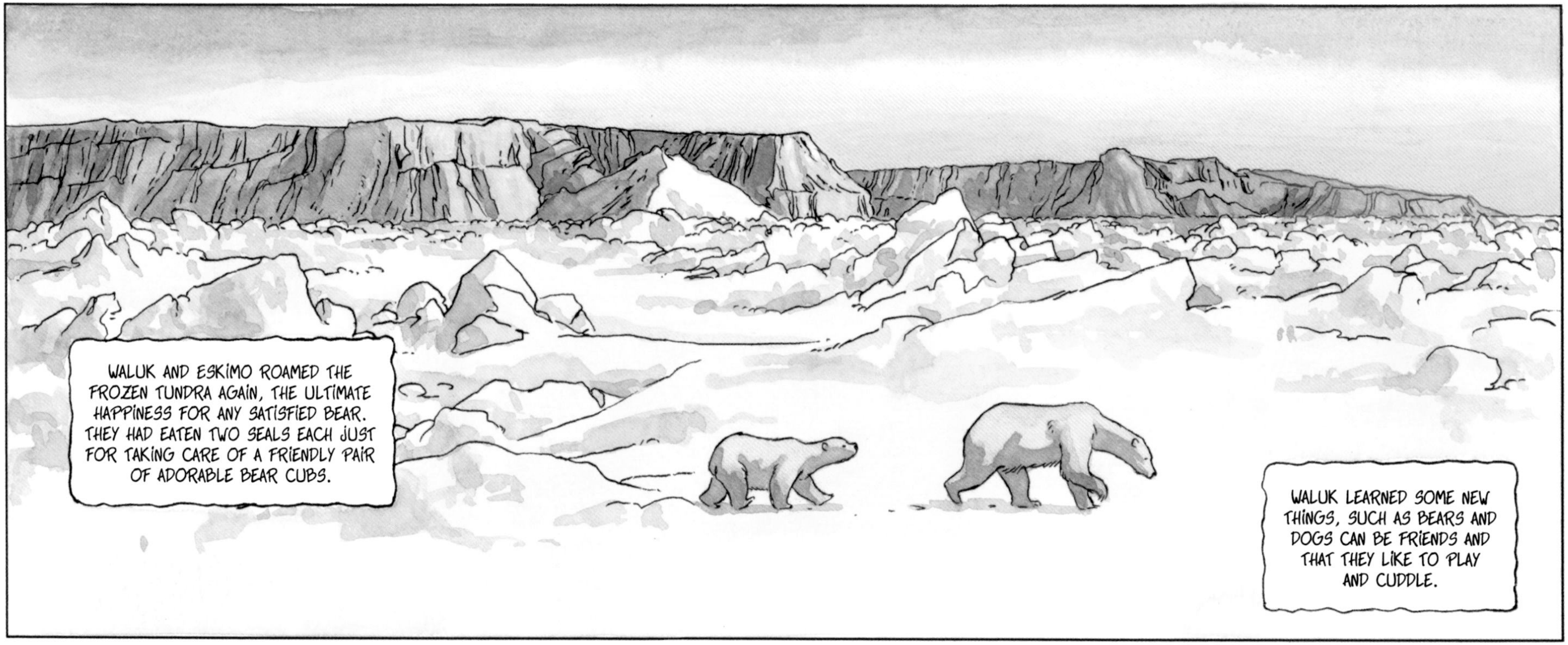
WALUK AND ESKIMO ROAMED THE FROZEN TUNDRA AGAIN, THE ULTIMATE HAPPINESS FOR ANY SATISFIED BEAR. THEY HAD EATEN TWO SEALS EACH JUST FOR TAKING CARE OF A FRIENDLY PAIR OF ADORABLE BEAR CUBS.
WALUK LEARNED SOME NEW THINGS, SUCH AS BEARS AND DOGS CAN BE FRIENDS AND THAT THEY LIKE TO PLAY AND CUDDLE.

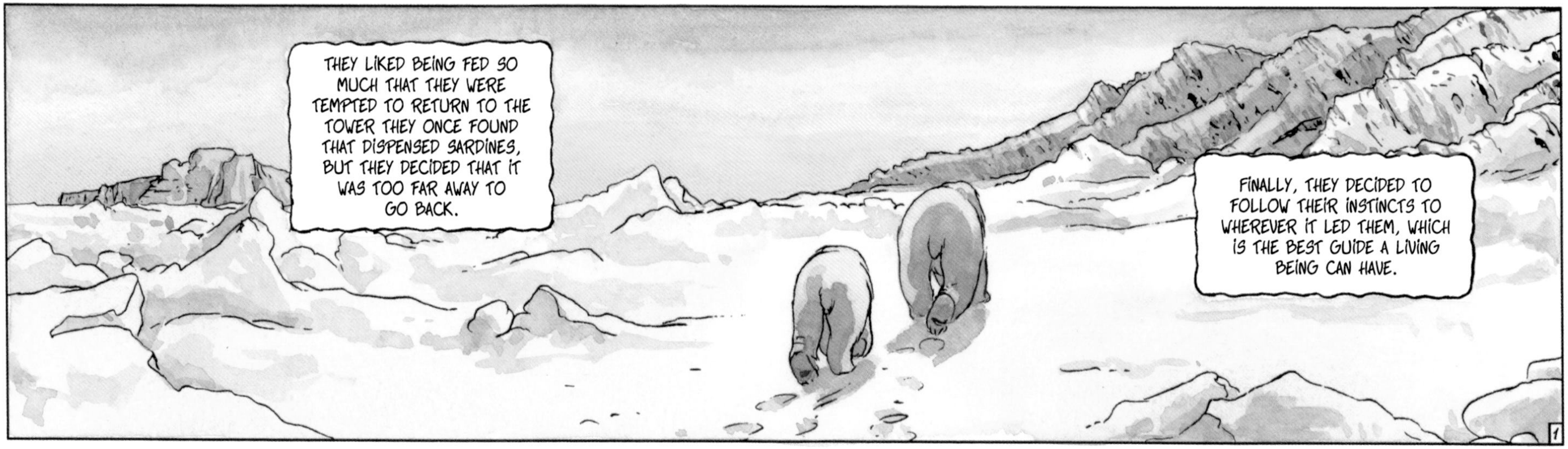
THEY LIKED BEING FED SO MUCH THAT THEY WERE TEMPTED TO RETURN TO THE TOWER THEY ONCE FOUND THAT DISPENSED SARDINES, BUT THEY DECIDED THAT IT WAS TOO FAR AWAY TO GO BACK.
FINALLY, THEY DECIDED TO FOLLOW THEIR INSTINCTS TO WHEREVER IT LED THEM, WHICH IS THE BEST GUIDE A LIVING BEING CAN HAVE.
1

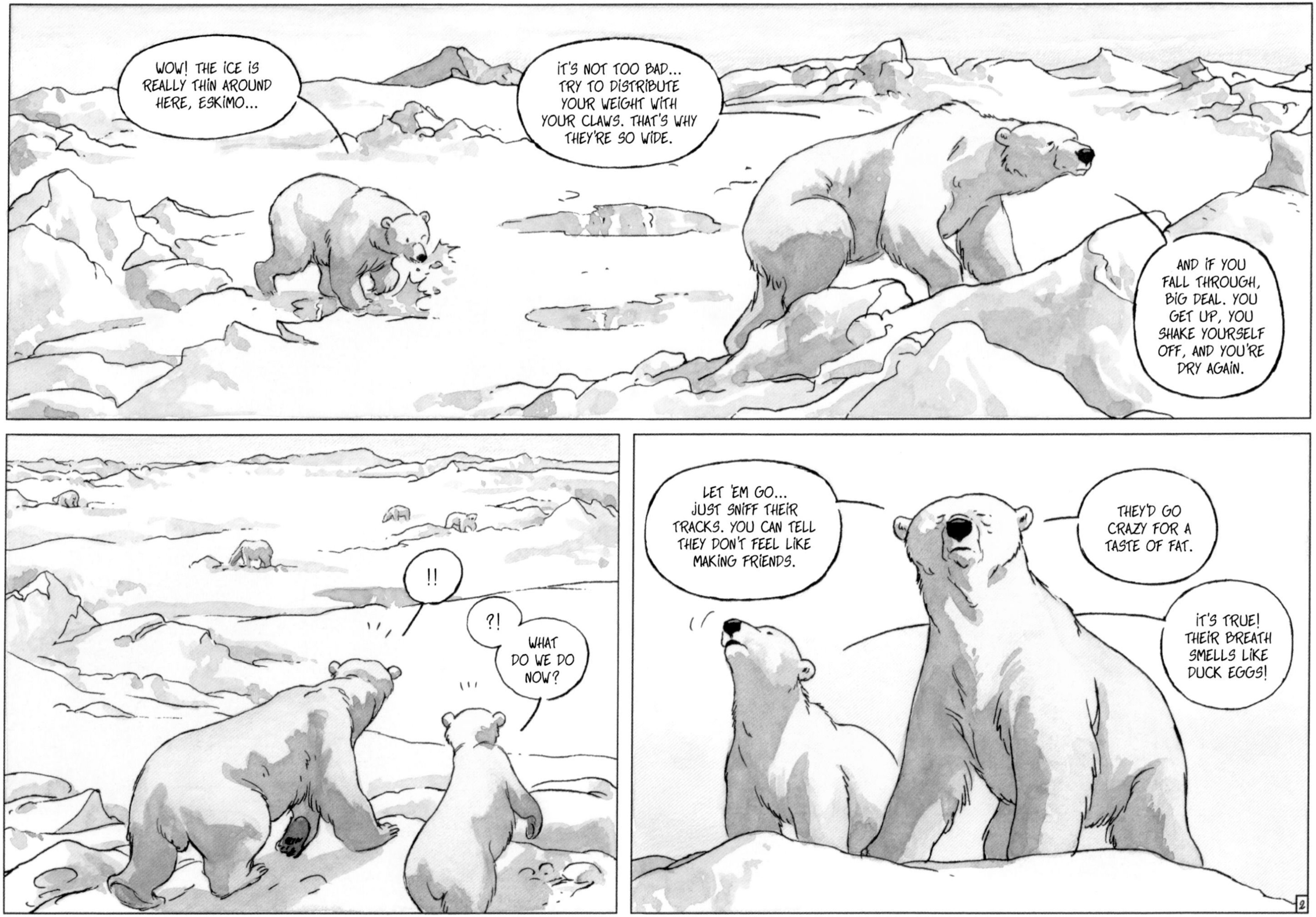
WOW! THE ICE IS REALLY THIN AROUND HERE, ESKIMO...
IT'S NOT TOO BAD... TRY TO DISTRIBUTE YOUR WEIGHT WITH YOUR CLAWS. THAT'S WHY THEY'RE SO WIDE.
AND IF YOU FALL THROUGH, BIG DEAL. YOU GET UP, YOU SHAKE YOURSELF OFF, AND YOU'RE DRY AGAIN.
!!
?!
WHAT DO WE DO NOW?
LET 'EM GO... JUST SNIFF THEIR TRACKS. YOU CAN TELL THEY DON'T FEEL LIKE MAKING FRIENDS.
THEY'D GO CRAZY FOR A TASTE OF FAT.
IT'S TRUE! THEIR BREATH SMELLS LIKE DUCK EGGS!

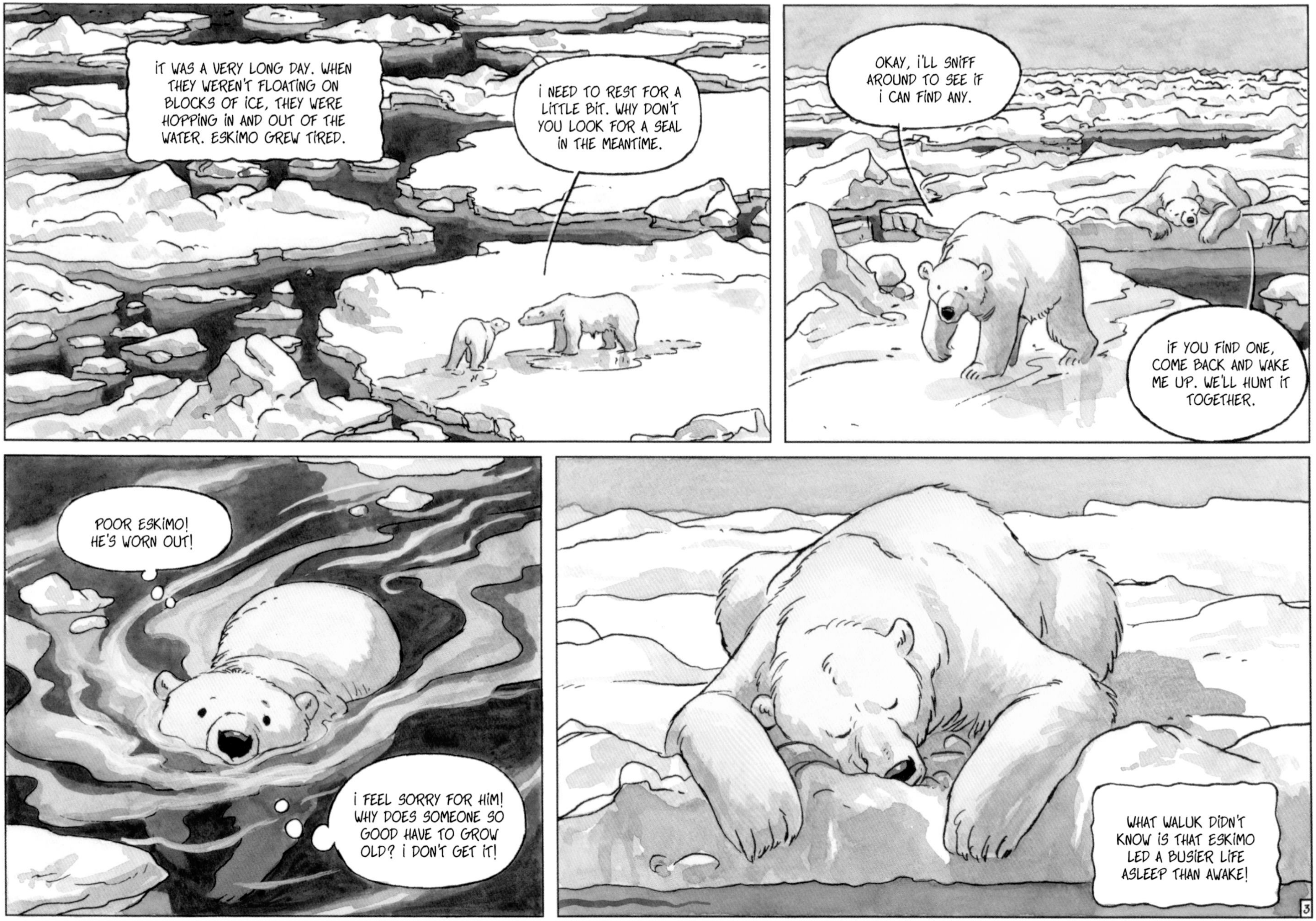
IT WAS A VERY LONG DAY. WHEN THEY WEREN'T FLOATING ON BLOCKS OF ICE, THEY WERE HOPPING IN AND OUT OF THE WATER. ESKIMO GREW TIRED.
I NEED TO REST FOR A LITTLE BIT. WHY DON'T YOU LOOK FOR A SEAL IN THE MEANTIME.
OKAY, I'LL SNIFF AROUND TO SEE IF I CAN FIND ANY.
IF YOU FIND ONE, COME BACK AND WAKE ME UP. WE'LL HUNT IT TOGETHER.
POOR ESKIMO! HE'S WORN OUT!
I FEEL SORRY FOR HIM! WHY DOES SOMEONE SO GOOD HAVE TO GROW OLD? I DON'T GET IT!
WHAT WALUK DIDN'T KNOW IS THAT ESKIMO LED A BUSIER LIFE ASLEEP THAN AWAKE!
3

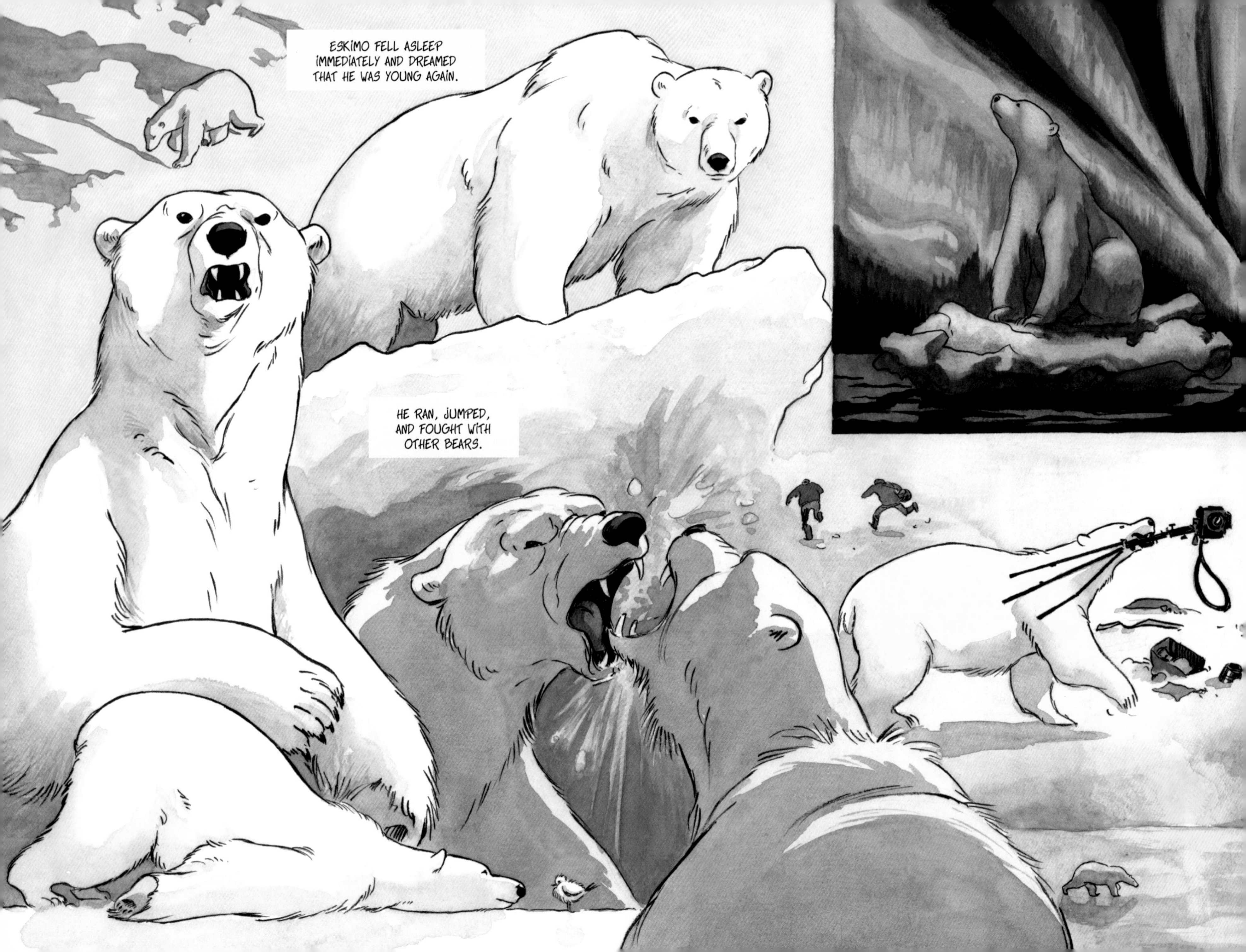
ESKIMO FELL ASLEEP IMMEDIATELY AND DREAMED THAT HE WAS YOUNG AGAIN.
HE RAN, JUMPED, AND FOUGHT WITH OTHER BEARS.

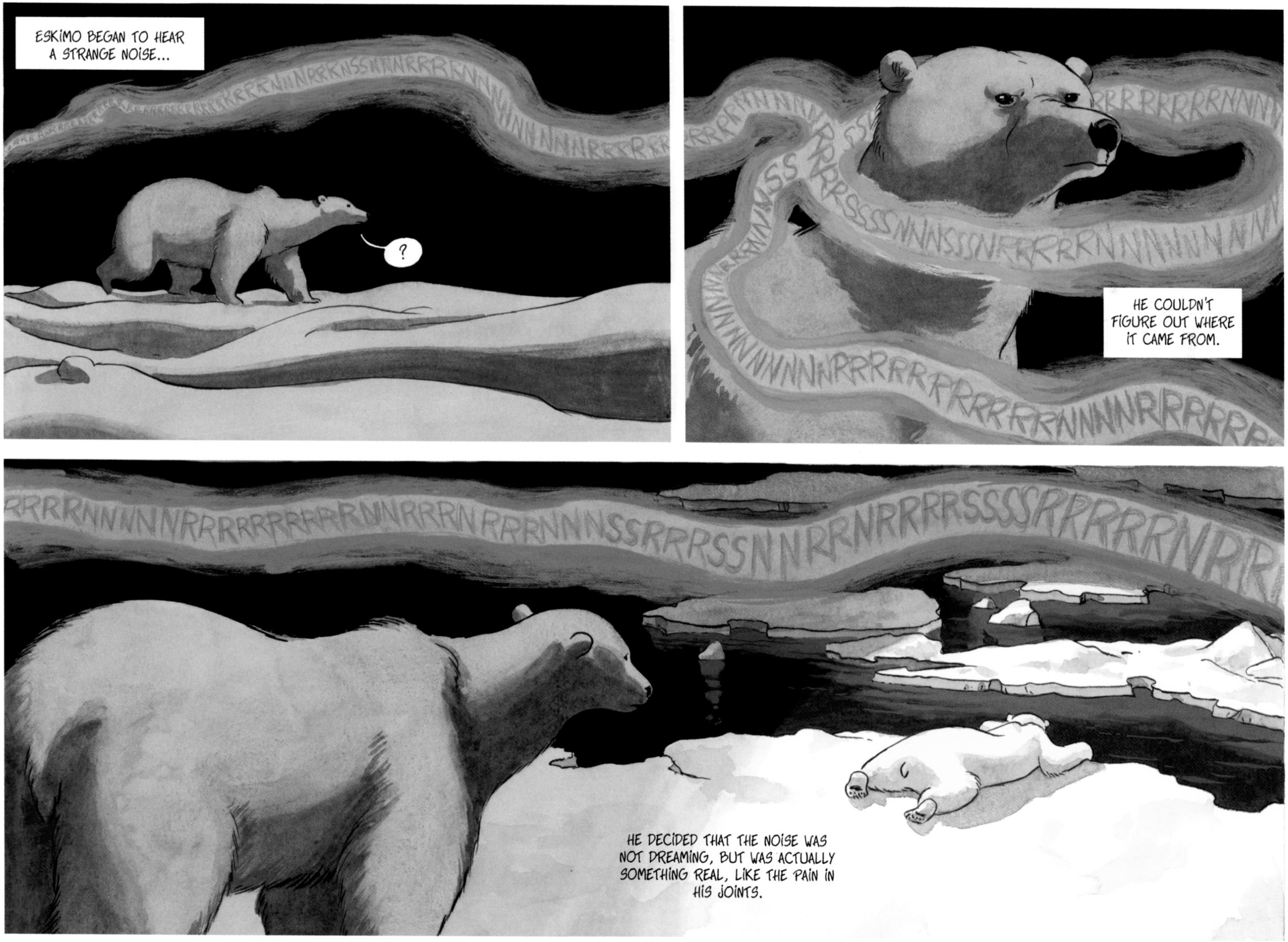
ESKIMO BEGAN TO HEAR A STRANGE NOISE...
?
HE COULDN'T FIGURE OUT WHERE IT CAME FROM.
HE DECIDED THAT THE NOISE WAS NOT DREAMING, BUT WAS ACTUALLY SOMETHING REAL, LIKE THE PAIN IN HIS JOINTS.

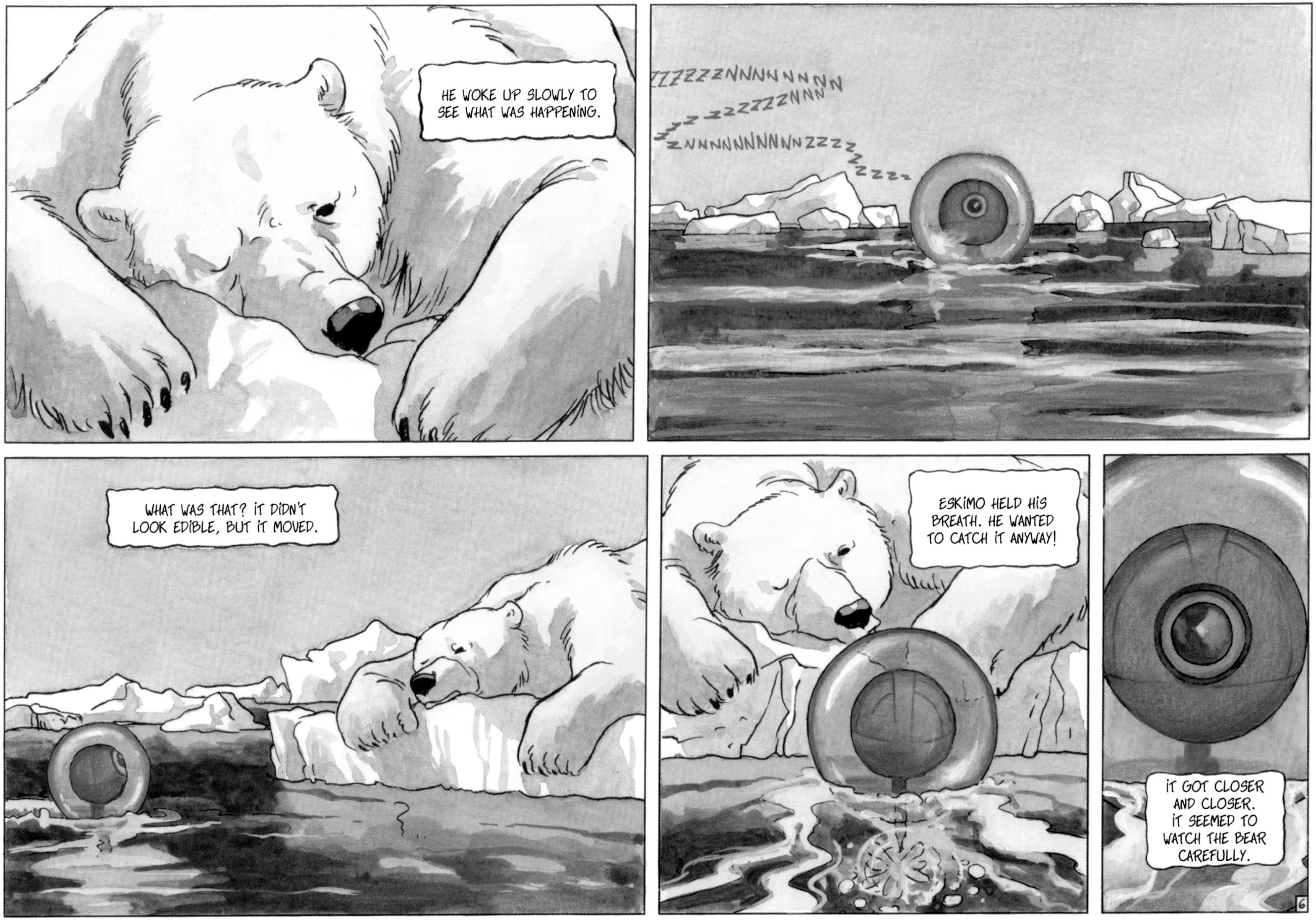
HE WOKE UP SLOWLY TO SEE WHAT WAS HAPPENING.
ZZZZZZNNNNNNNN
ZZZZZZZZZNNN
ZNNNNNNNNNNZZZZ
ZZZZ
WHAT WAS THAT? IT DIDN'T LOOK EDIBLE, BUT IT MOVED.
ESKIMO HELD HIS BREATH. HE WANTED TO CATCH IT ANYWAY!
IT GOT CLOSER AND CLOSER. IT SEEMED TO WATCH THE BEAR CAREFULLY.
6

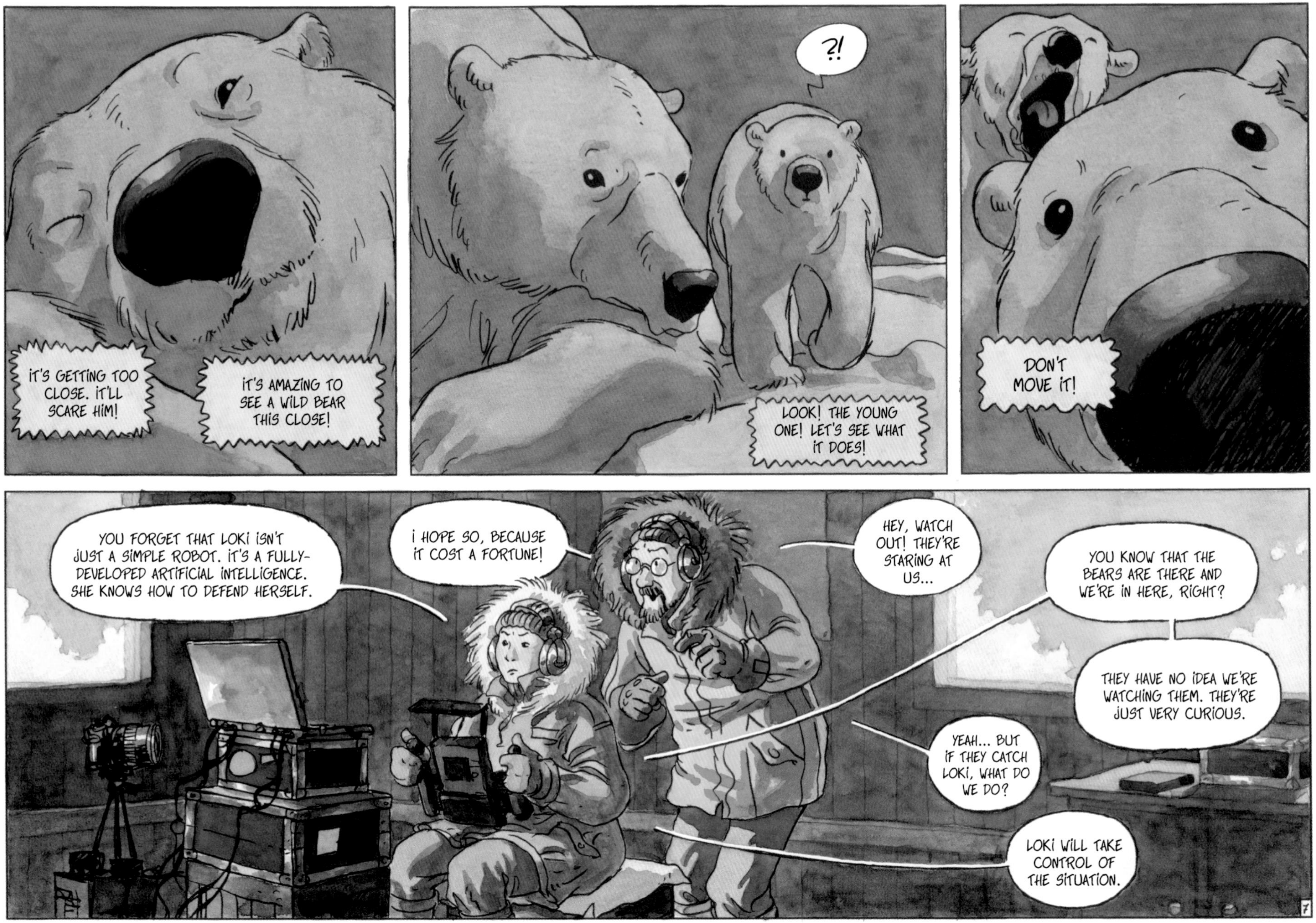
IT'S GETTING TOO CLOSE. IT'LL SCARE HIM!
IT'S AMAZING TO SEE A WILD BEAR THIS CLOSE!
?!
LOOK! THE YOUNG ONE! LET'S SEE WHAT IT DOES!
DON'T MOVE IT!
YOU FORGET THAT LOKI ISN'T JUST A SIMPLE ROBOT. IT'S A FULLY-DEVELOPED ARTIFICIAL INTELLIGENCE. SHE KNOWS HOW TO DEFEND HERSELF.
I HOPE SO, BECAUSE IT COST A FORTUNE!
HEY, WATCH OUT! THEY'RE STARING AT US...
YOU KNOW THAT THE BEARS ARE THERE AND WE'RE IN HERE, RIGHT?
THEY HAVE NO IDEA WE'RE WATCHING THEM. THEY'RE JUST VERY CURIOUS.
YEAH... BUT IF THEY CATCH LOKI, WHAT DO WE DO?
LOKI WILL TAKE CONTROL OF THE SITUATION.
7

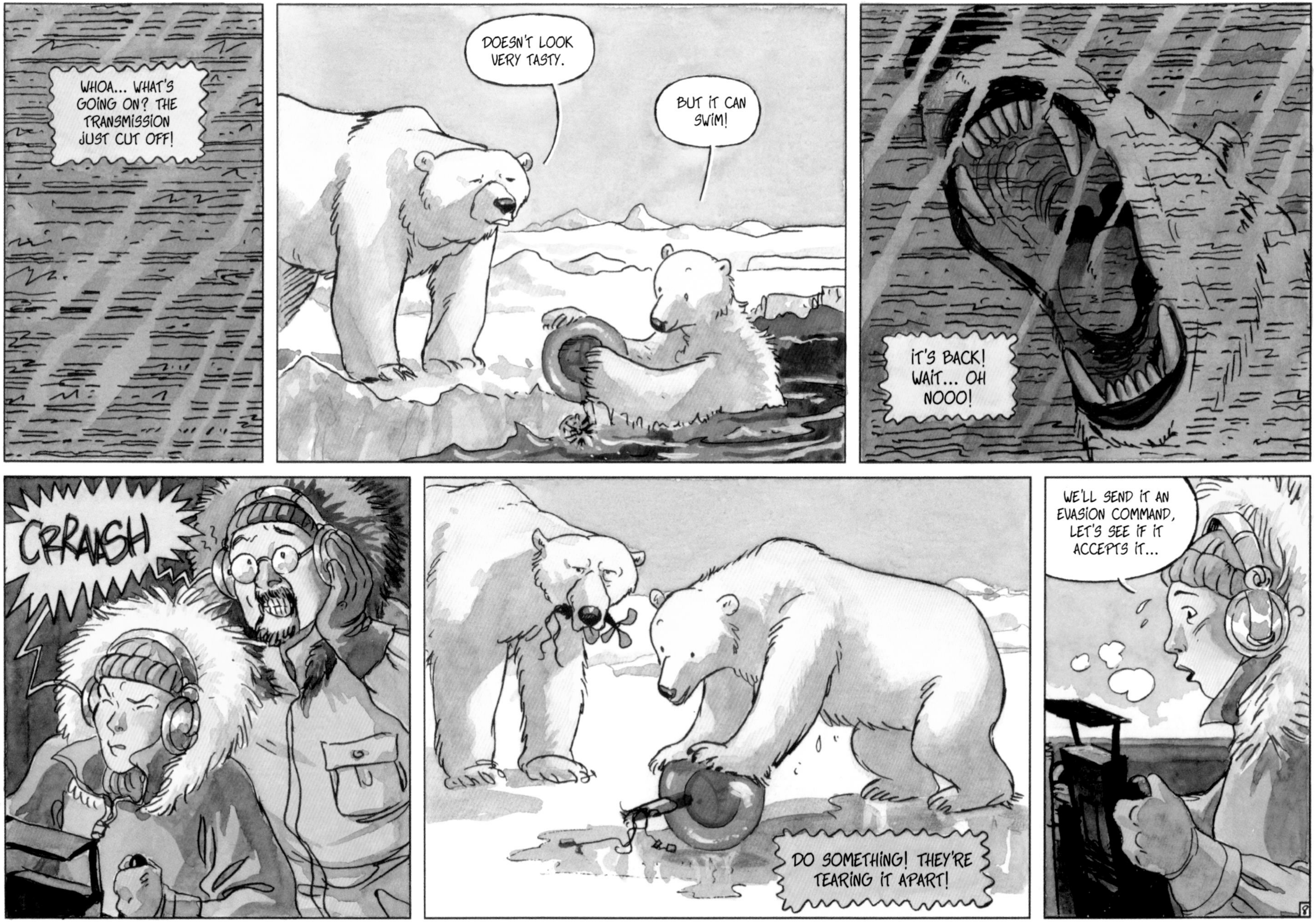
WHOA... WHAT'S GOING ON? THE TRANSMISSION JUST CUT OFF!
DOESN'T LOOK VERY TASTY.
BUT IT CAN SWIM!
IT'S BACK! WAIT... OH NOOO!
CRRAASH
DO SOMETHING! THEY'RE TEARING IT APART!
WE'LL SEND IT AN EVASION COMMAND, LET'S SEE IF IT ACCEPTS IT...

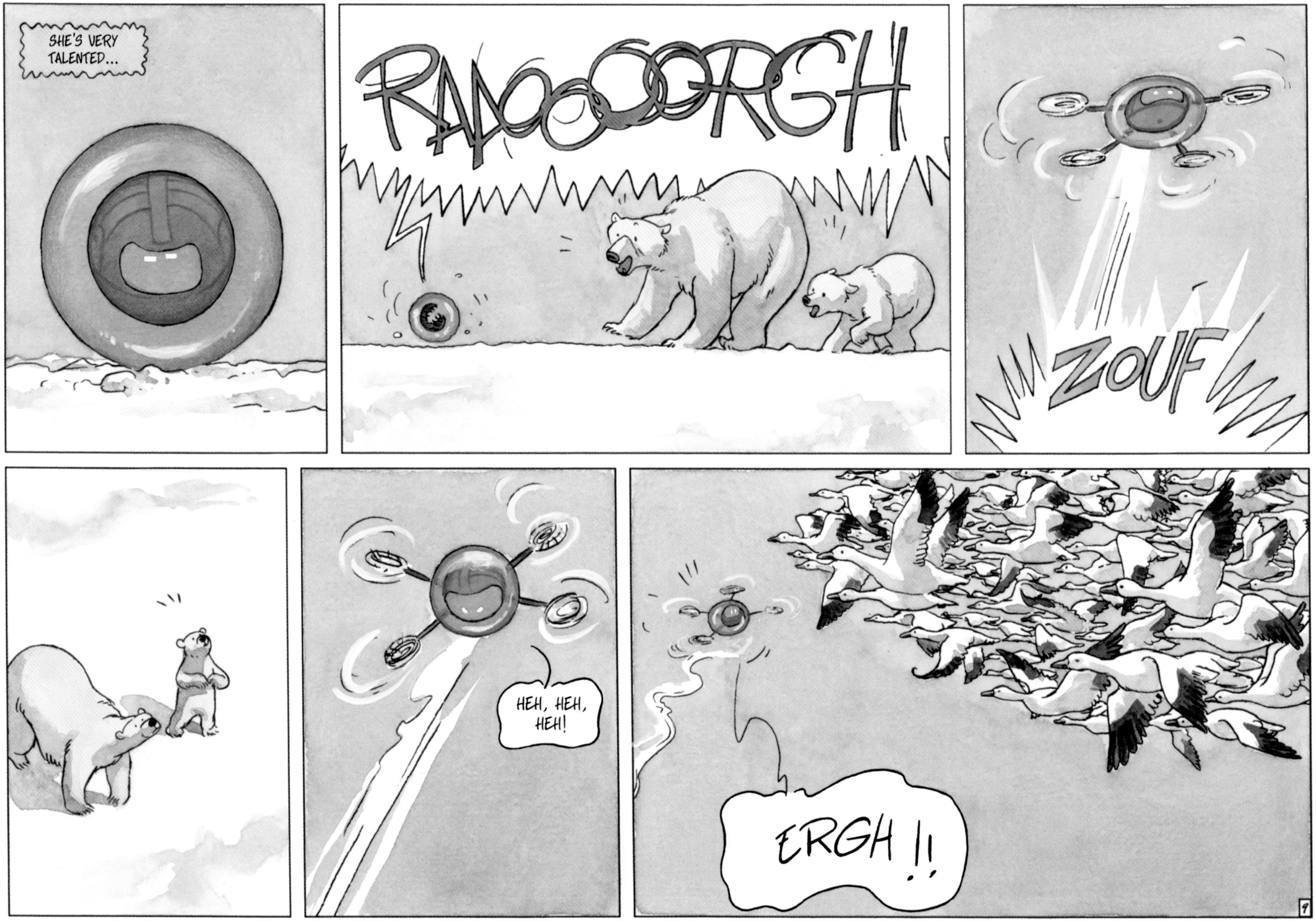
SHE'S VERY TALENTED...
RAAOOOOORGH
ZOUF
HEH, HEH, HEH!
ERGH !!
9

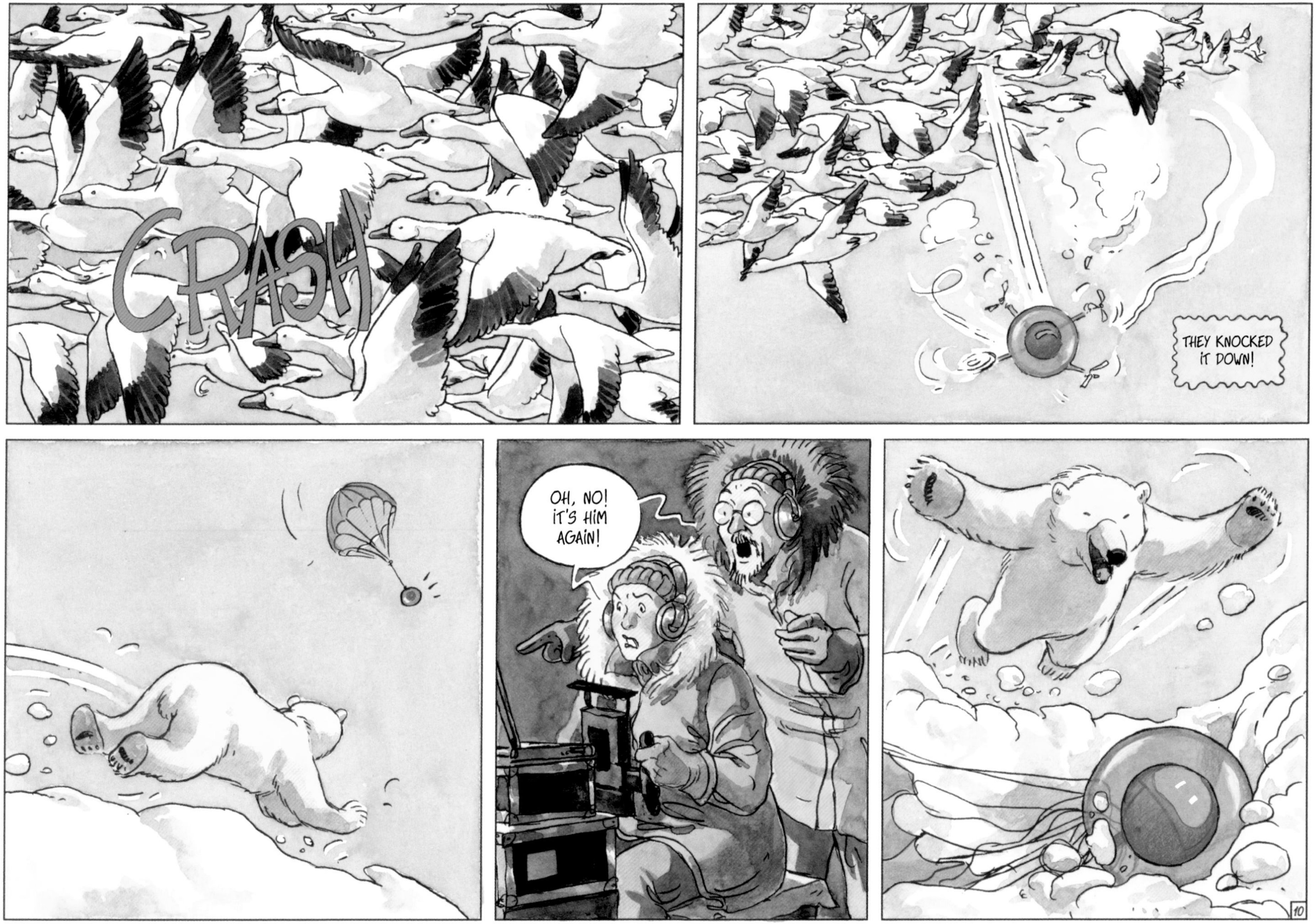
CRASH
THEY KNOCKED IT DOWN!
OH, NO! IT'S HIM AGAIN!
10

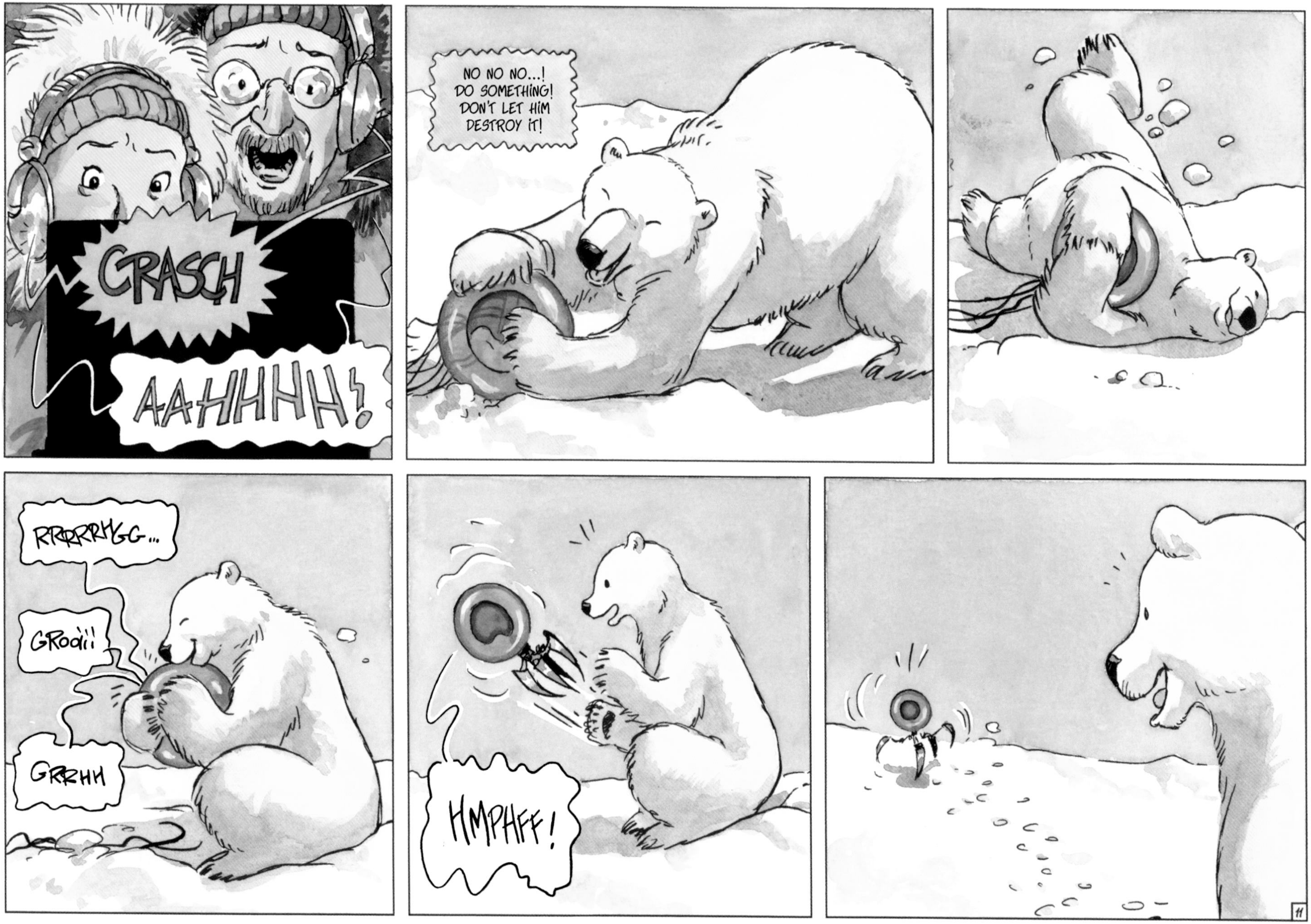
CRASCH
AAHHHH!
NO NO NO...! DO SOMETHING! DON'T LET HIM DESTROY IT!
RRRRRHGG...
GROOiii
GRRHH
HMPHFF!
11

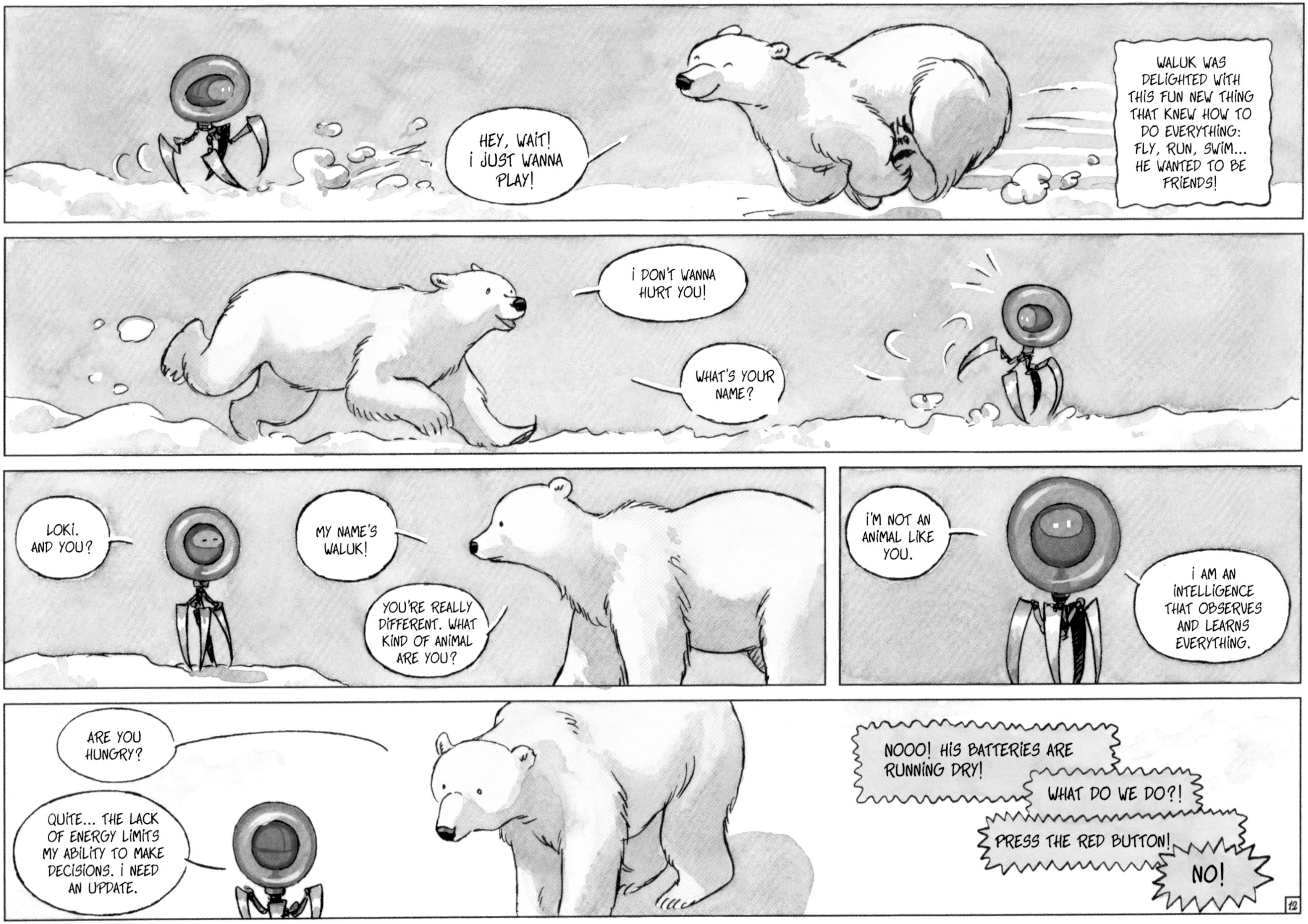
WALUK WAS DELIGHTED WITH THIS FUN NEW THING THAT KNEW HOW TO DO EVERYTHING: FLY, RUN, SWIM... HE WANTED TO BE FRIENDS!
HEY, WAIT! I JUST WANNA PLAY!
I DON'T WANNA HURT YOU!
WHAT'S YOUR NAME?
LOKI. AND YOU?
MY NAME'S WALUK!
YOU'RE REALLY DIFFERENT. WHAT KIND OF ANIMAL ARE YOU?
I'M NOT AN ANIMAL LIKE YOU.
I AM AN INTELLIGENCE THAT OBSERVES AND LEARNS EVERYTHING.
ARE YOU HUNGRY?
QUITE... THE LACK OF ENERGY LIMITS MY ABILITY TO MAKE DECISIONS. I NEED AN UPDATE.
NOOO! HIS BATTERIES ARE RUNNING DRY!
WHAT DO WE DO?!
PRESS THE RED BUTTON!
NO!
12

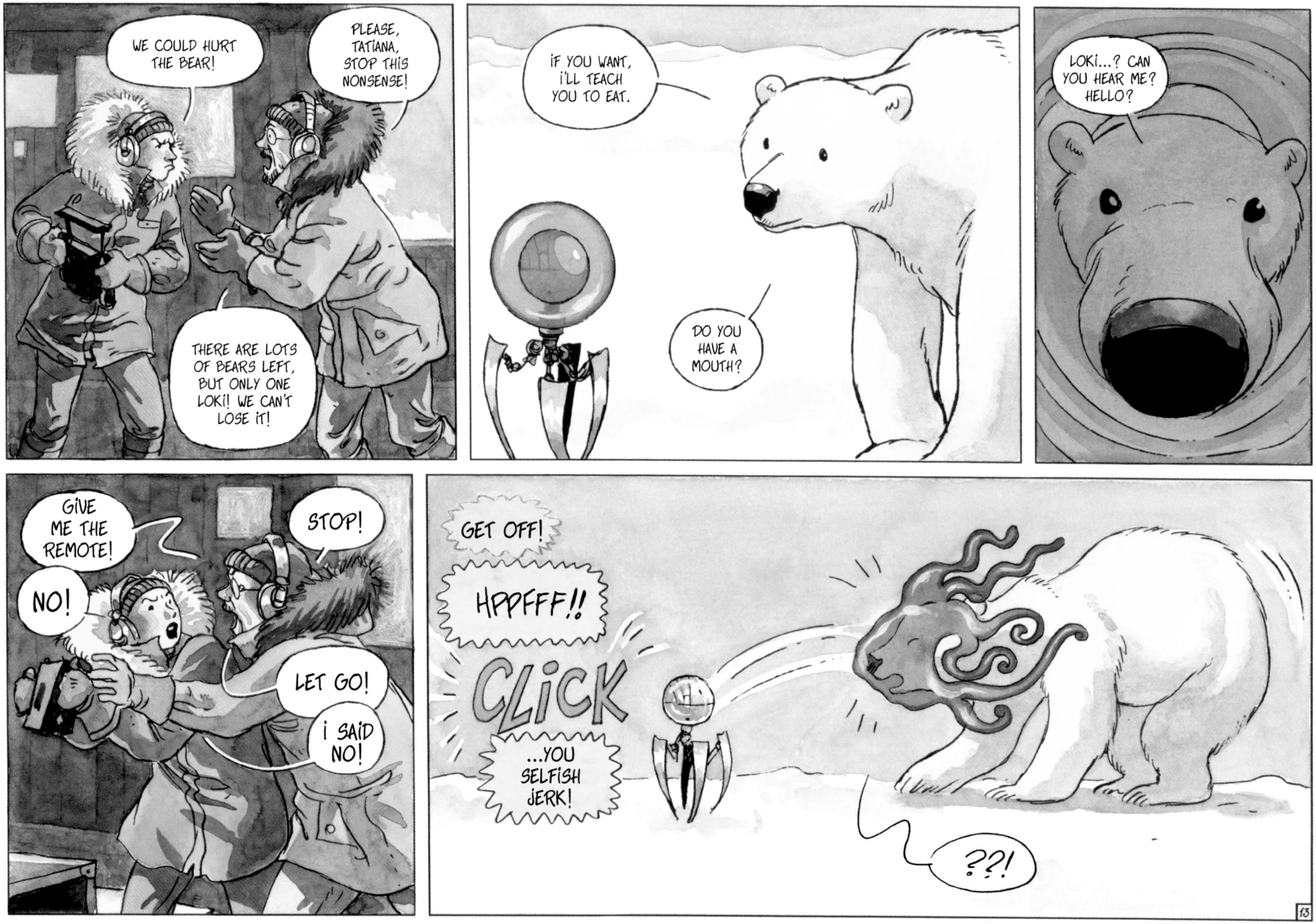
WE COULD HURT THE BEAR!
PLEASE, TATIANA, STOP THIS NONSENSE!
THERE ARE LOTS OF BEARS LEFT, BUT ONLY ONE LOKI! WE CAN'T LOSE IT!
IF YOU WANT, I'LL TEACH YOU TO EAT.
DO YOU HAVE A MOUTH?
LOKI...? CAN YOU HEAR ME? HELLO?
GIVE ME THE REMOTE!
STOP!
NO!
LET GO!
I SAID NO!
GET OFF!
HPPFFF!!
CLICK
...YOU SELFISH JERK!
??!
13

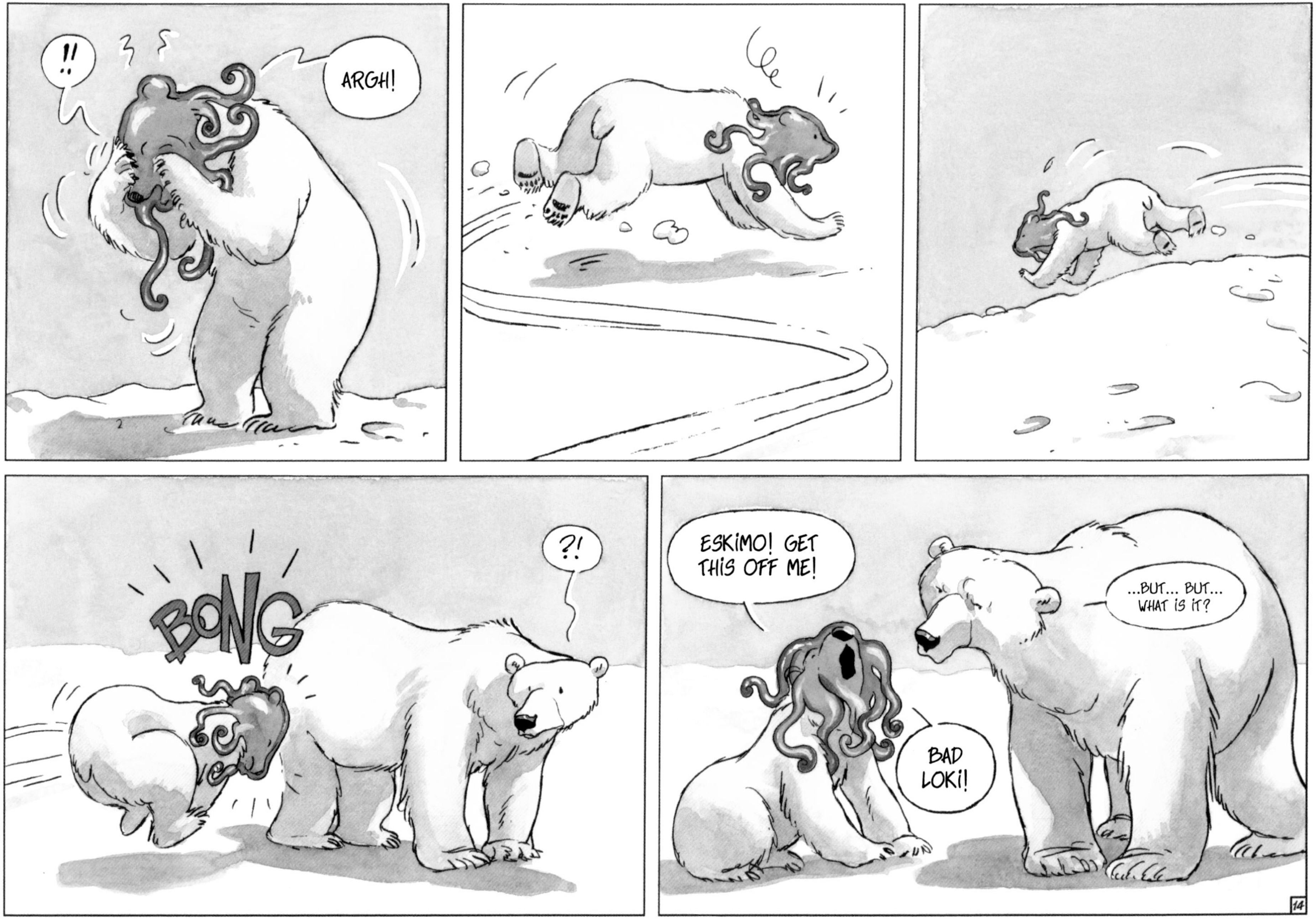
!!
ARGH!
BONG
?!
ESKiMO! GET THiS OFF ME!
...BUT... BUT... WHAT iS iT?
BAD LOKi!
14

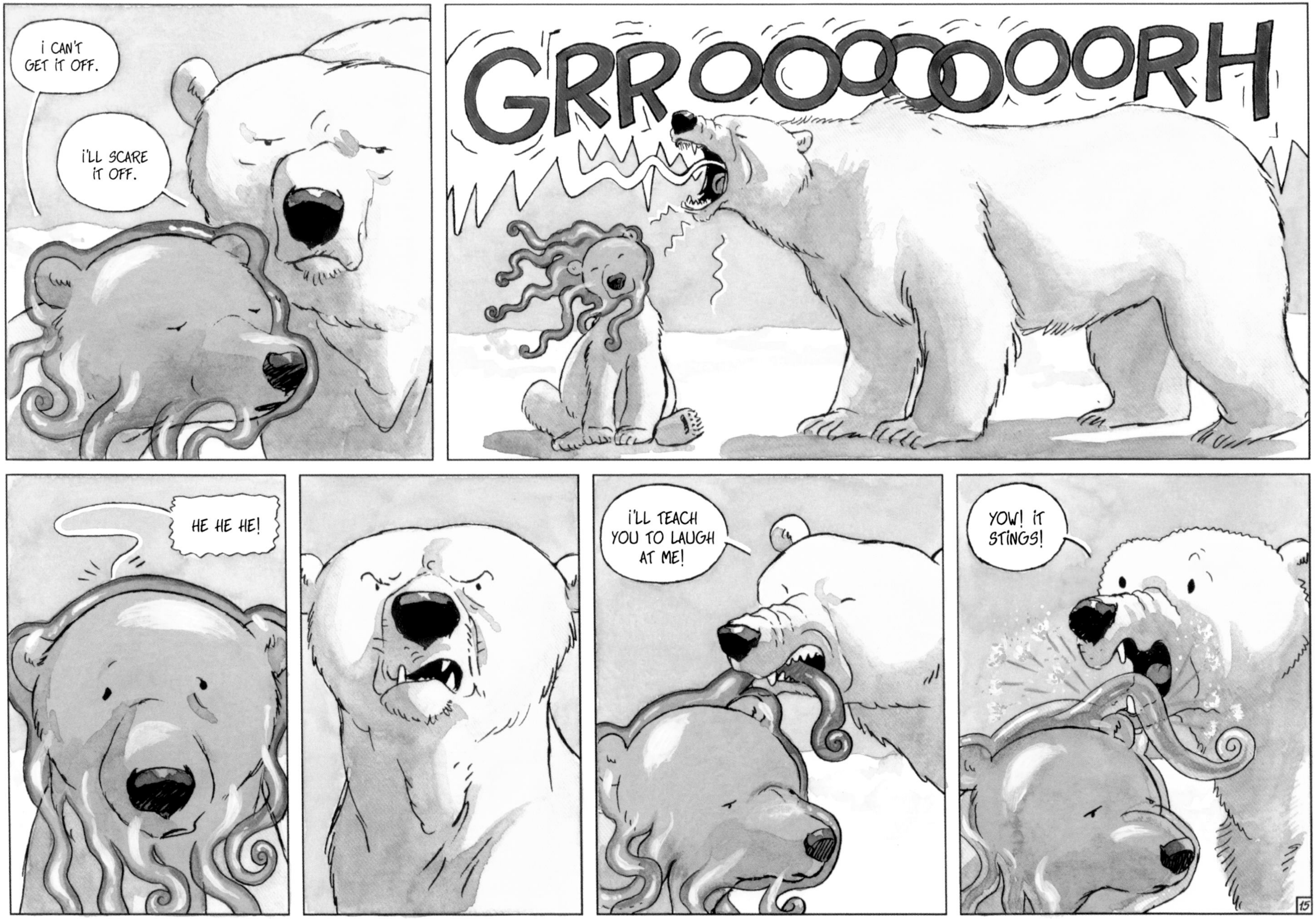
I CAN'T GET IT OFF.
I'LL SCARE IT OFF.
GRROOOOOOORH
HE HE HE!
I'LL TEACH YOU TO LAUGH AT ME!
YOW! IT STINGS!
15

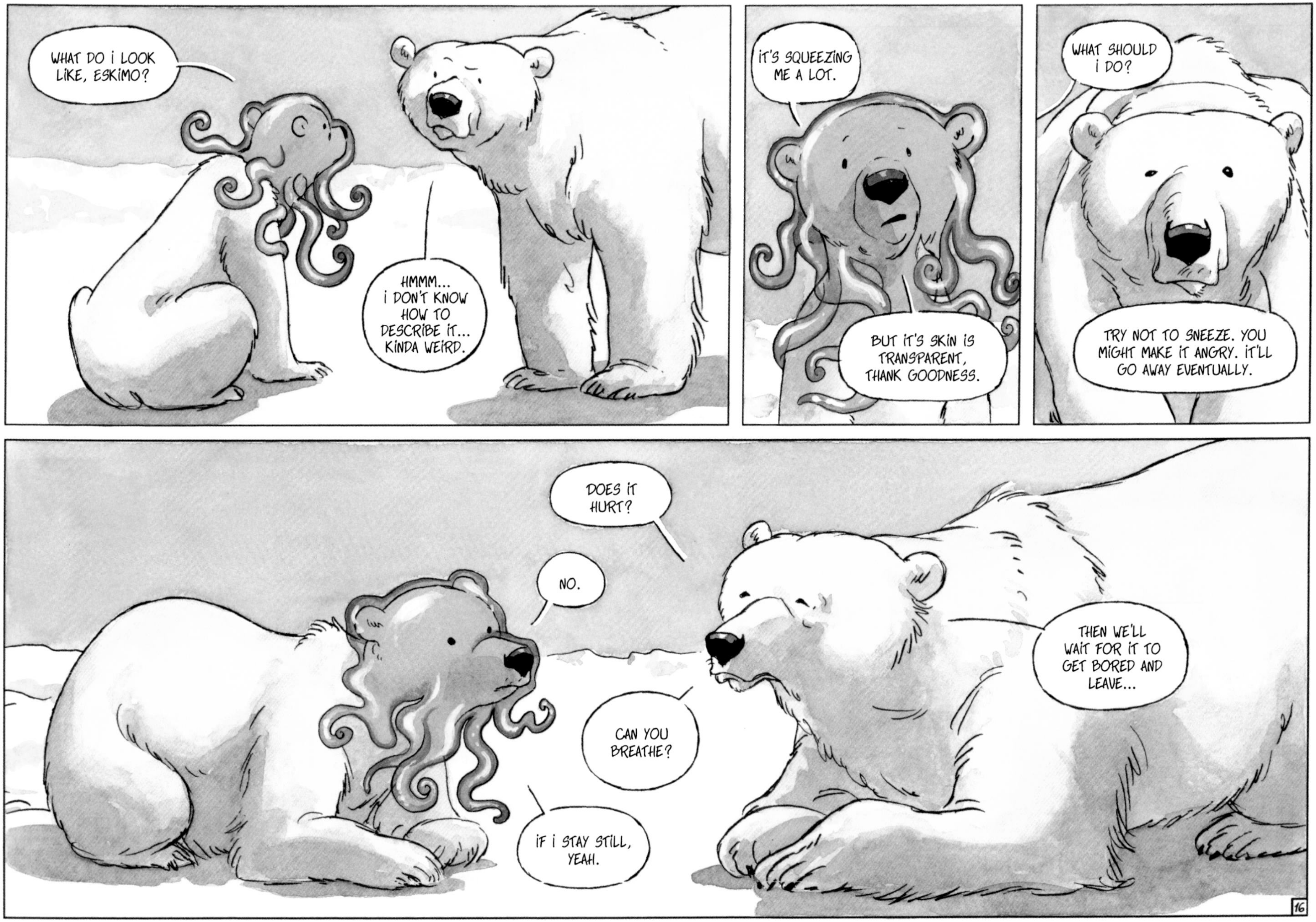
WHAT DO i LOOK LIKE, ESKiMO?
HMMM... i DON'T KNOW HOW TO DESCRiBE iT... KiNDA WEiRD.
iT'S SQUEEZiNG ME A LOT.
BUT iT'S SKiN iS TRANSPARENT, THANK GOODNESS.
WHAT SHOULD i DO?
TRY NOT TO SNEEZE. YOU MiGHT MAKE iT ANGRY. iT'LL GO AWAY EVENTUALLY.
DOES iT HURT?
NO.
CAN YOU BREATHE?
iF i STAY STiLL, YEAH.
THEN WE'LL WAiT FOR iT TO GET BORED AND LEAVE...
16

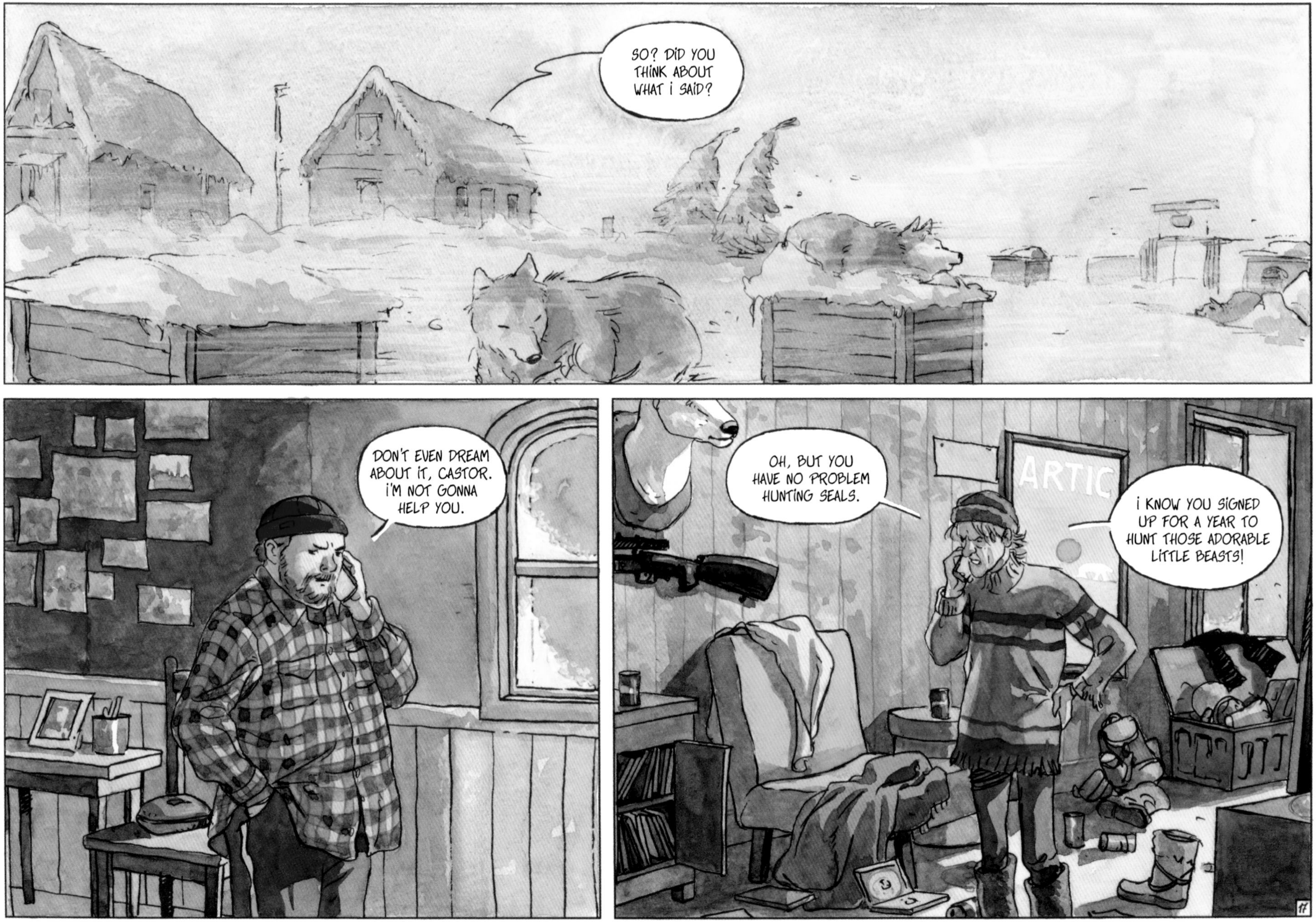
SO? DID YOU THINK ABOUT WHAT I SAID?
DON'T EVEN DREAM ABOUT IT, CASTOR. I'M NOT GONNA HELP YOU.
OH, BUT YOU HAVE NO PROBLEM HUNTING SEALS.
ARTIC
I KNOW YOU SIGNED UP FOR A YEAR TO HUNT THOSE ADORABLE LITTLE BEASTS!
17

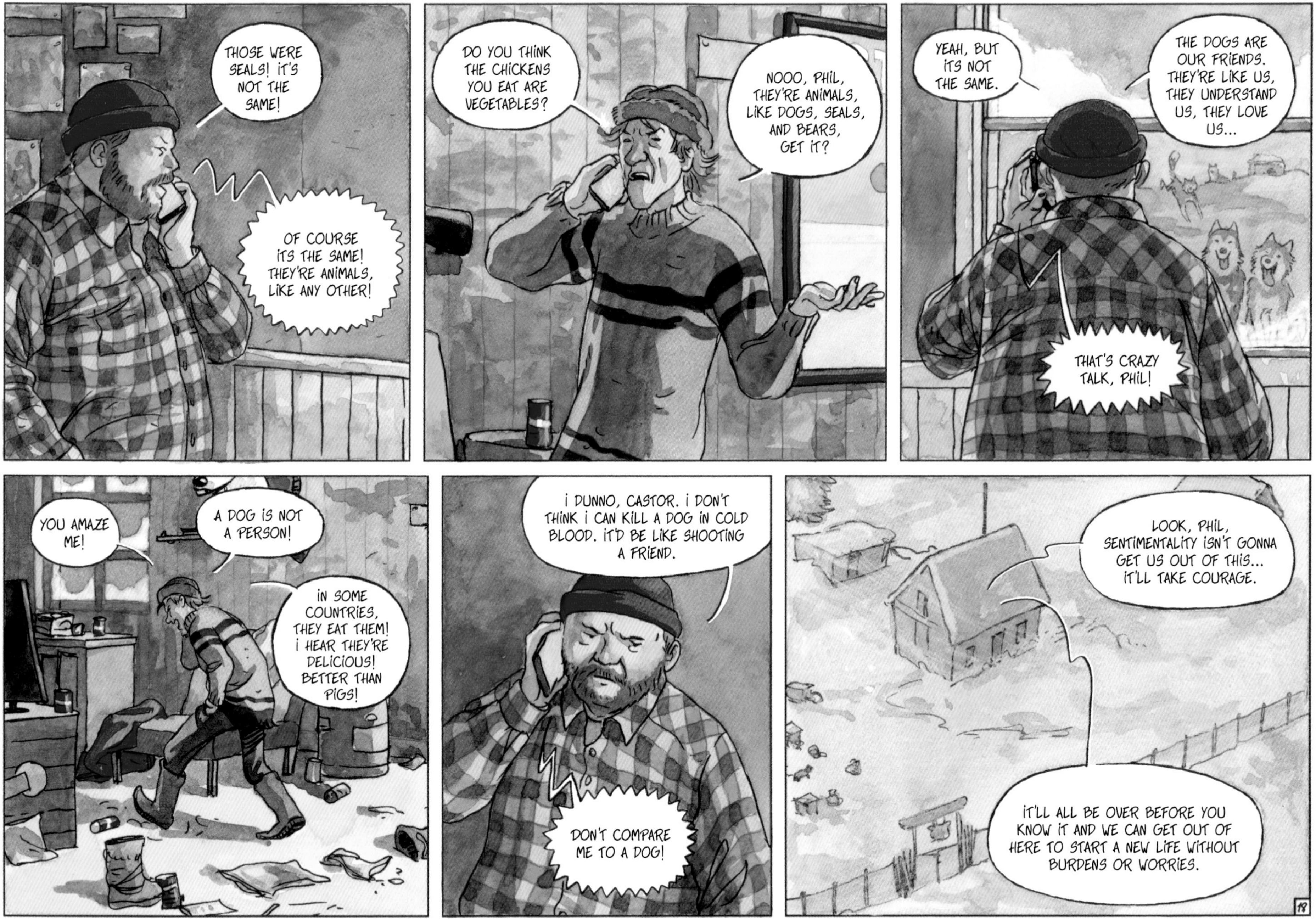
THOSE WERE SEALS! IT'S NOT THE SAME!
OF COURSE IT'S THE SAME! THEY'RE ANIMALS, LIKE ANY OTHER!
DO YOU THINK THE CHICKENS YOU EAT ARE VEGETABLES?
NOOO, PHIL, THEY'RE ANIMALS, LIKE DOGS, SEALS, AND BEARS, GET IT?
YEAH, BUT IT'S NOT THE SAME.
THE DOGS ARE OUR FRIENDS. THEY'RE LIKE US, THEY UNDERSTAND US, THEY LOVE US...
THAT'S CRAZY TALK, PHIL!
YOU AMAZE ME!
A DOG IS NOT A PERSON!
IN SOME COUNTRIES, THEY EAT THEM! I HEAR THEY'RE DELICIOUS! BETTER THAN PIGS!
I DUNNO, CASTOR. I DON'T THINK I CAN KILL A DOG IN COLD BLOOD. IT'D BE LIKE SHOOTING A FRIEND.
DON'T COMPARE ME TO A DOG!
LOOK, PHIL, SENTIMENTALITY ISN'T GONNA GET US OUT OF THIS... IT'LL TAKE COURAGE.
IT'LL ALL BE OVER BEFORE YOU KNOW IT AND WE CAN GET OUT OF HERE TO START A NEW LIFE WITHOUT BURDENS OR WORRIES.
19

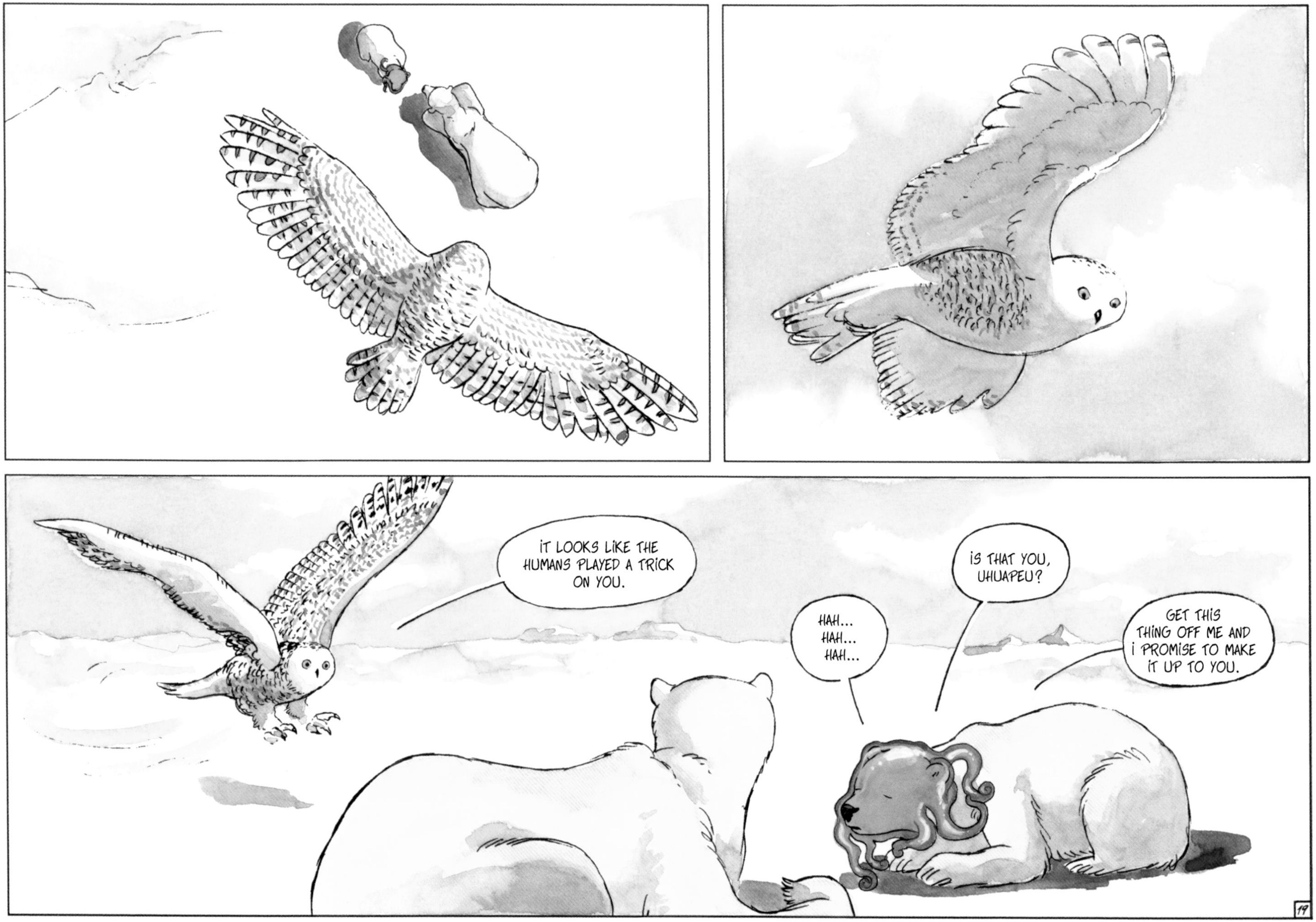
IT LOOKS LIKE THE HUMANS PLAYED A TRICK ON YOU.
IS THAT YOU, UHUAPEU?
HAH... HAH... HAH...
GET THIS THING OFF ME AND I PROMISE TO MAKE IT UP TO YOU.
19

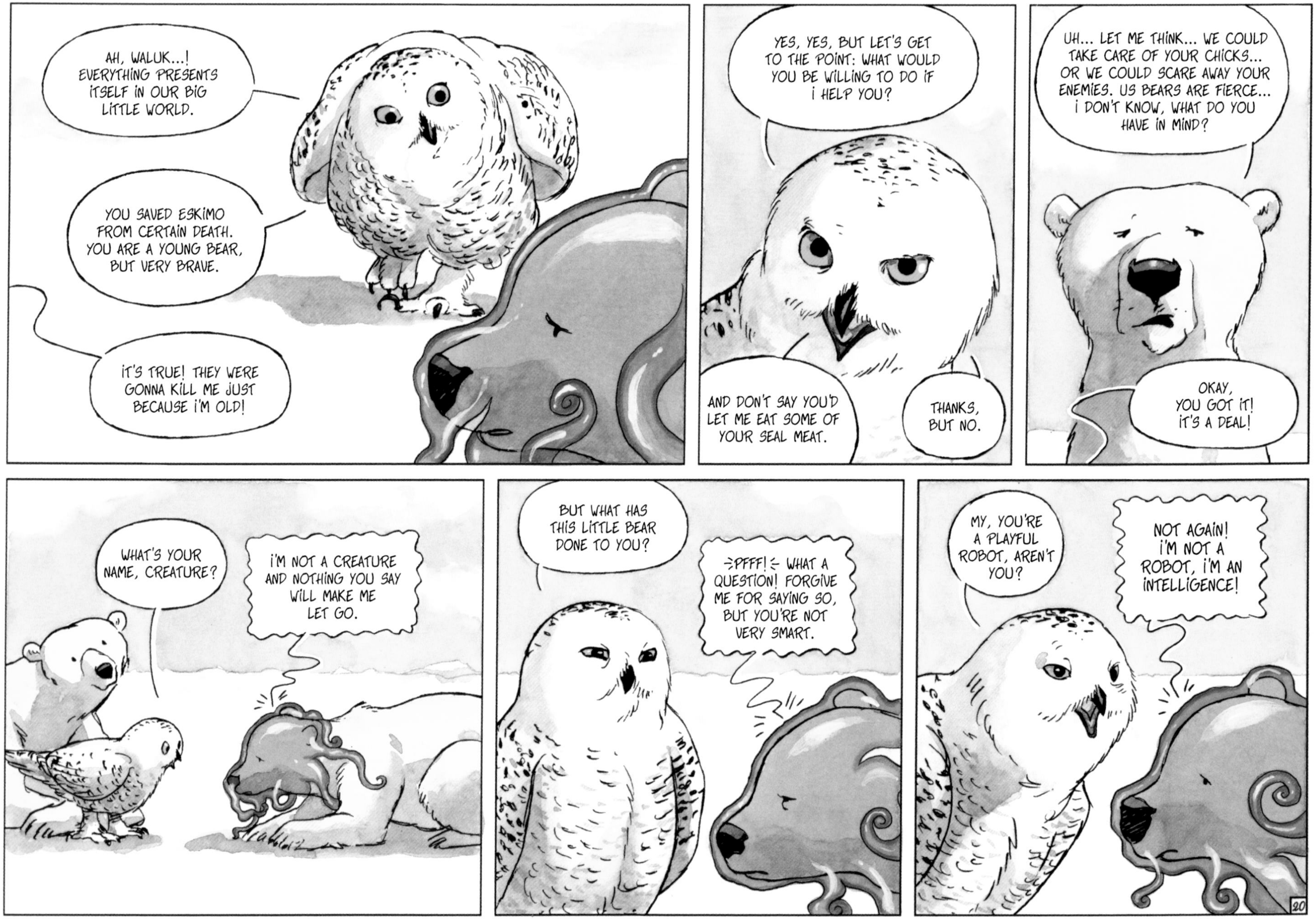

AH, WALUK...! EVERYTHING PRESENTS ITSELF IN OUR BIG LITTLE WORLD.
YOU SAVED ESKIMO FROM CERTAIN DEATH. YOU ARE A YOUNG BEAR, BUT VERY BRAVE.
IT'S TRUE! THEY WERE GONNA KILL ME JUST BECAUSE I'M OLD!
YES, YES, BUT LET'S GET TO THE POINT: WHAT WOULD YOU BE WILLING TO DO IF I HELP YOU?
AND DON'T SAY YOU'D LET ME EAT SOME OF YOUR SEAL MEAT.
THANKS, BUT NO.
UH... LET ME THINK... WE COULD TAKE CARE OF YOUR CHICKS... OR WE COULD SCARE AWAY YOUR ENEMIES. US BEARS ARE FIERCE... I DON'T KNOW, WHAT DO YOU HAVE IN MIND?
OKAY, YOU GOT IT! IT'S A DEAL!
WHAT'S YOUR NAME, CREATURE?
I'M NOT A CREATURE AND NOTHING YOU SAY WILL MAKE ME LET GO.
BUT WHAT HAS THIS LITTLE BEAR DONE TO YOU?
⇒PFFF!⇐ WHAT A QUESTION! FORGIVE ME FOR SAYING SO, BUT YOU'RE NOT VERY SMART.
MY, YOU'RE A PLAYFUL ROBOT, AREN'T YOU?
NOT AGAIN! I'M NOT A ROBOT, I'M AN INTELLIGENCE!
20

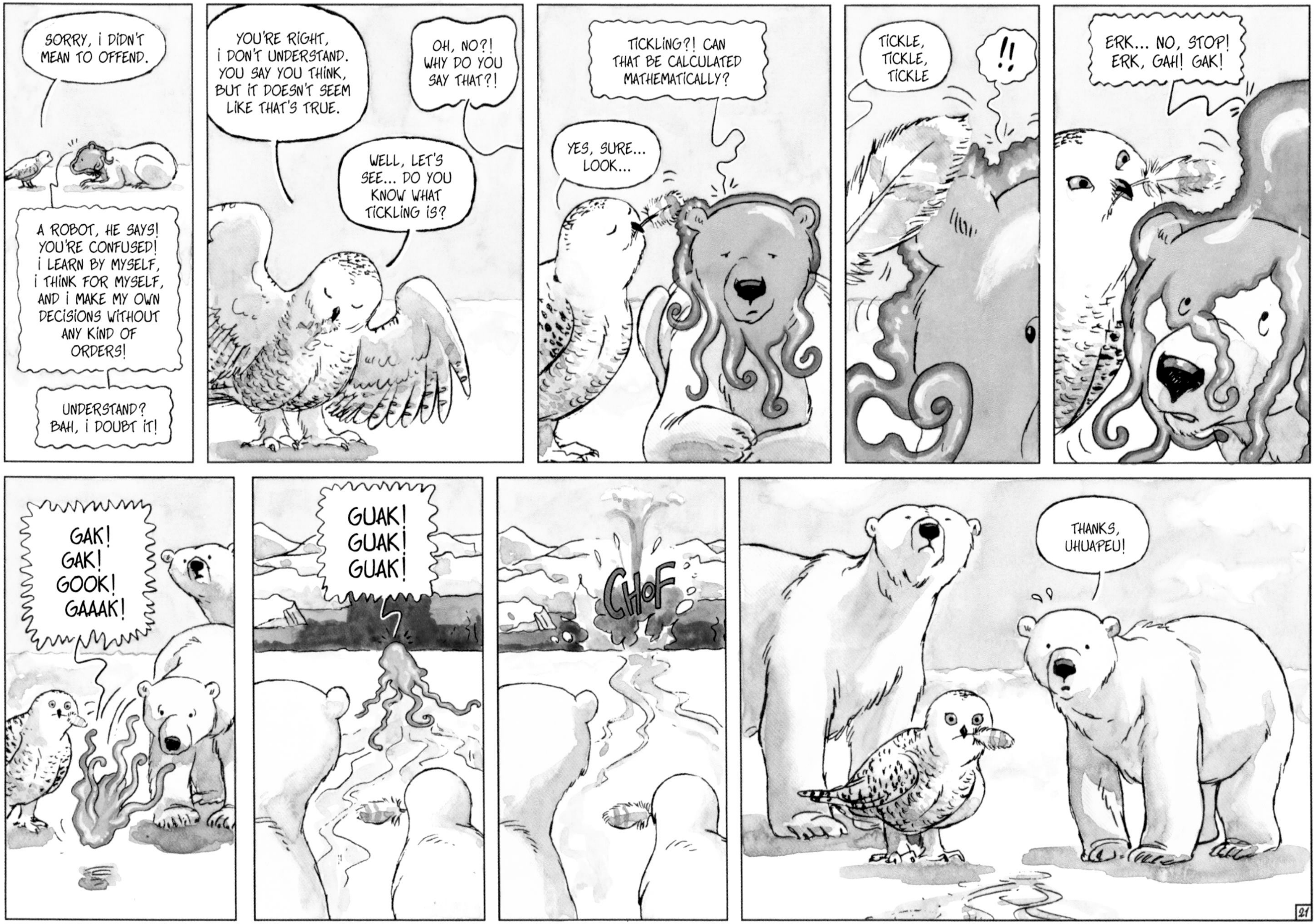
SORRY, I DIDN'T MEAN TO OFFEND.
A ROBOT, HE SAYS! YOU'RE CONFUSED! I LEARN BY MYSELF, I THINK FOR MYSELF, AND I MAKE MY OWN DECISIONS WITHOUT ANY KIND OF ORDERS!
UNDERSTAND? BAH, I DOUBT IT!
YOU'RE RIGHT, I DON'T UNDERSTAND. YOU SAY YOU THINK, BUT IT DOESN'T SEEM LIKE THAT'S TRUE.
OH, NO?! WHY DO YOU SAY THAT?!
WELL, LET'S SEE... DO YOU KNOW WHAT TICKLING IS?
TICKLING?! CAN THAT BE CALCULATED MATHEMATICALLY?
YES, SURE... LOOK...
TICKLE, TICKLE, TICKLE
!!
ERK... NO, STOP! ERK, GAH! GAK!
GAK! GAK! GOOK! GAAAK!
GUAK! GUAK! GUAK!
CHOF
THANKS, UHUAPEU!
21

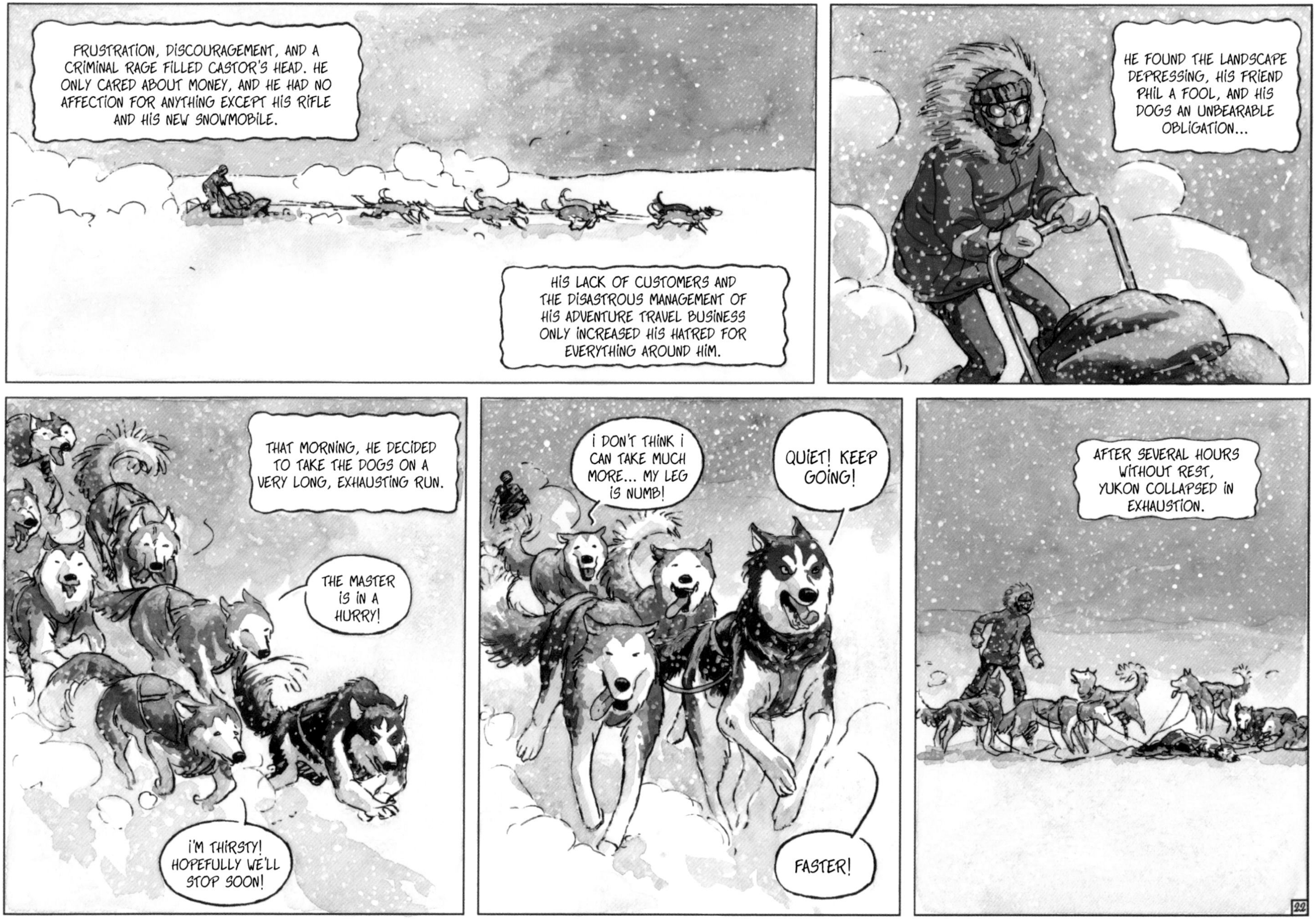
FRUSTRATION, DISCOURAGEMENT, AND A CRIMINAL RAGE FILLED CASTOR'S HEAD. HE ONLY CARED ABOUT MONEY, AND HE HAD NO AFFECTION FOR ANYTHING EXCEPT HIS RIFLE AND HIS NEW SNOWMOBILE.
HIS LACK OF CUSTOMERS AND THE DISASTROUS MANAGEMENT OF HIS ADVENTURE TRAVEL BUSINESS ONLY INCREASED HIS HATRED FOR EVERYTHING AROUND HIM.
HE FOUND THE LANDSCAPE DEPRESSING, HIS FRIEND PHIL A FOOL, AND HIS DOGS AN UNBEARABLE OBLIGATION...
THAT MORNING, HE DECIDED TO TAKE THE DOGS ON A VERY LONG, EXHAUSTING RUN.
THE MASTER IS IN A HURRY!
I'M THIRSTY! HOPEFULLY WE'LL STOP SOON!
I DON'T THINK I CAN TAKE MUCH MORE... MY LEG IS NUMB!
QUIET! KEEP GOING!
FASTER!
AFTER SEVERAL HOURS WITHOUT REST, YUKON COLLAPSED IN EXHAUSTION.
22

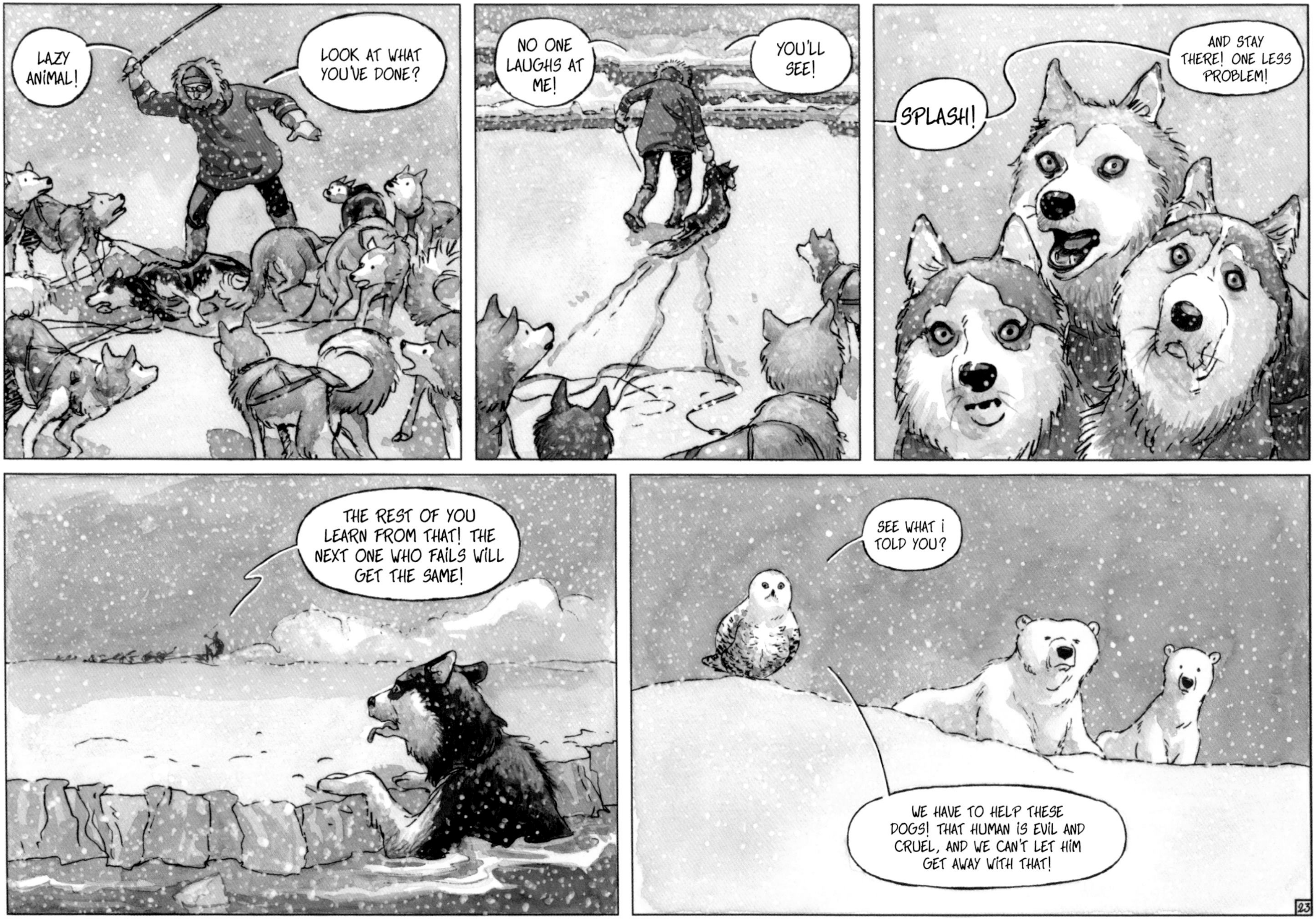
LAZY ANIMAL!
LOOK AT WHAT YOU'VE DONE?
NO ONE LAUGHS AT ME!
YOU'LL SEE!
SPLASH!
AND STAY THERE! ONE LESS PROBLEM!
THE REST OF YOU LEARN FROM THAT! THE NEXT ONE WHO FAILS WILL GET THE SAME!
SEE WHAT I TOLD YOU?
WE HAVE TO HELP THESE DOGS! THAT HUMAN IS EVIL AND CRUEL, AND WE CAN'T LET HIM GET AWAY WITH THAT!
23

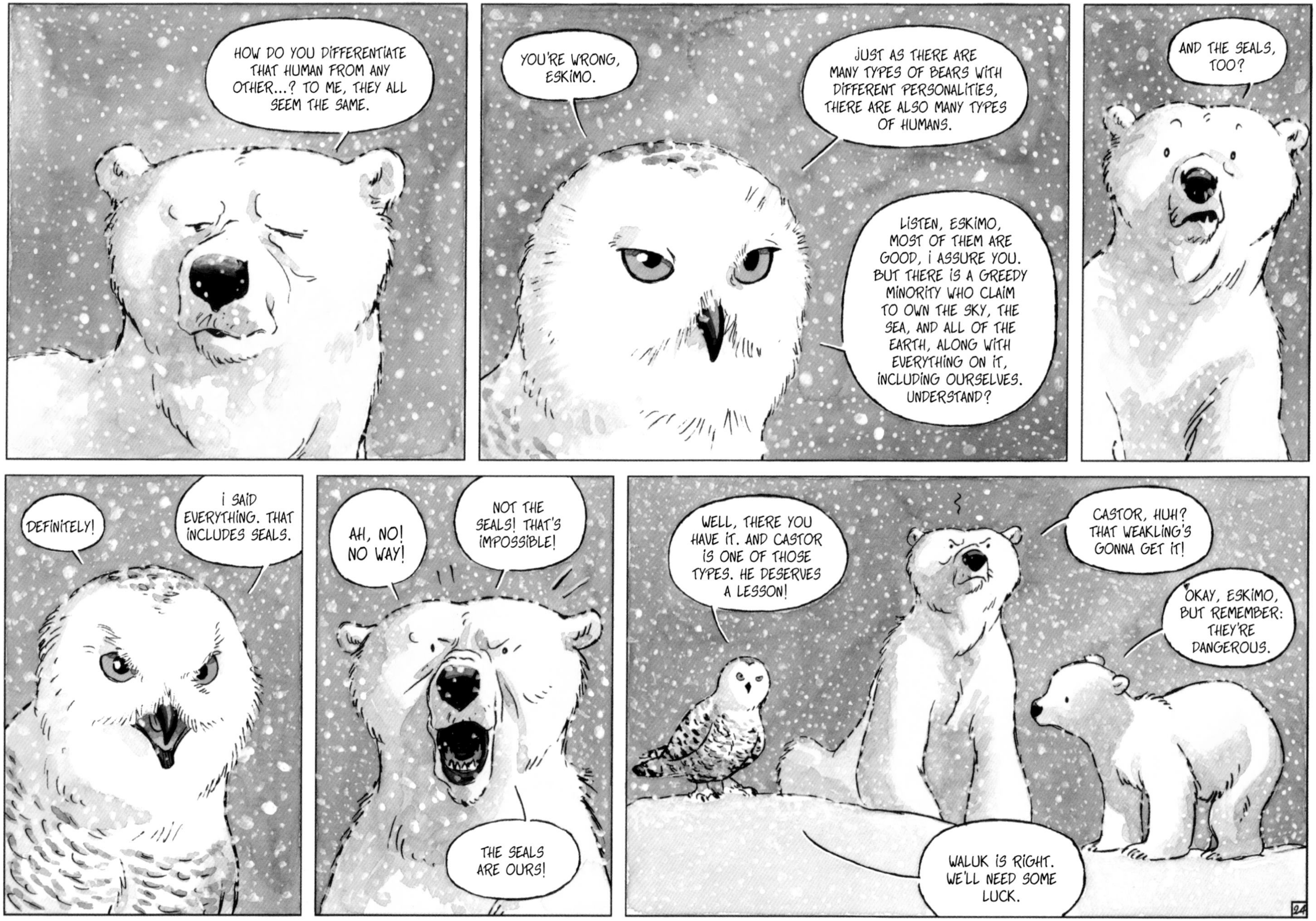
HOW DO YOU DIFFERENTIATE THAT HUMAN FROM ANY OTHER...? TO ME, THEY ALL SEEM THE SAME.
YOU'RE WRONG, ESKIMO.
JUST AS THERE ARE MANY TYPES OF BEARS WITH DIFFERENT PERSONALITIES, THERE ARE ALSO MANY TYPES OF HUMANS.
LISTEN, ESKIMO, MOST OF THEM ARE GOOD, I ASSURE YOU. BUT THERE IS A GREEDY MINORITY WHO CLAIM TO OWN THE SKY, THE SEA, AND ALL OF THE EARTH, ALONG WITH EVERYTHING ON IT, INCLUDING OURSELVES. UNDERSTAND?
AND THE SEALS, TOO?
DEFINITELY!
I SAID EVERYTHING. THAT INCLUDES SEALS.
AH, NO! NO WAY!
NOT THE SEALS! THAT'S IMPOSSIBLE!
THE SEALS ARE OURS!
WELL, THERE YOU HAVE IT. AND CASTOR IS ONE OF THOSE TYPES. HE DESERVES A LESSON!
CASTOR, HUH? THAT WEAKLING'S GONNA GET IT!
OKAY, ESKIMO, BUT REMEMBER: THEY'RE DANGEROUS.
WALUK IS RIGHT. WE'LL NEED SOME LUCK.
24

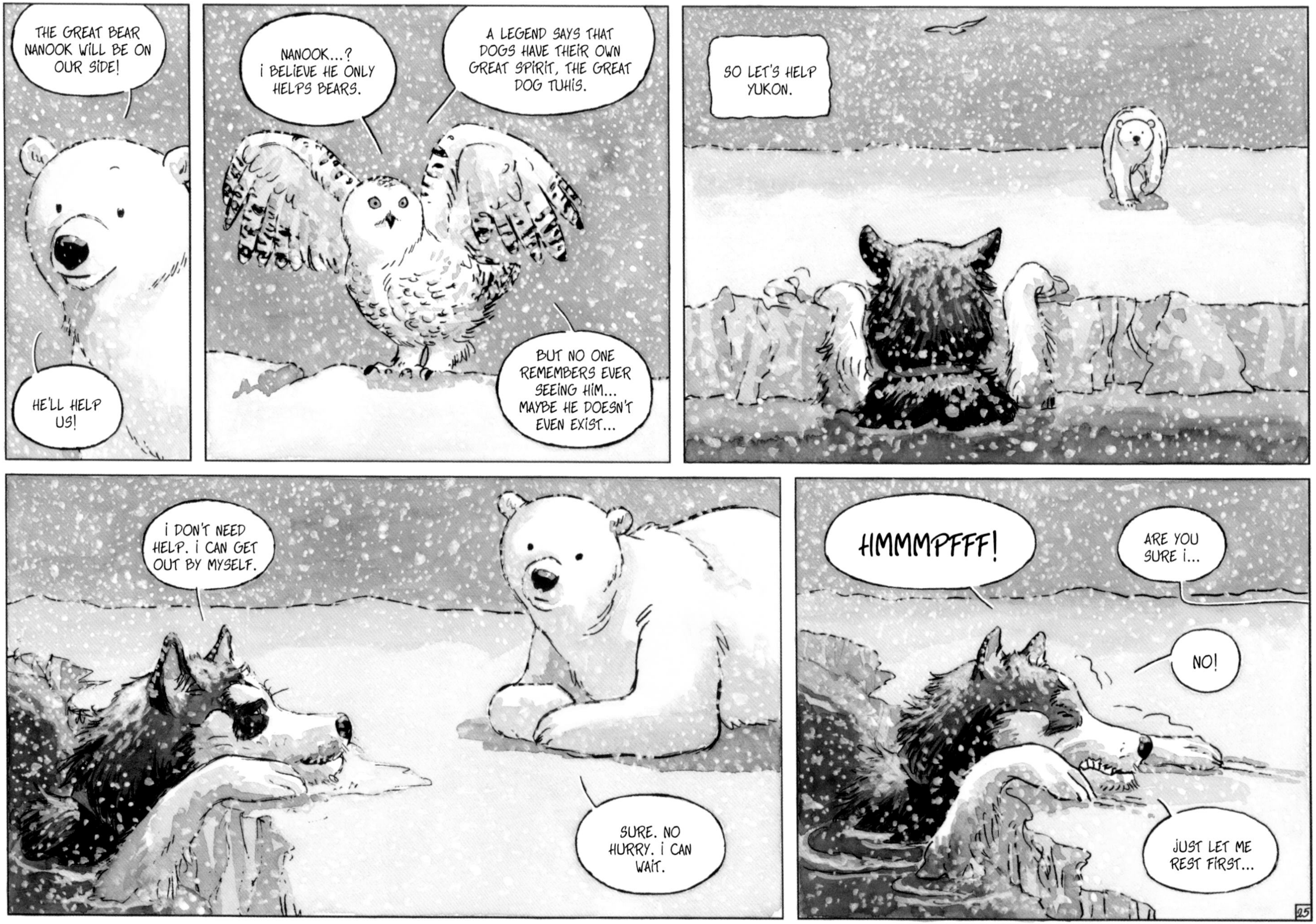
THE GREAT BEAR NANOOK WILL BE ON OUR SIDE!
HE'LL HELP US!
NANOOK...? I BELIEVE HE ONLY HELPS BEARS.
A LEGEND SAYS THAT DOGS HAVE THEIR OWN GREAT SPIRIT, THE GREAT DOG TUHIS.
BUT NO ONE REMEMBERS EVER SEEING HIM... MAYBE HE DOESN'T EVEN EXIST...
SO LET'S HELP YUKON.
I DON'T NEED HELP. I CAN GET OUT BY MYSELF.
SURE. NO HURRY. I CAN WAIT.
HMMMPFFF!
ARE YOU SURE I...
NO!
JUST LET ME REST FIRST...
25

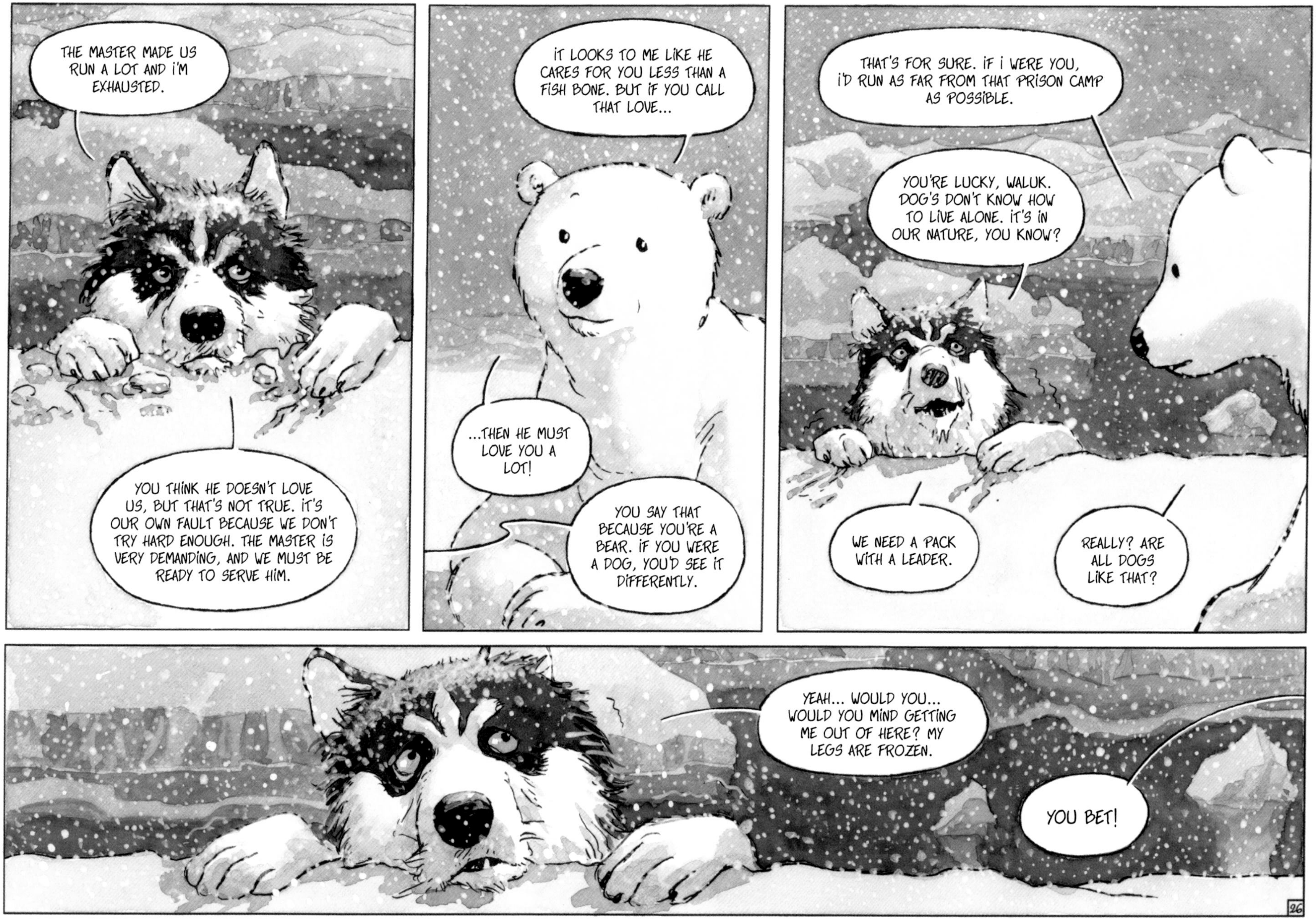
THE MASTER MADE US RUN A LOT AND I'M EXHAUSTED.
YOU THINK HE DOESN'T LOVE US, BUT THAT'S NOT TRUE. IT'S OUR OWN FAULT BECAUSE WE DON'T TRY HARD ENOUGH. THE MASTER IS VERY DEMANDING, AND WE MUST BE READY TO SERVE HIM.
IT LOOKS TO ME LIKE HE CARES FOR YOU LESS THAN A FISH BONE. BUT IF YOU CALL THAT LOVE...
...THEN HE MUST LOVE YOU A LOT!
YOU SAY THAT BECAUSE YOU'RE A BEAR. IF YOU WERE A DOG, YOU'D SEE IT DIFFERENTLY.
THAT'S FOR SURE. IF I WERE YOU, I'D RUN AS FAR FROM THAT PRISON CAMP AS POSSIBLE.
YOU'RE LUCKY, WALUK. DOG'S DON'T KNOW HOW TO LIVE ALONE. IT'S IN OUR NATURE, YOU KNOW?
WE NEED A PACK WITH A LEADER.
REALLY? ARE ALL DOGS LIKE THAT?
YEAH... WOULD YOU... WOULD YOU MIND GETTING ME OUT OF HERE? MY LEGS ARE FROZEN.
YOU BET!
26

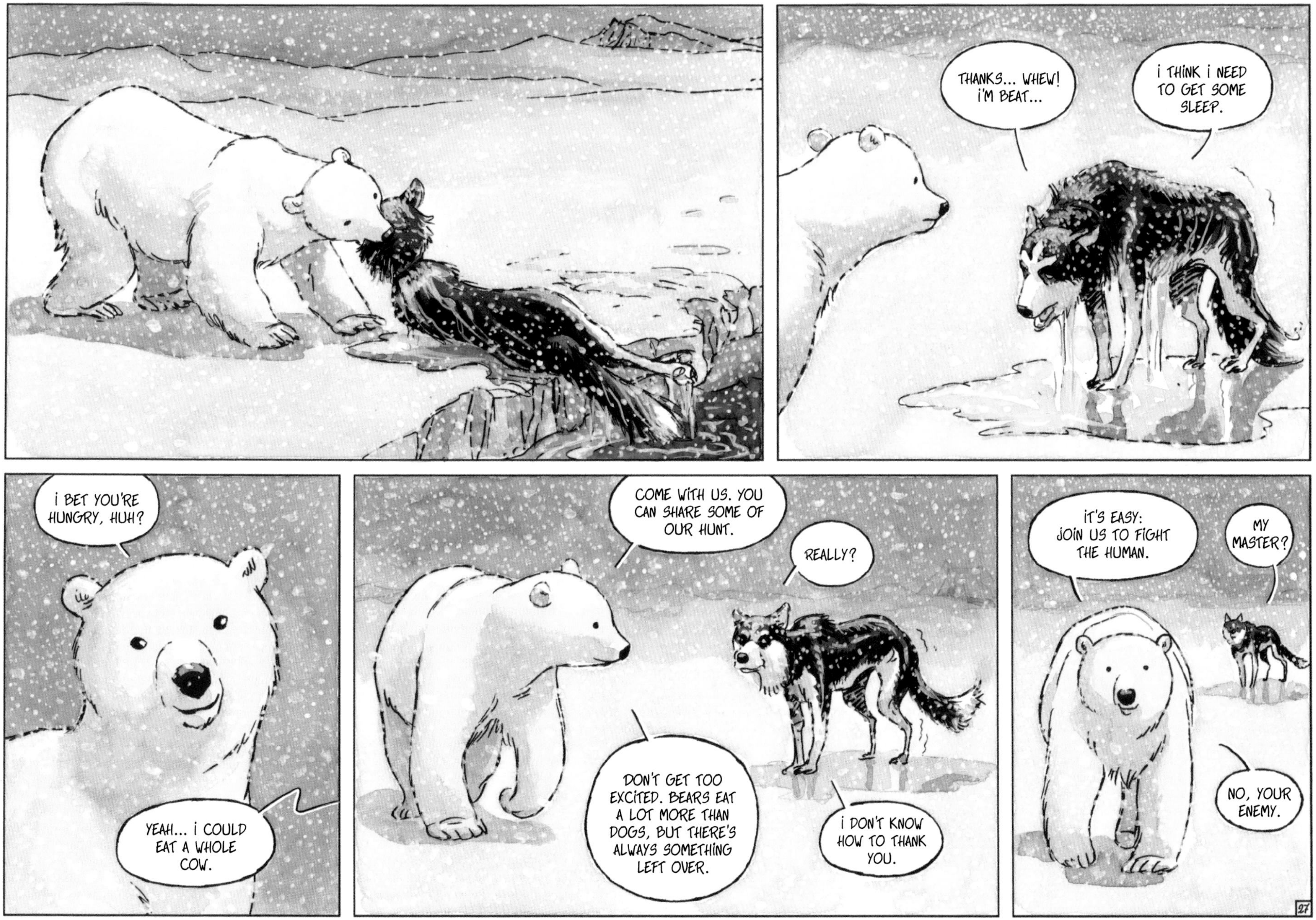
THANKS... WHEW! I'M BEAT...
I THINK I NEED TO GET SOME SLEEP.
I BET YOU'RE HUNGRY, HUH?
YEAH... I COULD EAT A WHOLE COW.
COME WITH US. YOU CAN SHARE SOME OF OUR HUNT.
REALLY?
DON'T GET TOO EXCITED. BEARS EAT A LOT MORE THAN DOGS, BUT THERE'S ALWAYS SOMETHING LEFT OVER.
I DON'T KNOW HOW TO THANK YOU.
IT'S EASY: JOIN US TO FIGHT THE HUMAN.
MY MASTER?
NO, YOUR ENEMY.
27

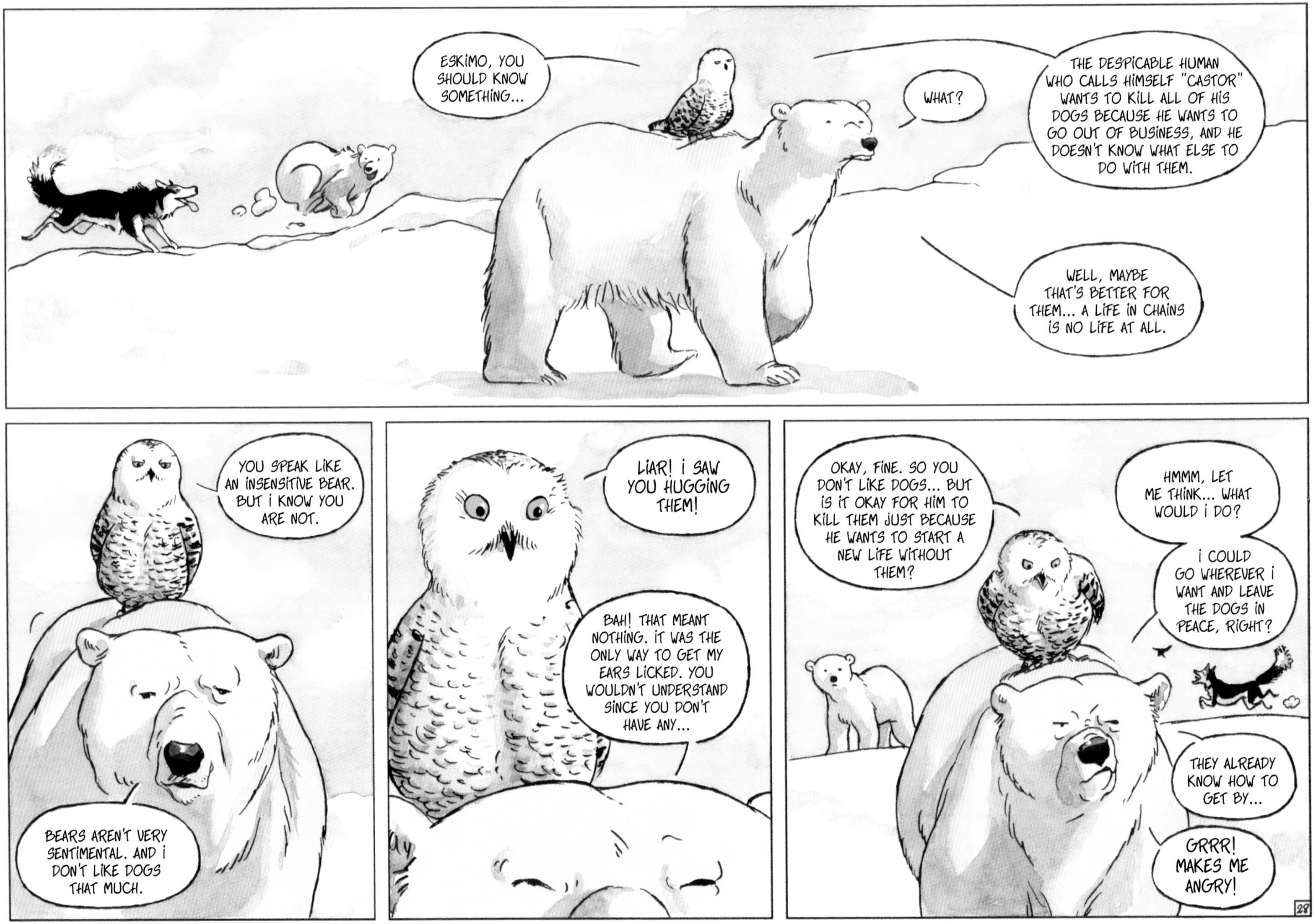
ESKIMO, YOU SHOULD KNOW SOMETHING...
WHAT?
THE DESPICABLE HUMAN WHO CALLS HIMSELF "CASTOR" WANTS TO KILL ALL OF HIS DOGS BECAUSE HE WANTS TO GO OUT OF BUSINESS, AND HE DOESN'T KNOW WHAT ELSE TO DO WITH THEM.
WELL, MAYBE THAT'S BETTER FOR THEM... A LIFE IN CHAINS IS NO LIFE AT ALL.
YOU SPEAK LIKE AN INSENSITIVE BEAR. BUT I KNOW YOU ARE NOT.
BEARS AREN'T VERY SENTIMENTAL. AND I DON'T LIKE DOGS THAT MUCH.
LIAR! I SAW YOU HUGGING THEM!
BAH! THAT MEANT NOTHING. IT WAS THE ONLY WAY TO GET MY EARS LICKED. YOU WOULDN'T UNDERSTAND SINCE YOU DON'T HAVE ANY...
OKAY, FINE. SO YOU DON'T LIKE DOGS... BUT IS IT OKAY FOR HIM TO KILL THEM JUST BECAUSE HE WANTS TO START A NEW LIFE WITHOUT THEM?
HMMM, LET ME THINK... WHAT WOULD I DO?
I COULD GO WHEREVER I WANT AND LEAVE THE DOGS IN PEACE, RIGHT?
THEY ALREADY KNOW HOW TO GET BY...
GRRR! MAKES ME ANGRY!
28

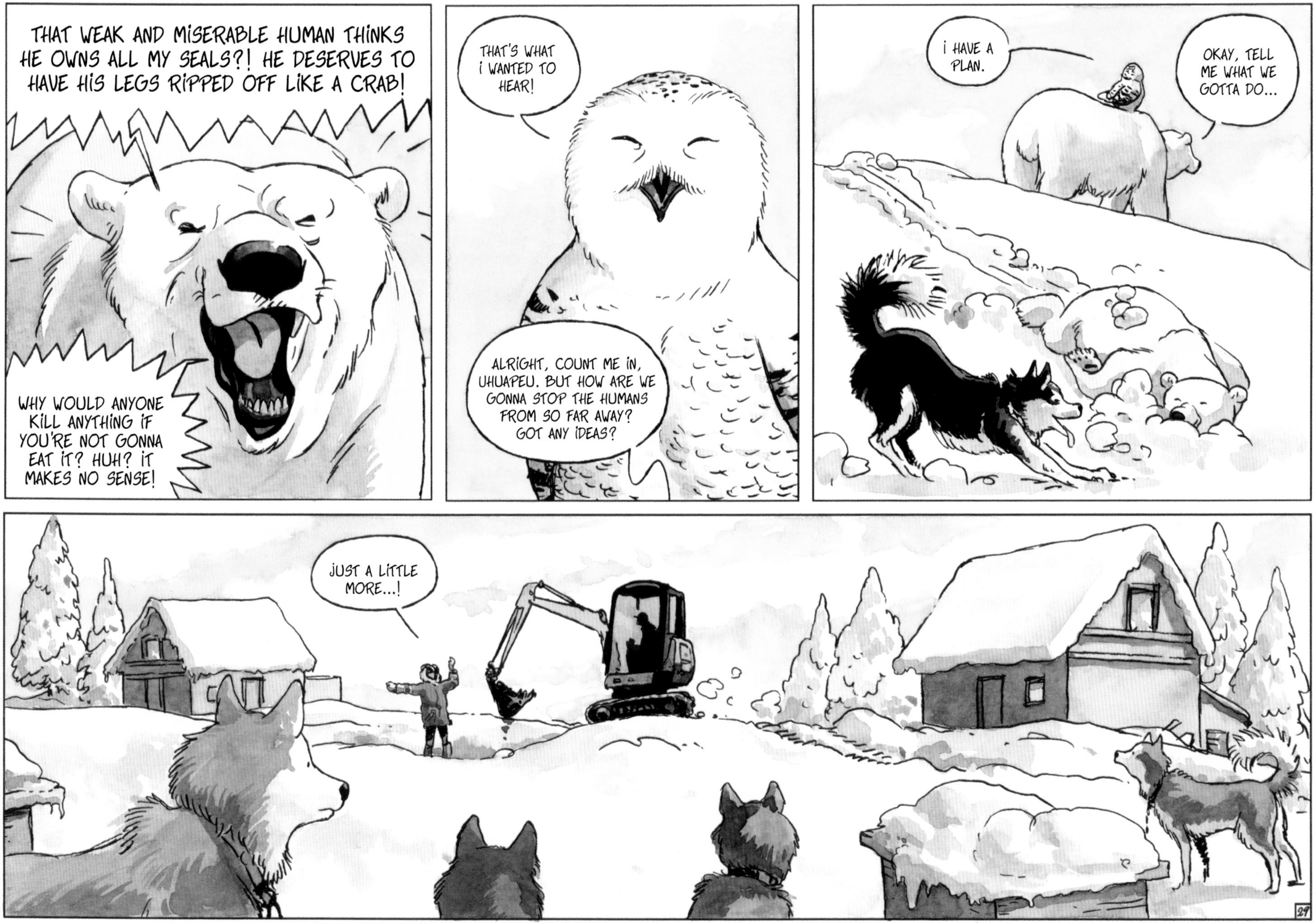
THAT WEAK AND MISERABLE HUMAN THINKS HE OWNS ALL MY SEALS?! HE DESERVES TO HAVE HIS LEGS RIPPED OFF LIKE A CRAB!
WHY WOULD ANYONE KILL ANYTHING IF YOU'RE NOT GONNA EAT IT? HUH? IT MAKES NO SENSE!
THAT'S WHAT I WANTED TO HEAR!
ALRIGHT, COUNT ME IN, UHUAPEU. BUT HOW ARE WE GONNA STOP THE HUMANS FROM SO FAR AWAY? GOT ANY IDEAS?
I HAVE A PLAN.
OKAY, TELL ME WHAT WE GOTTA DO...
JUST A LITTLE MORE...!
29

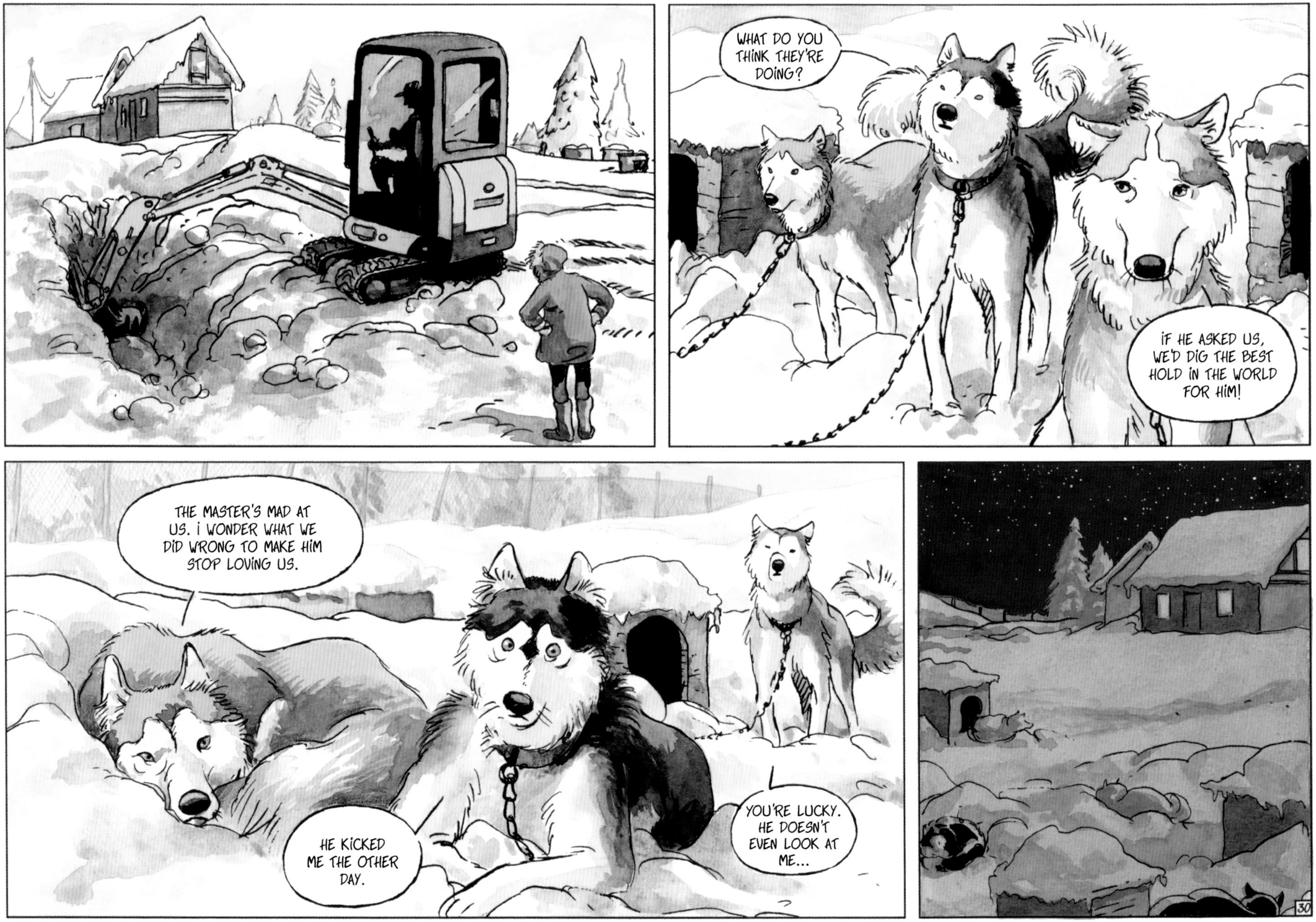
WHAT DO YOU THINK THEY'RE DOING?
IF HE ASKED US, WE'D DIG THE BEST HOLD IN THE WORLD FOR HIM!
THE MASTER'S MAD AT US. I WONDER WHAT WE DID WRONG TO MAKE HIM STOP LOVING US.
HE KICKED ME THE OTHER DAY.
YOU'RE LUCKY. HE DOESN'T EVEN LOOK AT ME...
30

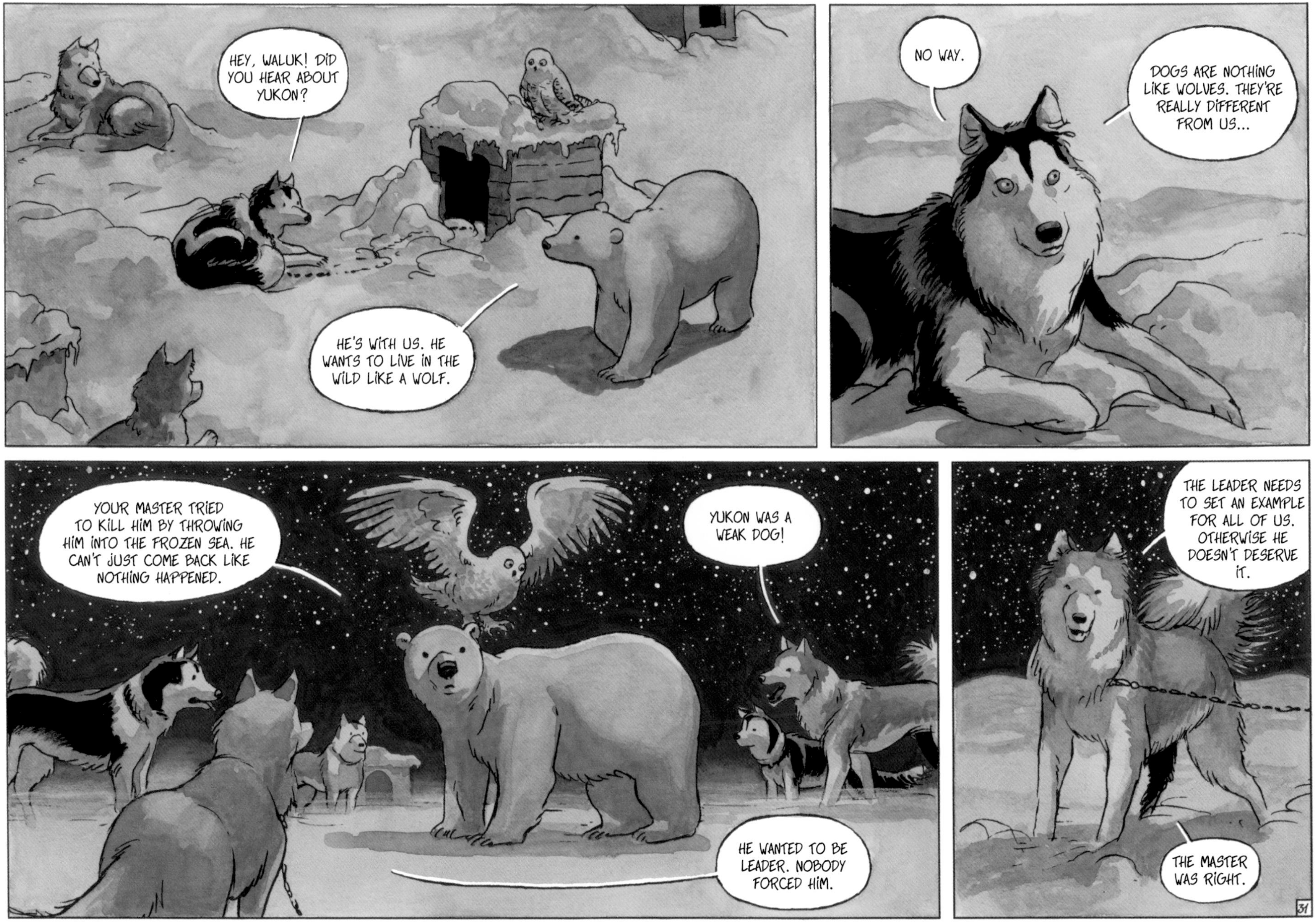
HEY, WALUK! DID YOU HEAR ABOUT YUKON?
HE'S WITH US. HE WANTS TO LIVE IN THE WILD LIKE A WOLF.
NO WAY.
DOGS ARE NOTHING LIKE WOLVES. THEY'RE REALLY DIFFERENT FROM US...
YOUR MASTER TRIED TO KILL HIM BY THROWING HIM INTO THE FROZEN SEA. HE CAN'T JUST COME BACK LIKE NOTHING HAPPENED.
YUKON WAS A WEAK DOG!
HE WANTED TO BE LEADER. NOBODY FORCED HIM.
THE LEADER NEEDS TO SET AN EXAMPLE FOR ALL OF US. OTHERWISE HE DOESN'T DESERVE IT.
THE MASTER WAS RIGHT.
31

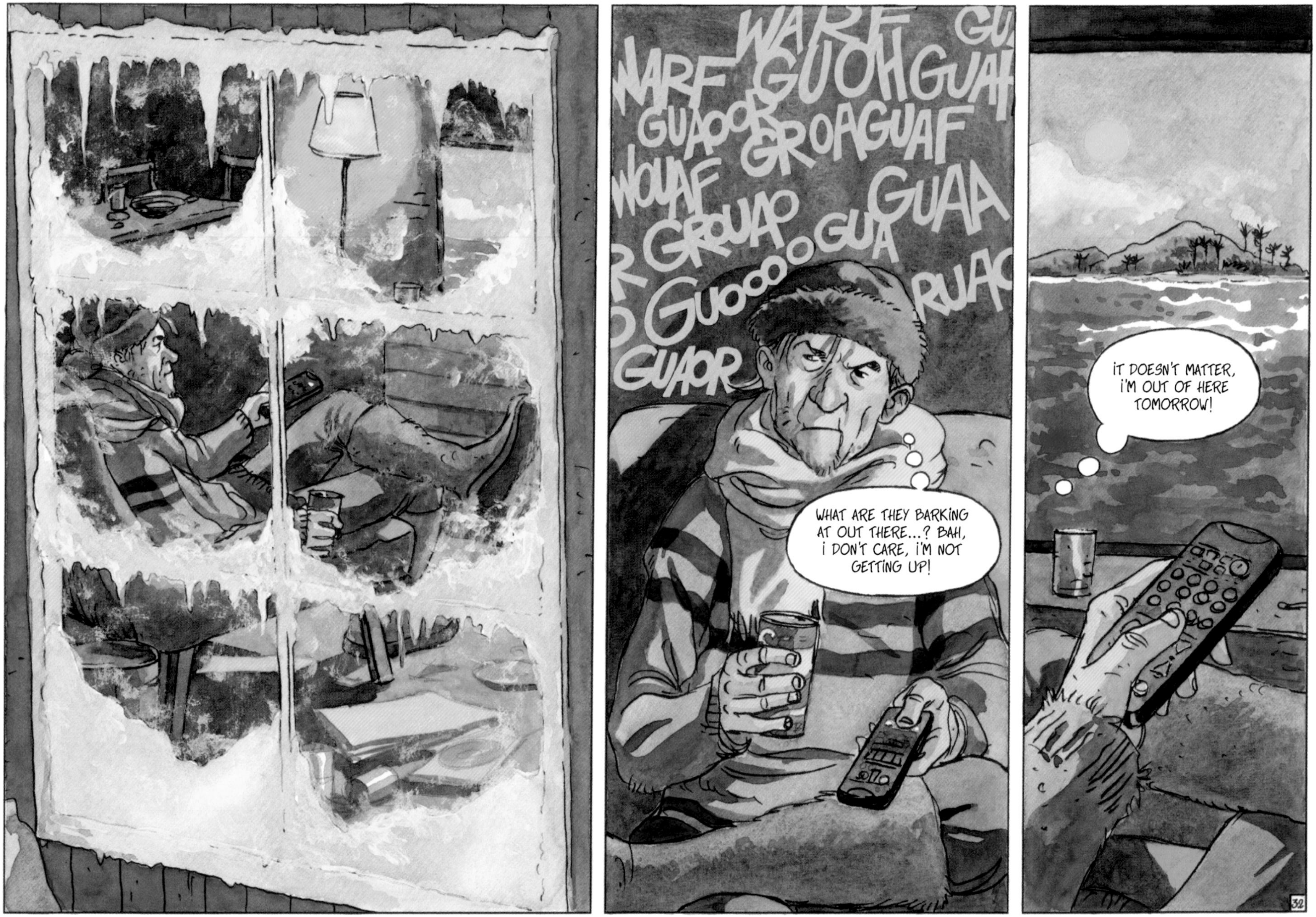
WARF
WARF GUOH GUAH
GUAOOR GROAGUAF
WOUAF
GROUAP GUAA
GROUAP OOGUA
GUoooo
RUAC
GUAOR
WHAT ARE THEY BARKING AT OUT THERE...? BAH, I DON'T CARE, I'M NOT GETTING UP!
IT DOESN'T MATTER, I'M OUT OF HERE TOMORROW!
32

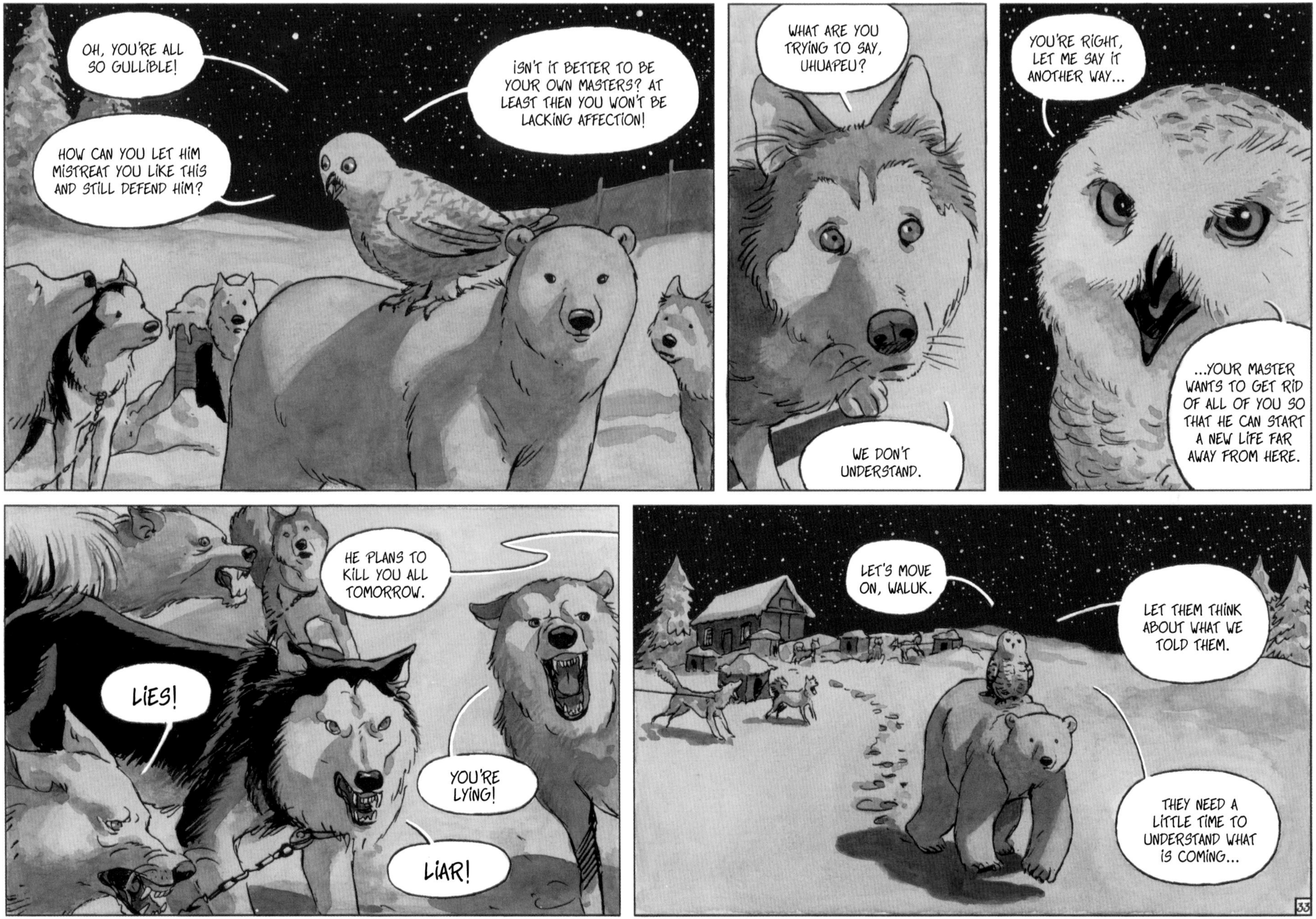
OH, YOU'RE ALL SO GULLIBLE!
ISN'T IT BETTER TO BE YOUR OWN MASTERS? AT LEAST THEN YOU WON'T BE LACKING AFFECTION!
HOW CAN YOU LET HIM MISTREAT YOU LIKE THIS AND STILL DEFEND HIM?
WHAT ARE YOU TRYING TO SAY, UHUAPEU?
WE DON'T UNDERSTAND.
YOU'RE RIGHT, LET ME SAY IT ANOTHER WAY...
...YOUR MASTER WANTS TO GET RID OF ALL OF YOU SO THAT HE CAN START A NEW LIFE FAR AWAY FROM HERE.
HE PLANS TO KILL YOU ALL TOMORROW.
LIES!
YOU'RE LYING!
LIAR!
LET'S MOVE ON, WALUK.
LET THEM THINK ABOUT WHAT WE TOLD THEM.
THEY NEED A LITTLE TIME TO UNDERSTAND WHAT IS COMING...
33

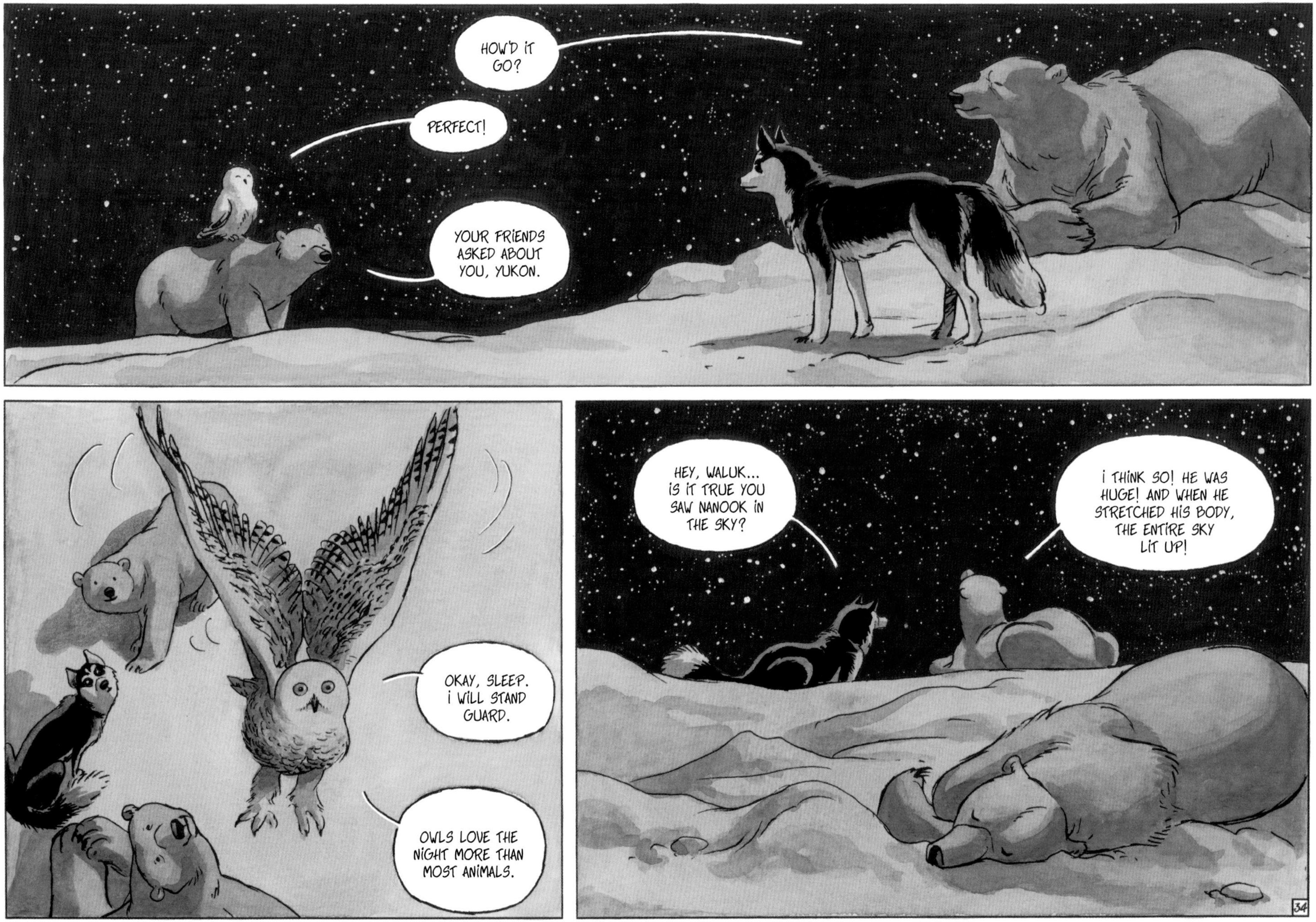
HOW'D IT GO?
PERFECT!
YOUR FRIENDS ASKED ABOUT YOU, YUKON.
OKAY, SLEEP. I WILL STAND GUARD.
OWLS LOVE THE NIGHT MORE THAN MOST ANIMALS.
HEY, WALUK... IS IT TRUE YOU SAW NANOOK IN THE SKY?
I THINK SO! HE WAS HUGE! AND WHEN HE STRETCHED HIS BODY, THE ENTIRE SKY LIT UP!
34

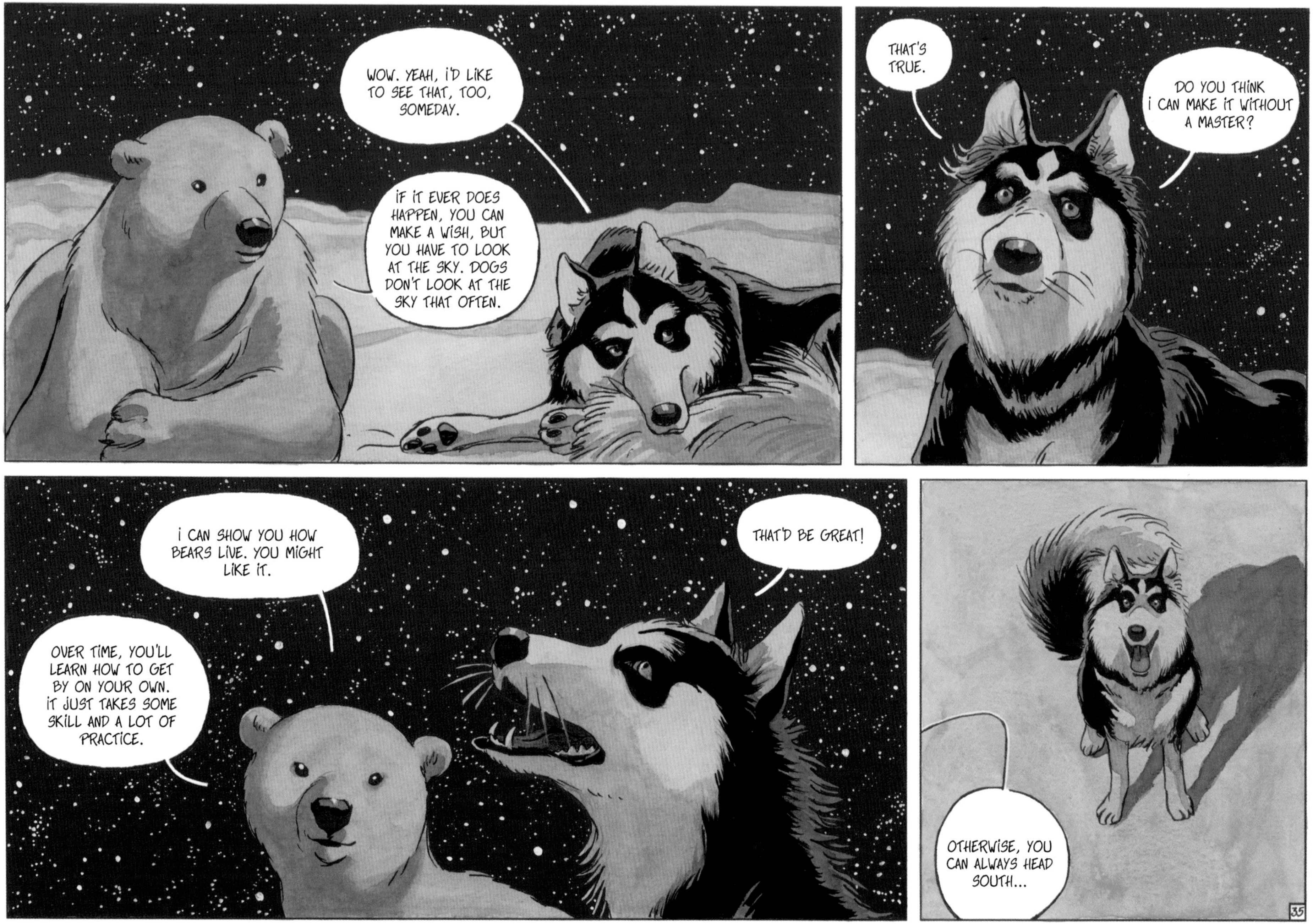
WOW. YEAH, I'D LIKE TO SEE THAT, TOO, SOMEDAY.
IF IT EVER DOES HAPPEN, YOU CAN MAKE A WISH, BUT YOU HAVE TO LOOK AT THE SKY. DOGS DON'T LOOK AT THE SKY THAT OFTEN.
THAT'S TRUE.
DO YOU THINK I CAN MAKE IT WITHOUT A MASTER?
I CAN SHOW YOU HOW BEARS LIVE. YOU MIGHT LIKE IT.
THAT'D BE GREAT!
OVER TIME, YOU'LL LEARN HOW TO GET BY ON YOUR OWN. IT JUST TAKES SOME SKILL AND A LOT OF PRACTICE.
OTHERWISE, YOU CAN ALWAYS HEAD SOUTH...
35

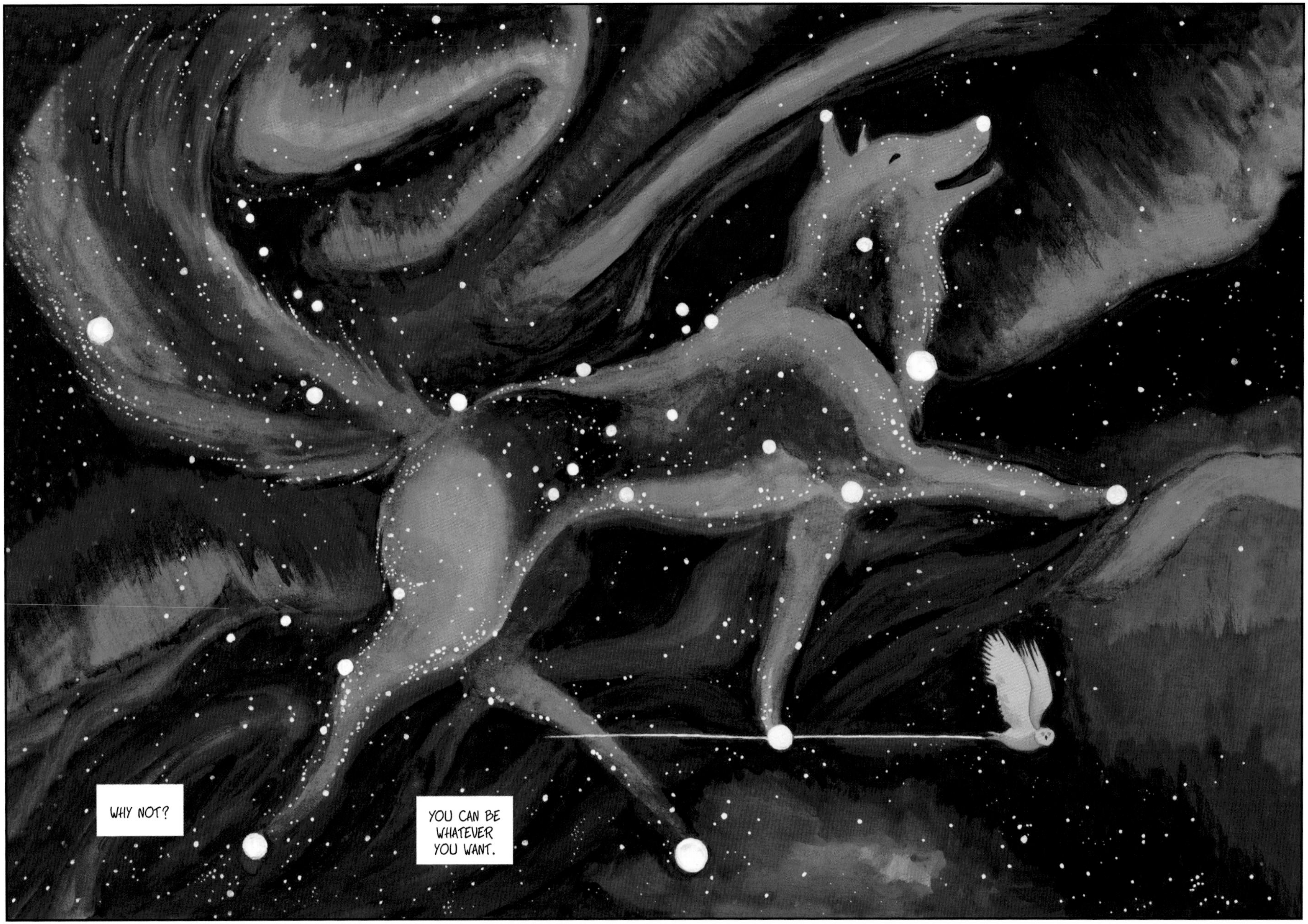
WHY NOT?
YOU CAN BE WHATEVER YOU WANT.

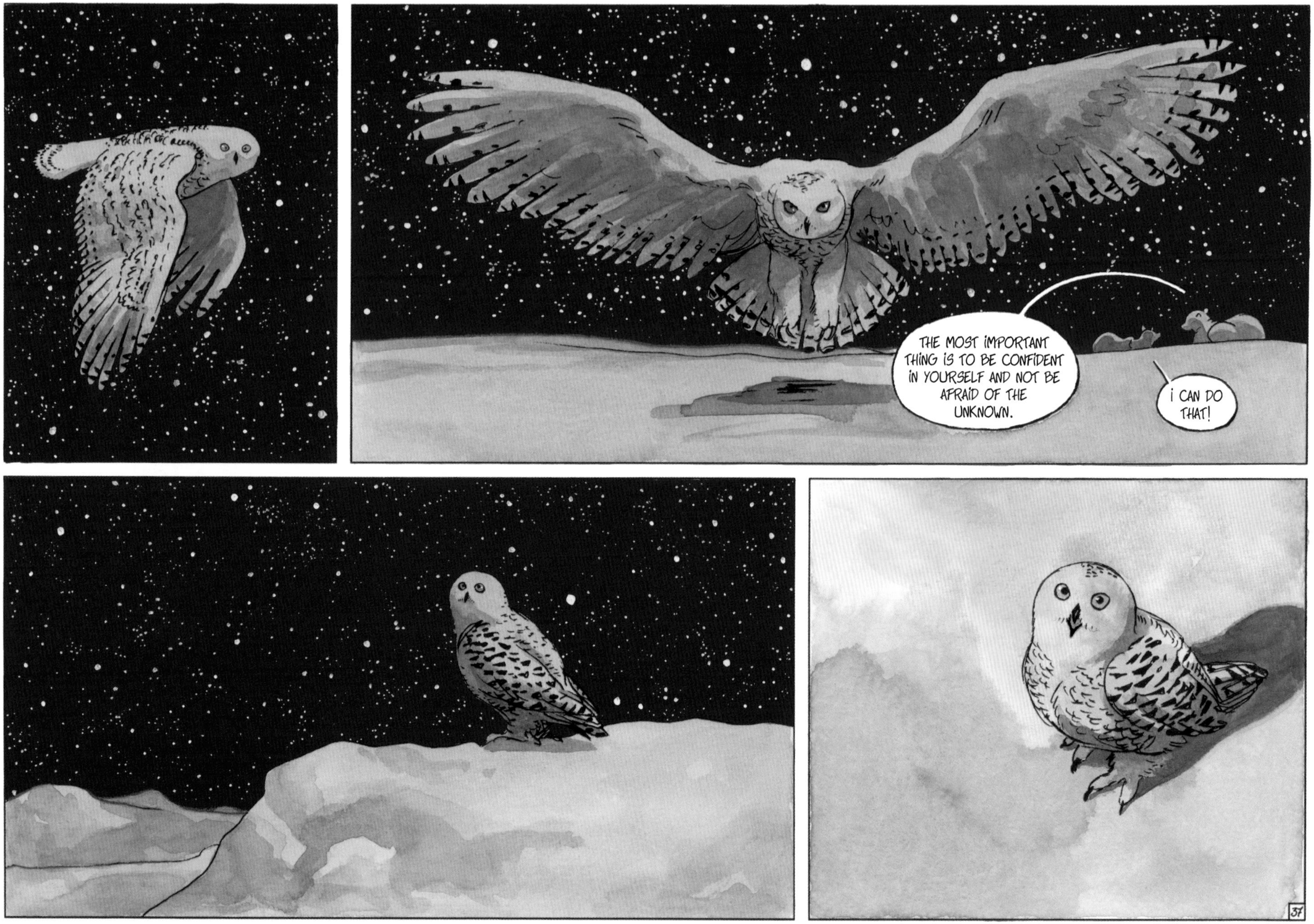
THE MOST IMPORTANT THING IS TO BE CONFIDENT IN YOURSELF AND NOT BE AFRAID OF THE UNKNOWN.
I CAN DO THAT!
37

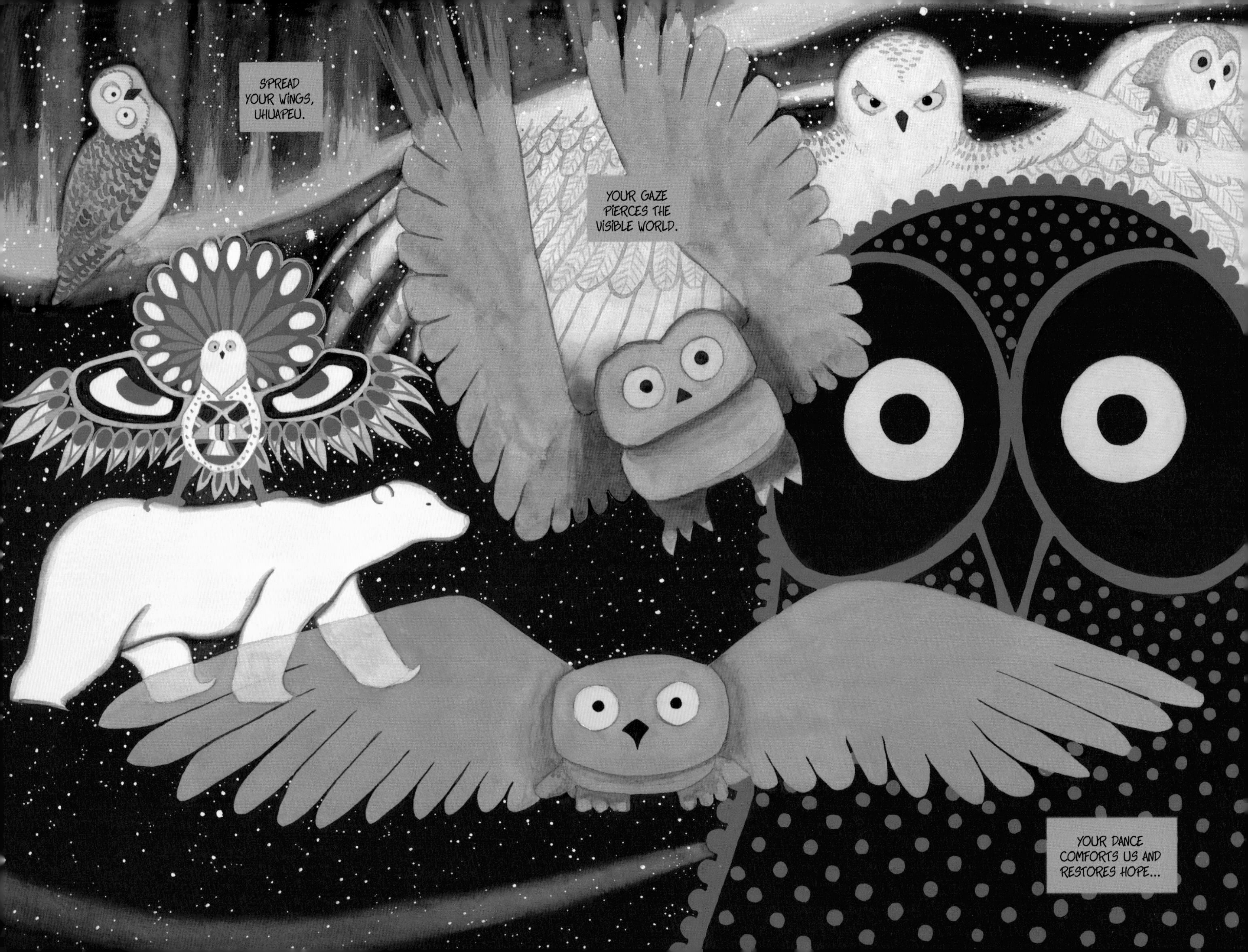
SPREAD YOUR WINGS, UHUAPEU.
YOUR GAZE PIERCES THE VISIBLE WORLD.
YOUR DANCE COMFORTS US AND RESTORES HOPE...

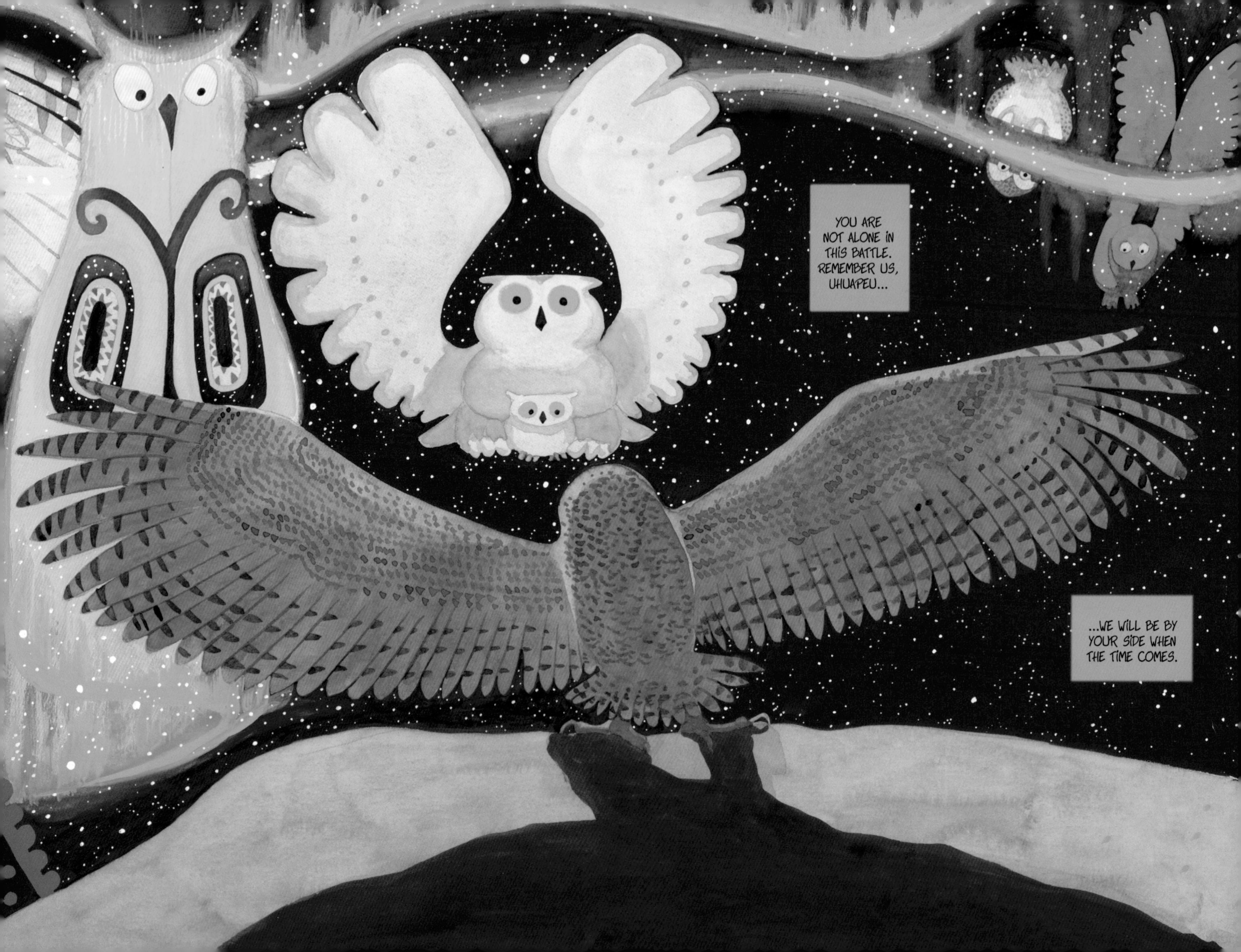
YOU ARE NOT ALONE IN THIS BATTLE. REMEMBER US, UHUAPEU...
...WE WILL BE BY YOUR SIDE WHEN THE TIME COMES.

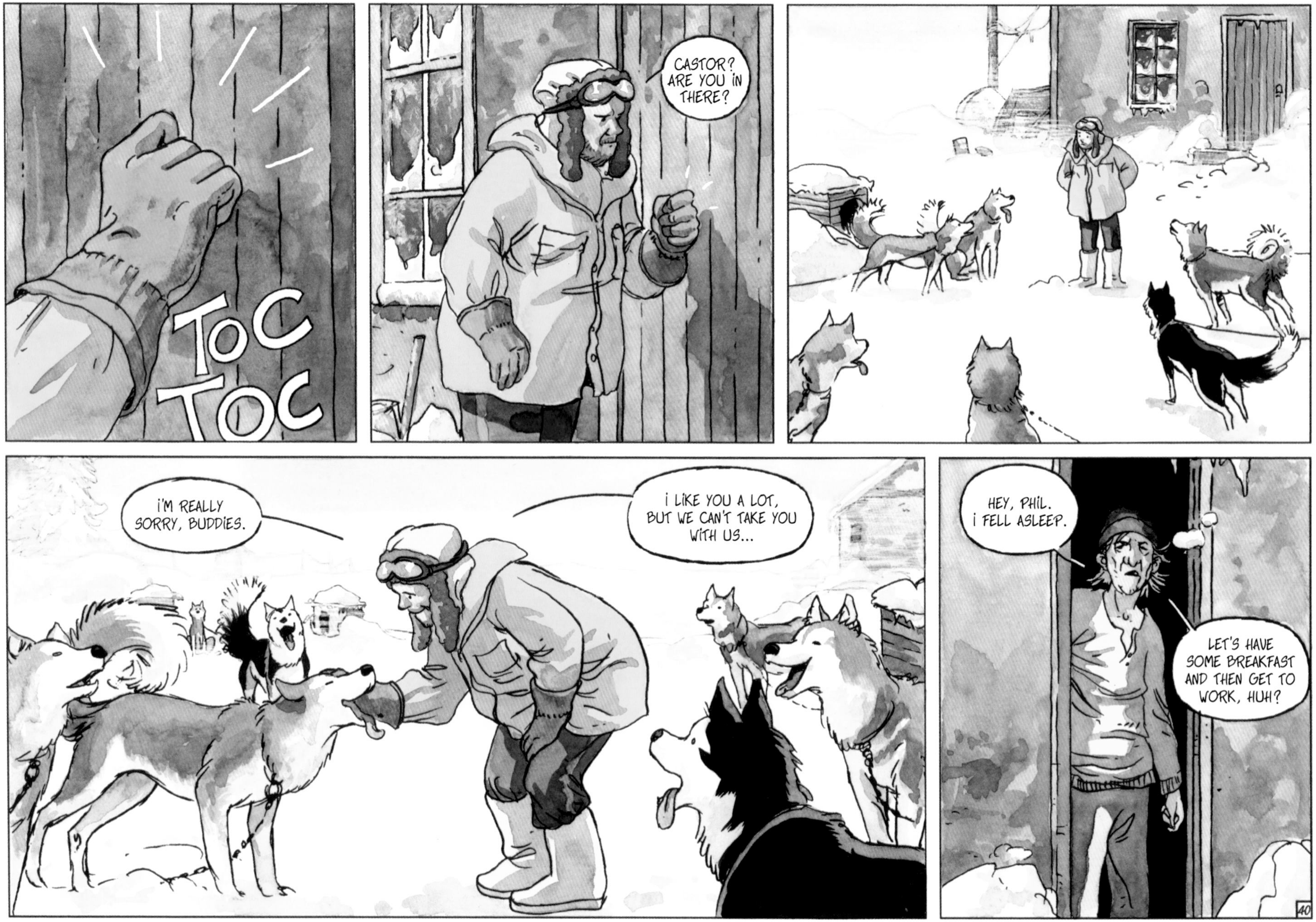
TOC
TOC
CASTOR? ARE YOU IN THERE?
I'M REALLY SORRY, BUDDIES.
I LIKE YOU A LOT, BUT WE CAN'T TAKE YOU WITH US...
HEY, PHIL. I FELL ASLEEP.
LET'S HAVE SOME BREAKFAST AND THEN GET TO WORK, HUH?
40

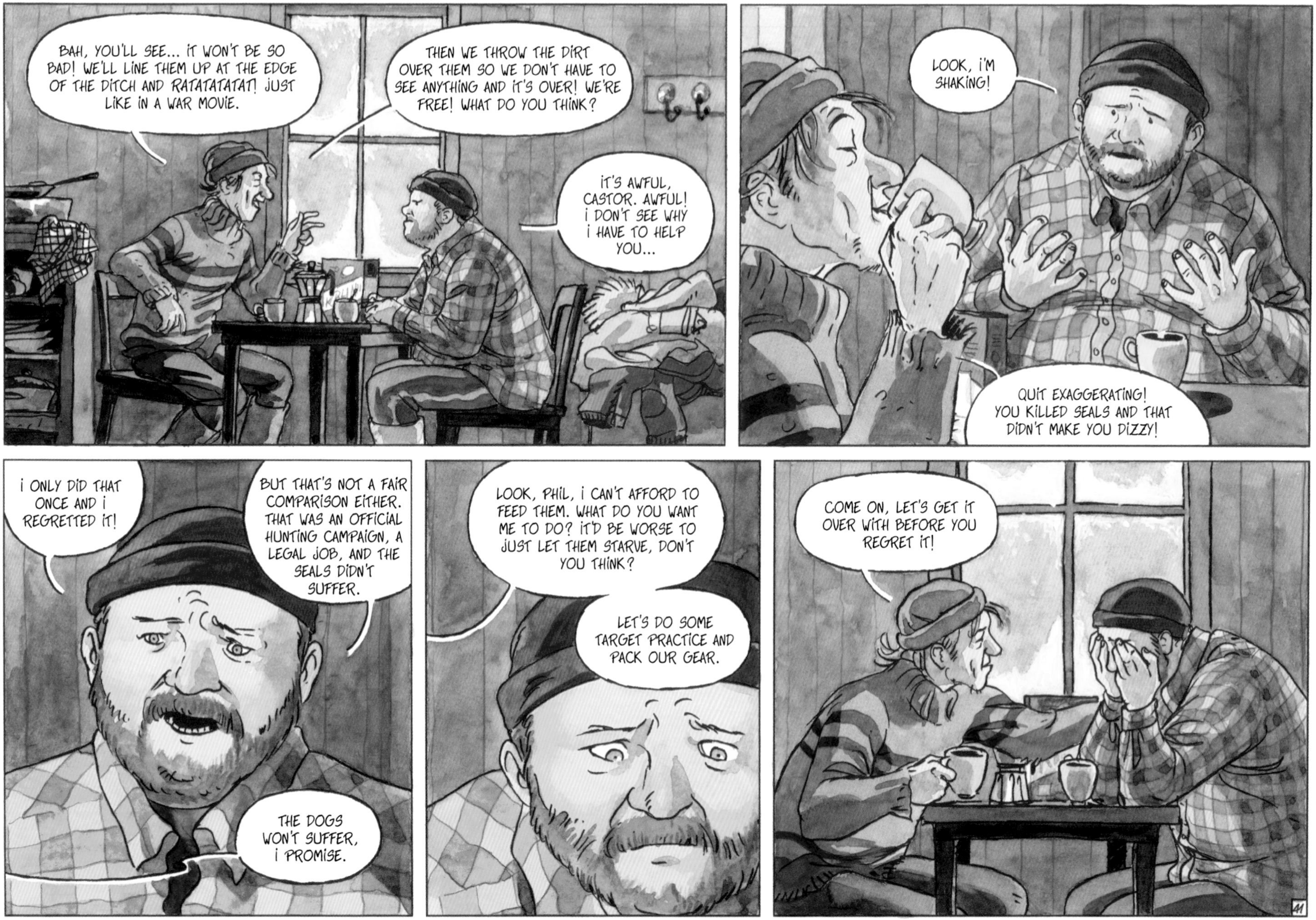
BAH, YOU'LL SEE... IT WON'T BE SO BAD! WE'LL LINE THEM UP AT THE EDGE OF THE DITCH AND RATATATATAT! JUST LIKE IN A WAR MOVIE.
THEN WE THROW THE DIRT OVER THEM SO WE DON'T HAVE TO SEE ANYTHING AND IT'S OVER! WE'RE FREE! WHAT DO YOU THINK?
IT'S AWFUL, CASTOR. AWFUL! I DON'T SEE WHY I HAVE TO HELP YOU...
LOOK, I'M SHAKING!
QUIT EXAGGERATING! YOU KILLED SEALS AND THAT DIDN'T MAKE YOU DIZZY!
I ONLY DID THAT ONCE AND I REGRETTED IT!
BUT THAT'S NOT A FAIR COMPARISON EITHER. THAT WAS AN OFFICIAL HUNTING CAMPAIGN, A LEGAL JOB, AND THE SEALS DIDN'T SUFFER.
THE DOGS WON'T SUFFER, I PROMISE.
LOOK, PHIL, I CAN'T AFFORD TO FEED THEM. WHAT DO YOU WANT ME TO DO? IT'D BE WORSE TO JUST LET THEM STARVE, DON'T YOU THINK?
LET'S DO SOME TARGET PRACTICE AND PACK OUR GEAR.
COME ON, LET'S GET IT OVER WITH BEFORE YOU REGRET IT!

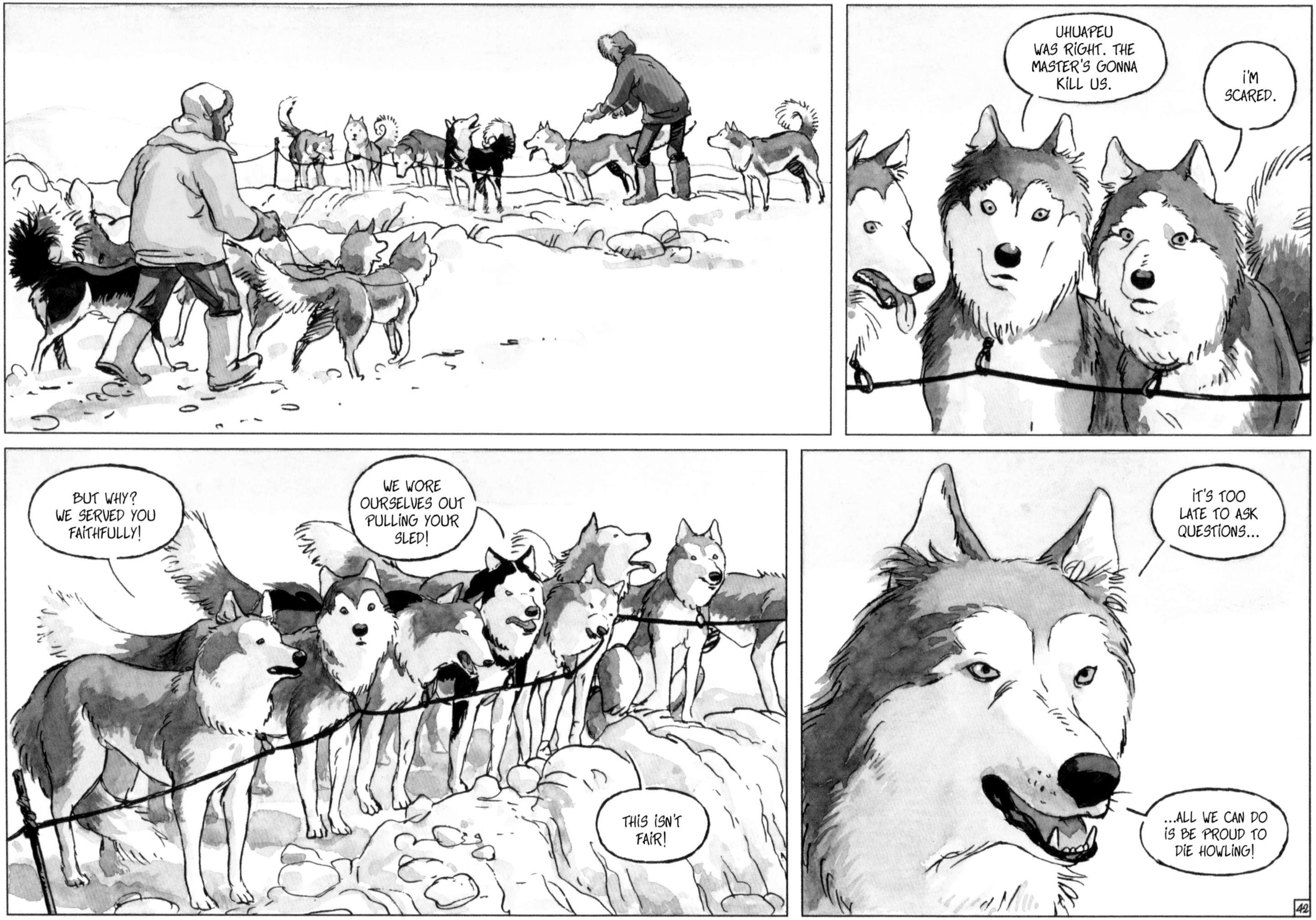
UHUAPEU WAS RIGHT. THE MASTER'S GONNA KILL US.
I'M SCARED.
BUT WHY? WE SERVED YOU FAITHFULLY!
WE WORE OURSELVES OUT PULLING YOUR SLED!
THIS ISN'T FAIR!
IT'S TOO LATE TO ASK QUESTIONS...
...ALL WE CAN DO IS BE PROUD TO DIE HOWLING!
42

AAAAAAUUUU

UUHHHUUUHHHHHHUUUUUHH
AAAAAUUUUUUUUUUHHHHAP
UUUUUHH

HUUUUUUUU
HAAAAAUUHH

?!!

THEY KNOW!

SHUT UP FOR ONCE!

JUST SIT DOWN FOR A MINUTE. I'LL GO GET THE RIFLES...

AAAHHUUUUUUUUUUHHHHAAAAAAHUUUUUU
UUHHHUUU AAAHHHHUU UUUU AAA
AUUUGHHHUU

!!

43

113

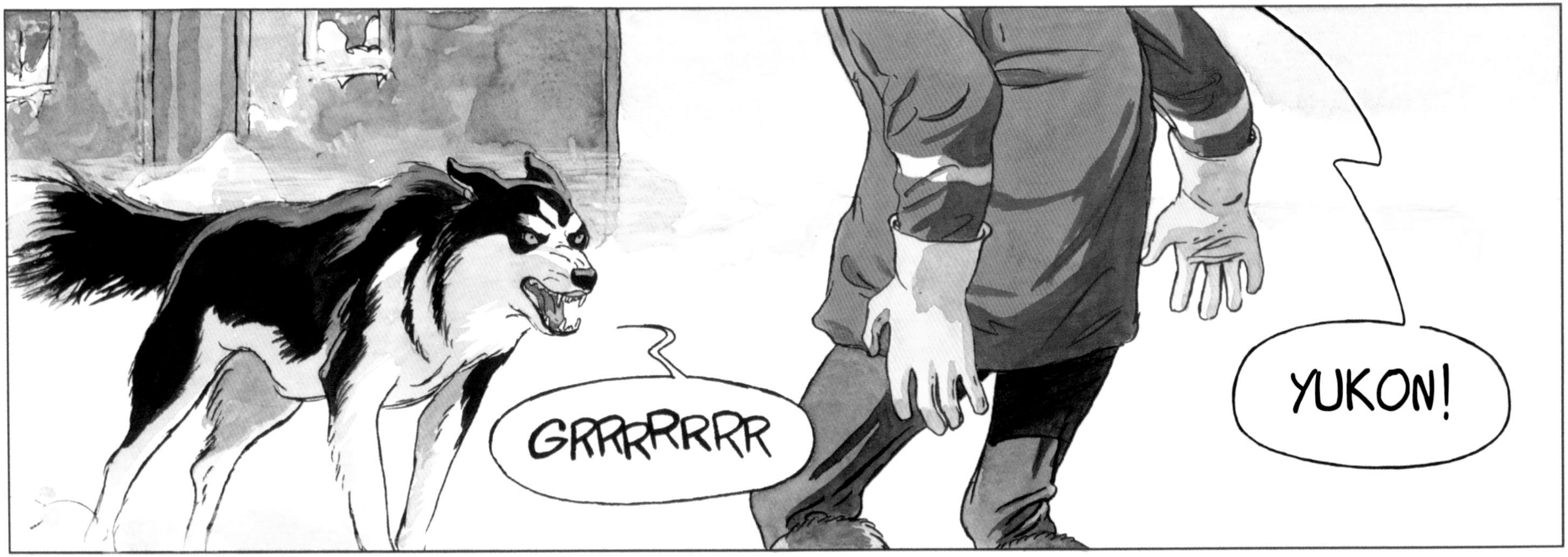
GRRRRRRR
YUKON!

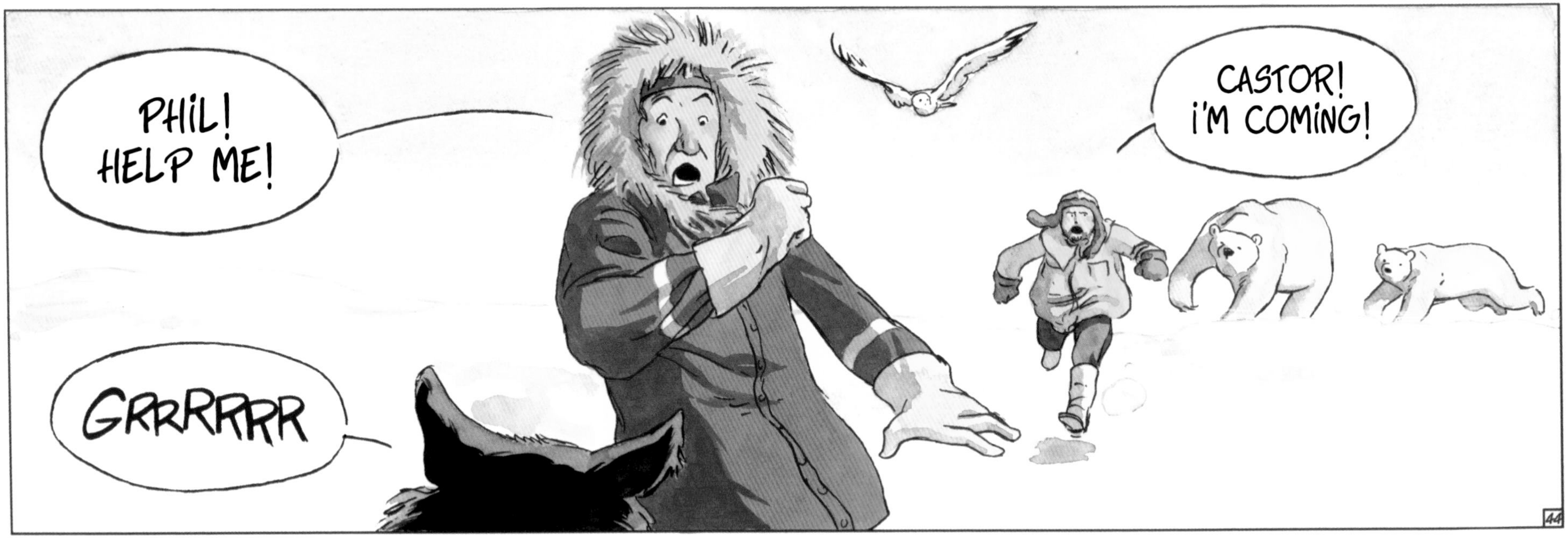
PHIL! HELP ME!
CASTOR! I'M COMING!
GRRRRRR

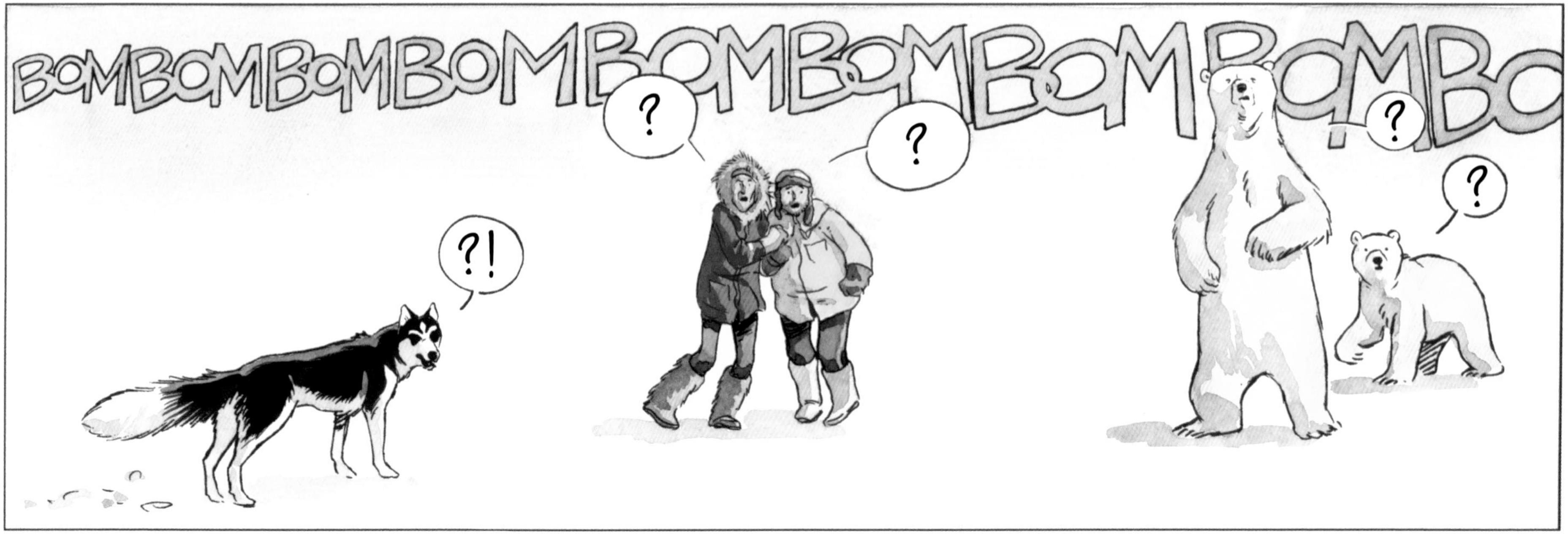
BOMBOMBOMBOMBOMBOMBOMBOMBOMBO
?!
?
?
?
?

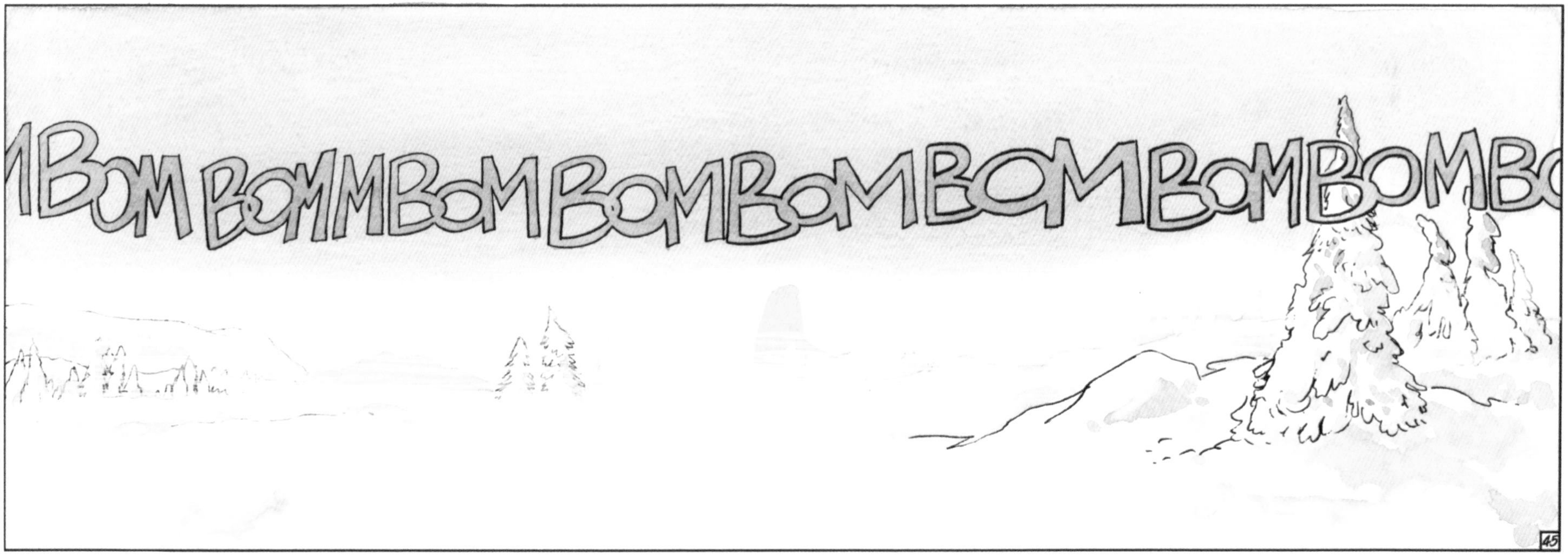
MBOM BOMMBOMBOMBOMBOMBOMBOMBO
45

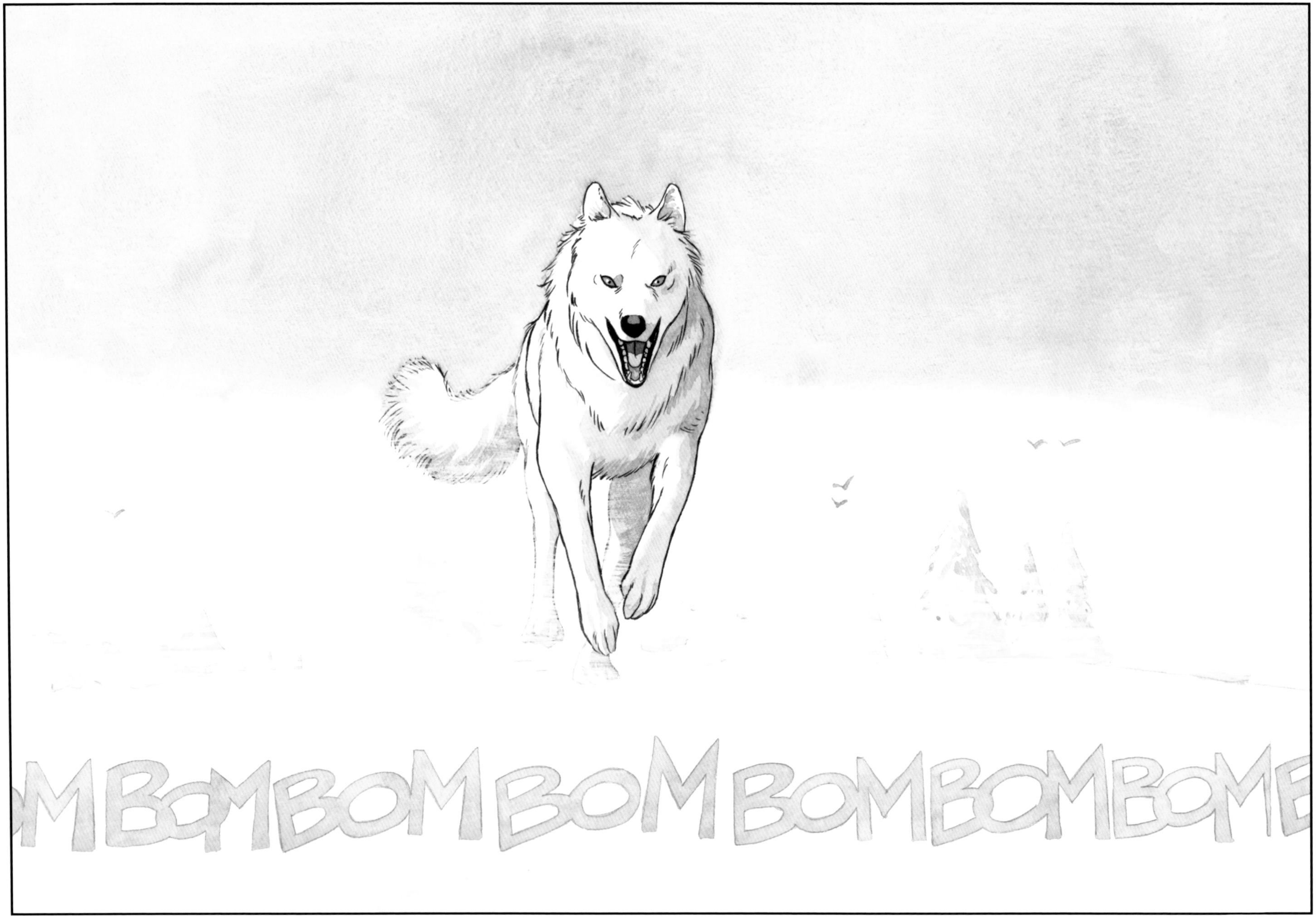
OMBOMBOMBOMBOMBOMBOMB

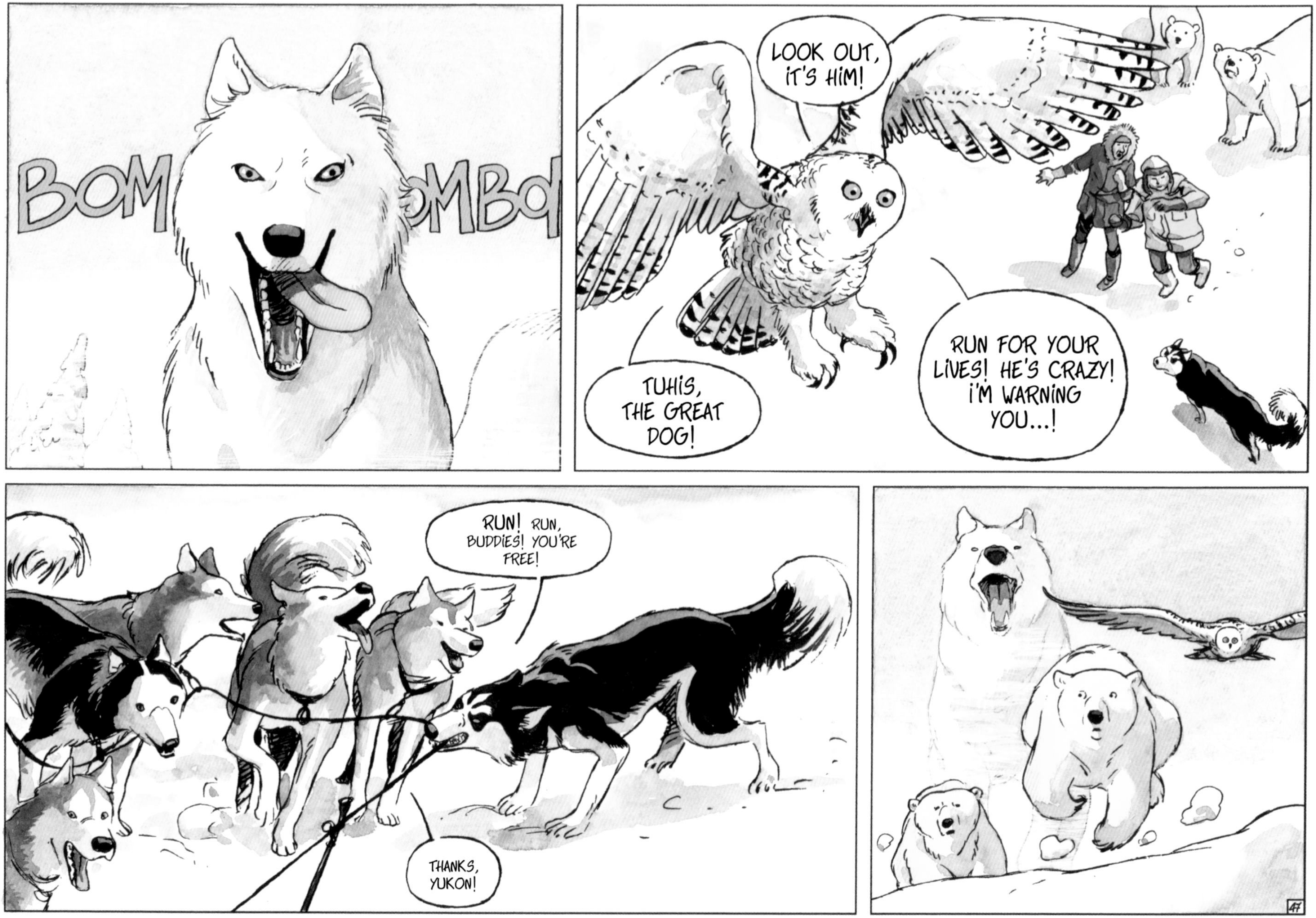
BOM
OMBO
LOOK OUT, IT'S HIM!
TUHIS, THE GREAT DOG!
RUN FOR YOUR LIVES! HE'S CRAZY! I'M WARNING YOU...!
RUN! RUN, BUDDIES! YOU'RE FREE!
THANKS, YUKON!
47

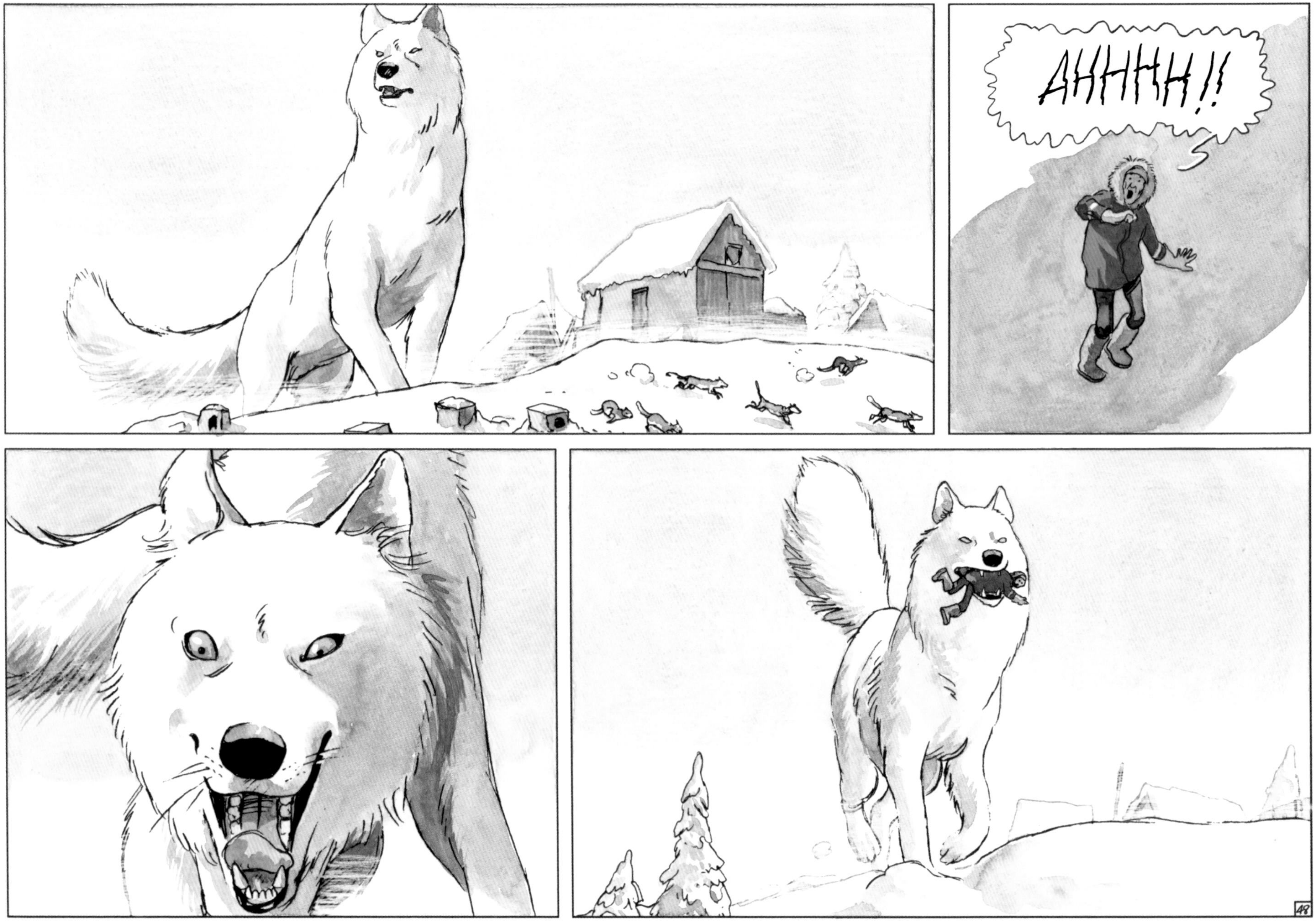
AHHHH!!
48

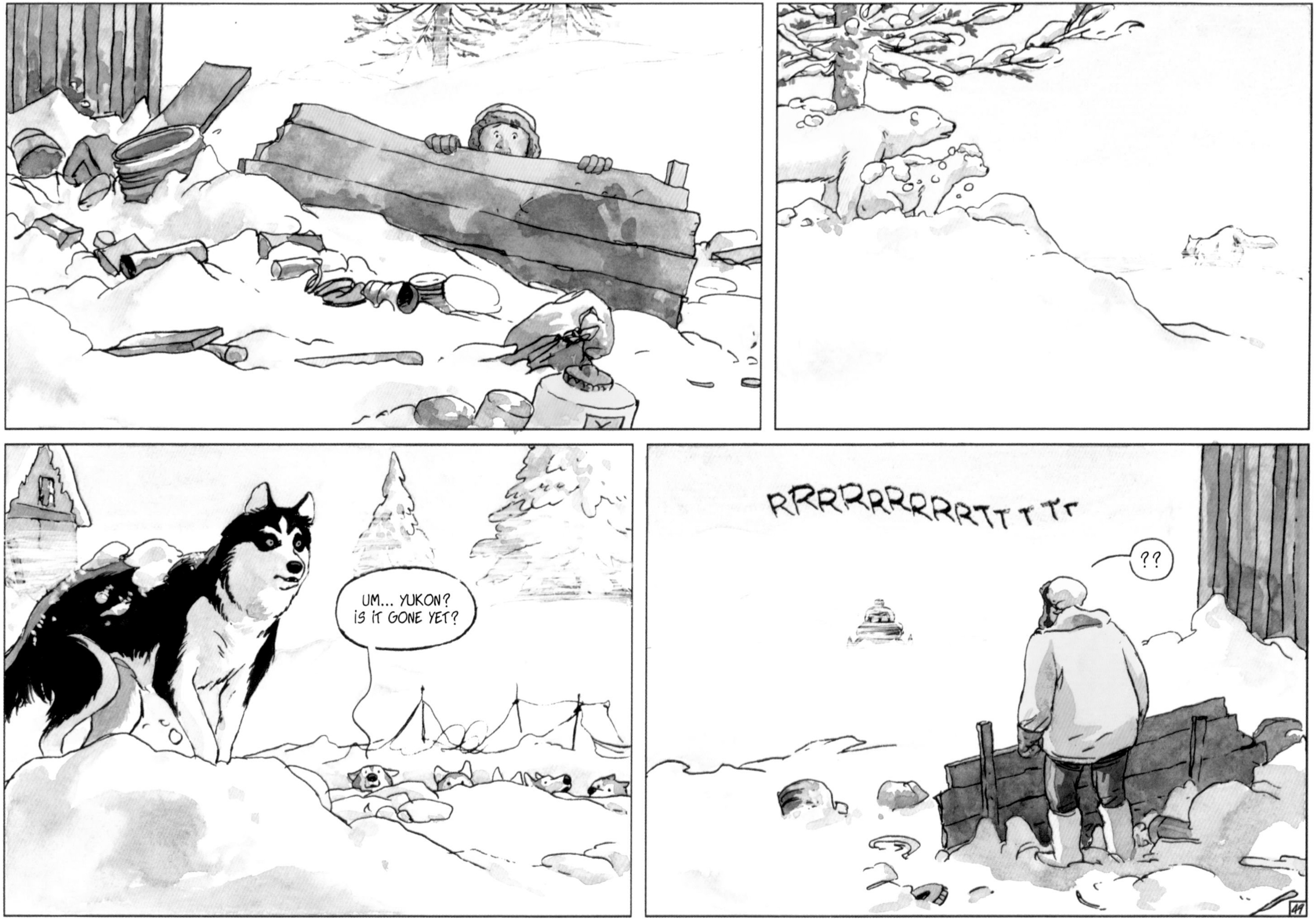
UM... YUKON?
IS IT GONE YET?
RRRRRRRRRRTTTTT
??

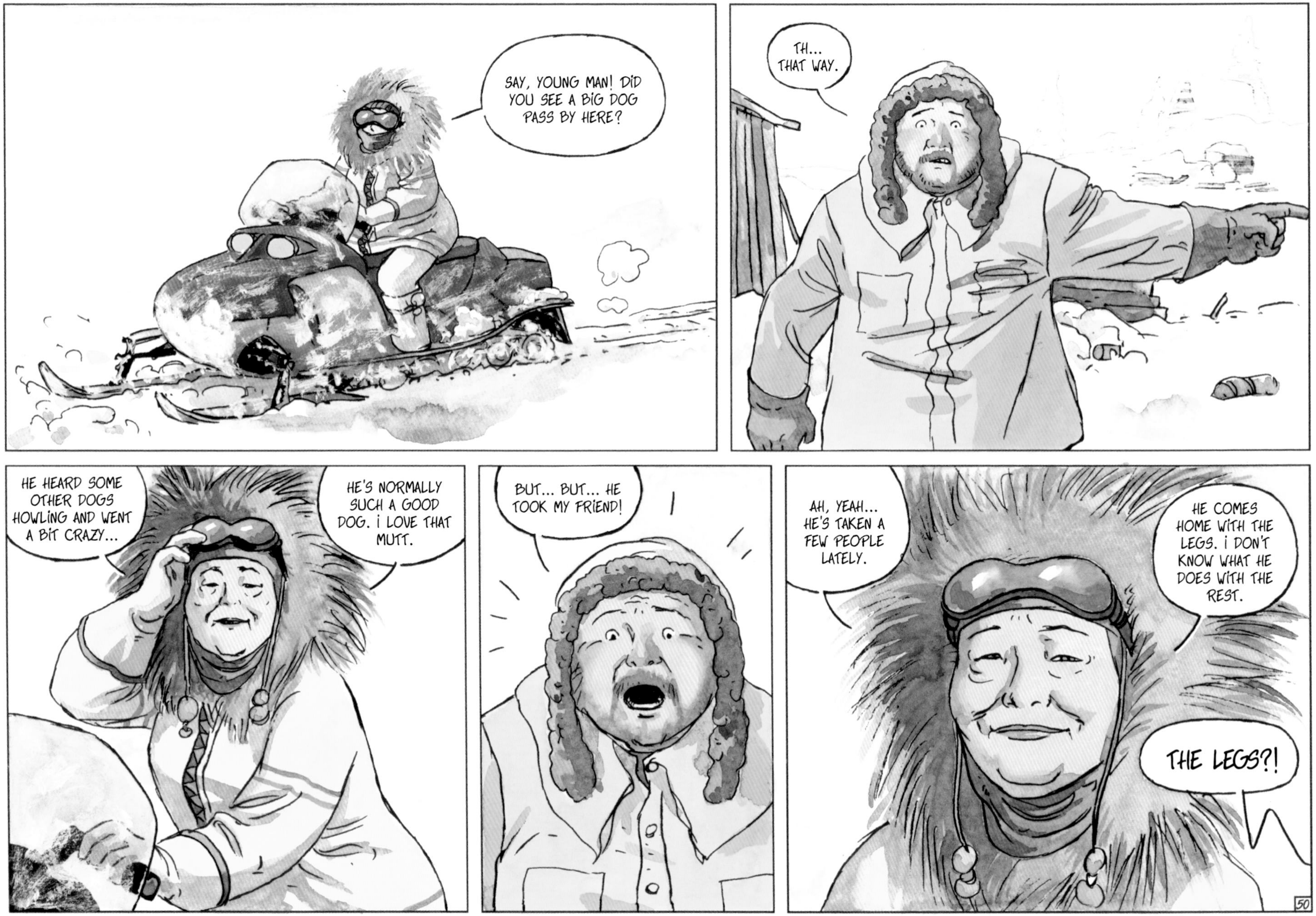
SAY, YOUNG MAN! DID YOU SEE A BIG DOG PASS BY HERE?
TH... THAT WAY.
HE HEARD SOME OTHER DOGS HOWLING AND WENT A BIT CRAZY...
HE'S NORMALLY SUCH A GOOD DOG. I LOVE THAT MUTT.
BUT... BUT... HE TOOK MY FRIEND!
AH, YEAH... HE'S TAKEN A FEW PEOPLE LATELY.
HE COMES HOME WITH THE LEGS. I DON'T KNOW WHAT HE DOES WITH THE REST.
THE LEGS?!
50

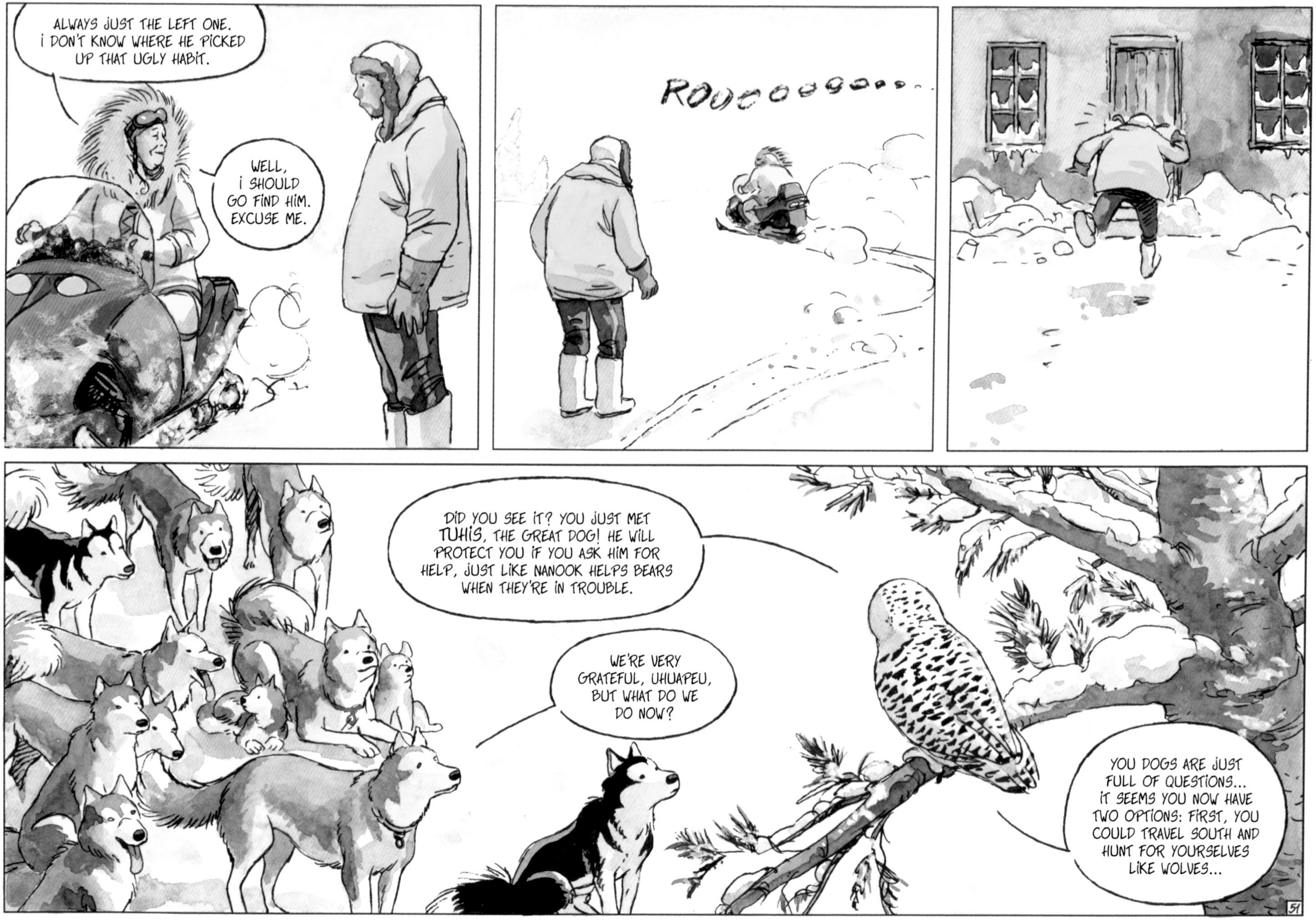
ALWAYS JUST THE LEFT ONE. I DON'T KNOW WHERE HE PICKED UP THAT UGLY HABIT.
WELL, I SHOULD GO FIND HIM. EXCUSE ME.
ROOOOOOOOO...
DID YOU SEE IT? YOU JUST MET TUHIS, THE GREAT DOG! HE WILL PROTECT YOU IF YOU ASK HIM FOR HELP, JUST LIKE NANOOK HELPS BEARS WHEN THEY'RE IN TROUBLE.
WE'RE VERY GRATEFUL, UHUAPEU, BUT WHAT DO WE DO NOW?
YOU DOGS ARE JUST FULL OF QUESTIONS... IT SEEMS YOU NOW HAVE TWO OPTIONS: FIRST, YOU COULD TRAVEL SOUTH AND HUNT FOR YOURSELVES LIKE WOLVES...
51

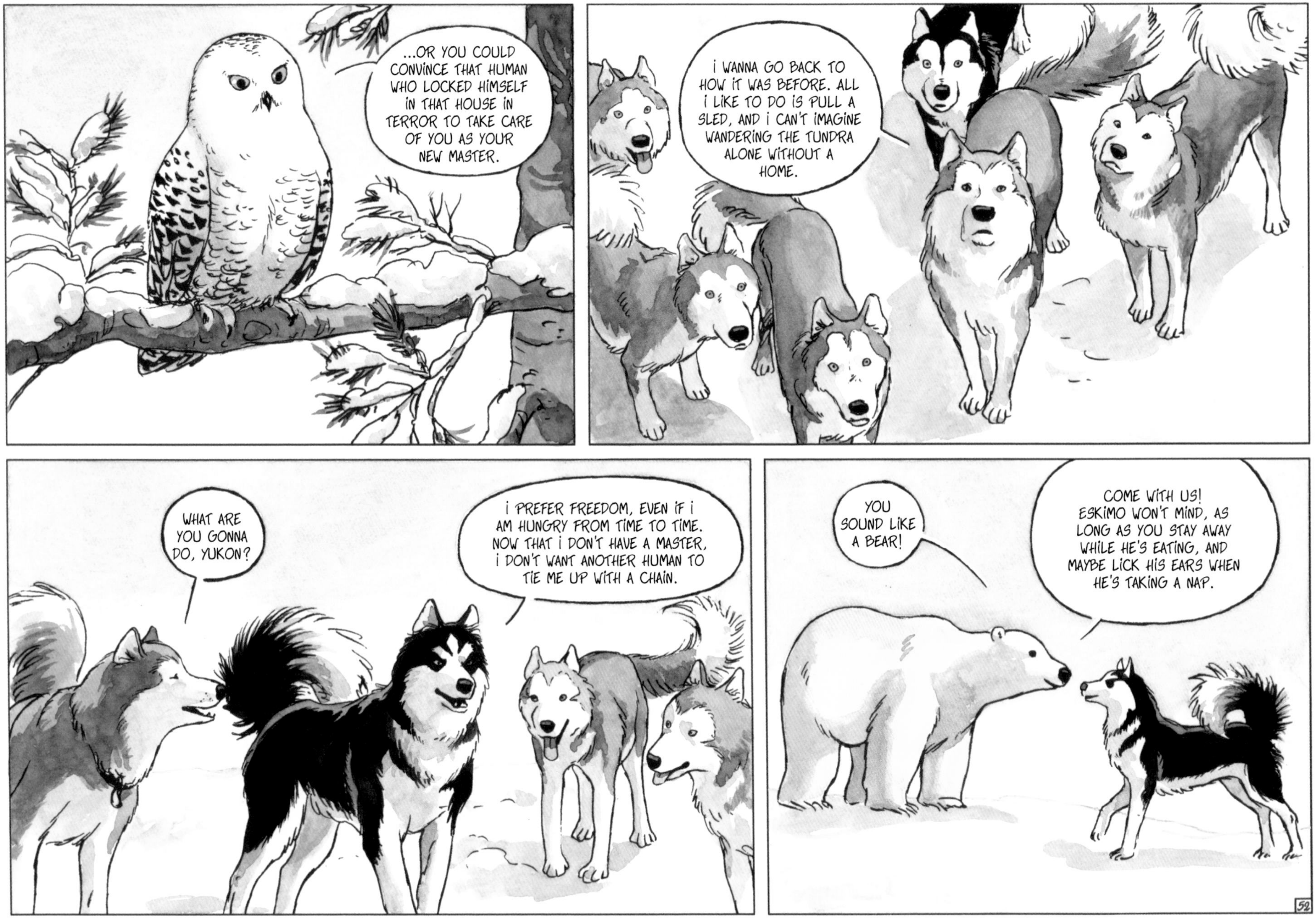
...OR YOU COULD CONVINCE THAT HUMAN WHO LOCKED HIMSELF IN THAT HOUSE IN TERROR TO TAKE CARE OF YOU AS YOUR NEW MASTER.
I WANNA GO BACK TO HOW IT WAS BEFORE. ALL I LIKE TO DO IS PULL A SLED, AND I CAN'T IMAGINE WANDERING THE TUNDRA ALONE WITHOUT A HOME.
WHAT ARE YOU GONNA DO, YUKON?
I PREFER FREEDOM, EVEN IF I AM HUNGRY FROM TIME TO TIME. NOW THAT I DON'T HAVE A MASTER, I DON'T WANT ANOTHER HUMAN TO TIE ME UP WITH A CHAIN.
YOU SOUND LIKE A BEAR!
COME WITH US! ESKIMO WON'T MIND, AS LONG AS YOU STAY AWAY WHILE HE'S EATING, AND MAYBE LICK HIS EARS WHEN HE'S TAKING A NAP.
52

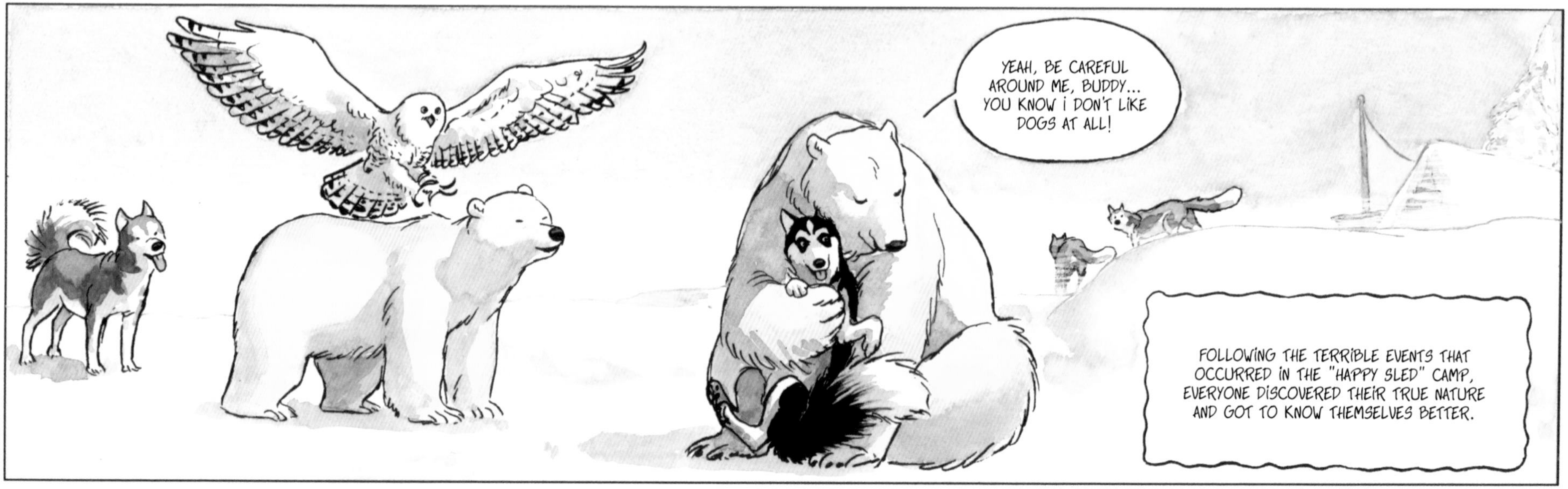
YEAH, BE CAREFUL AROUND ME, BUDDY... YOU KNOW I DON'T LIKE DOGS AT ALL!
FOLLOWING THE TERRIBLE EVENTS THAT OCCURRED IN THE "HAPPY SLED" CAMP, EVERYONE DISCOVERED THEIR TRUE NATURE AND GOT TO KNOW THEMSELVES BETTER.

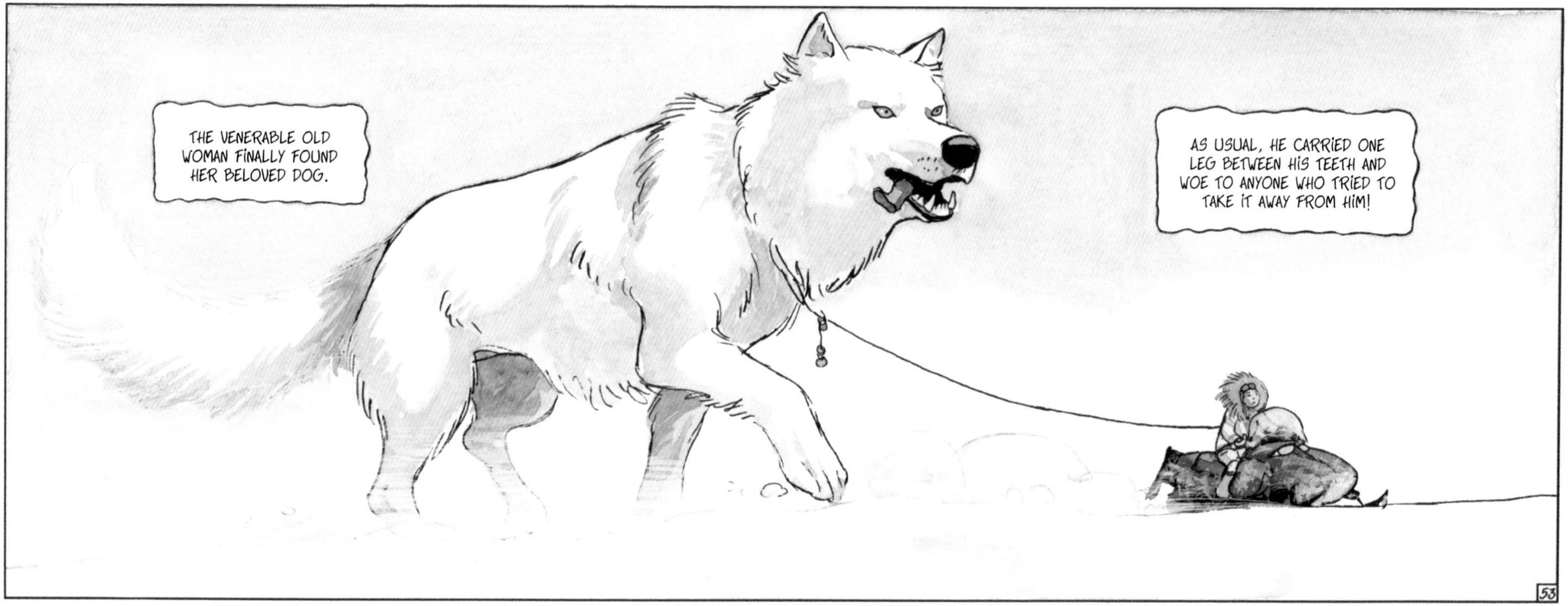
THE VENERABLE OLD WOMAN FINALLY FOUND HER BELOVED DOG.
AS USUAL, HE CARRIED ONE LEG BETWEEN HIS TEETH AND WOE TO ANYONE WHO TRIED TO TAKE IT AWAY FROM HIM!
53

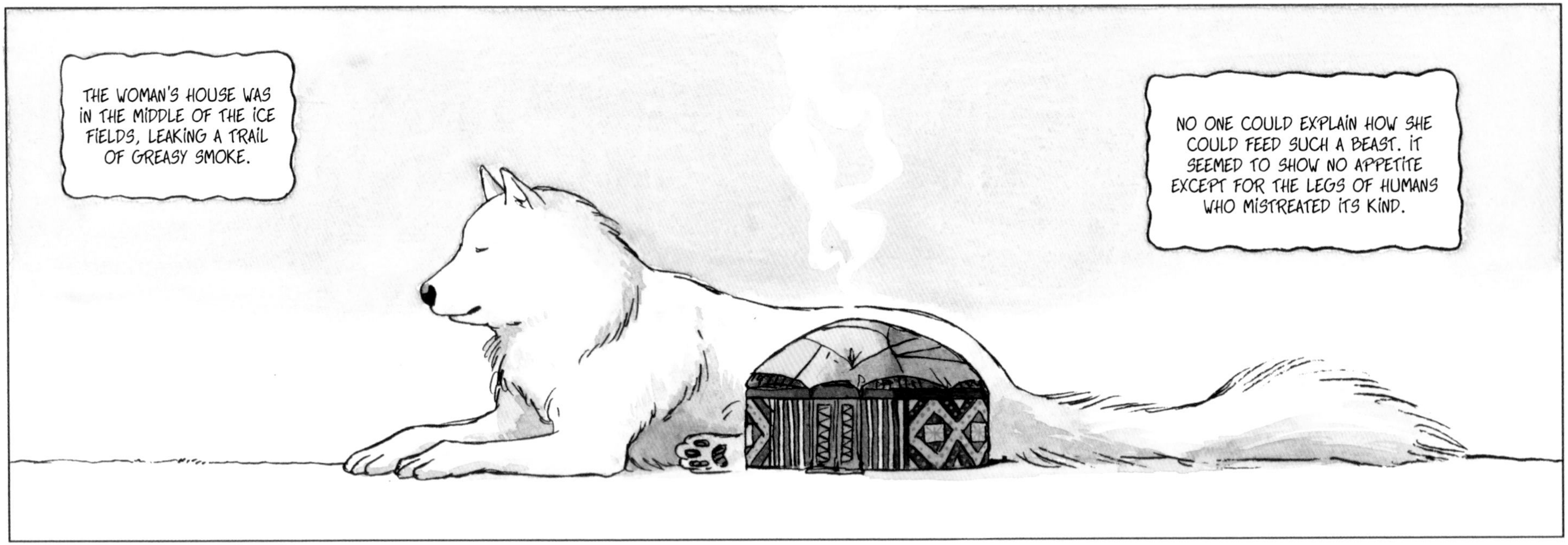
THE WOMAN'S HOUSE WAS IN THE MIDDLE OF THE ICE FIELDS, LEAKING A TRAIL OF GREASY SMOKE.
NO ONE COULD EXPLAIN HOW SHE COULD FEED SUCH A BEAST. IT SEEMED TO SHOW NO APPETITE EXCEPT FOR THE LEGS OF HUMANS WHO MISTREATED ITS KIND.

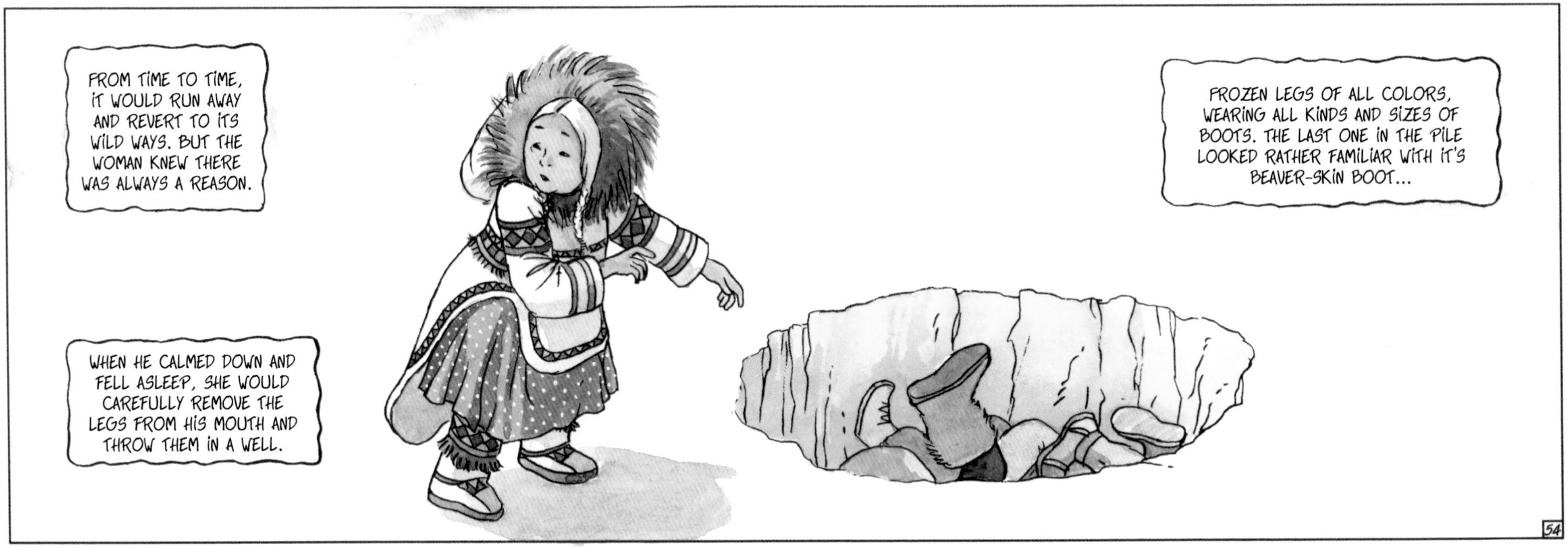
FROM TIME TO TIME, IT WOULD RUN AWAY AND REVERT TO ITS WILD WAYS. BUT THE WOMAN KNEW THERE WAS ALWAYS A REASON.
WHEN HE CALMED DOWN AND FELL ASLEEP, SHE WOULD CAREFULLY REMOVE THE LEGS FROM HIS MOUTH AND THROW THEM IN A WELL.
FROZEN LEGS OF ALL COLORS, WEARING ALL KINDS AND SIZES OF BOOTS. THE LAST ONE IN THE PILE LOOKED RATHER FAMILIAR WITH IT'S BEAVER-SKIN BOOT...
54

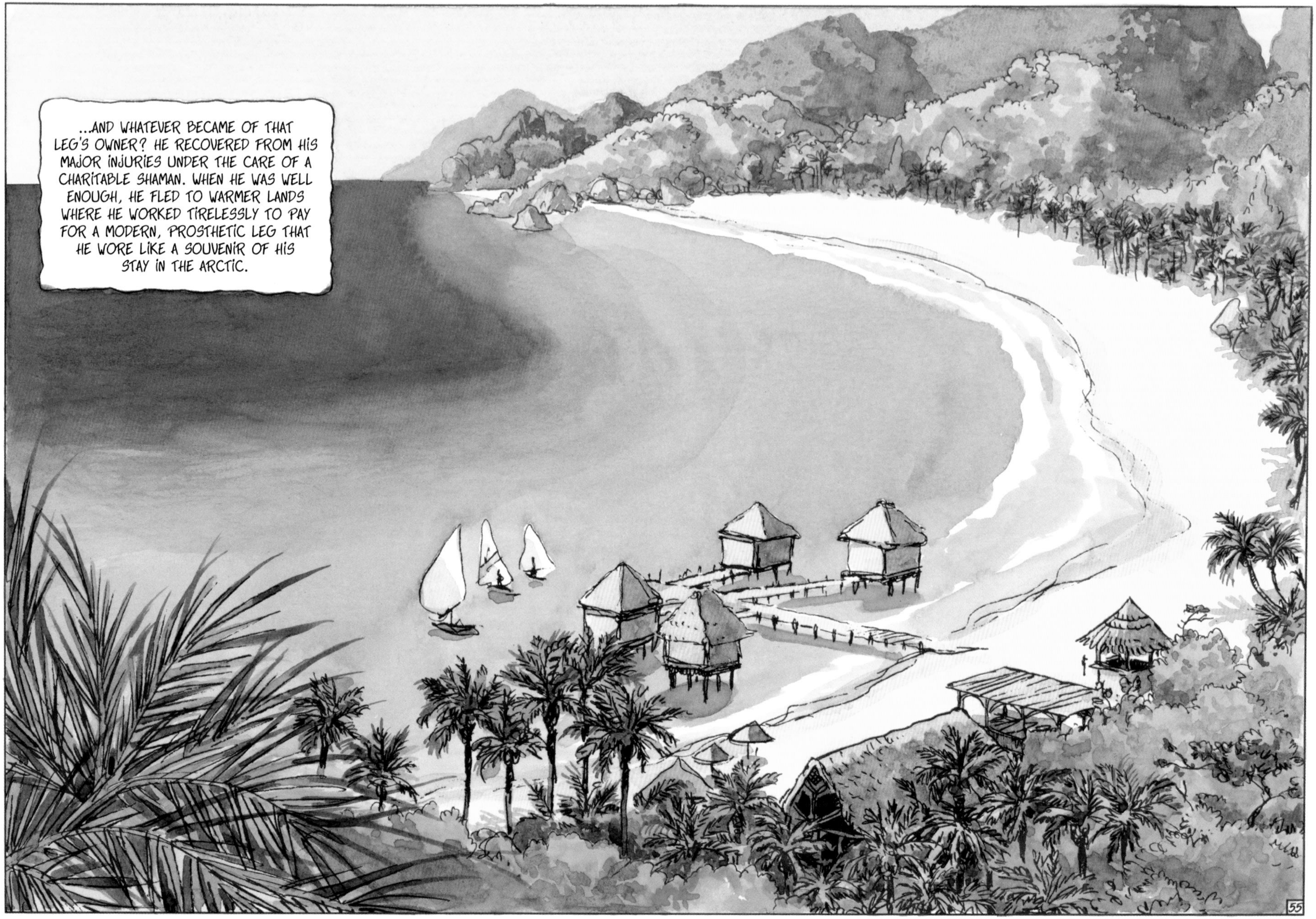
...AND WHATEVER BECAME OF THAT LEG'S OWNER? HE RECOVERED FROM HIS MAJOR INJURIES UNDER THE CARE OF A CHARITABLE SHAMAN. WHEN HE WAS WELL ENOUGH, HE FLED TO WARMER LANDS WHERE HE WORKED TIRELESSLY TO PAY FOR A MODERN, PROSTHETIC LEG THAT HE WORE LIKE A SOUVENIR OF HIS STAY IN THE ARCTIC.
55

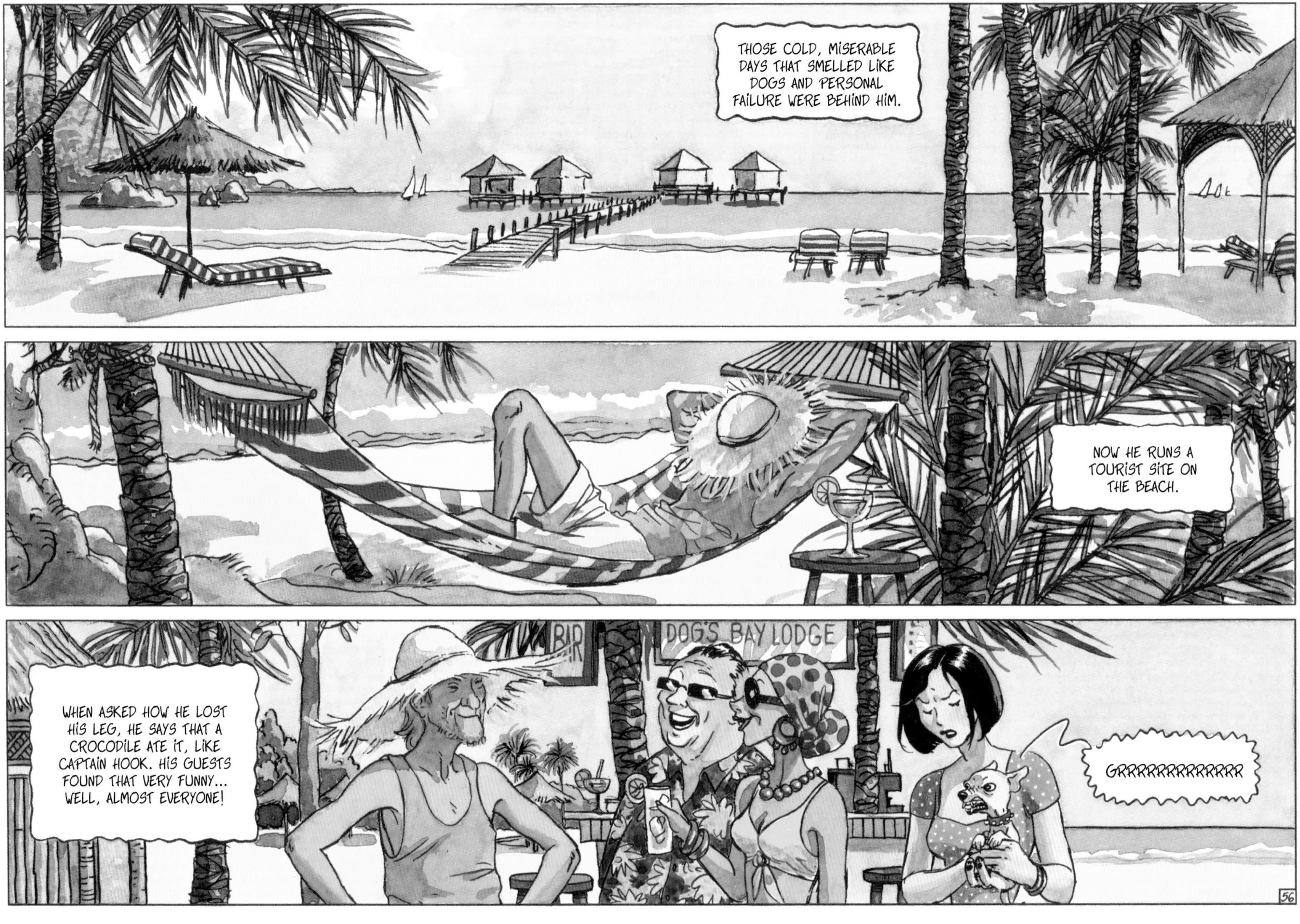
THOSE COLD, MISERABLE DAYS THAT SMELLED LIKE DOGS AND PERSONAL FAILURE WERE BEHIND HIM.
NOW HE RUNS A TOURIST SITE ON THE BEACH.
WHEN ASKED HOW HE LOST HIS LEG, HE SAYS THAT A CROCODILE ATE IT, LIKE CAPTAIN HOOK. HIS GUESTS FOUND THAT VERY FUNNY... WELL, ALMOST EVERYONE!
DOG'S BAY LODGE
GRRRRRRRRRRRR
56

**Ana Miralles** was born in 1959 and has dedicated herself to comics and illustration since 1982. She has written for such publishers as *Rambla, Madriz, Cairo, Acme Brand, Blue Press, Marie-Claire Spain, Vogue Spain* and *Je Bouquine*. A restless and prolific author, her early professional works include children's books, textbooks, posters, covers, magazine articles, advertising, and various other forms of graphic communication. She also contributed to theater and cinema as a costume designer, set designer, and storyboard artist.

Her work has been adapted and translated into many different languages and markets. She illustrated *The Eva Medusa Trilogy*, written by Antonio Segura, in addition to multiple collaborations with writer Emilio Ruiz. In 2001, she created the *Djinn* series with Belgian writer Jean Dufaux, which ran until 2016 with a total of 13 volumes selling over a million copies in France alone. In 2009, she became the first woman to be awarded the Barcelona Salon Grand Prize in recognition for her long career in the world of comics.

**Emilio Ruiz** was born in 1960. After studying Fine Arts in Valencia, he began a career as a photographer for an advertising agency, soon specializing in dance and theater photography. His photography began to lead him towards the prospects of visual storytelling, producing audiovisual presentations. In 2001, he worked on the Spanish television series *Cuéntame Cómo Pasó* as a documentary filmmaker and graphic designer for the first five seasons.

In the world of comics, he has written several scripts with Ana Miralles including *The Brightness of a Look* (1990) and the *In Search of the Unicorn* trilogy (1996-1999), *Hand to Hand, the Tale of a 20 Euro Banknote* (2009), *Muraqqa'* (2011) and the three volumes of the *Waluk* series (2011-2019) published to date.